AWOL

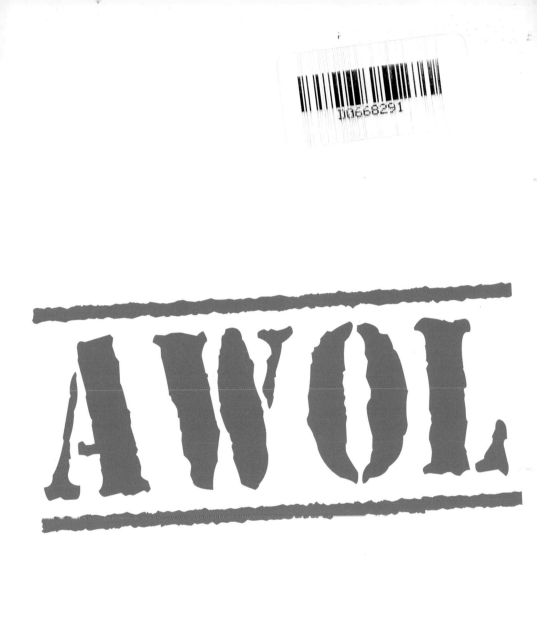

Marla Lesage

ORCA BOOK PUBLISHERS

For Marc,
who always takes me on the best adventures.
—M.L.

Text and illustrations copyright © Marla Lesage 2022

Published in Canada and the United States in 2022 by Orca Book Publishers.
orcabook.com

Library and Archives Canada Cataloguing in Publication
Title: AWOL / Marla Lesage.
Names: Lesage, Marla, author, artist.
Identifiers: Canadiana (print) 20210263369 | Canadiana (ebook) 20210263393 |
ISBN 9781459828391 (softcover) | ISBN 9781459828407 (PDF)
Subjects: LCGFT: Graphic novels.
Classification: LCC PN6733.L463 A98 2022 | DDC j741.5/971—dc23

Library of Congress Control Number: 2021941347

Summary: In this graphic novel for middle readers, everyone in eleven-year-old Leah's family is affected by her father's PTSD.

Orca Book Publishers is committed to reducing the consumption of nonrenewable resources in the production of our books. We make every effort to use materials that support a sustainable future.

Orca Book Publishers gratefully acknowledges the support for its publishing programs provided by the following agencies: the Government of Canada, the Canada Council for the Arts and the Province of British Columbia through the BC Arts Council and the Book Publishing Tax Credit.

Cover and interior illustrations by Marla Lesage

Edited by Tanya Trafford

Printed and bound in South Korea.

25 24 23 22 • 1 2 3 4

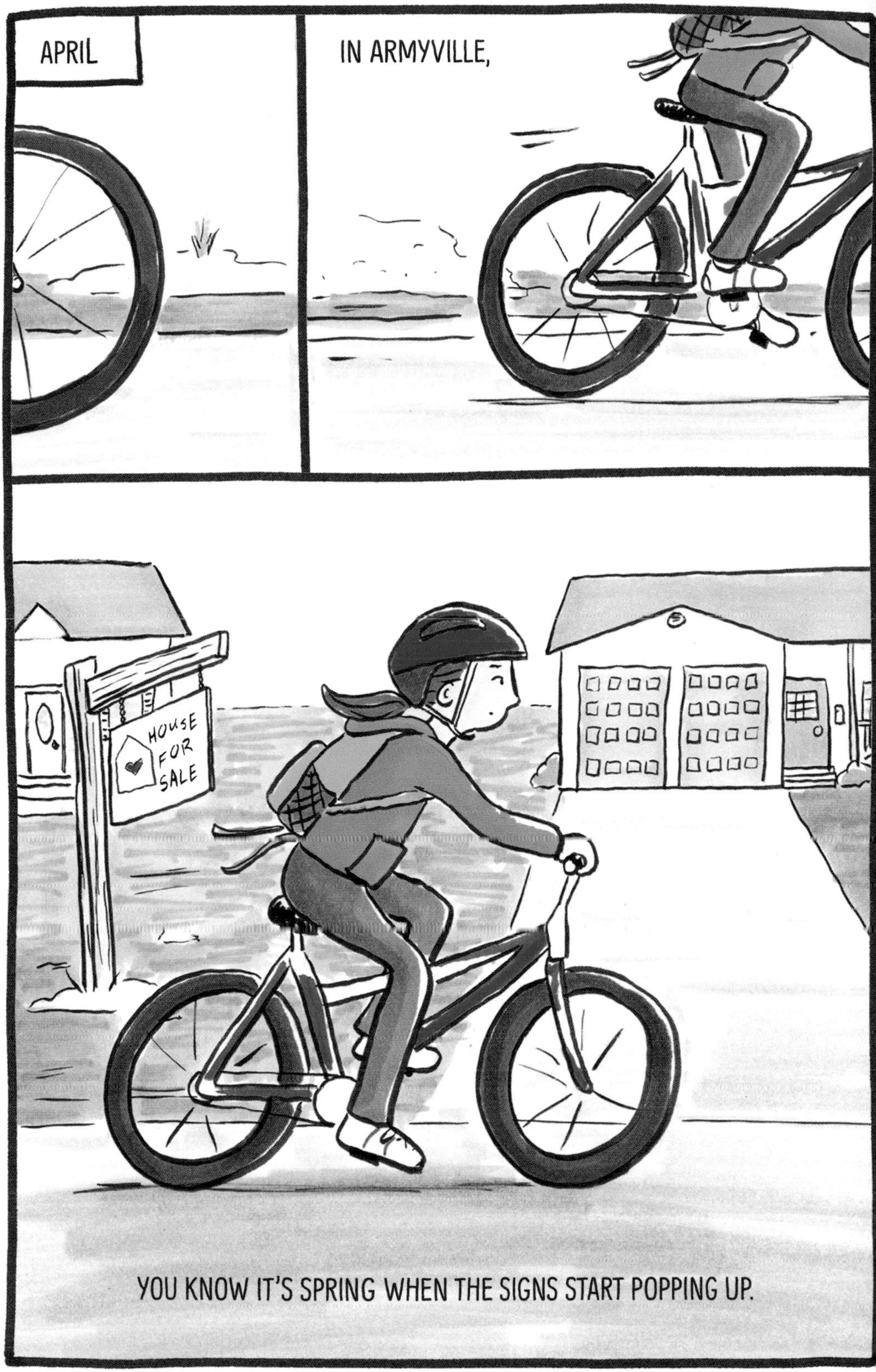
APRIL
IN ARMYVILLE,
HOUSE FOR SALE
YOU KNOW IT'S SPRING WHEN THE SIGNS START POPPING UP.

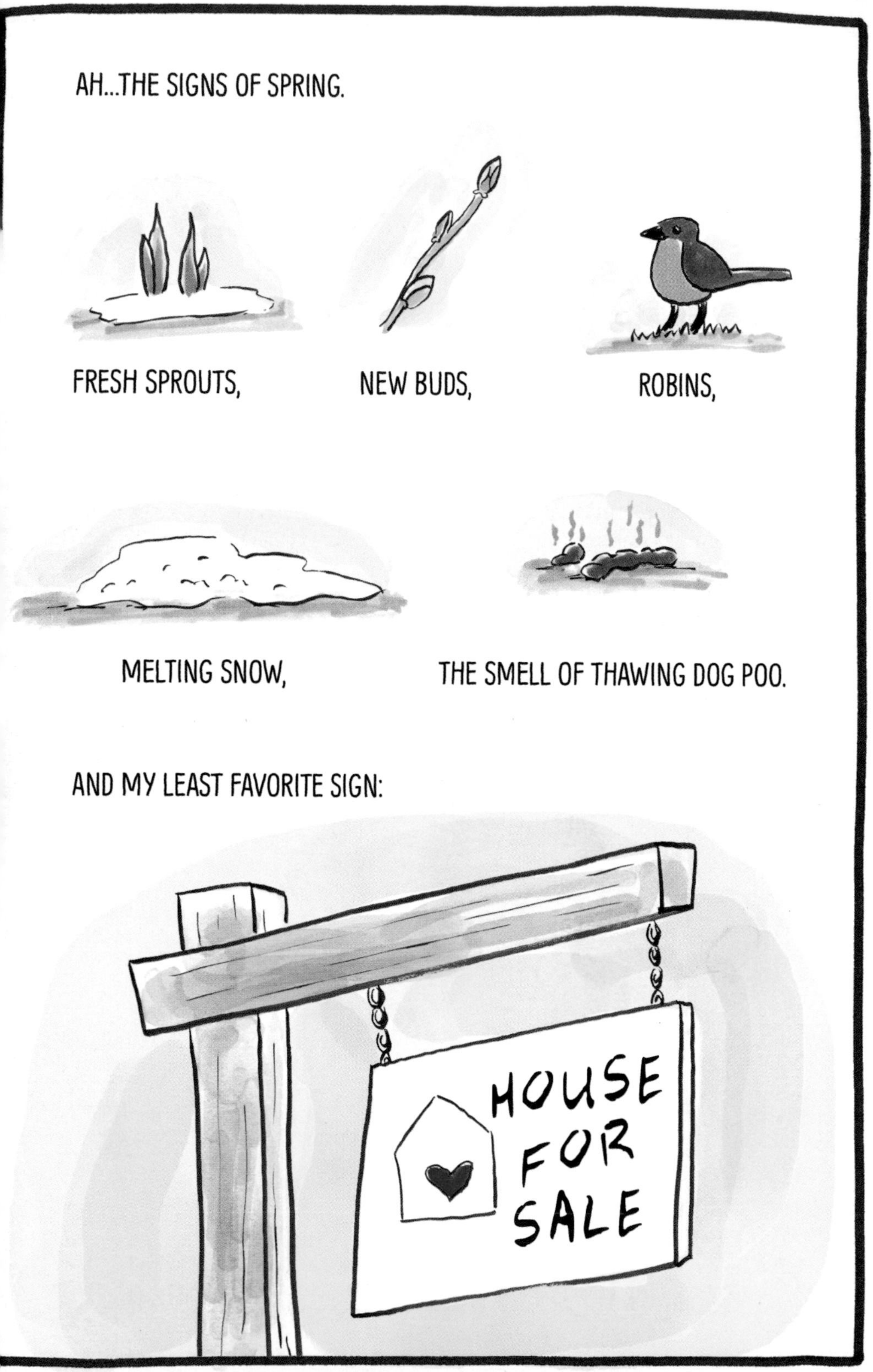
AH...THE SIGNS OF SPRING.
FRESH SPROUTS,
NEW BUDS,
ROBINS,
MELTING SNOW,
THE SMELL OF THAWING DOG POO.
AND MY LEAST FAVORITE SIGN:
HOUSE FOR SALE

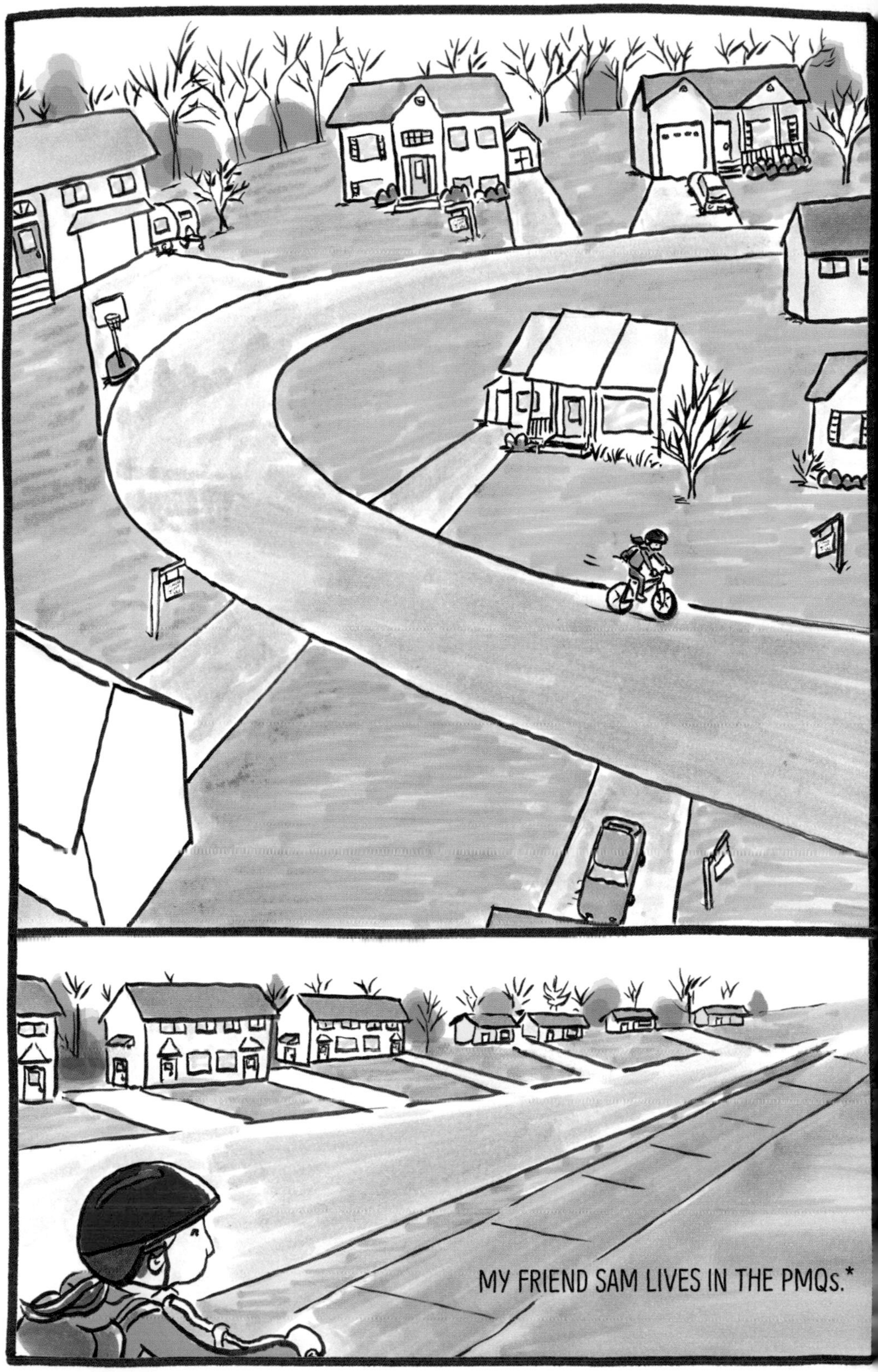
MY FRIEND SAM LIVES IN THE PMQs.*

*PMQ = Private married quarters, rental housing for military families

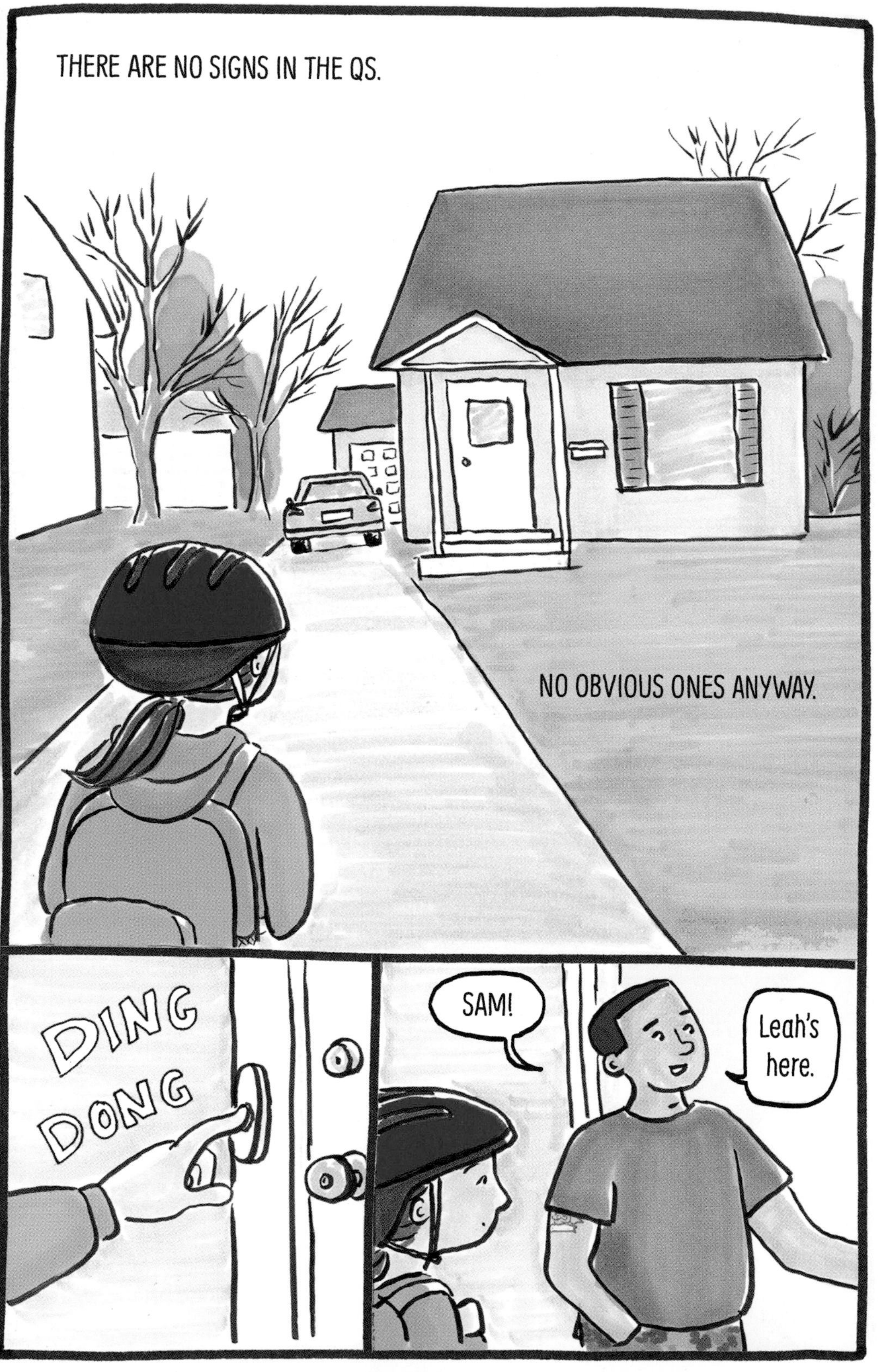
THERE ARE NO SIGNS IN THE QS.
NO OBVIOUS ONES ANYWAY.
DING DONG
SAM!
Leah's here.

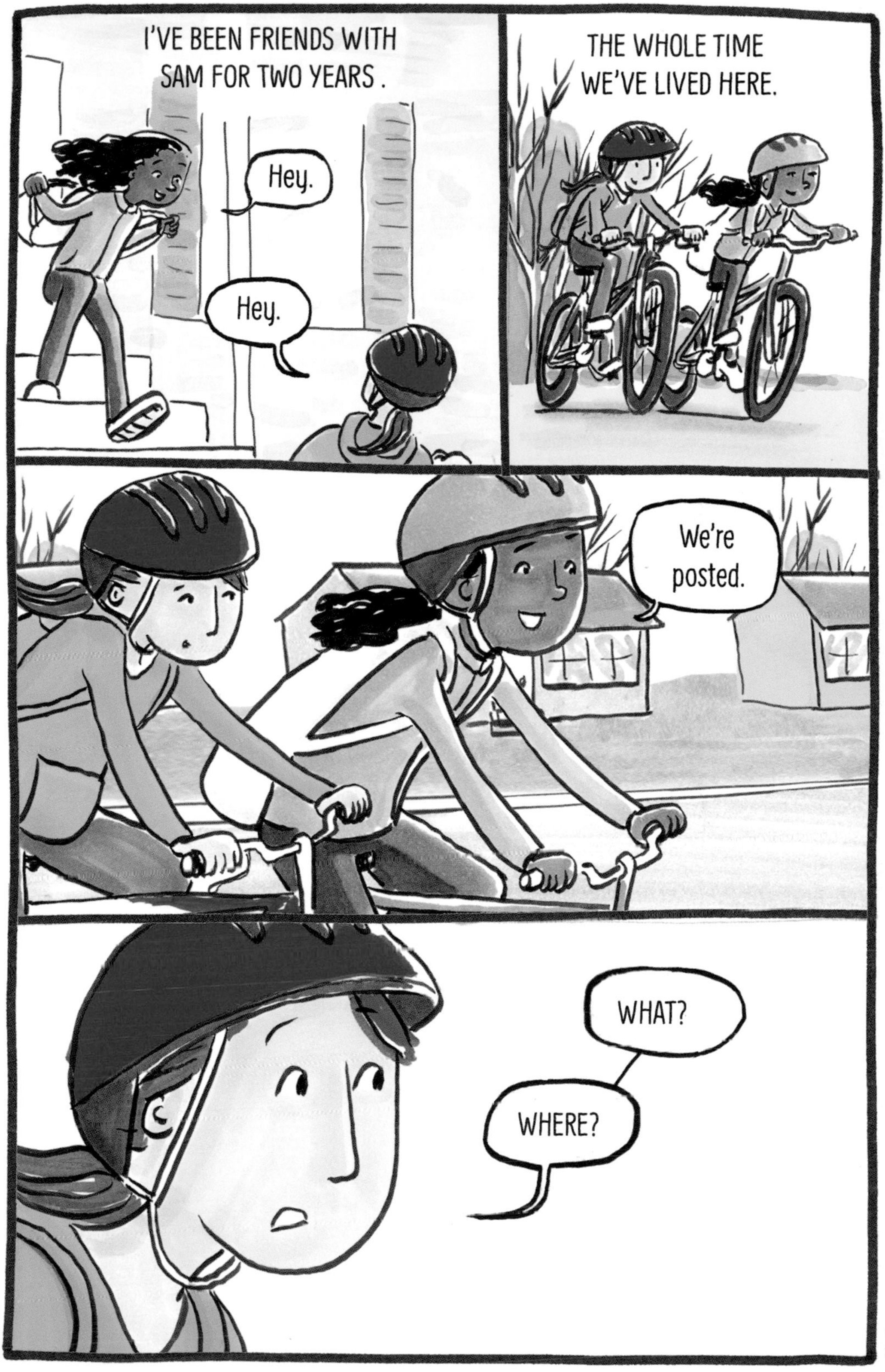
I'VE BEEN FRIENDS WITH SAM FOR TWO YEARS.
Hey.
Hey.
THE WHOLE TIME WE'VE LIVED HERE.
We're posted.
WHAT?
WHERE?

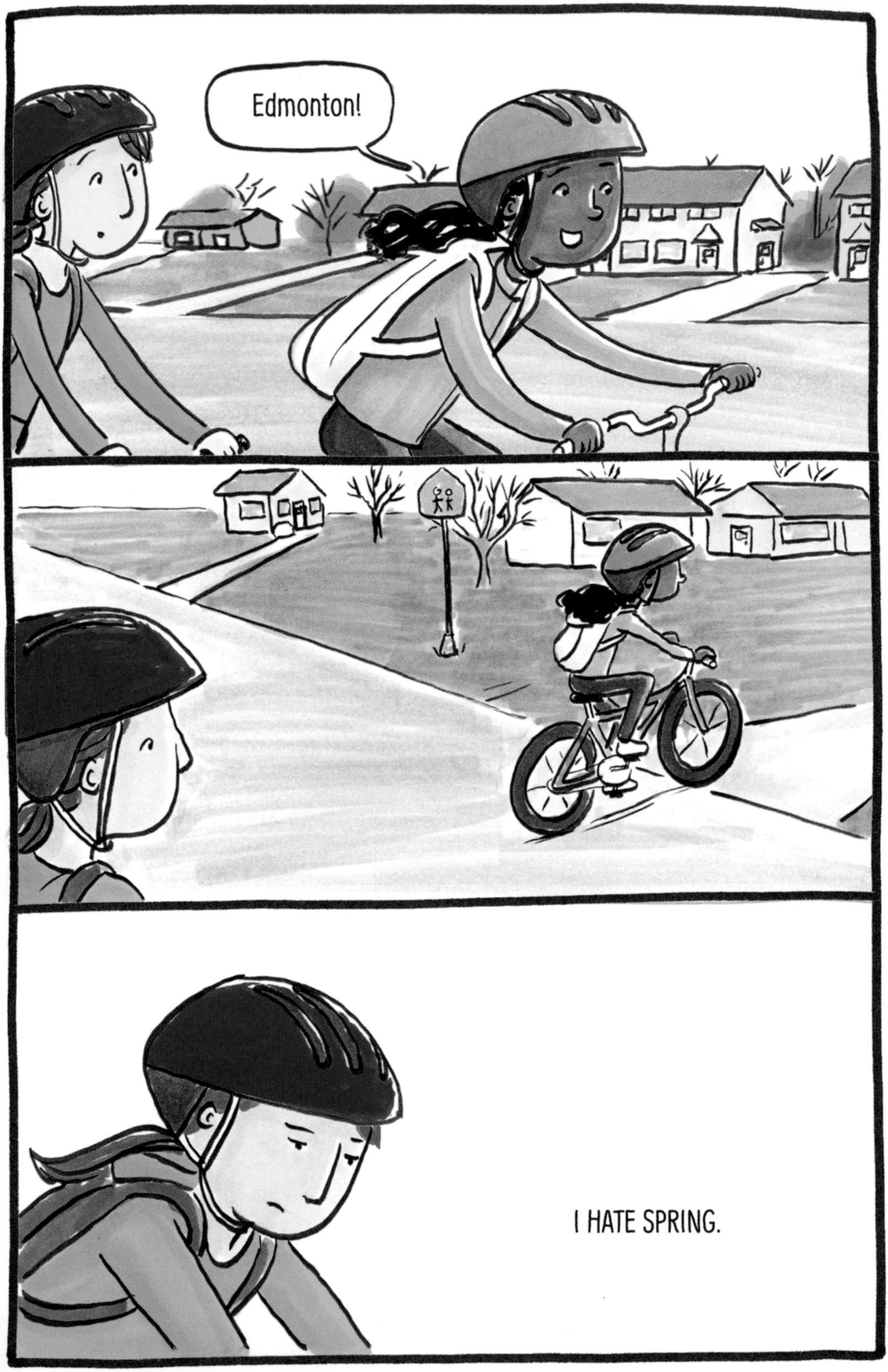
Edmonton!
I HATE SPRING.

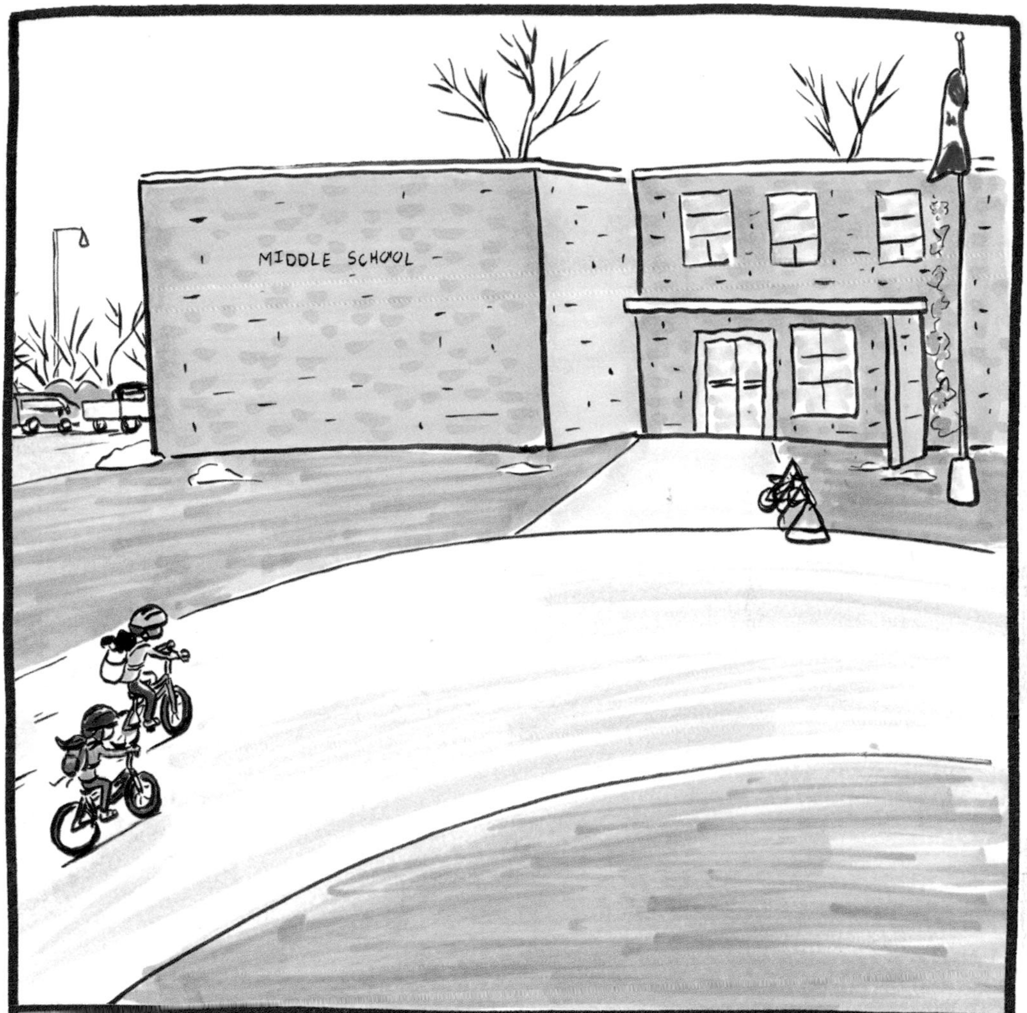
MIDDLE SCHOOL

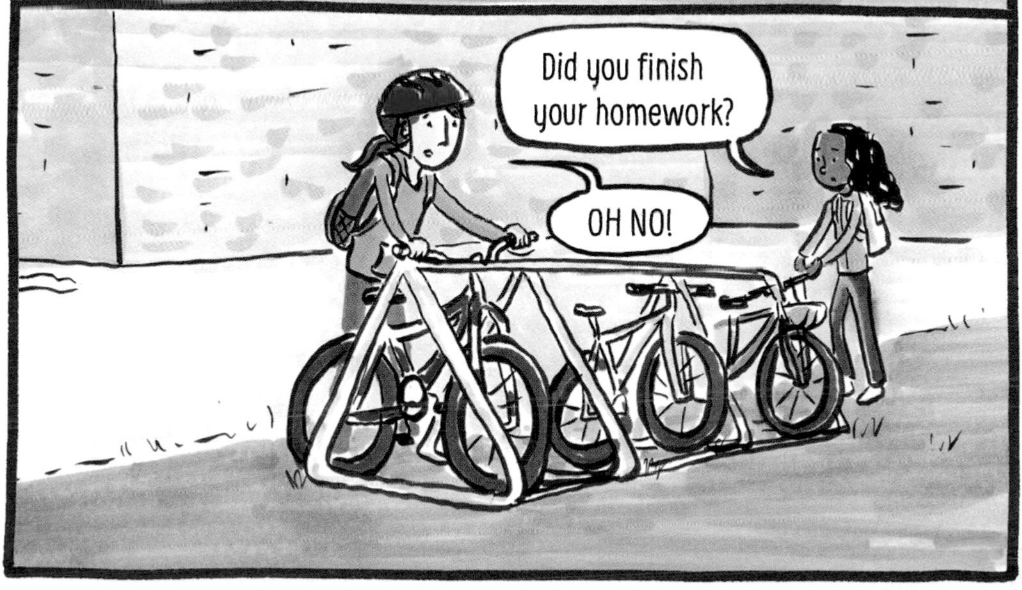
Did you finish
your homework?
OH NO!

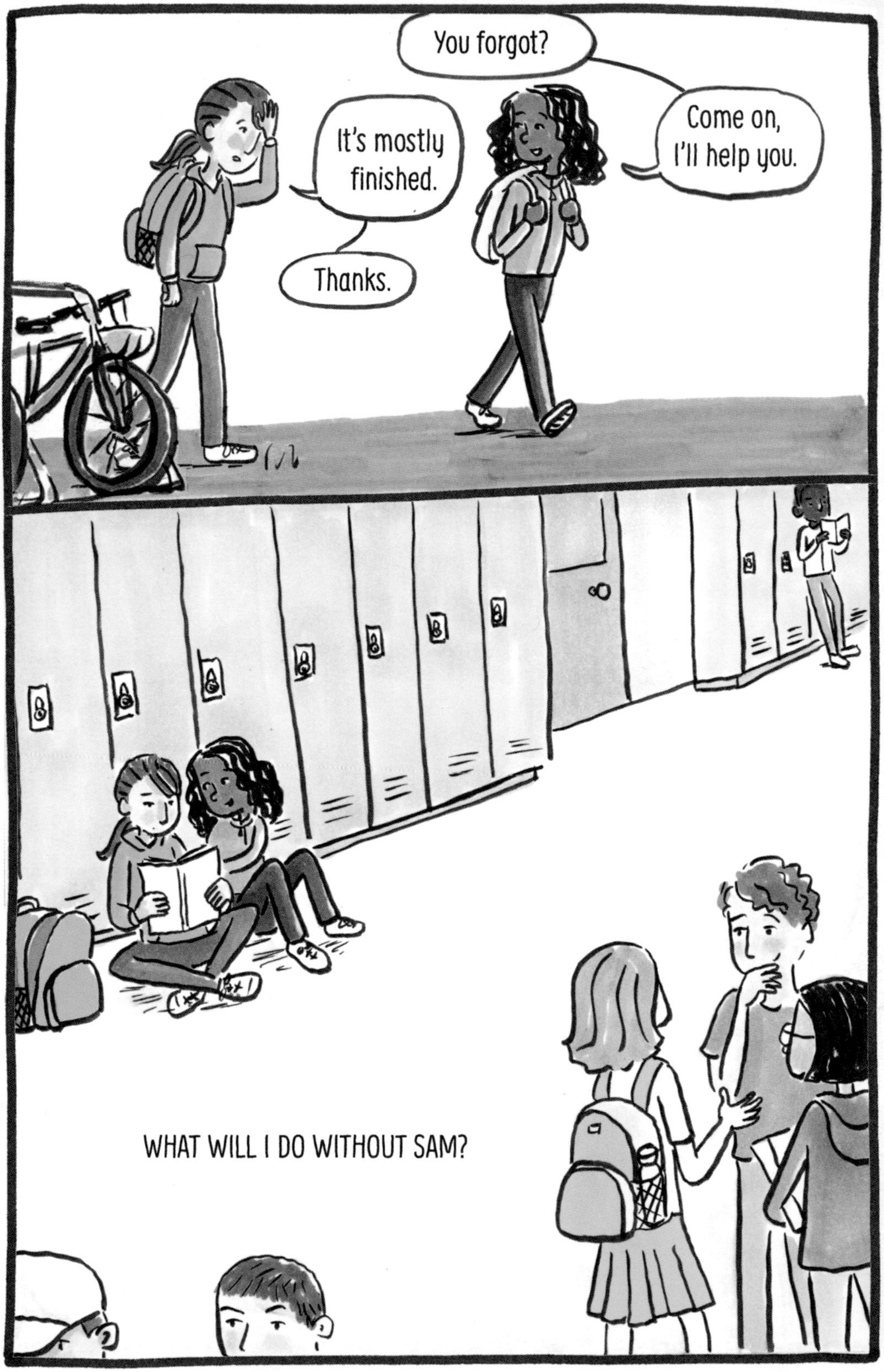
You forgot?
It's mostly finished.
Thanks.
Come on, I'll help you.
WHAT WILL I DO WITHOUT SAM?

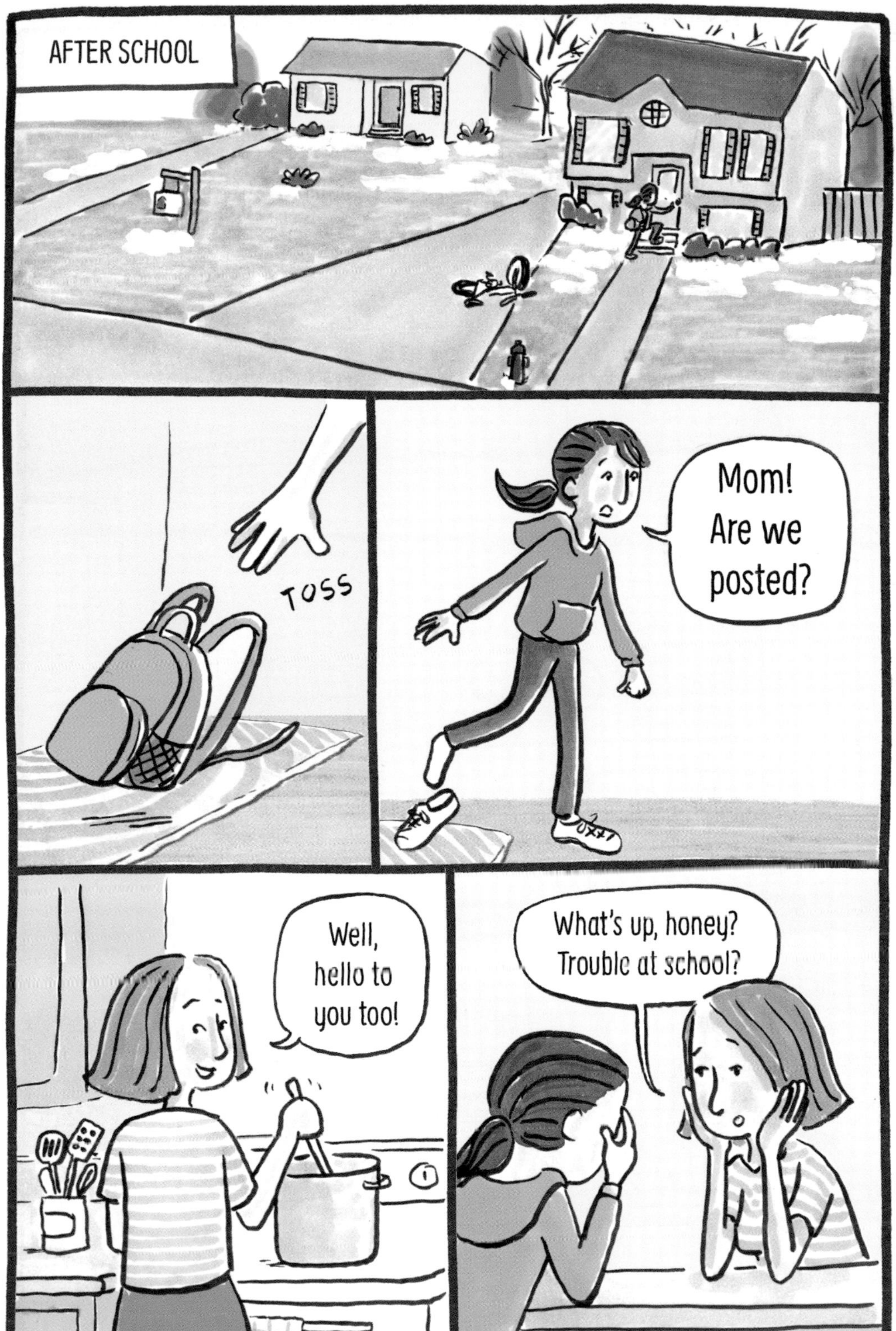
AFTER SCHOOL
TOSS
Mom! Are we posted?
Well, hello to you too!
What's up, honey? Trouble at school?

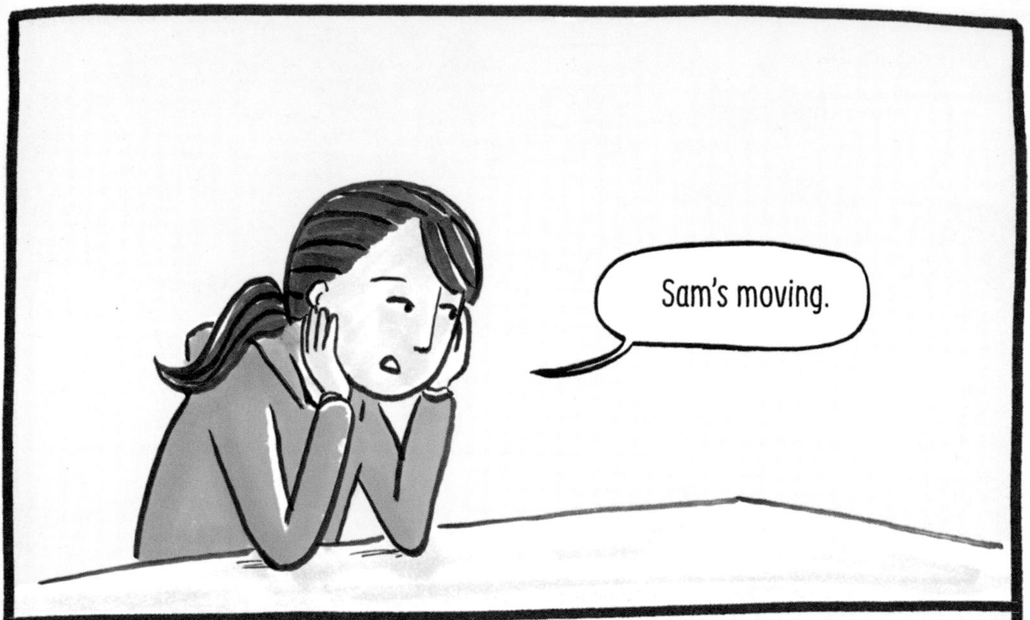
Sam's moving.

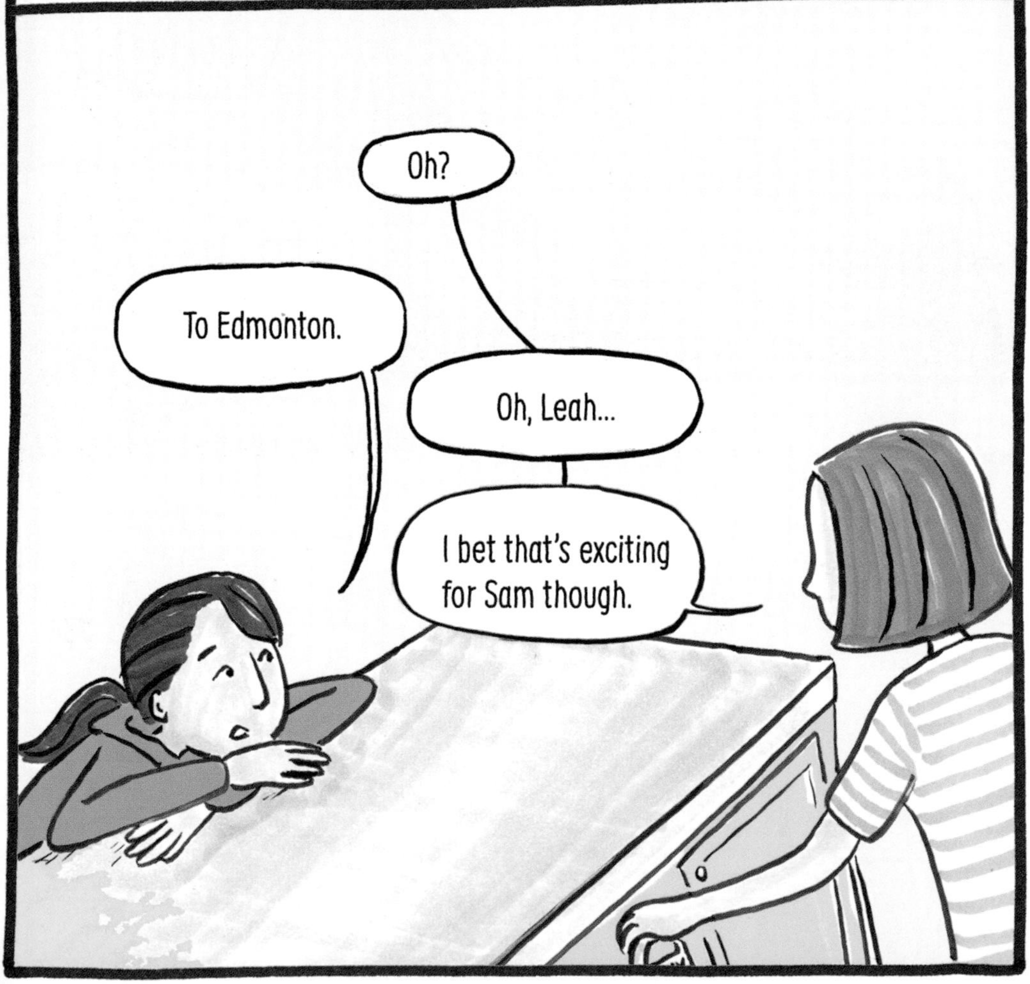
Oh?
To Edmonton.
Oh, Leah...
I bet that's exciting for Sam though.

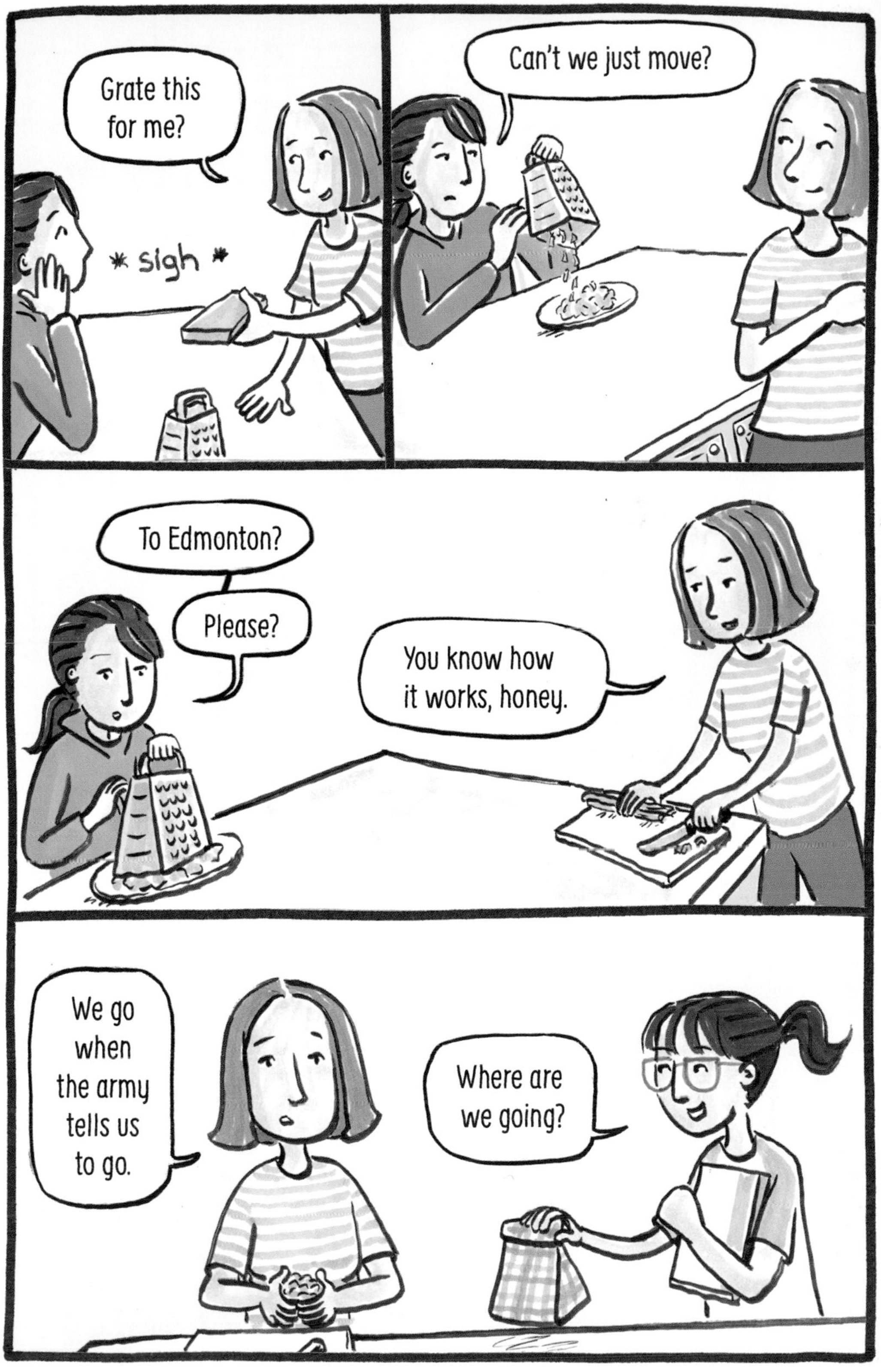
Grate this for me?
* sigh *
Can't we just move?
To Edmonton?
Please?
You know how it works, honey.
We go when the army tells us to go.
Where are we going?

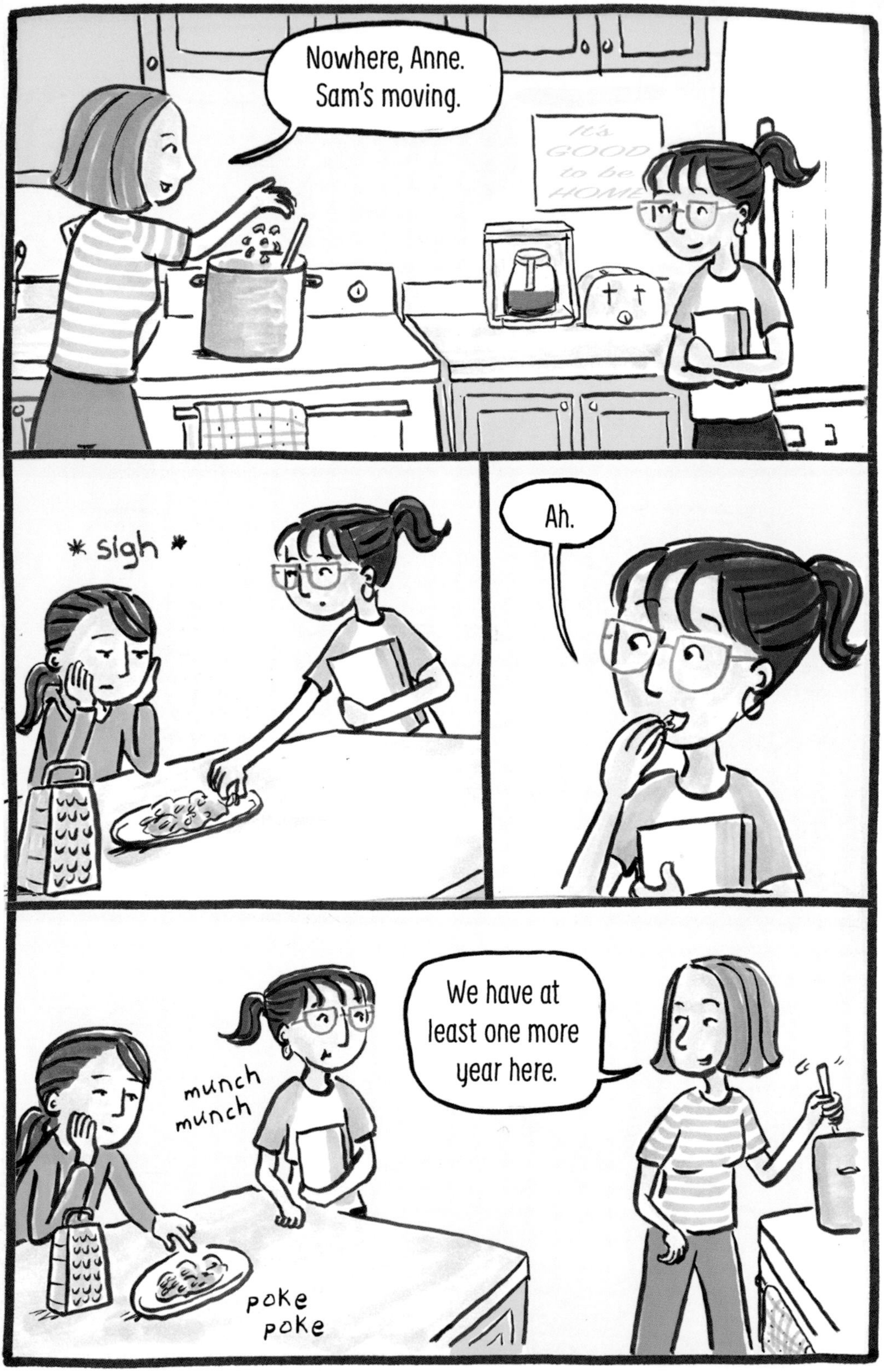
Nowhere, Anne.
Sam's moving.
It's GOOD to be HOME
* sigh *
Ah.
munch munch
We have at least one more year here.
poke poke

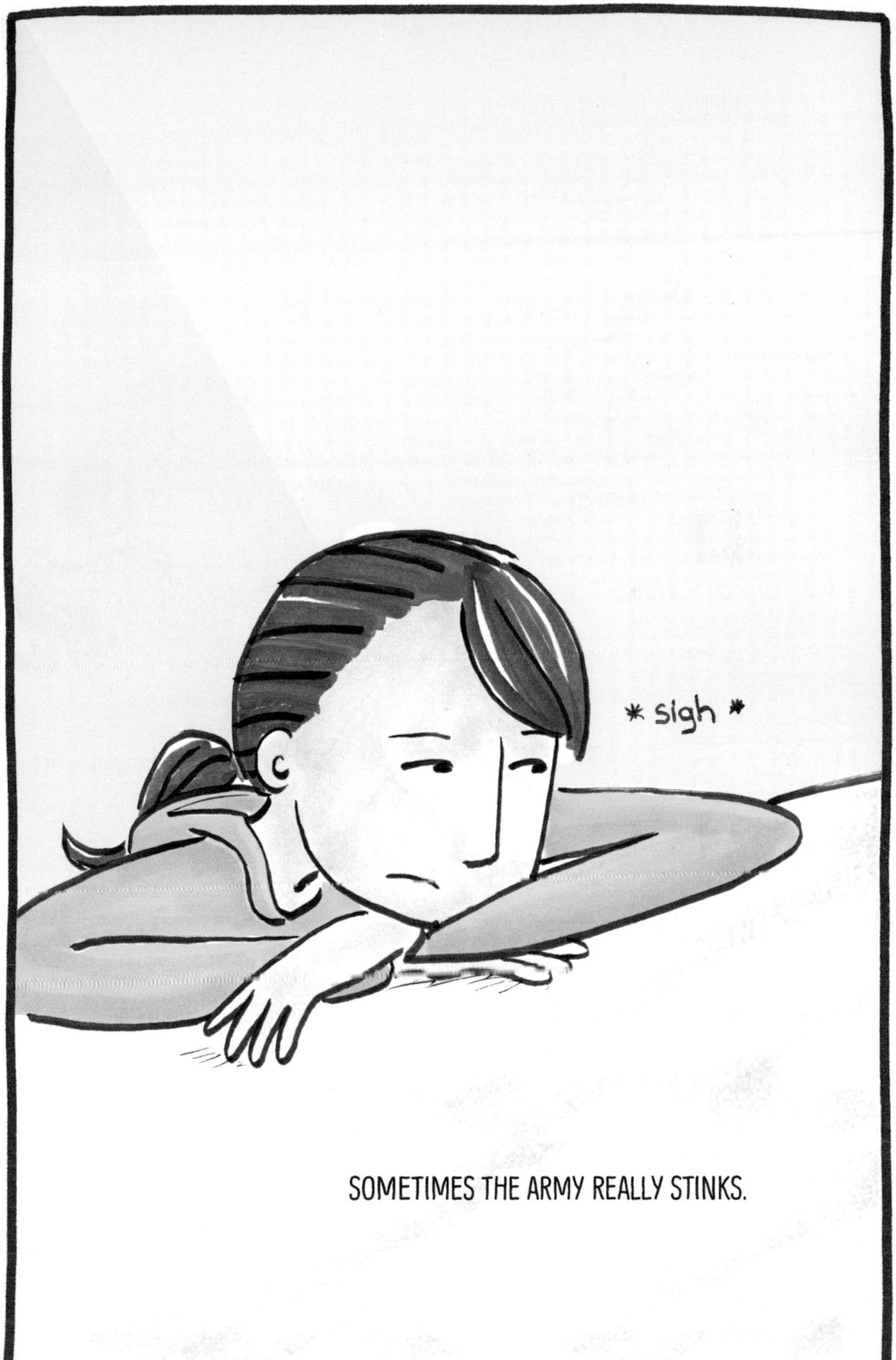
* sigh *
SOMETIMES THE ARMY REALLY STINKS.

FRIENDS I USED TO HAVE:

ARABELLA (PETAWAWA)

MAXIME & ANAÏS
(OROMOCTO – THE FIRST TIME I LIVED HERE)

DREW (OTTAWA)

THOMAS & MISAKI (KINGSTON)

I'M ONLY ELEVEN,
BUT I'VE ALREADY
MOVED FIVE TIMES.

NOUR (EDMONTON)

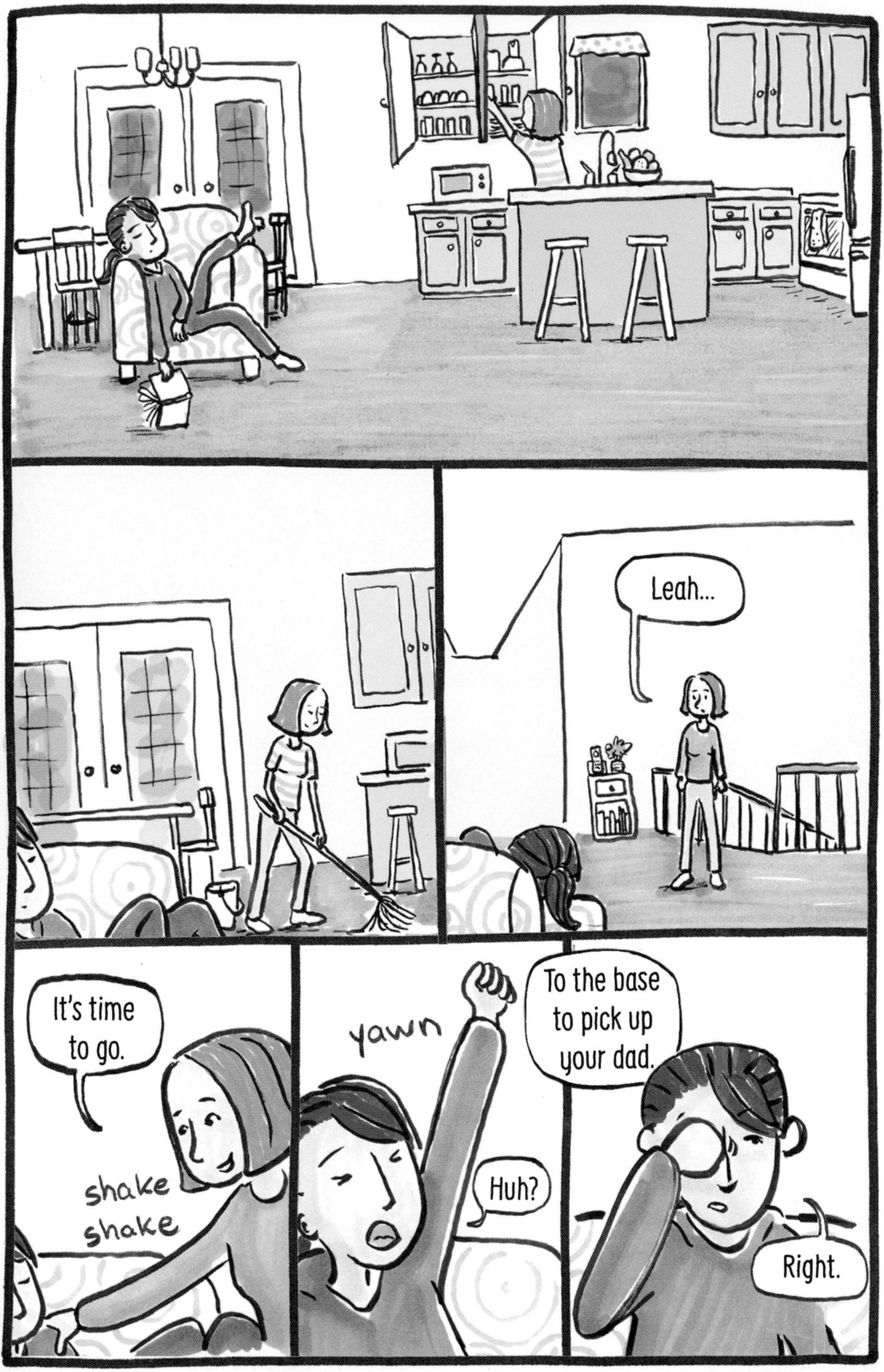
Leah...
It's time to go.
shake shake
yawn
Huh?
To the base to pick up your dad.
Right.

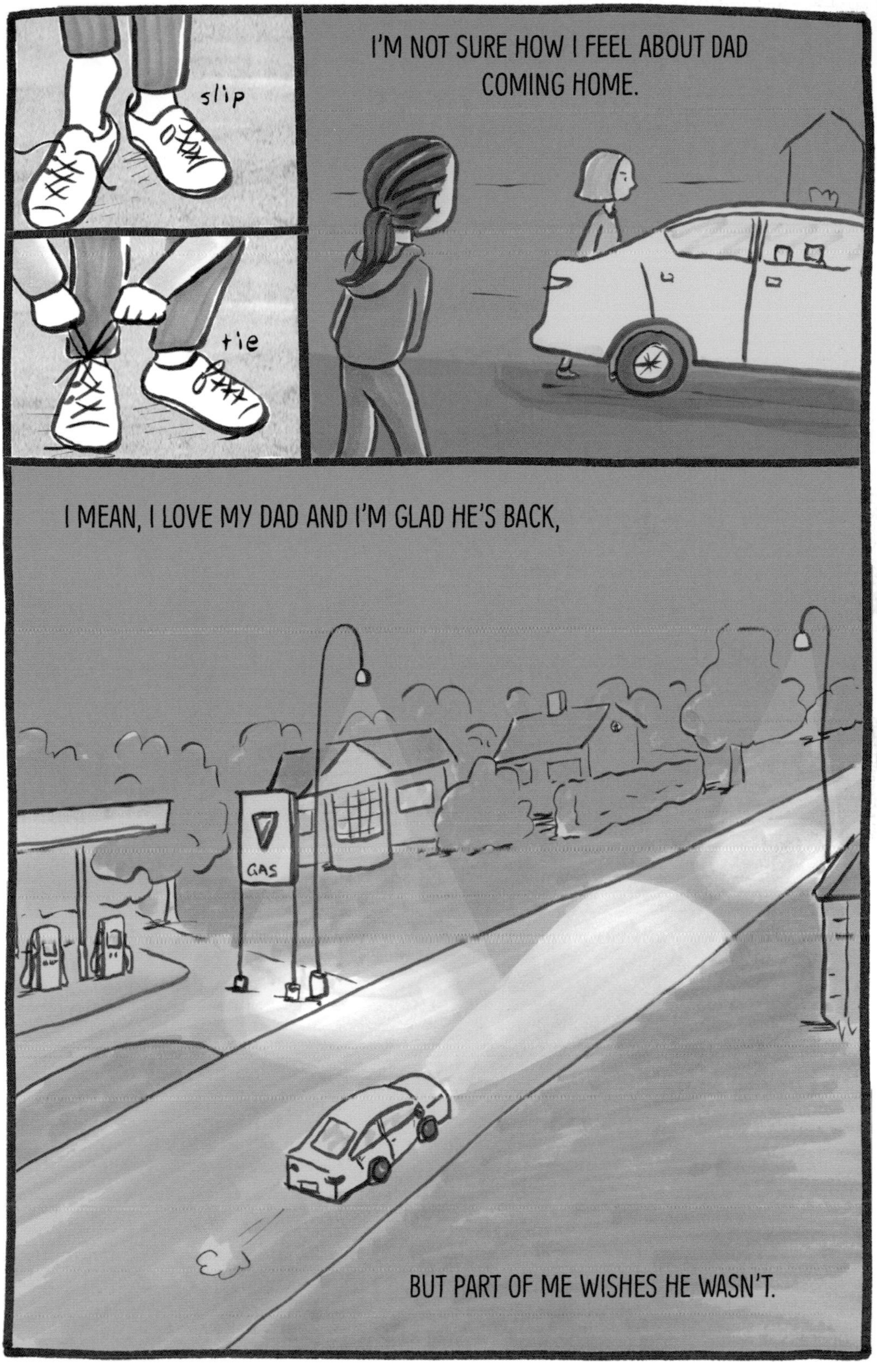
slip
tie
I'M NOT SURE HOW I FEEL ABOUT DAD COMING HOME.
I MEAN, I LOVE MY DAD AND I'M GLAD HE'S BACK,
GAS
BUT PART OF ME WISHES HE WASN'T.

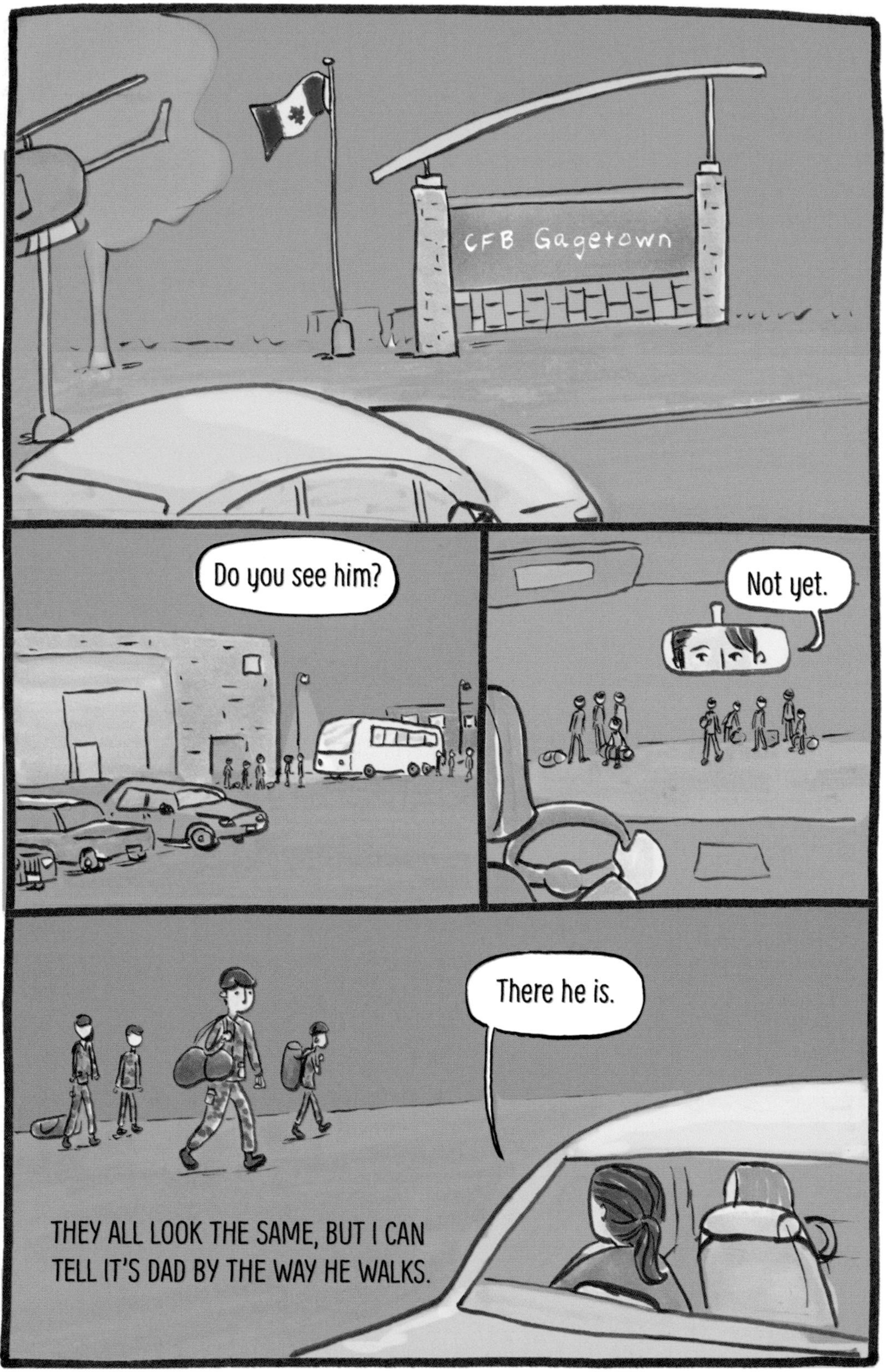
CFB Gagetown
Do you see him?
Not yet.
There he is.
THEY ALL LOOK THE SAME, BUT I CAN TELL IT'S DAD BY THE WAY HE WALKS.

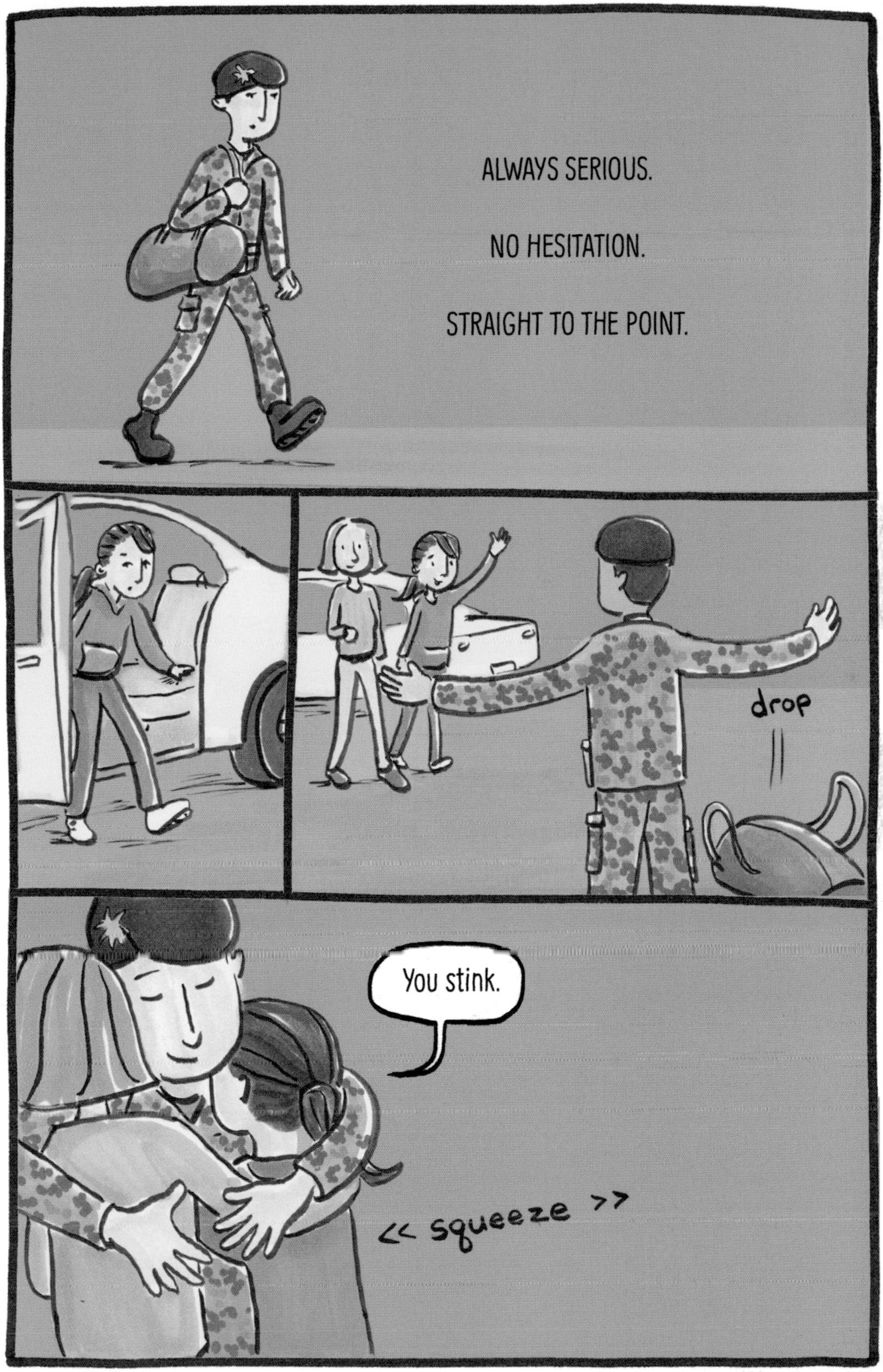
ALWAYS SERIOUS.
NO HESITATION.
STRAIGHT TO THE POINT.
drop
You stink.
<< squeeze >>

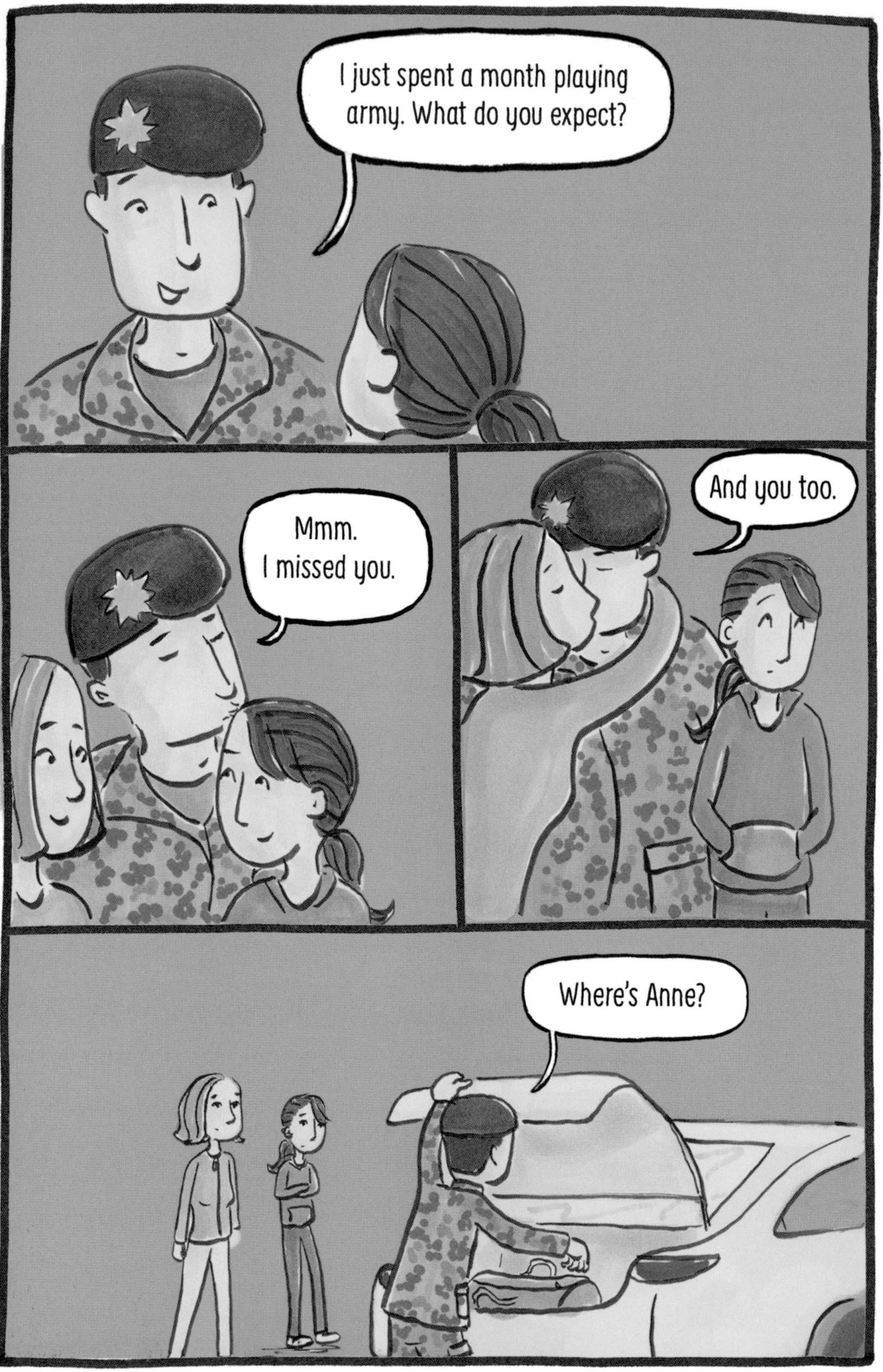
I just spent a month playing army. What do you expect?
Mmm. I missed you.
And you too.
Where's Anne?

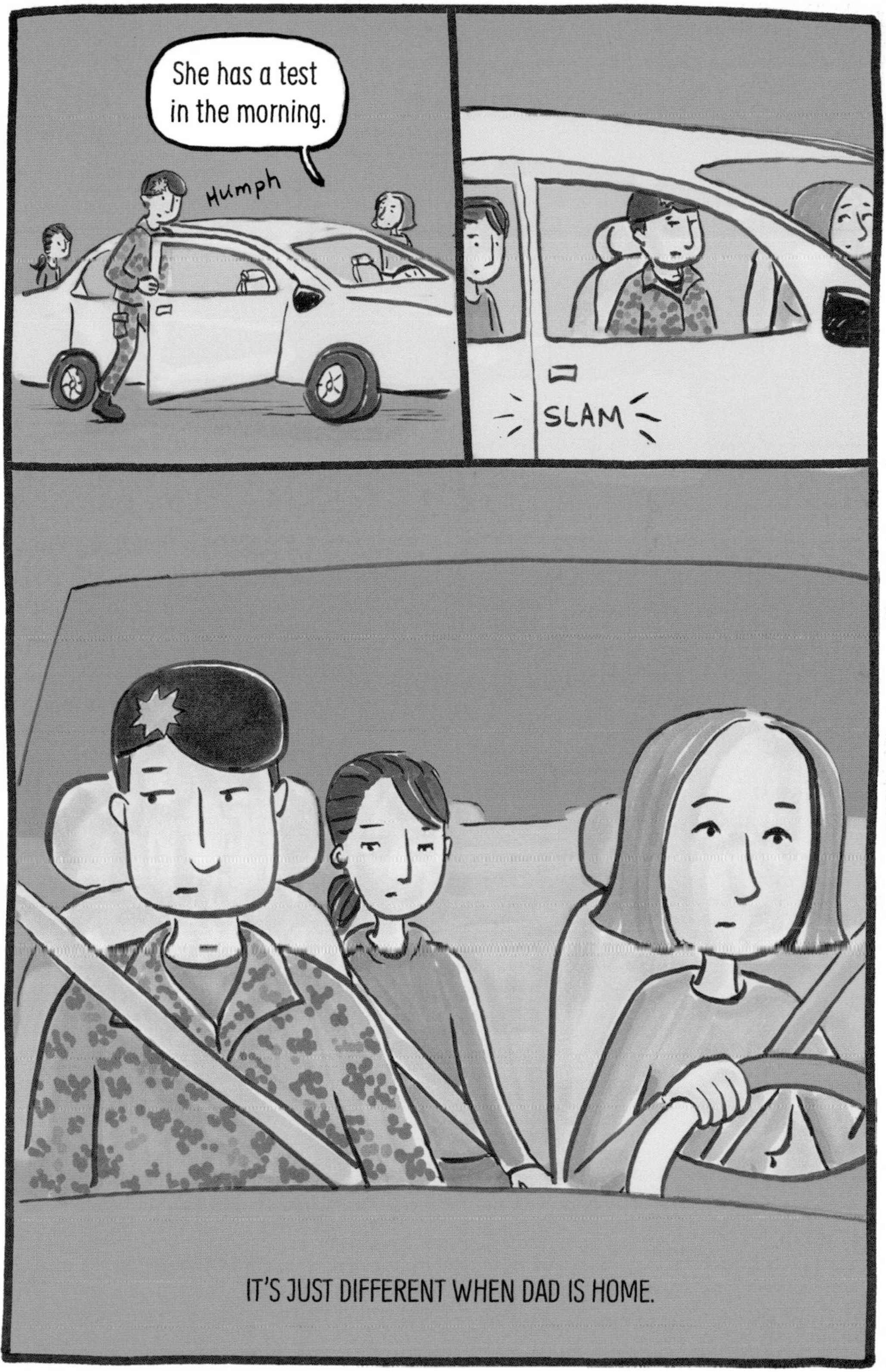
She has a test in the morning.
Humph
SLAM
IT'S JUST DIFFERENT WHEN DAD IS HOME.

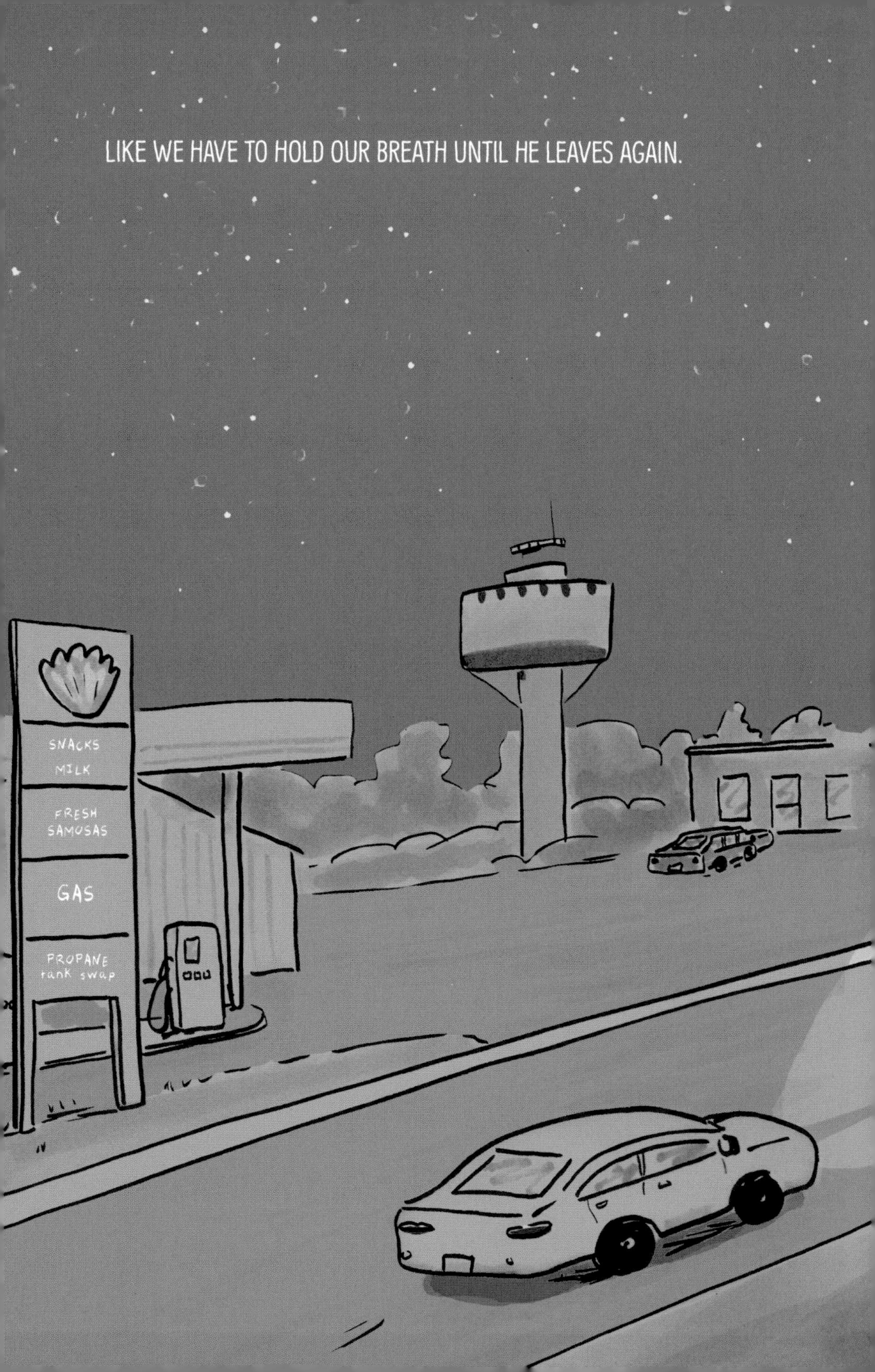
LIKE WE HAVE TO HOLD OUR BREATH UNTIL HE LEAVES AGAIN.
SNACKS
MILK
FRESH
SAMOSAS
GAS
PROPANE
tank swap

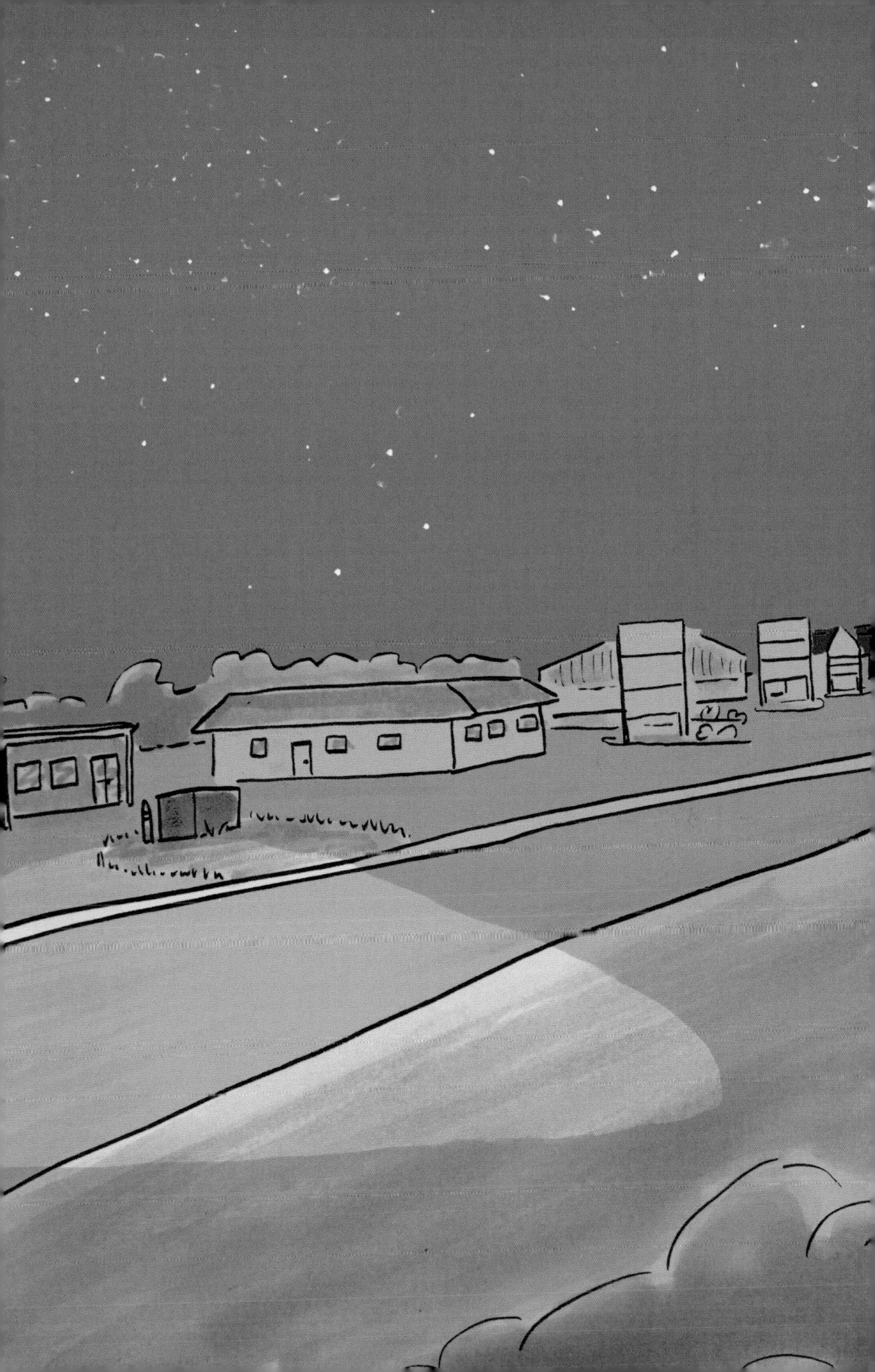

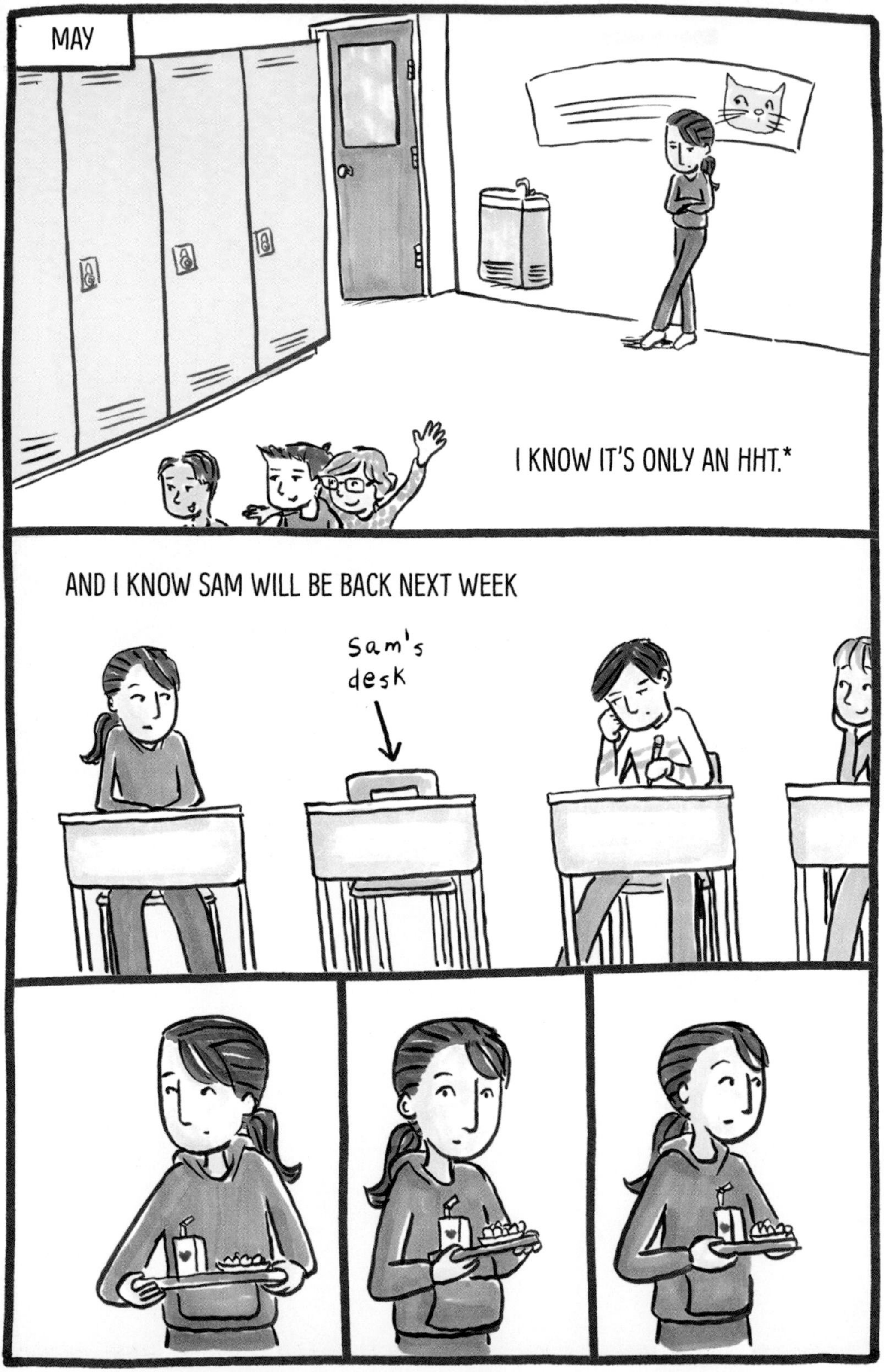
MAY
I KNOW IT'S ONLY AN HHT.*
AND I KNOW SAM WILL BE BACK NEXT WEEK
Sam's desk

*HHT = House Hunting Trip, a week-long not-a-vacation so your family can find a new place to live.

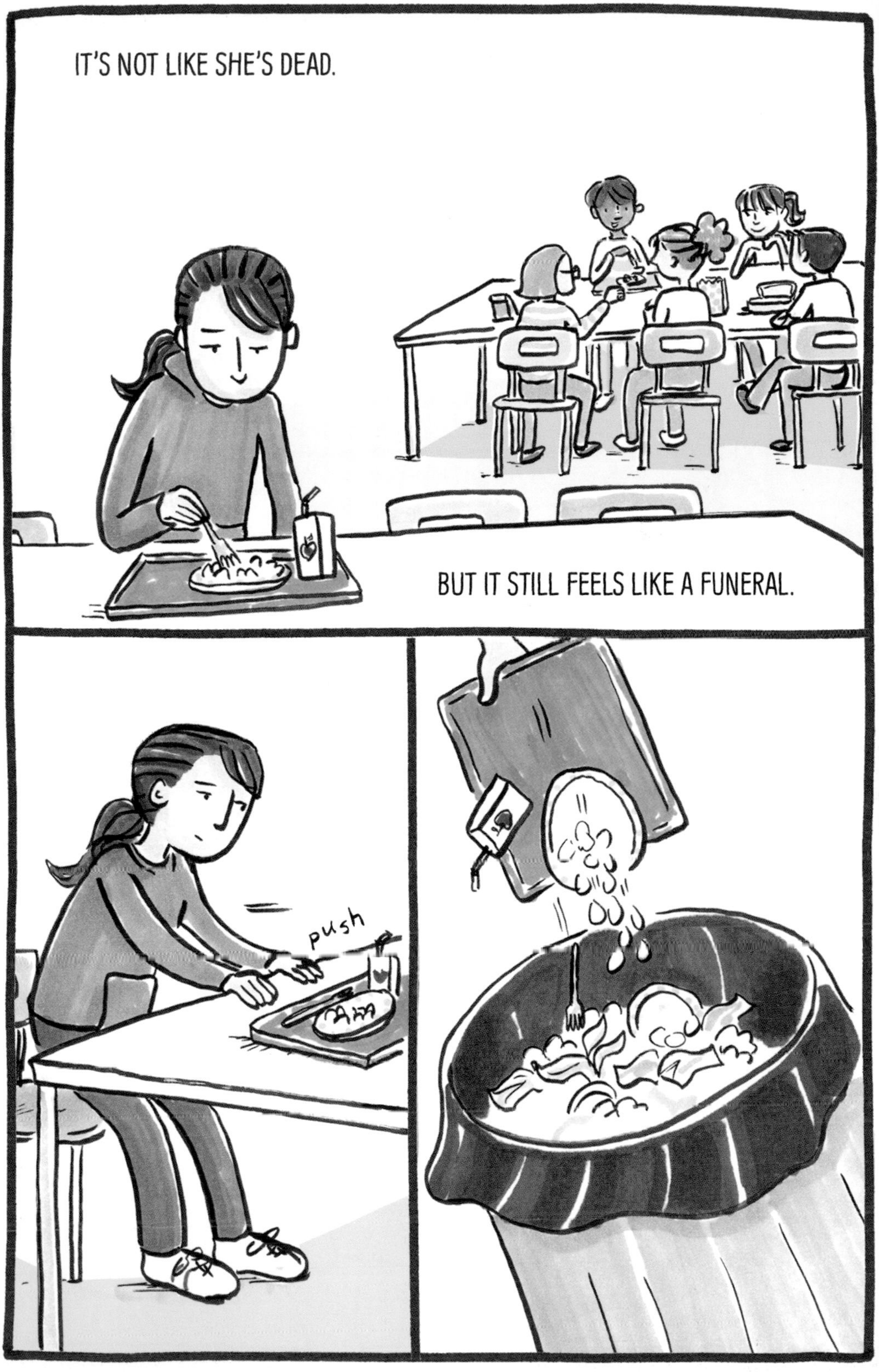
IT'S NOT LIKE SHE'S DEAD.
BUT IT STILL FEELS LIKE A FUNERAL.
push

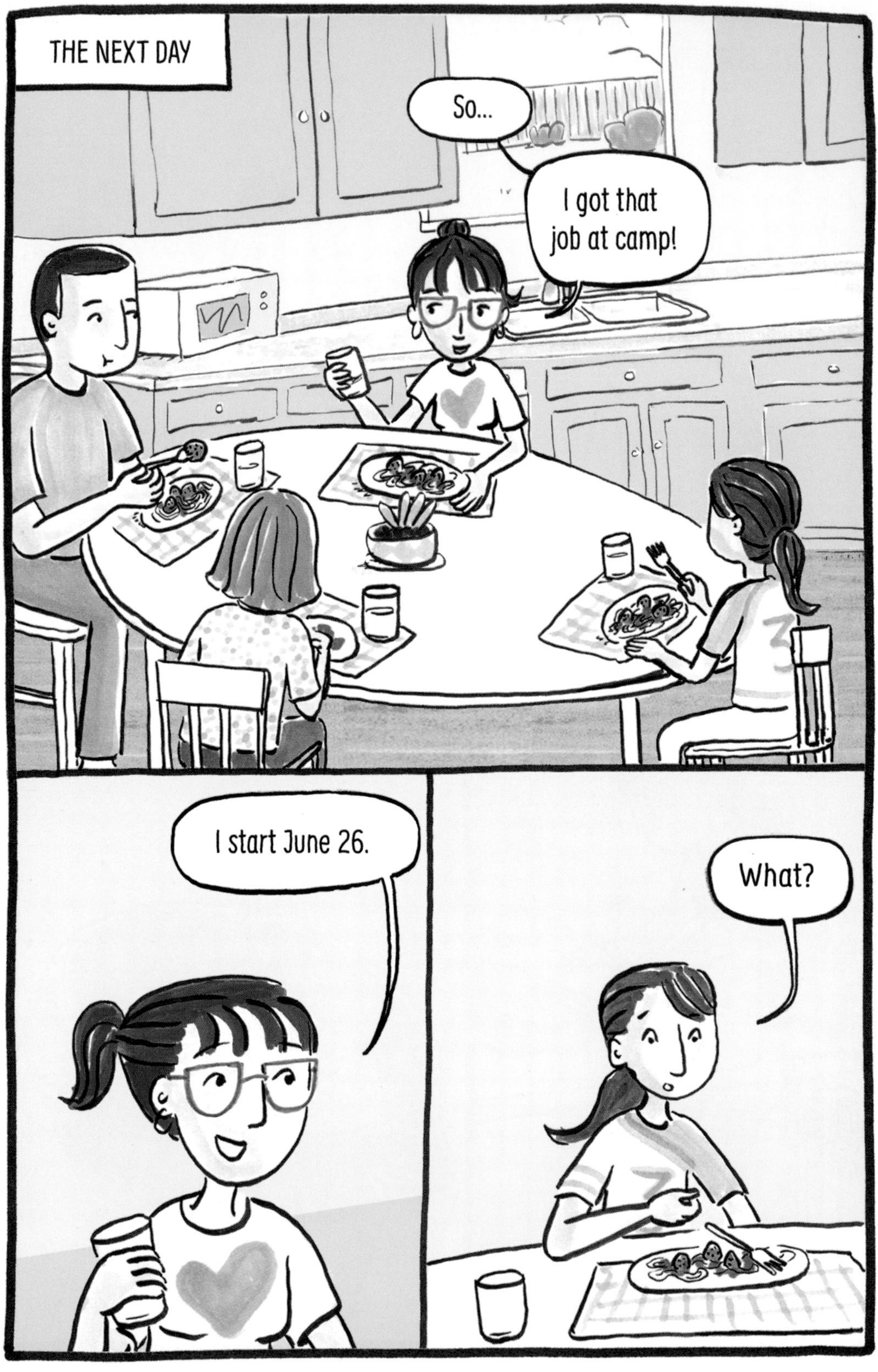
THE NEXT DAY
So...
I got that job at camp!
I start June 26.
What?

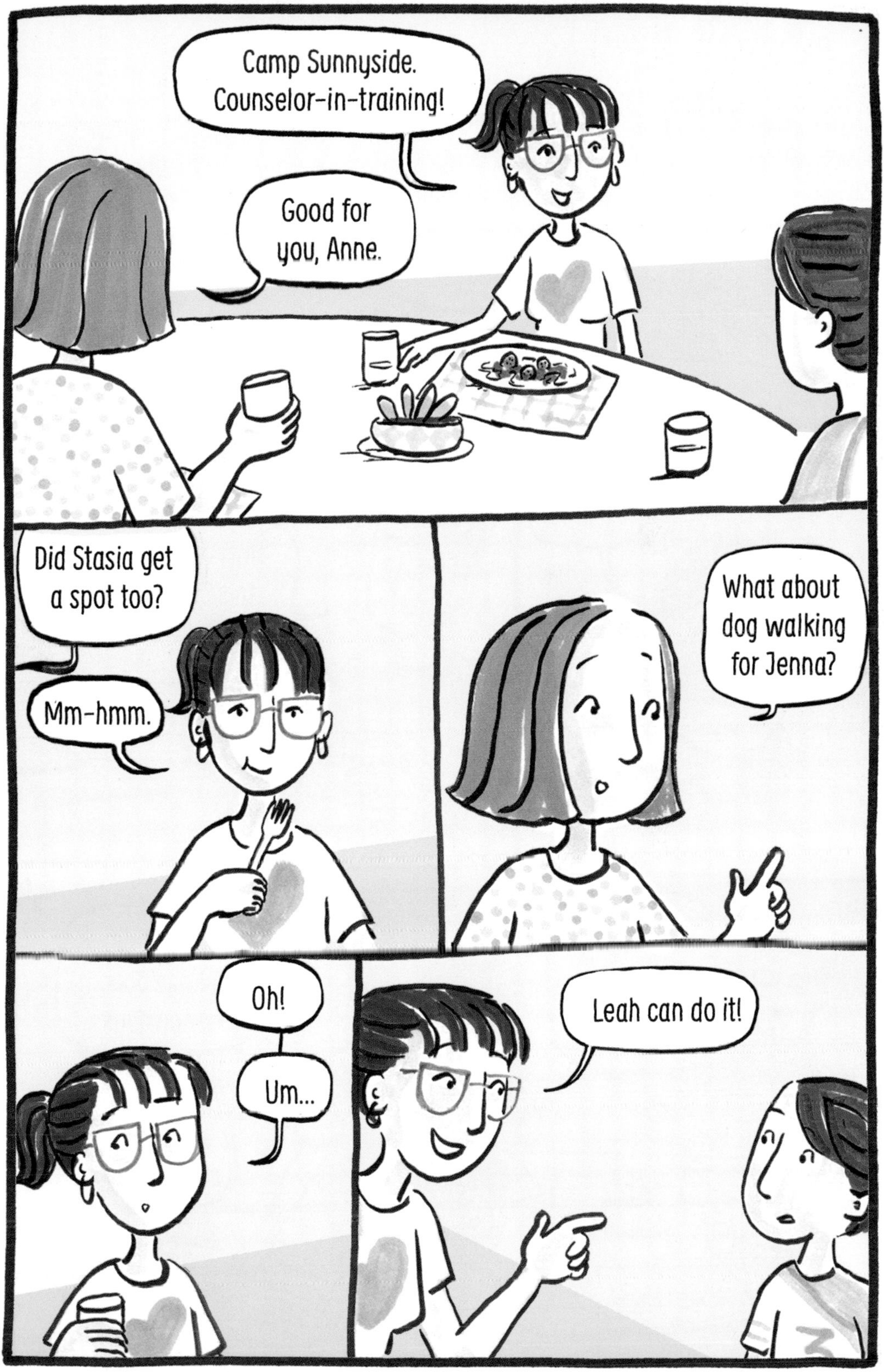
Camp Sunnyside. Counselor-in-training!
Good for you, Anne.
Did Stasia get a spot too?
Mm-hmm.
What about dog walking for Jenna?
Oh!
Um...
Leah can do it!

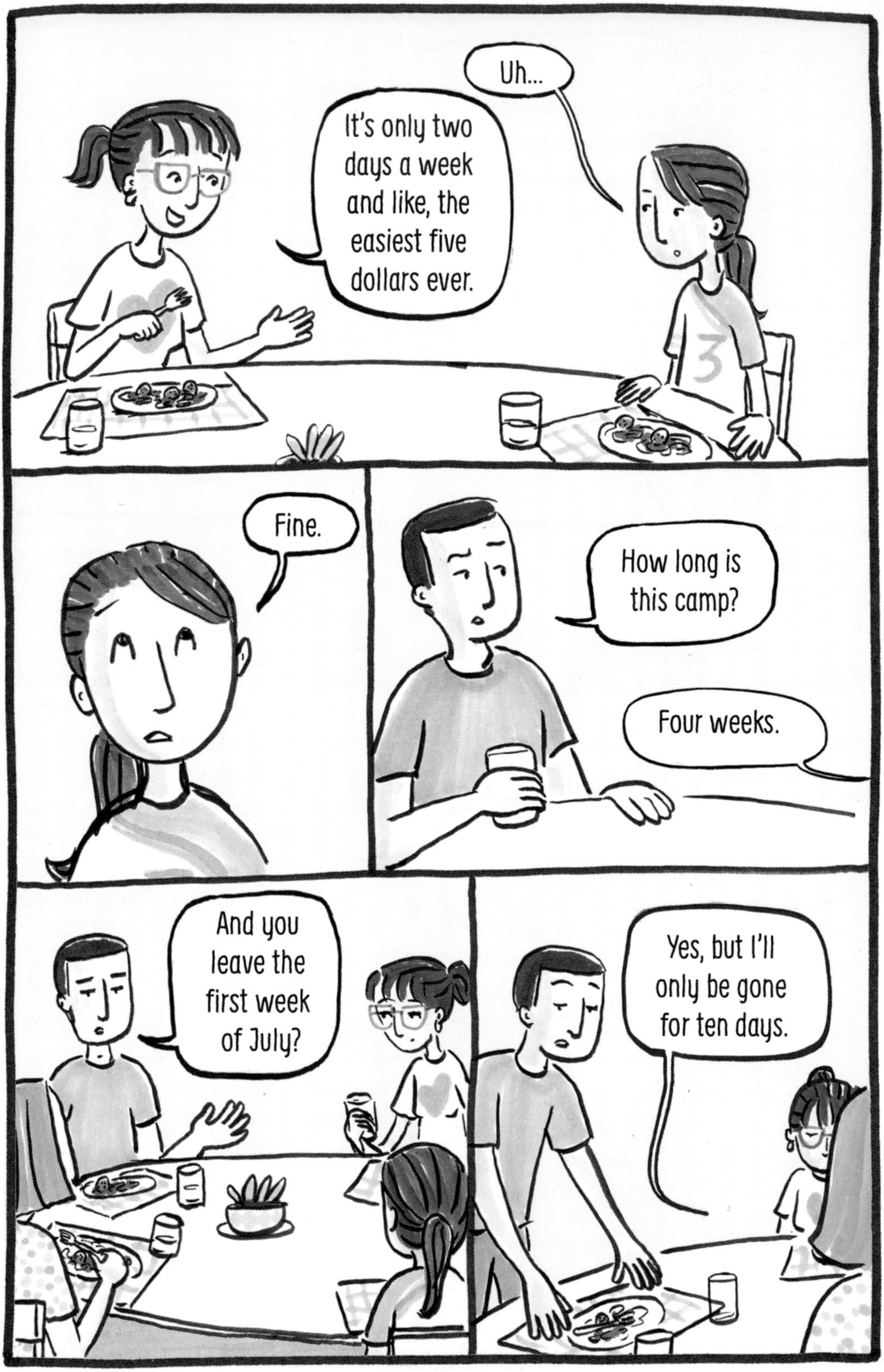
It's only two days a week and like, the easiest five dollars ever.
Uh...
Fine.
How long is this camp?
Four weeks.
And you leave the first week of July?
Yes, but I'll only be gone for ten days.

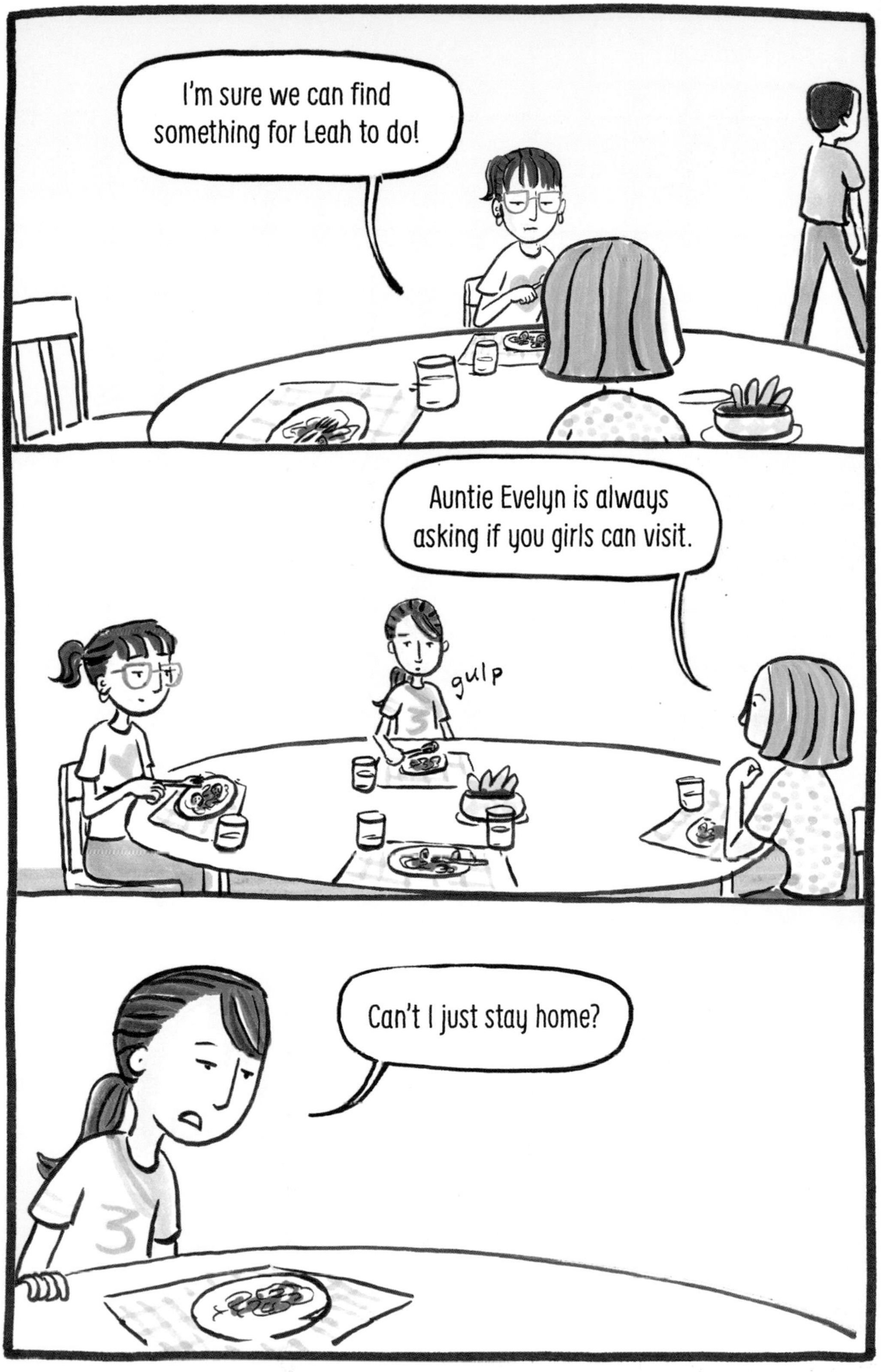
I'm sure we can find something for Leah to do!
Auntie Evelyn is always asking if you girls can visit.
gulp
Can't I just stay home?

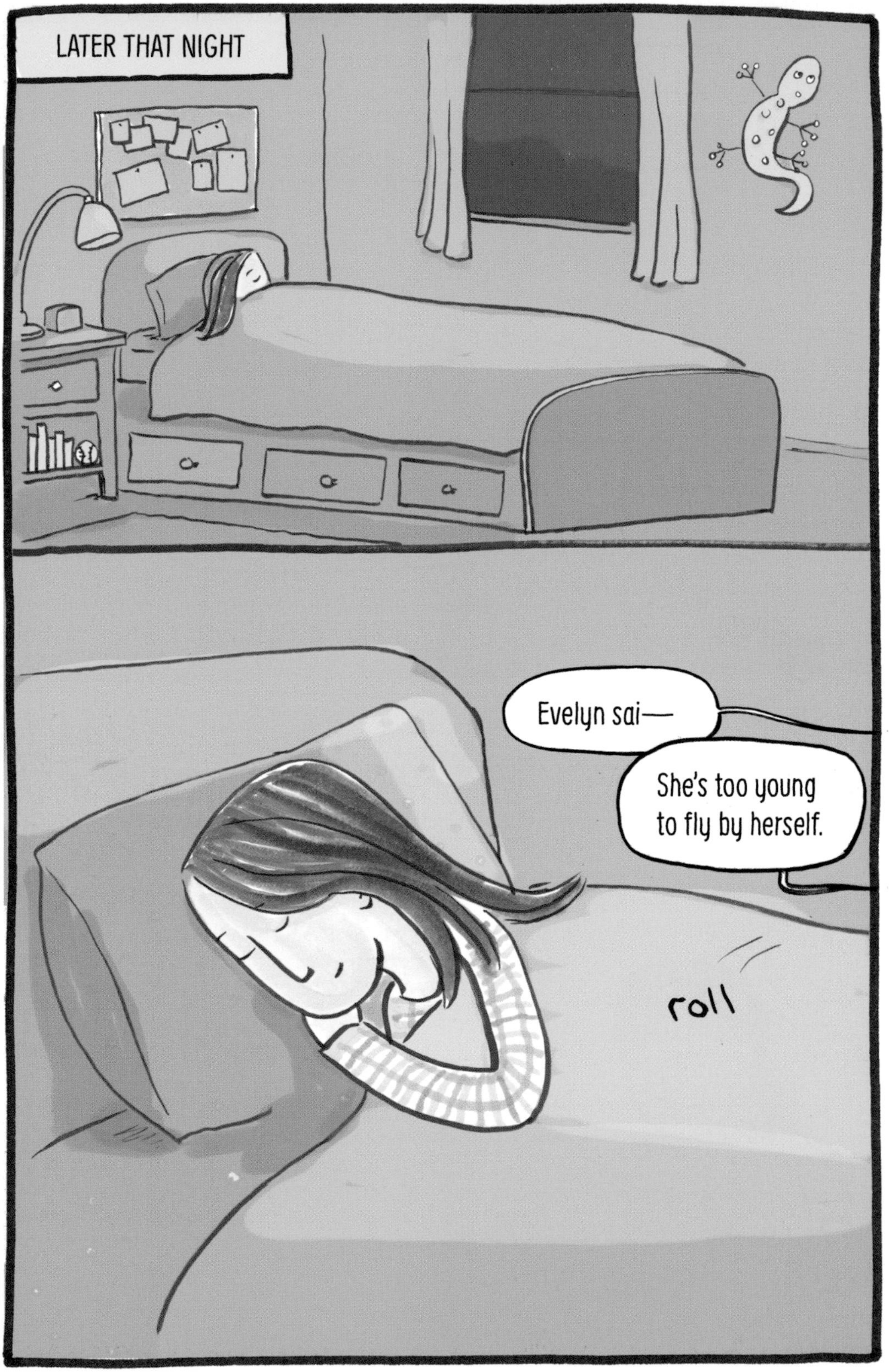
LATER THAT NIGHT
Evelyn sai—
She's too young to fly by herself.
roll

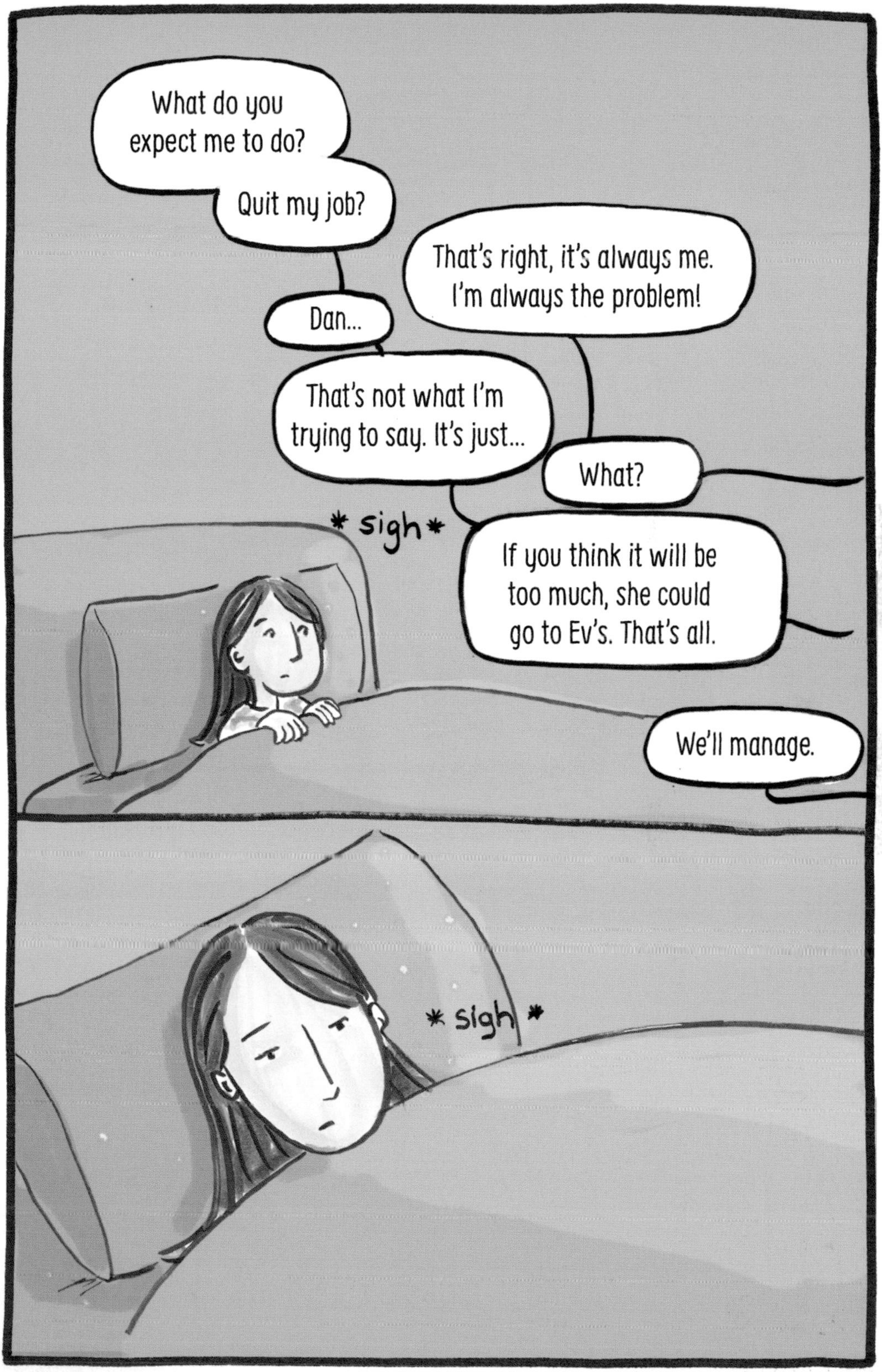
What do you expect me to do?
Quit my job?
Dan...
That's right, it's always me. I'm always the problem!
That's not what I'm trying to say. It's just...
What?
sigh
If you think it will be too much, she could go to Ev's. That's all.
We'll manage.
sigh

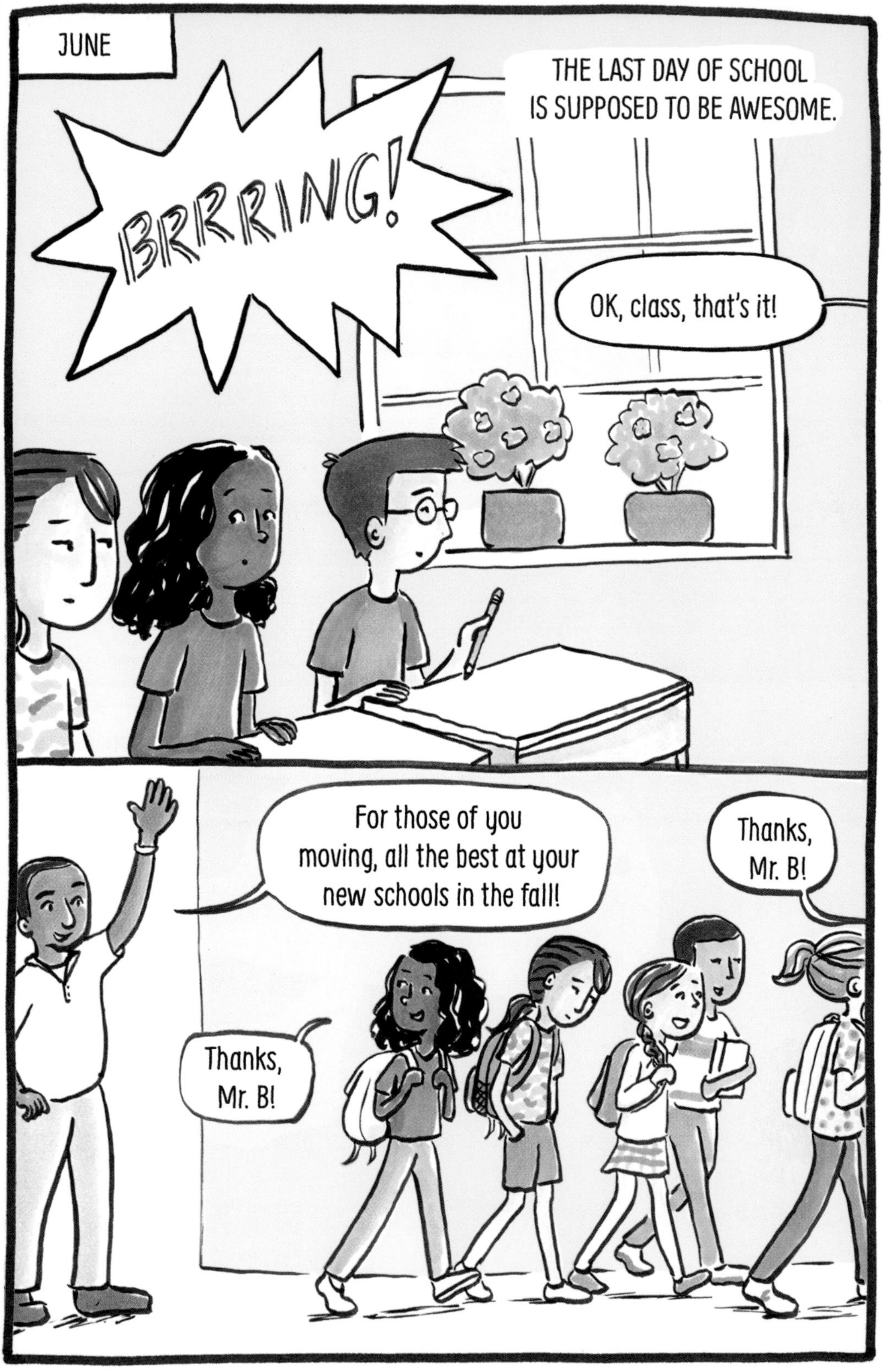
JUNE
THE LAST DAY OF SCHOOL IS SUPPOSED TO BE AWESOME.
BRRRING!
OK, class, that's it!
For those of you moving, all the best at your new schools in the fall!
Thanks, Mr. B!
Thanks, Mr. B!

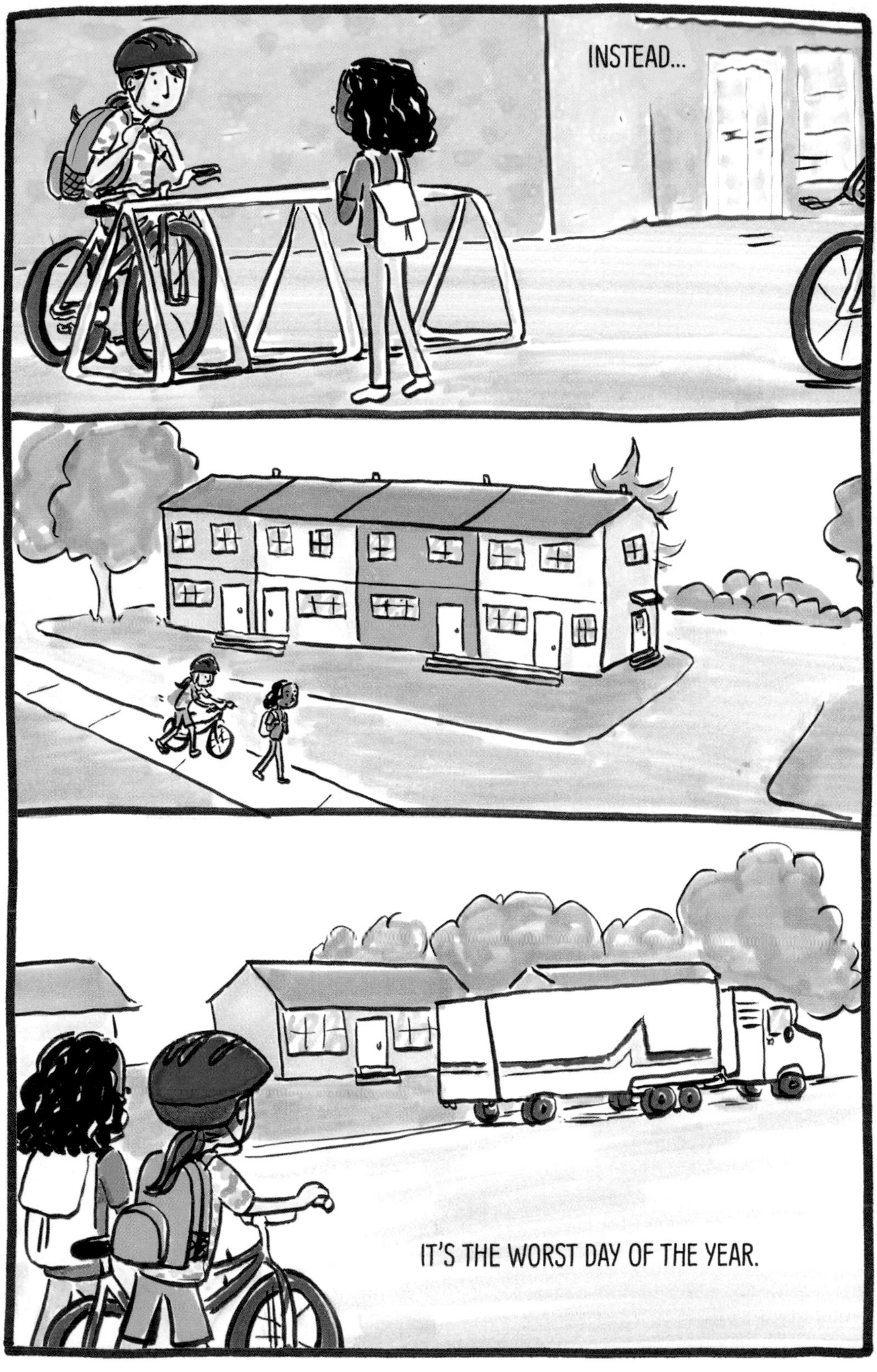
INSTEAD...
IT'S THE WORST DAY OF THE YEAR.

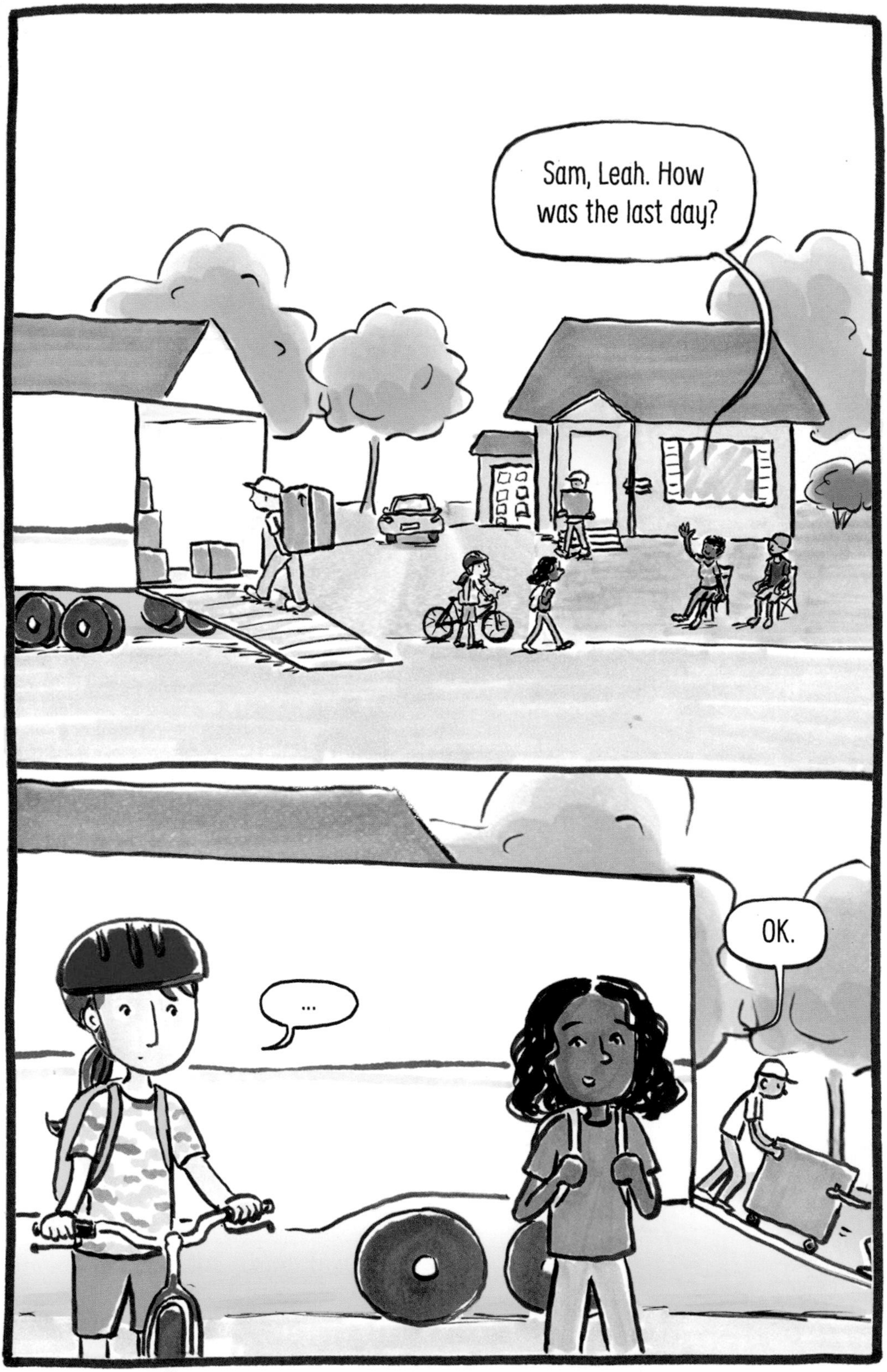
Sam, Leah. How was the last day?
...
OK.

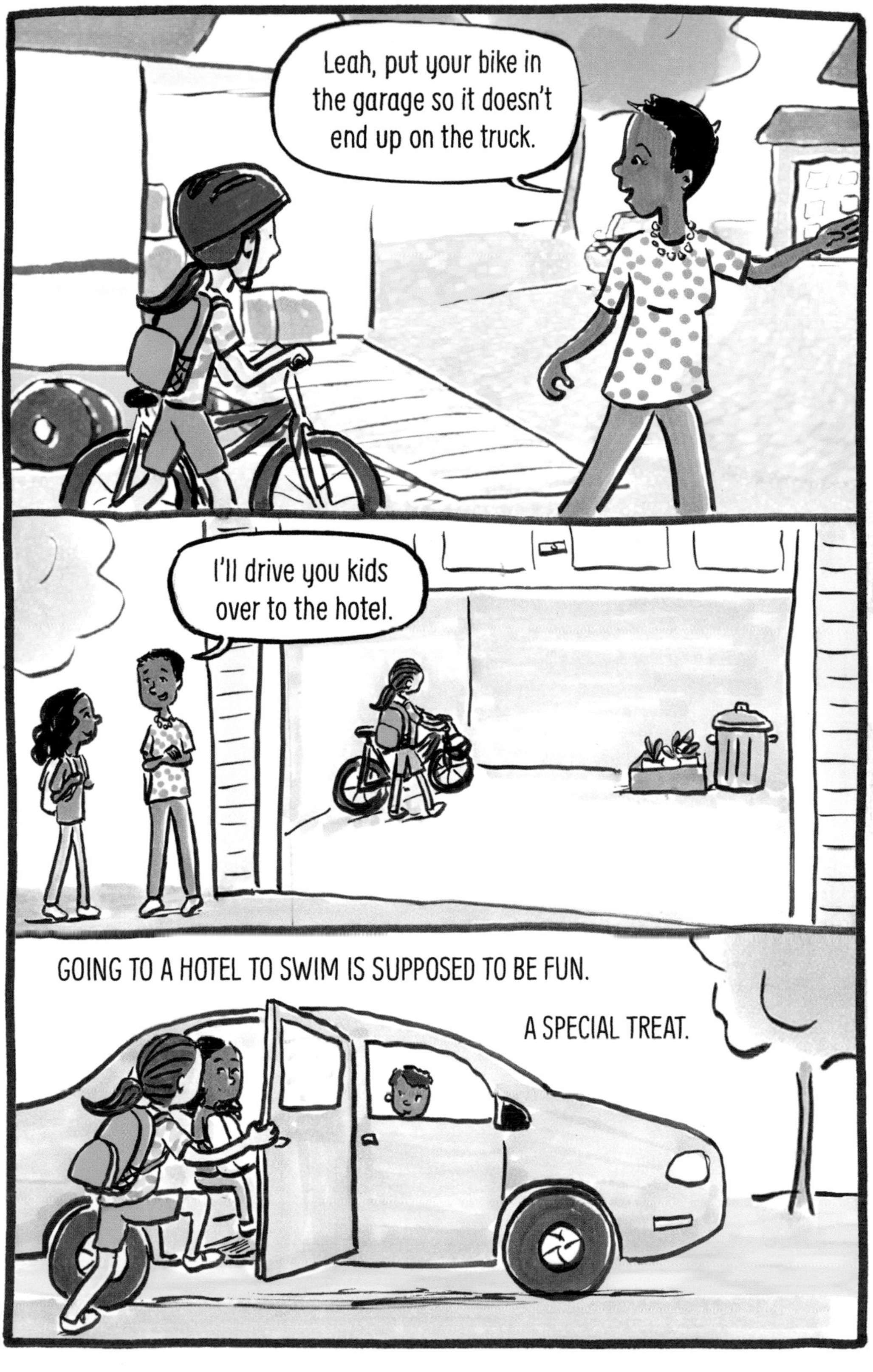
Leah, put your bike in the garage so it doesn't end up on the truck.
I'll drive you kids over to the hotel.
GOING TO A HOTEL TO SWIM IS SUPPOSED TO BE FUN.
A SPECIAL TREAT.

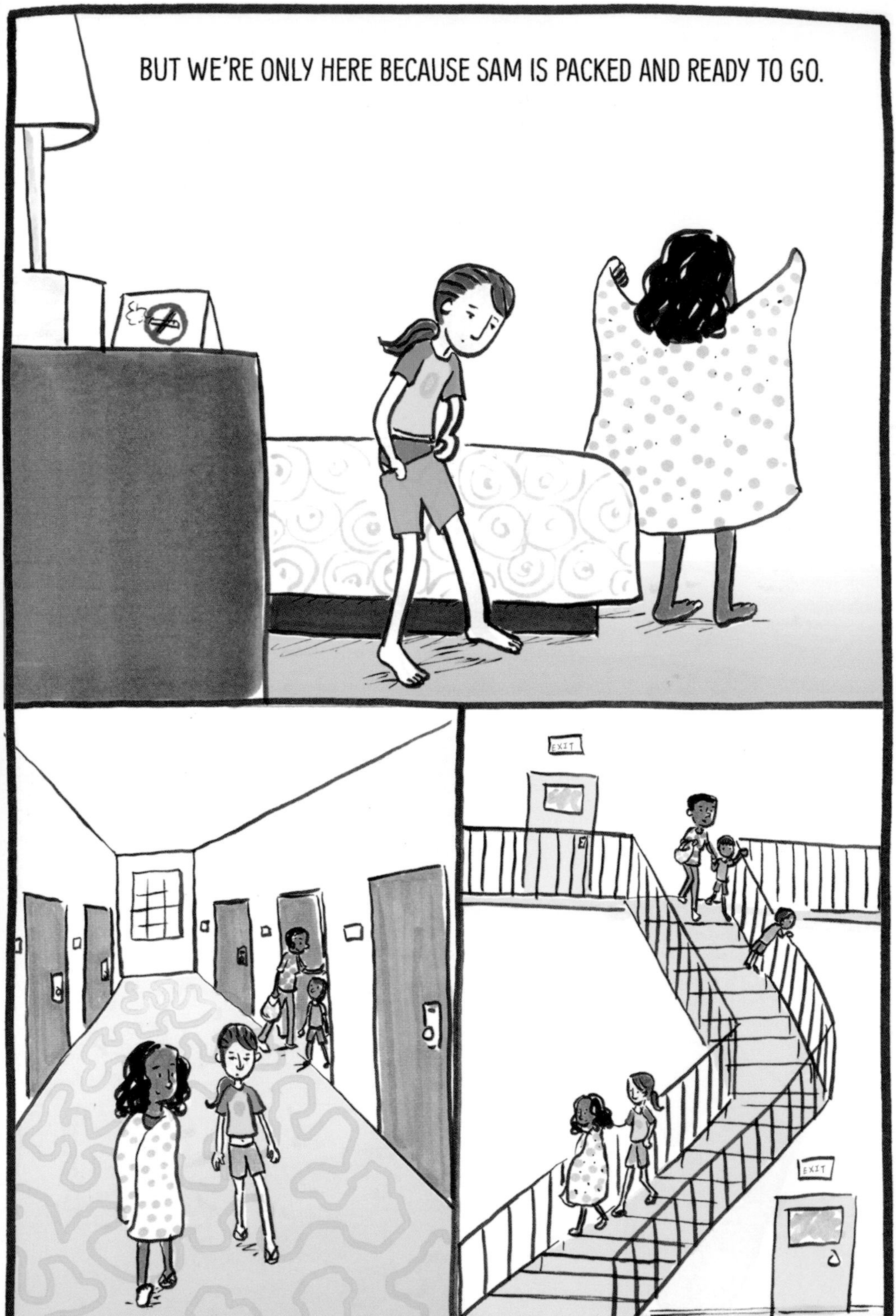
BUT WE'RE ONLY HERE BECAUSE SAM IS PACKED AND READY TO GO.
AND SHE'S LEAVING IN THE MORNING.
EXIT
EXIT

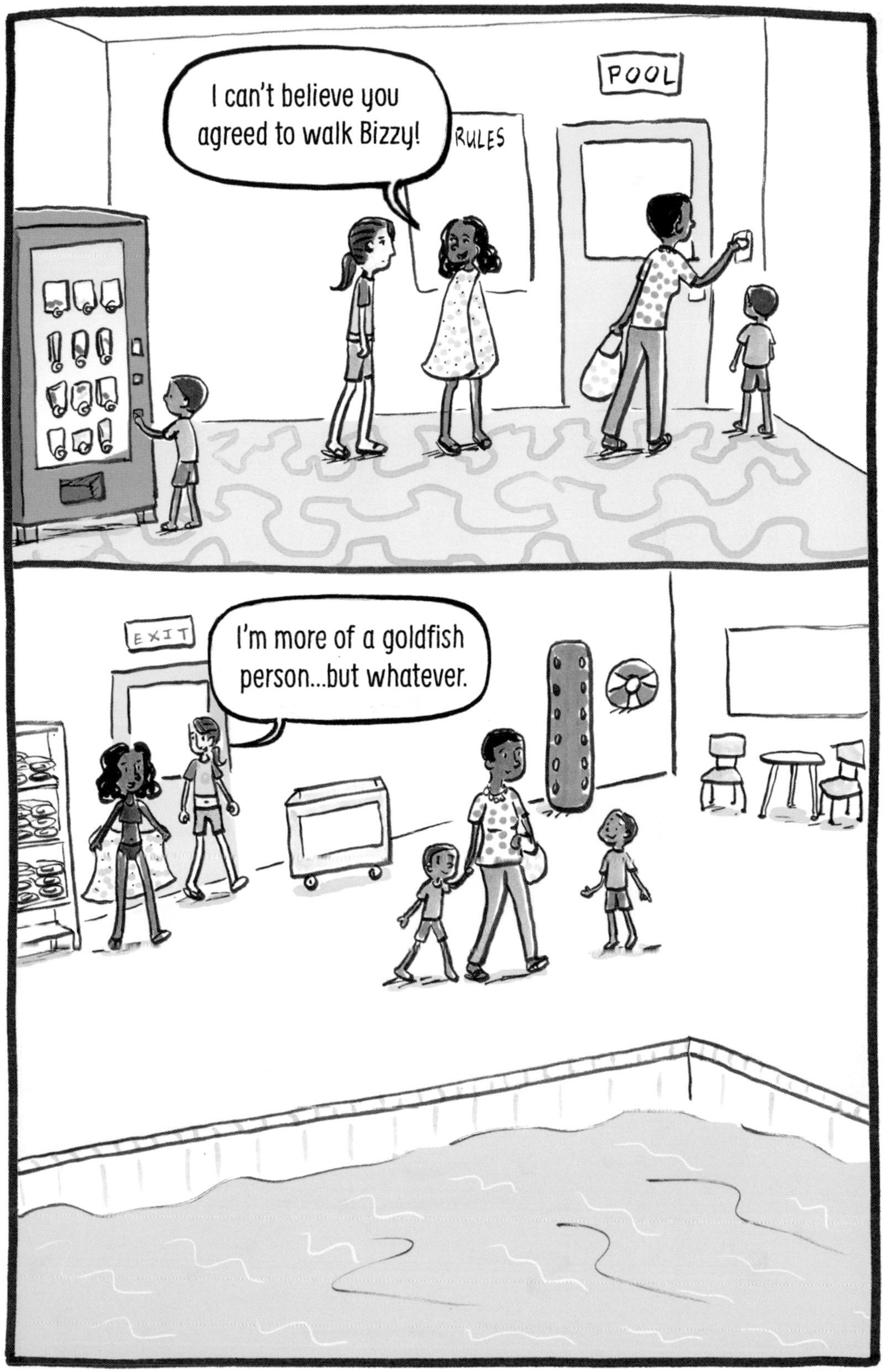
POOL
I can't believe you agreed to walk Bizzy!
RULES
EXIT
I'm more of a goldfish person...but whatever.

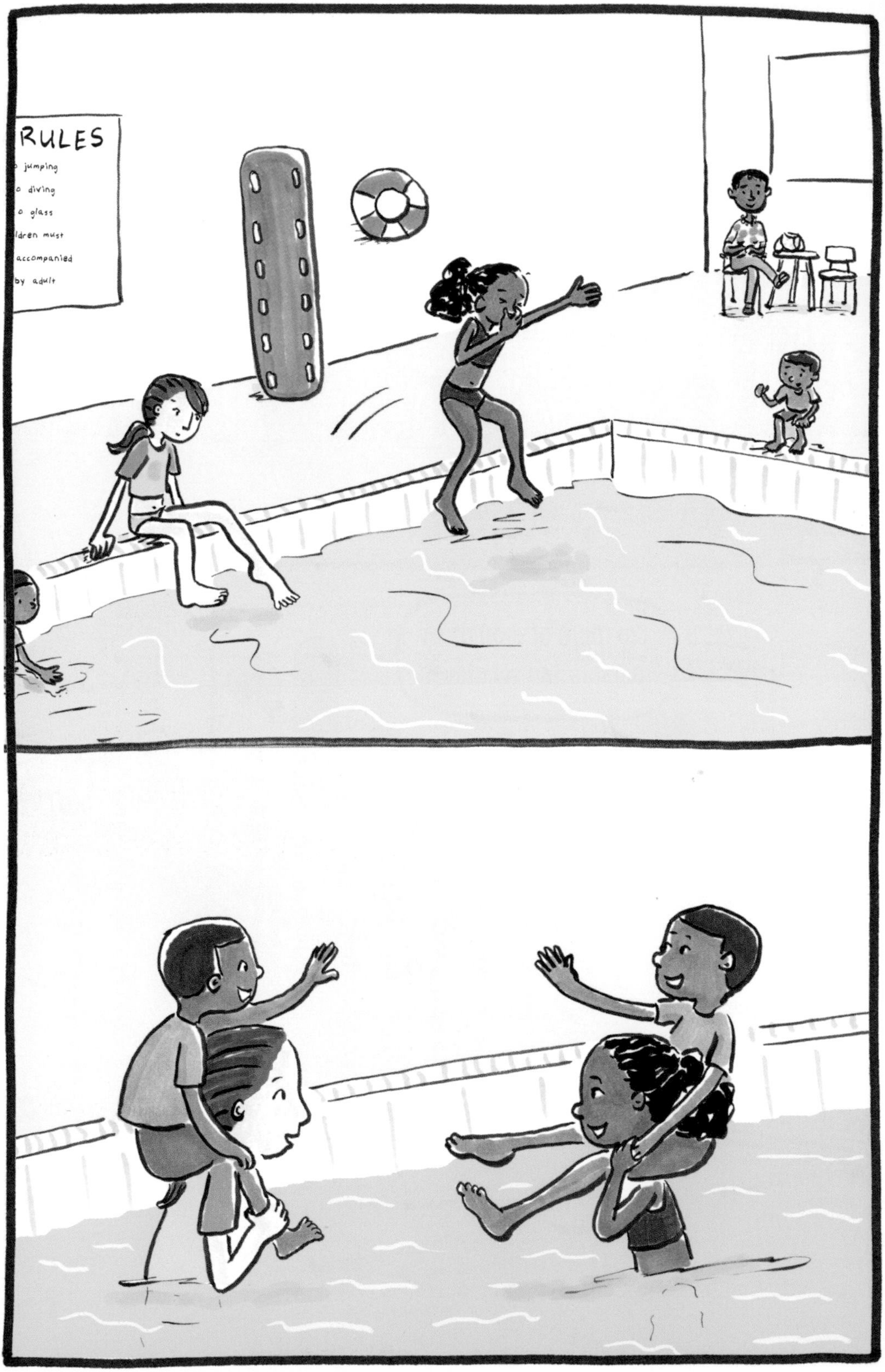
RULES
jumping
o diving
o glass
ldren must
accompanied
by adult

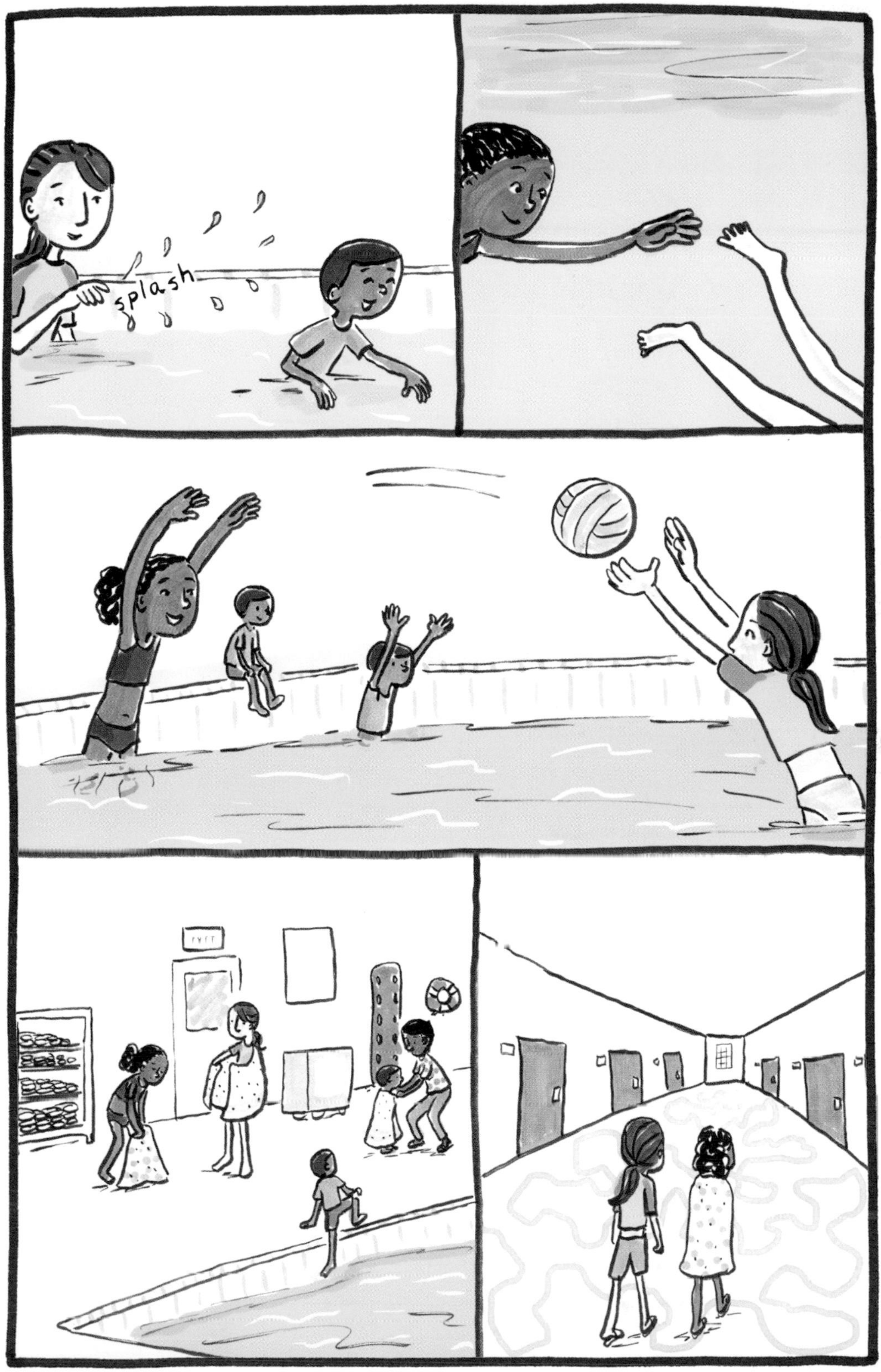
splash

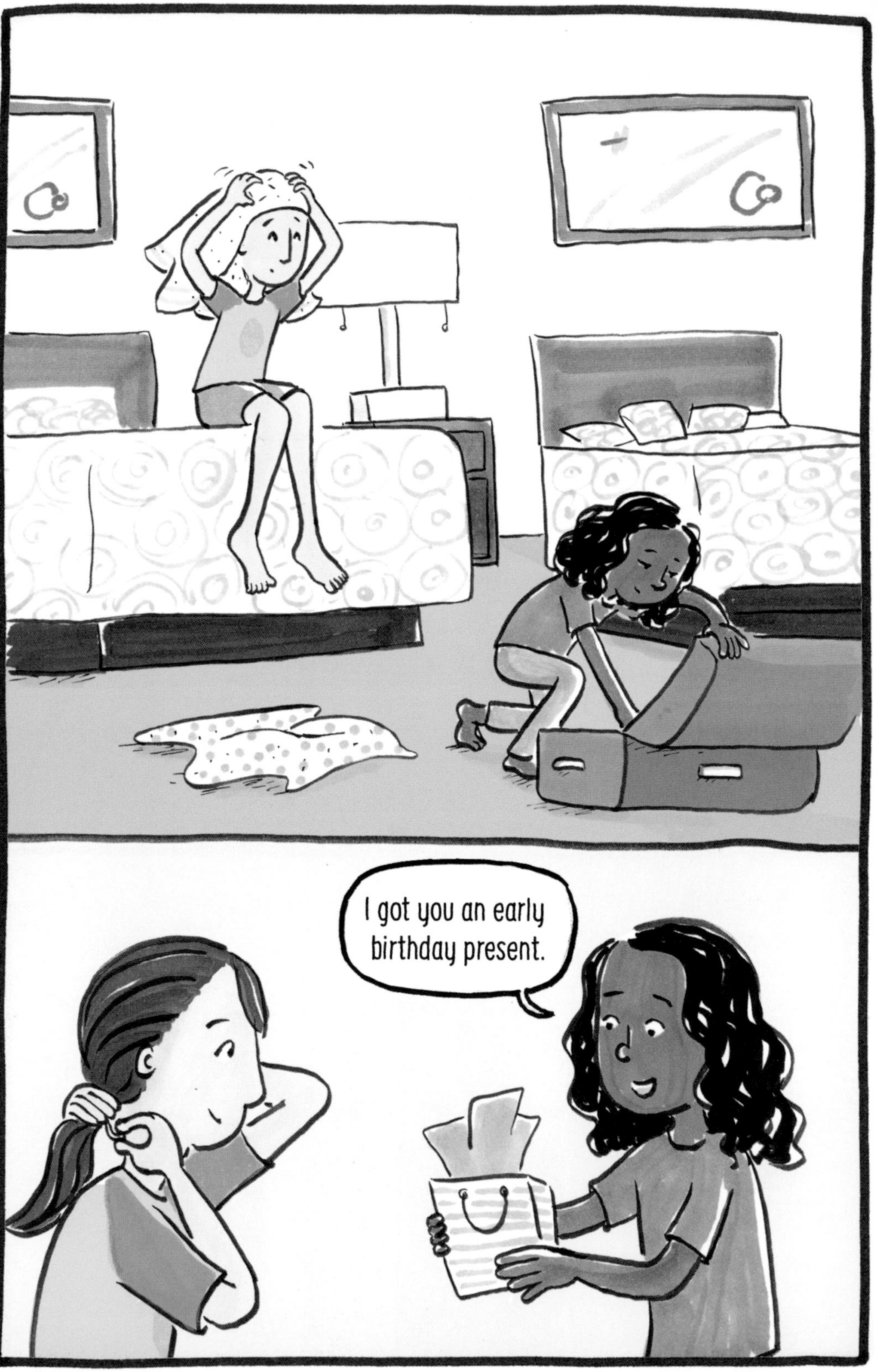
I got you an early birthday present.

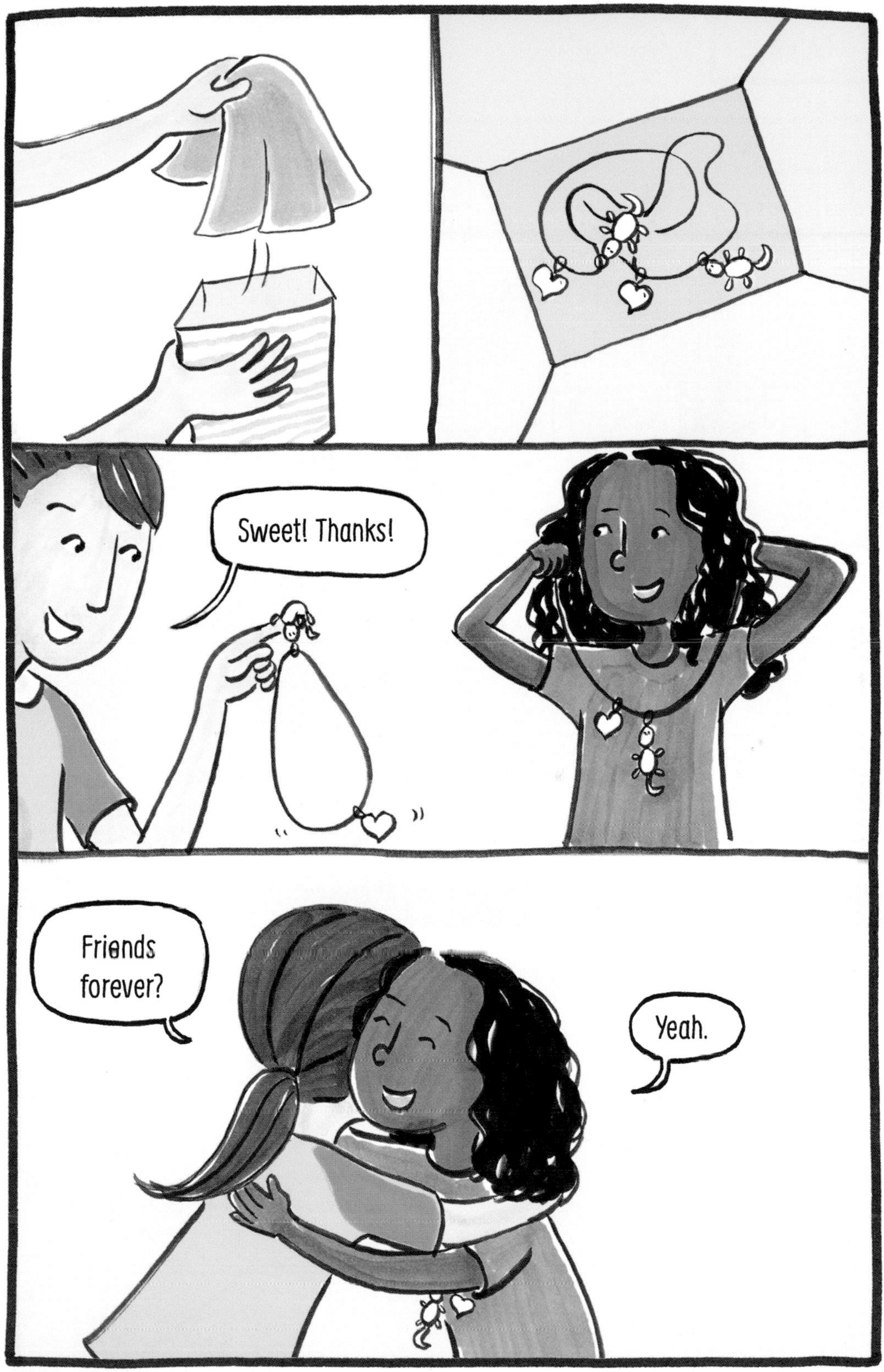
Sweet! Thanks!
Friends forever?
Yeah.

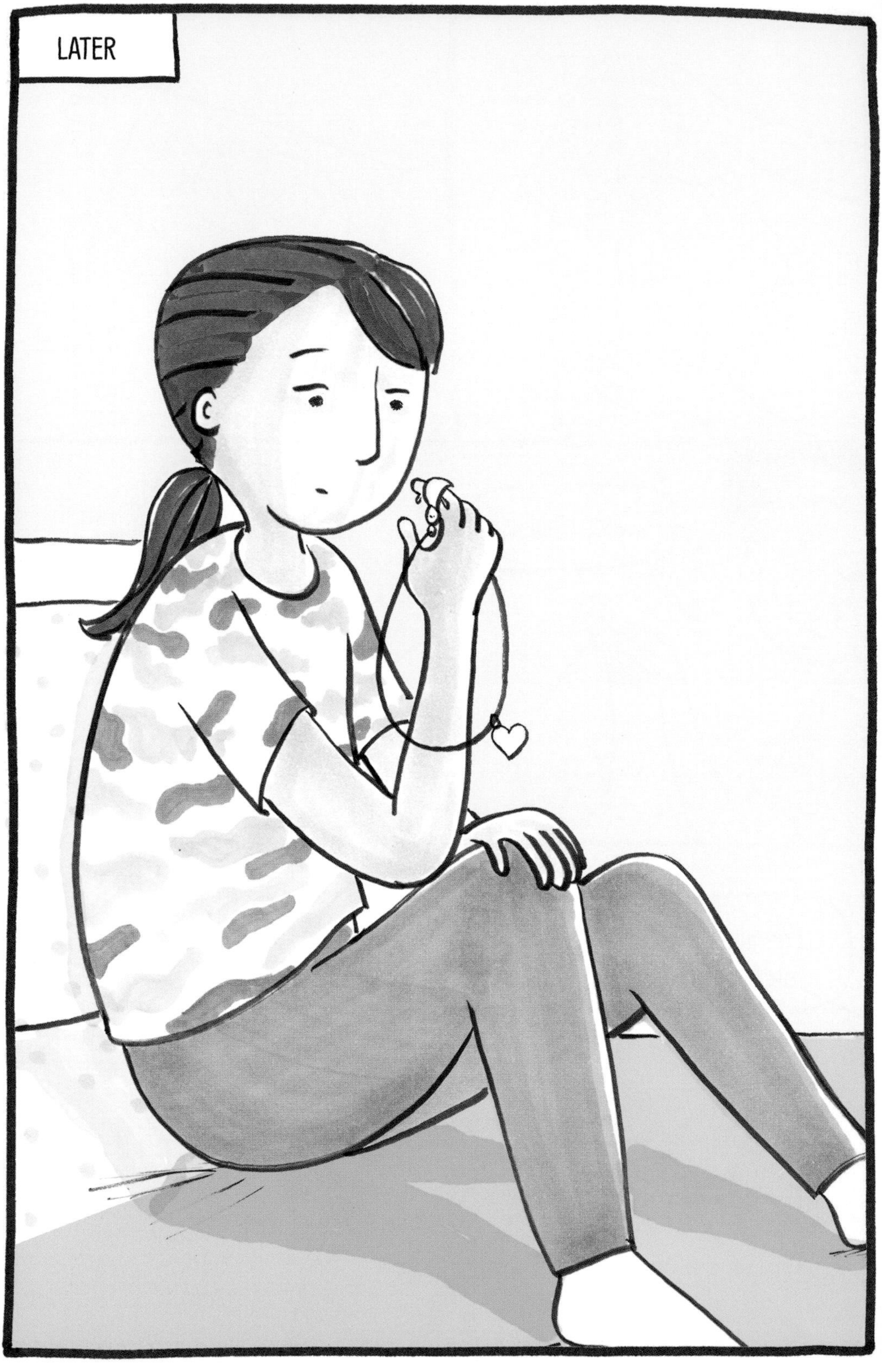
LATER

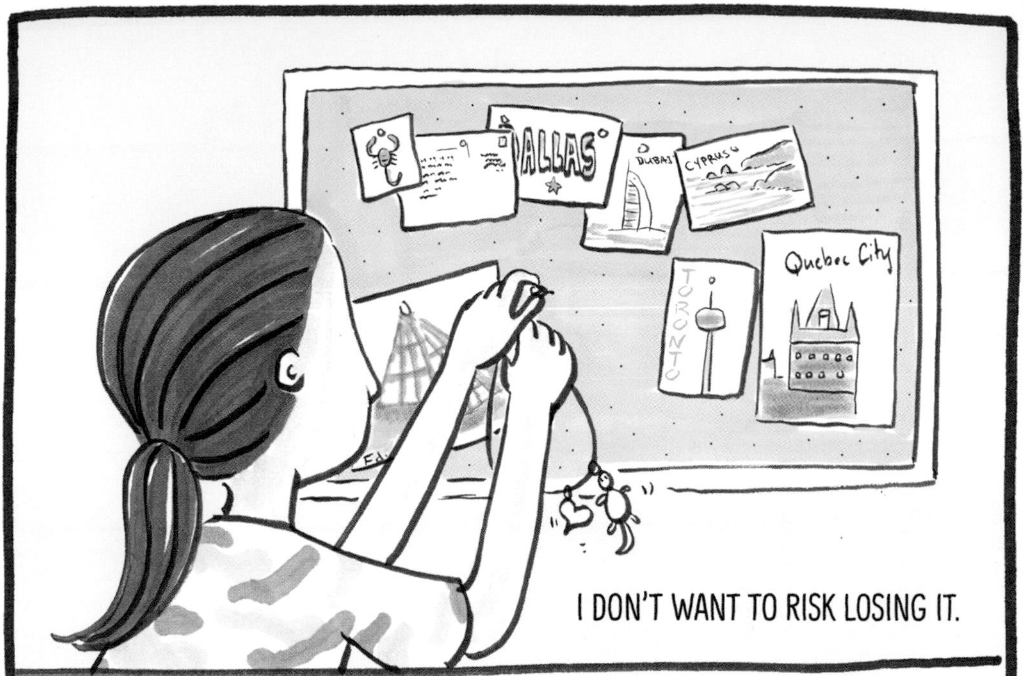
DUBAI
CYPRUS
TORONTO
Quebec City
I DON'T WANT TO RISK LOSING IT.

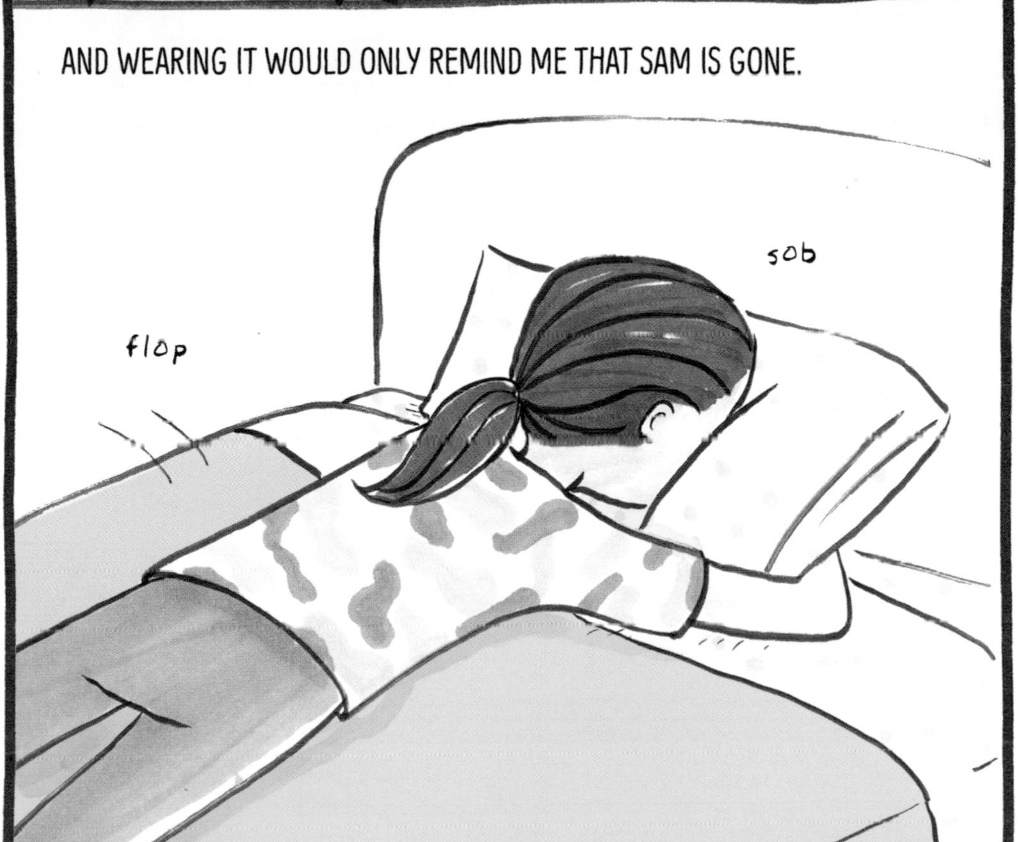
AND WEARING IT WOULD ONLY REMIND ME THAT SAM IS GONE.
sob
flop

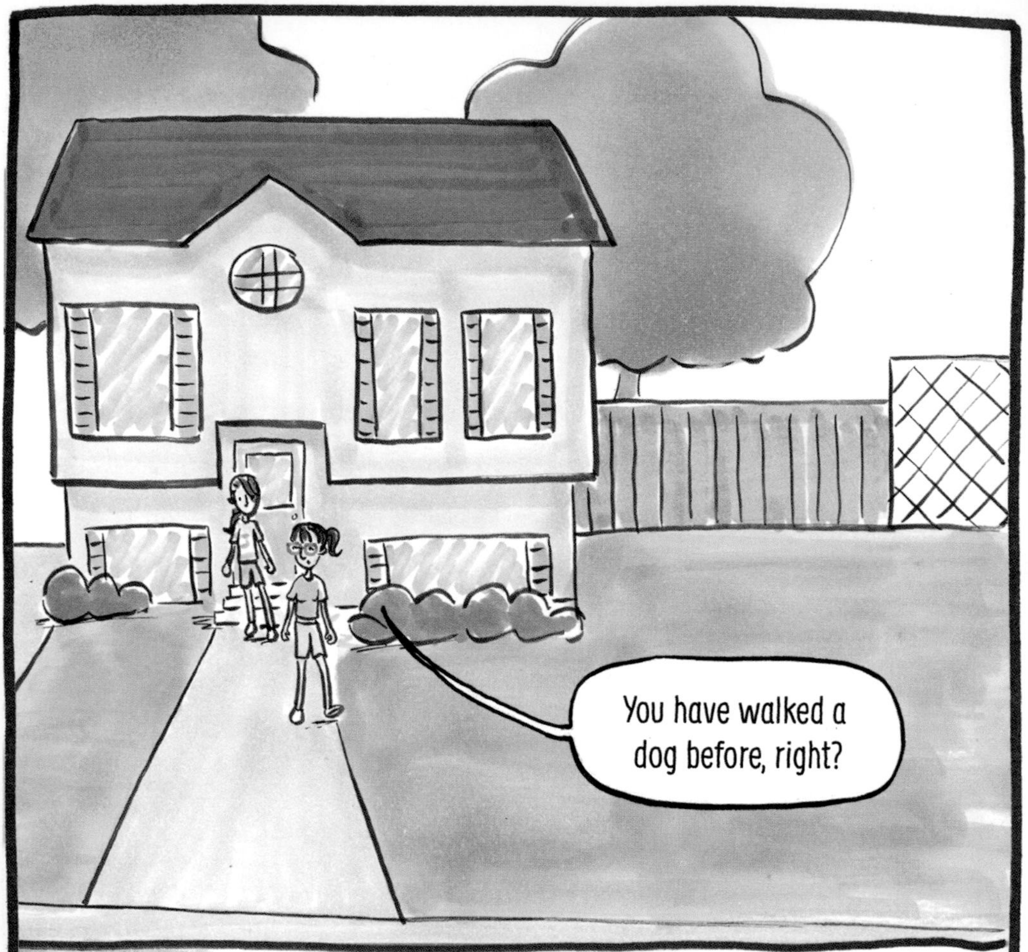
You have walked a dog before, right?

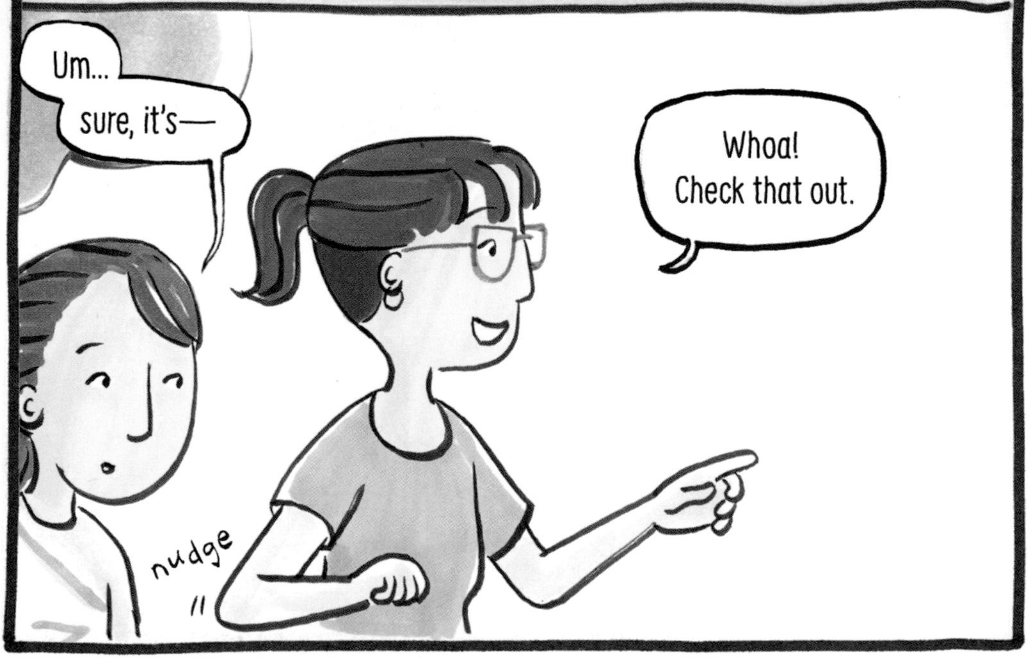
Um...
sure, it's—
Whoa! Check that out.
nudge

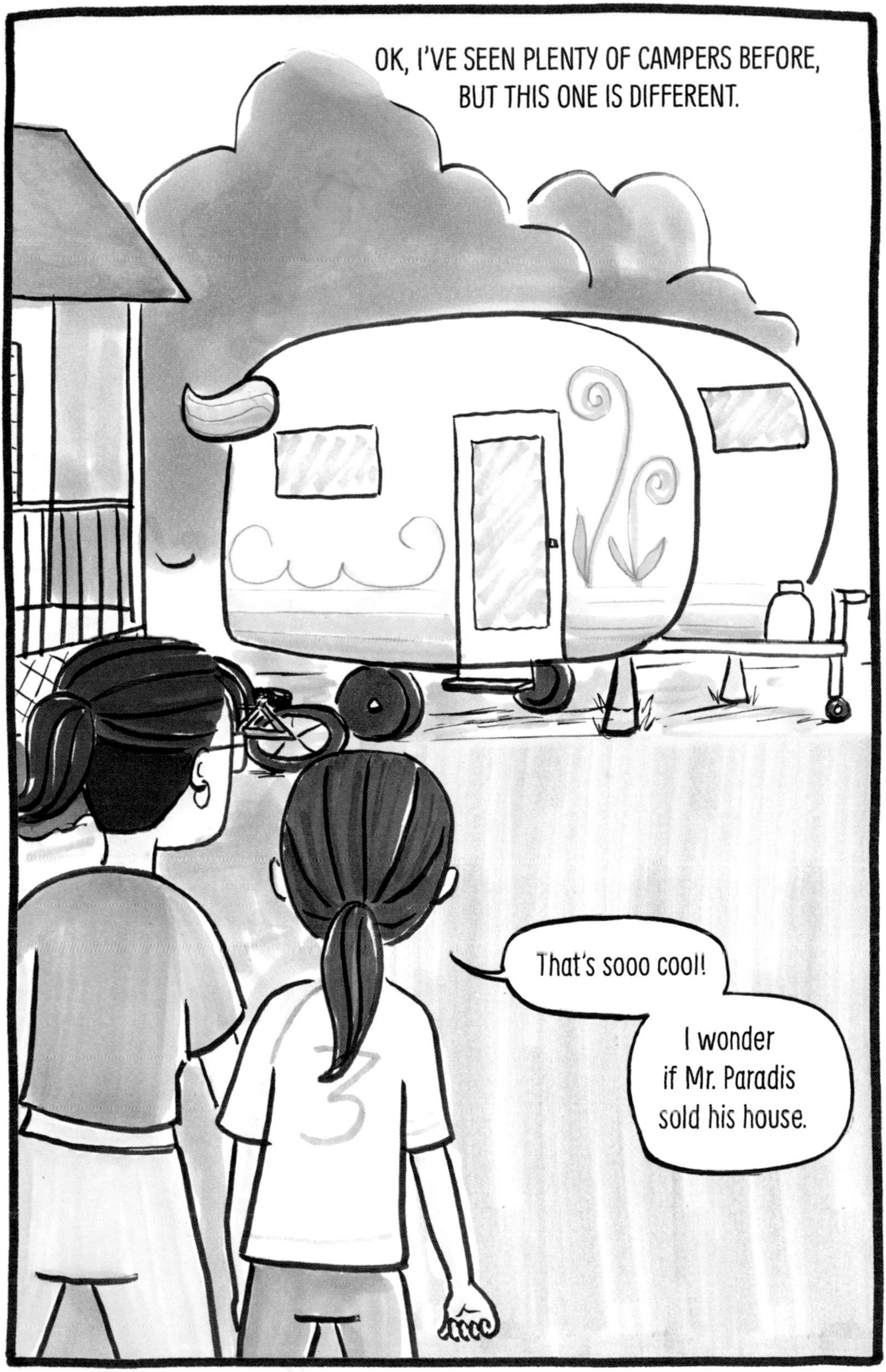
OK, I'VE SEEN PLENTY OF CAMPERS BEFORE, BUT THIS ONE IS DIFFERENT.
That's sooo cool!
I wonder if Mr. Paradis sold his house.

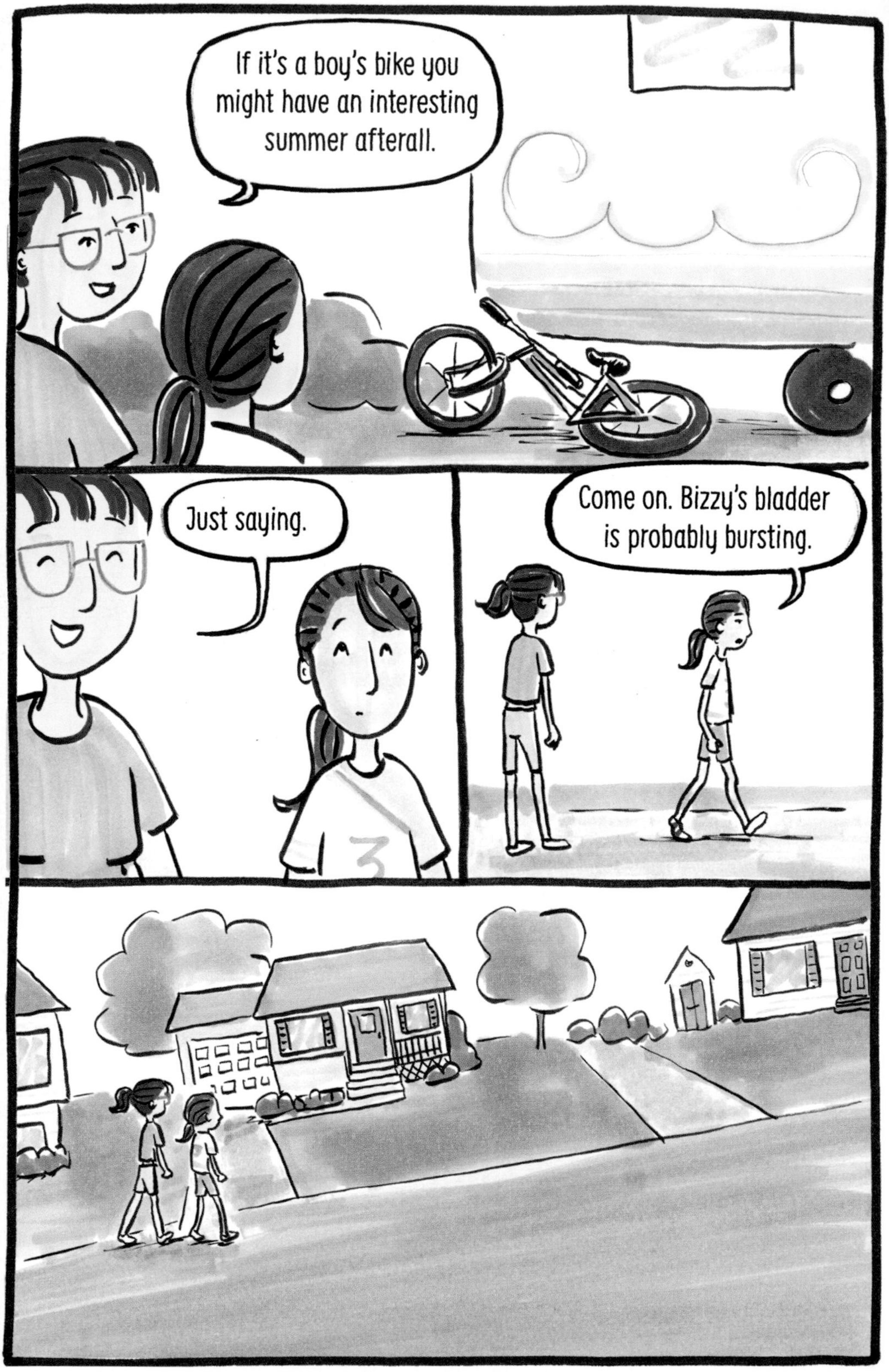
If it's a boy's bike you might have an interesting summer afterall.
Just saying.
Come on. Bizzy's bladder is probably bursting.

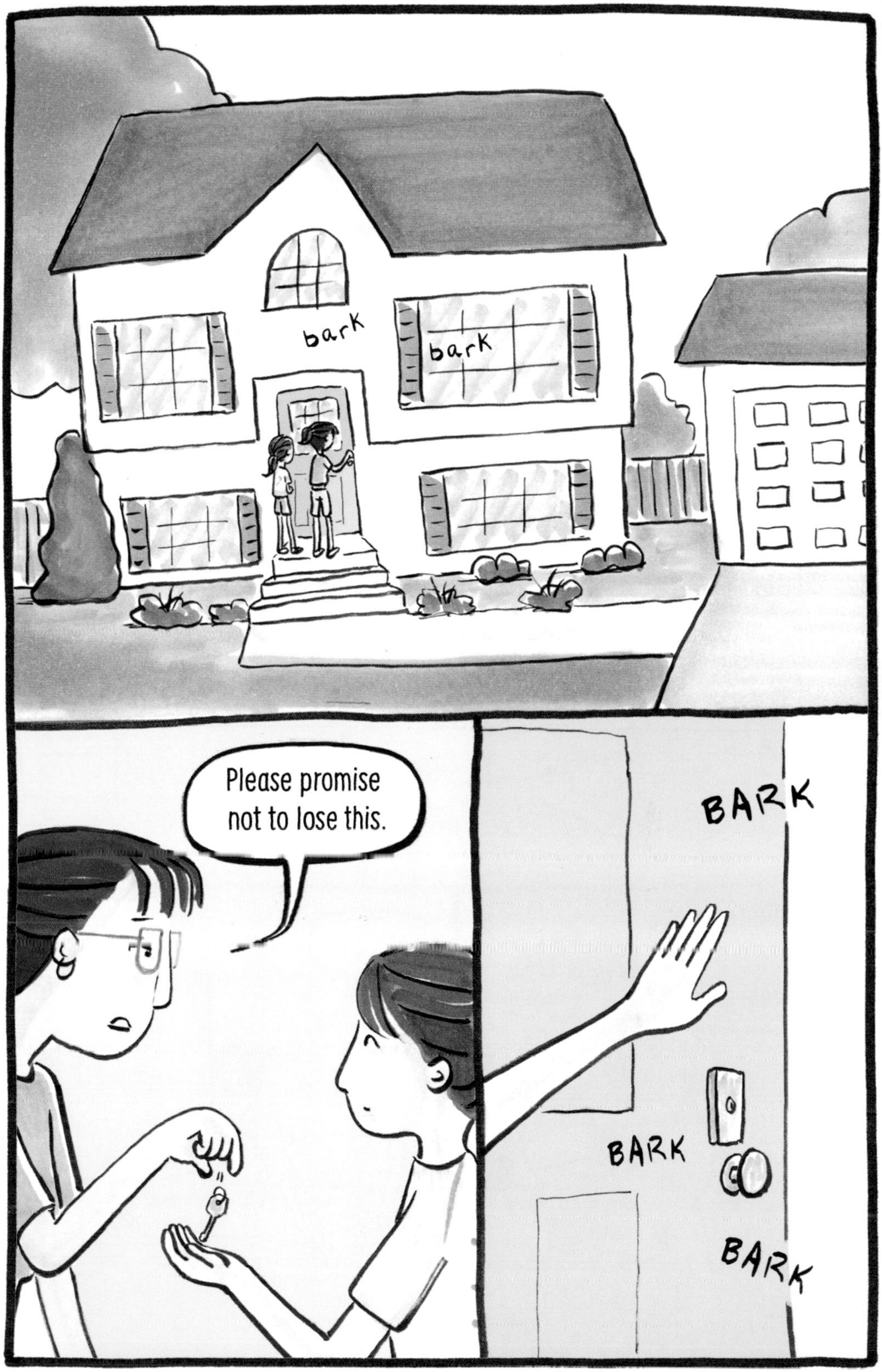

bark
bark
Please promise not to lose this.
BARK
BARK
BARK

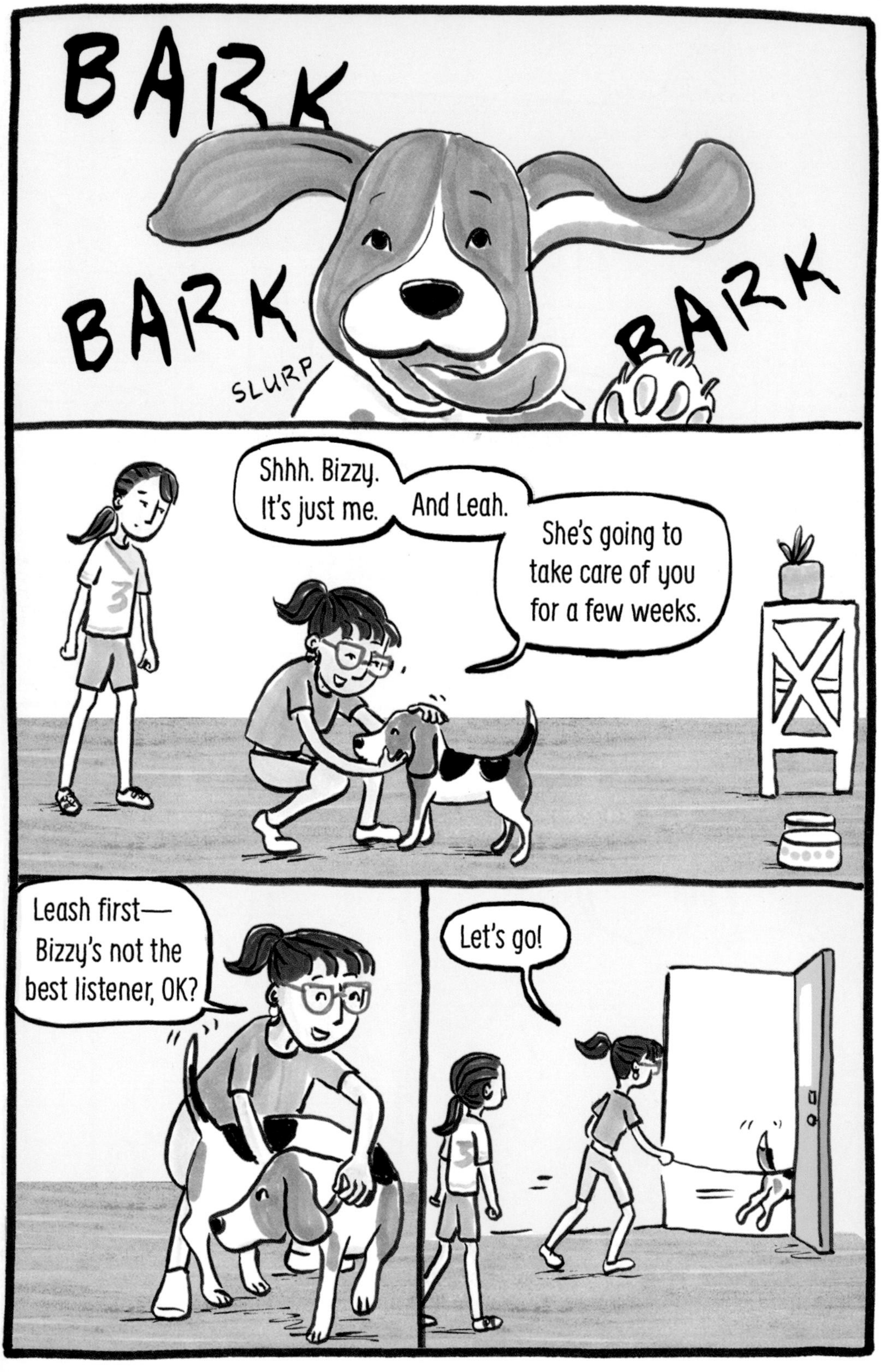
BARK
BARK
BARK
SLURP
Shhh. Bizzy. It's just me.
And Leah.
She's going to take care of you for a few weeks.
Leash first—Bizzy's not the best listener, OK?
Let's go!

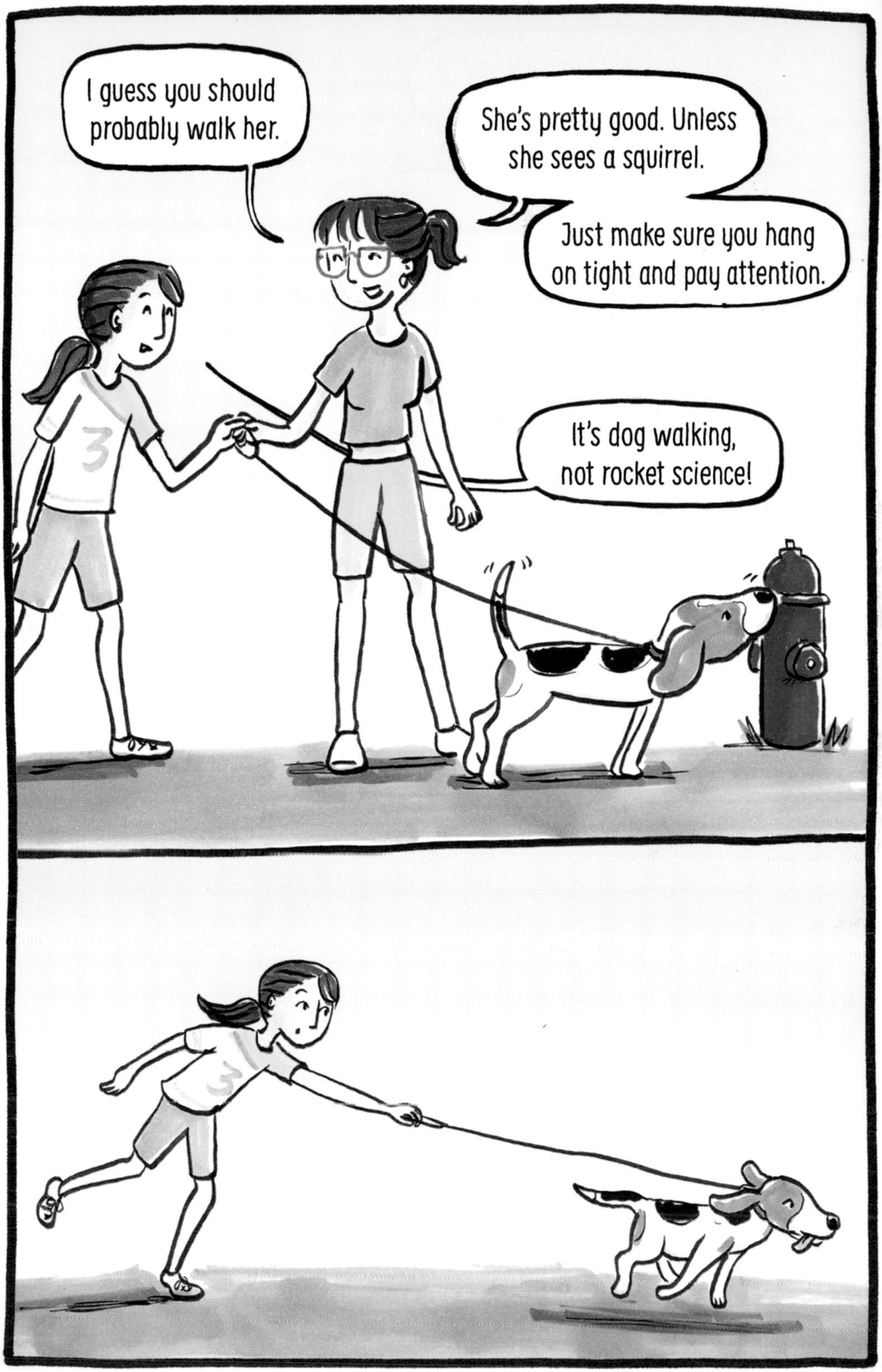
I guess you should probably walk her.
She's pretty good. Unless she sees a squirrel.
Just make sure you hang on tight and pay attention.
It's dog walking, not rocket science!

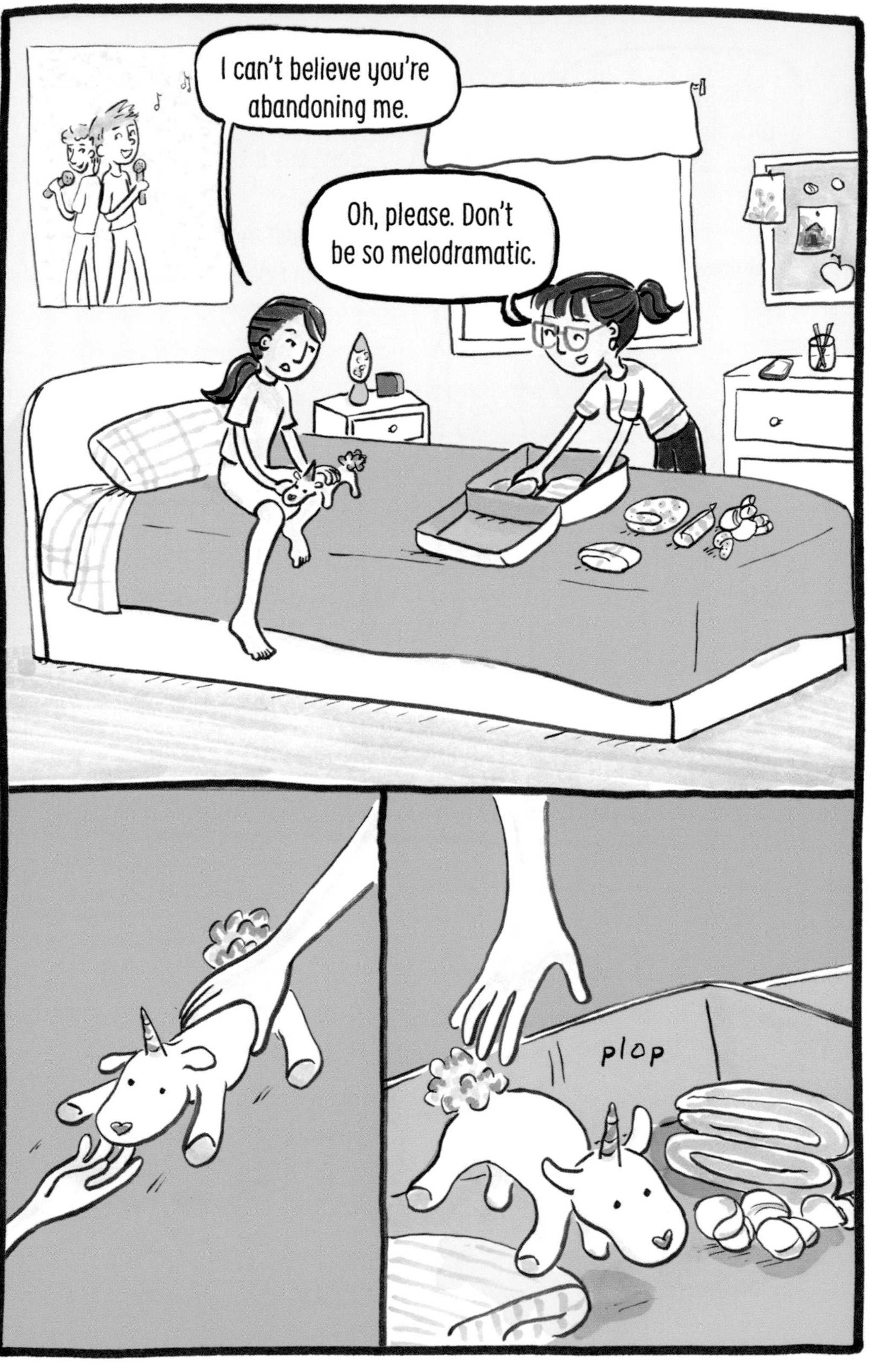
I can't believe you're abandoning me.
Oh, please. Don't be so melodramatic.
plop

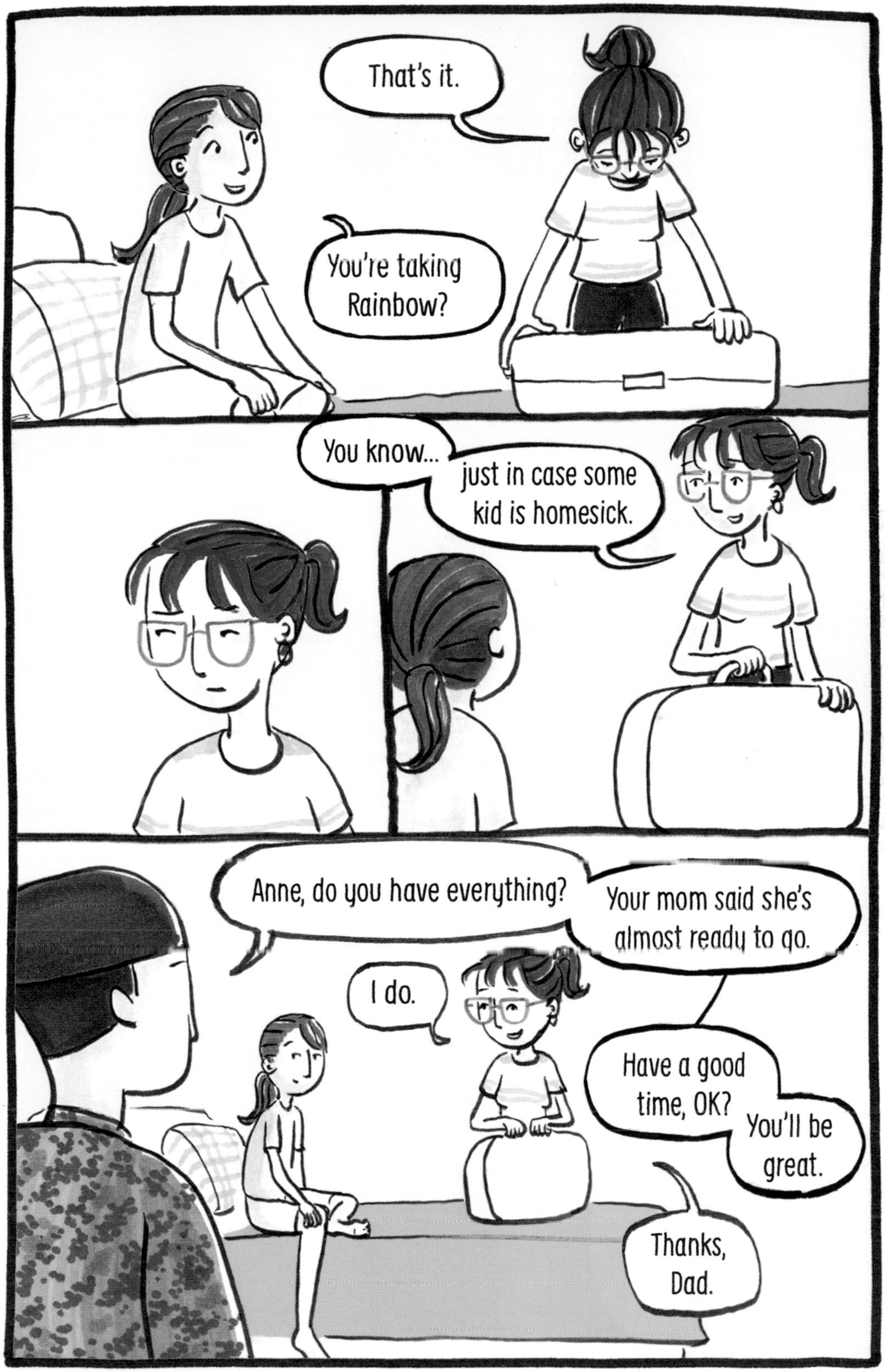
That's it.
You're taking Rainbow?
You know...
just in case some kid is homesick.
Anne, do you have everything?
Your mom said she's almost ready to go.
I do.
Have a good time, OK?
You'll be great.
Thanks, Dad.

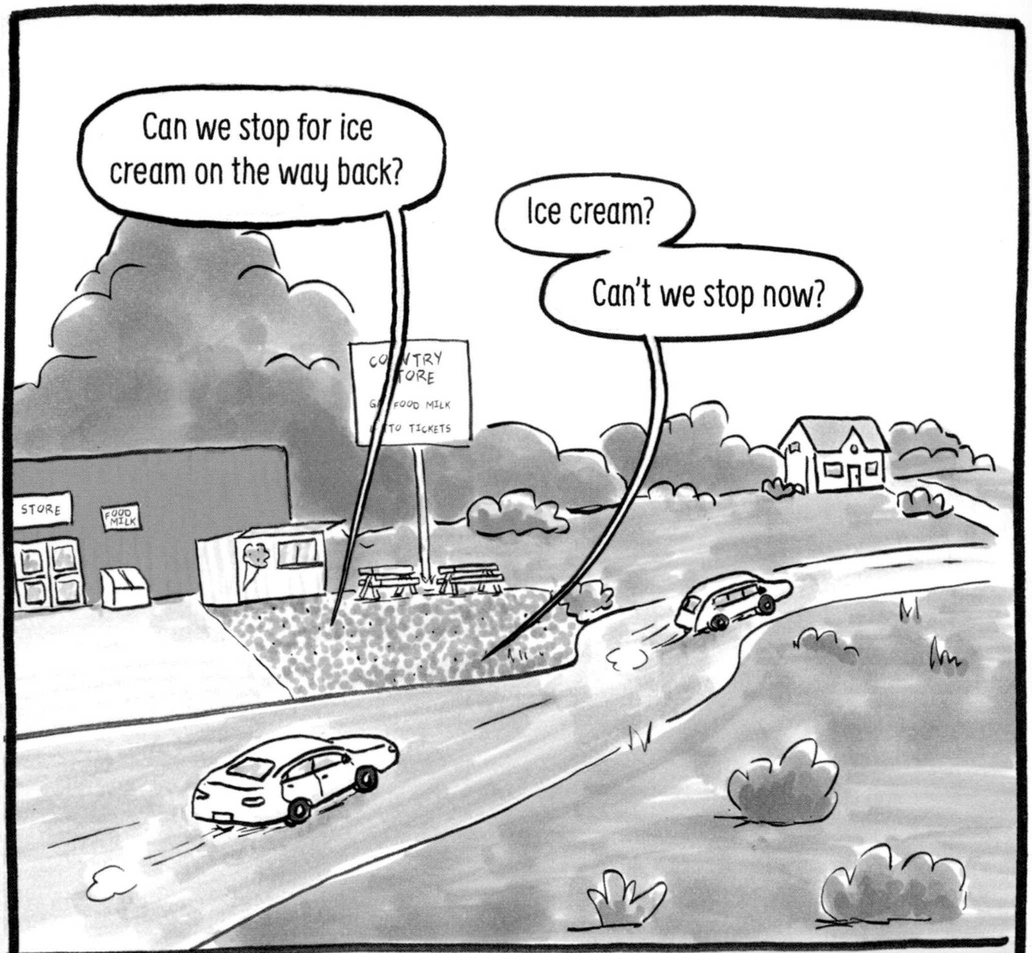
Can we stop for ice cream on the way back?
Ice cream?
Can't we stop now?
STORE
FOOD MILK

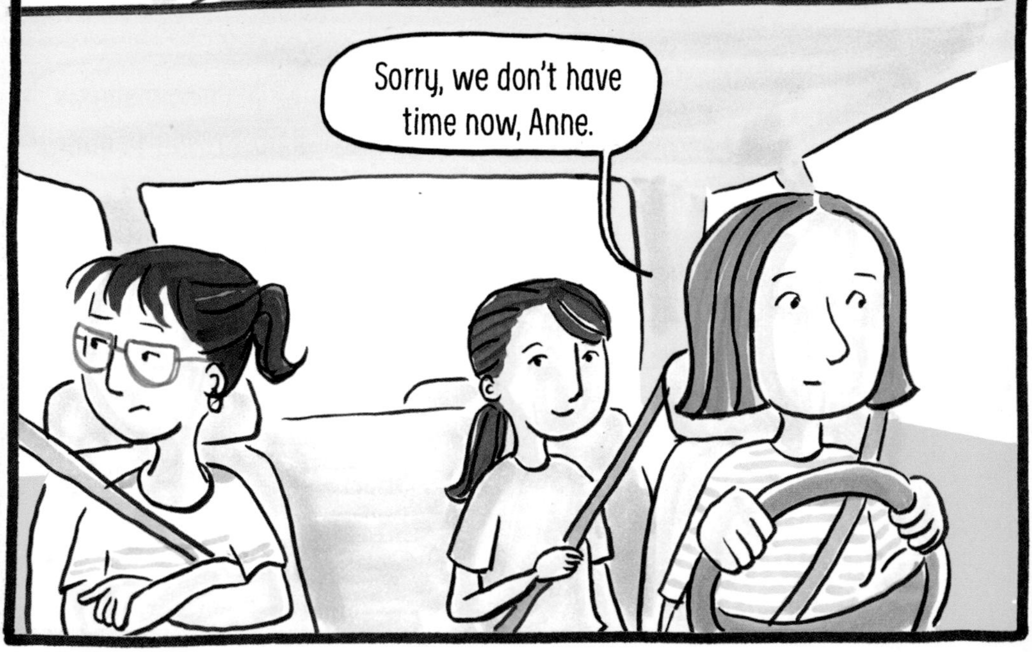
Sorry, we don't have time now, Anne.

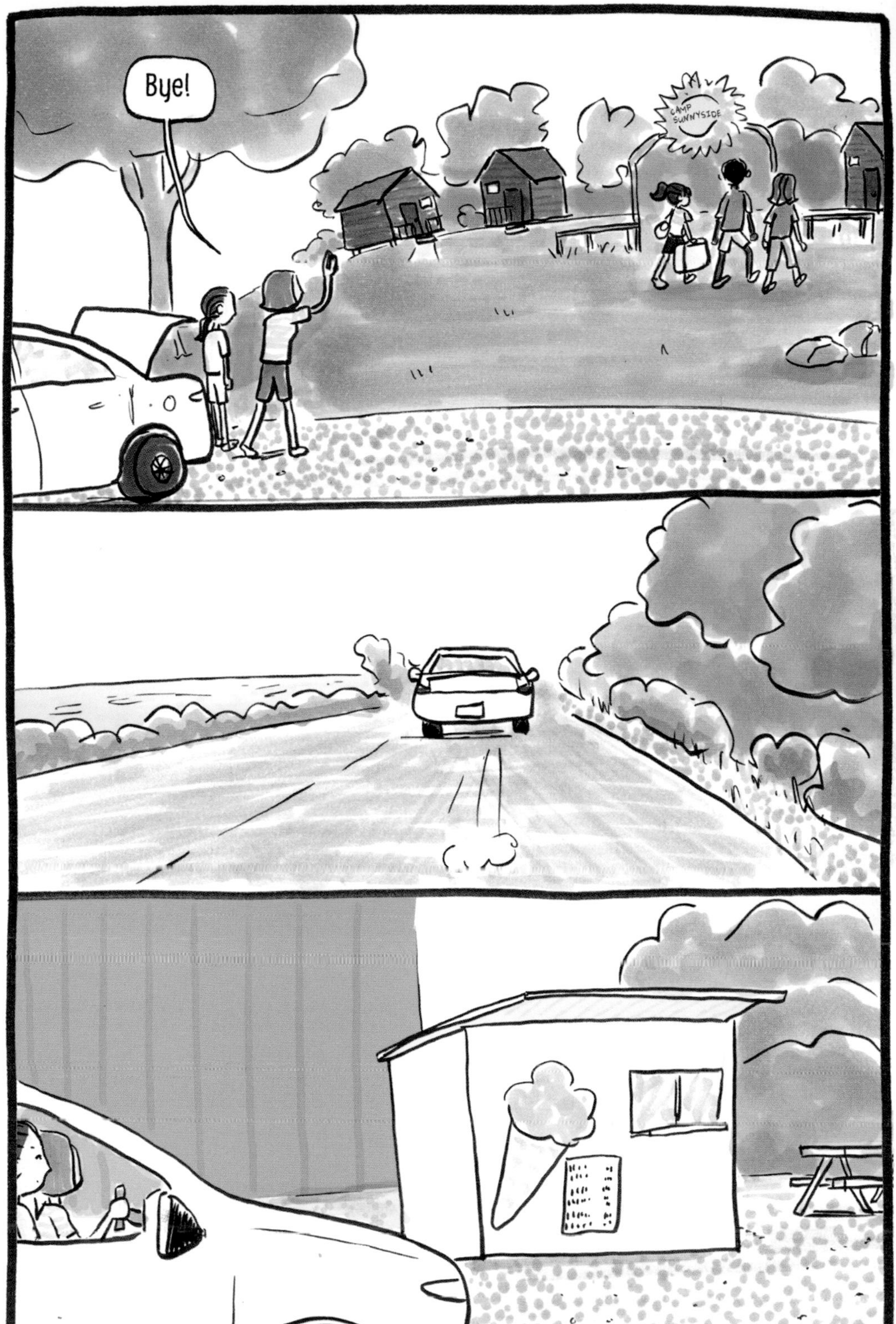
Bye!
CAMP SUNNYSIDE

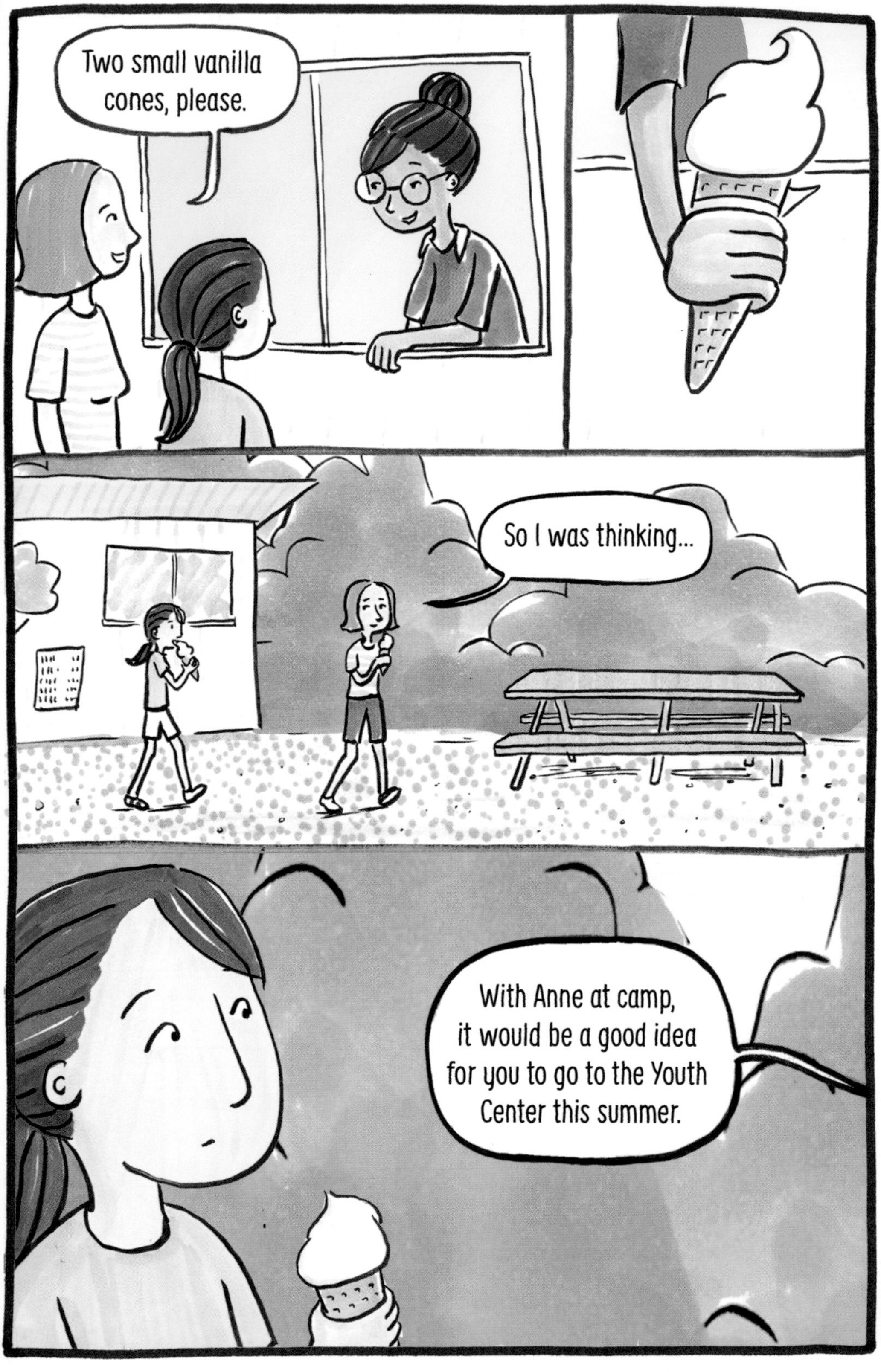
Two small vanilla cones, please.
So I was thinking...
With Anne at camp, it would be a good idea for you to go to the Youth Center this summer.

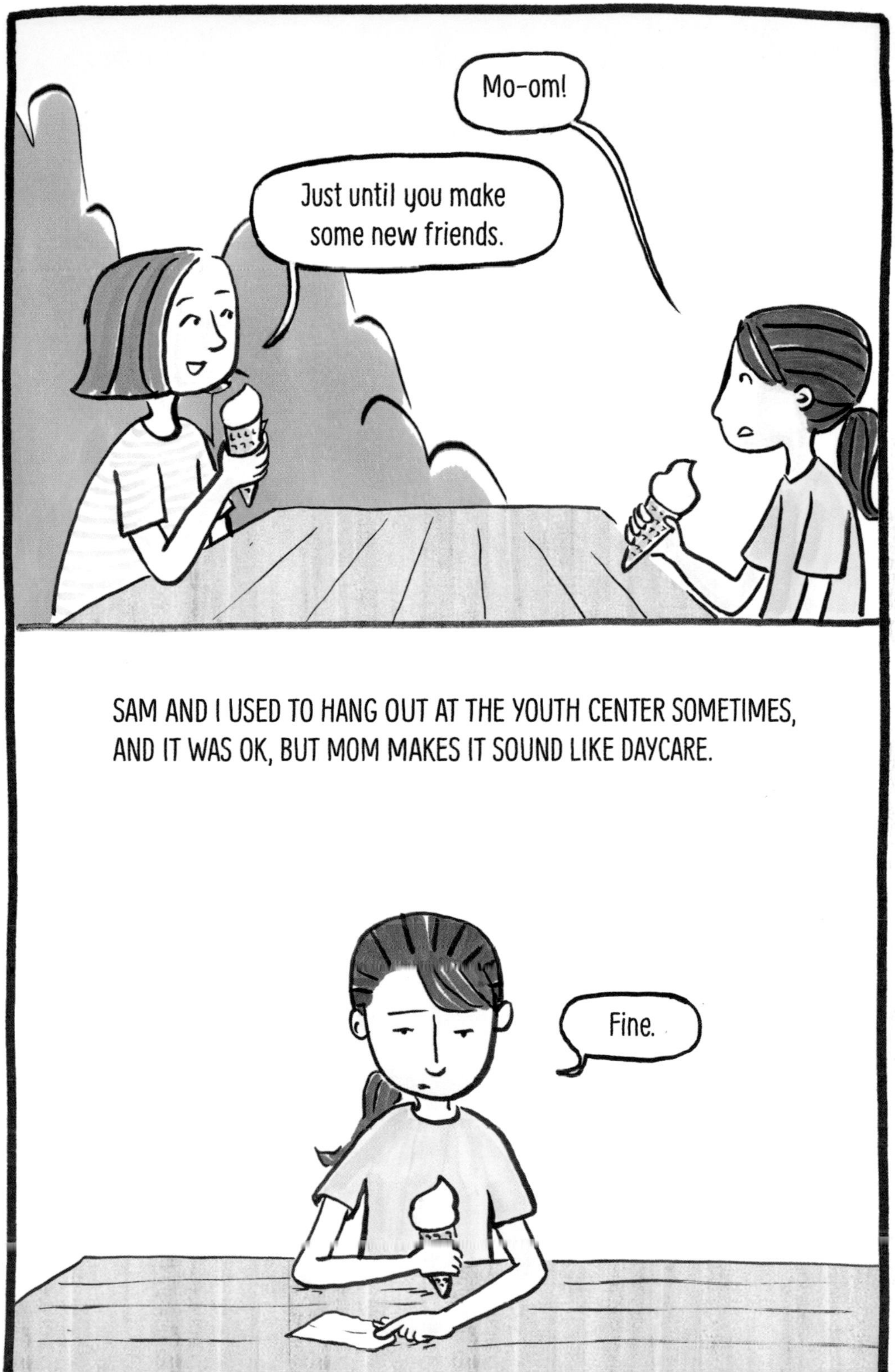
Mo-om!
Just until you make some new friends.
SAM AND I USED TO HANG OUT AT THE YOUTH CENTER SOMETIMES, AND IT WAS OK, BUT MOM MAKES IT SOUND LIKE DAYCARE.
Fine.

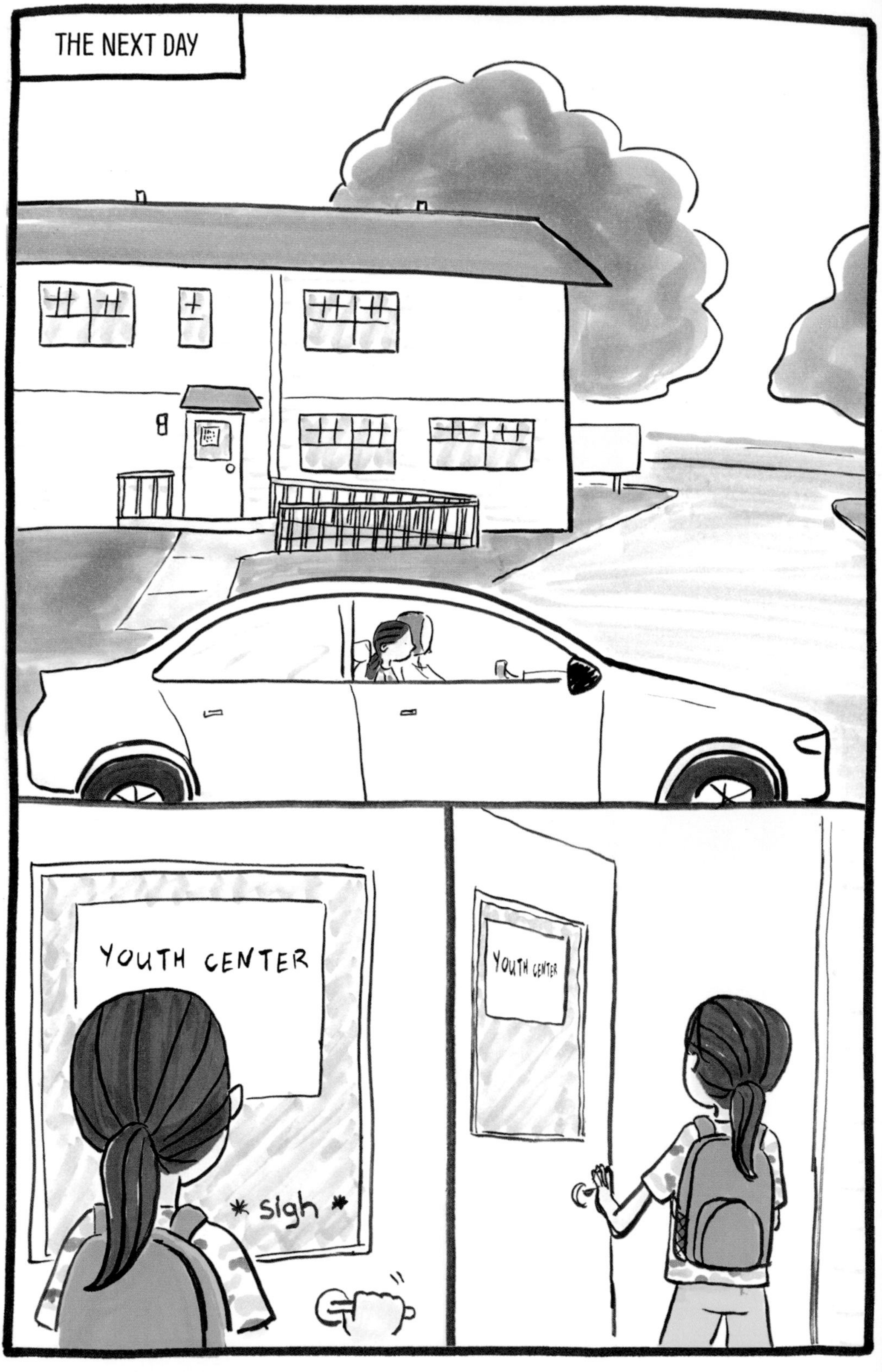
THE NEXT DAY
YOUTH CENTER
sigh
YOUTH CENTER

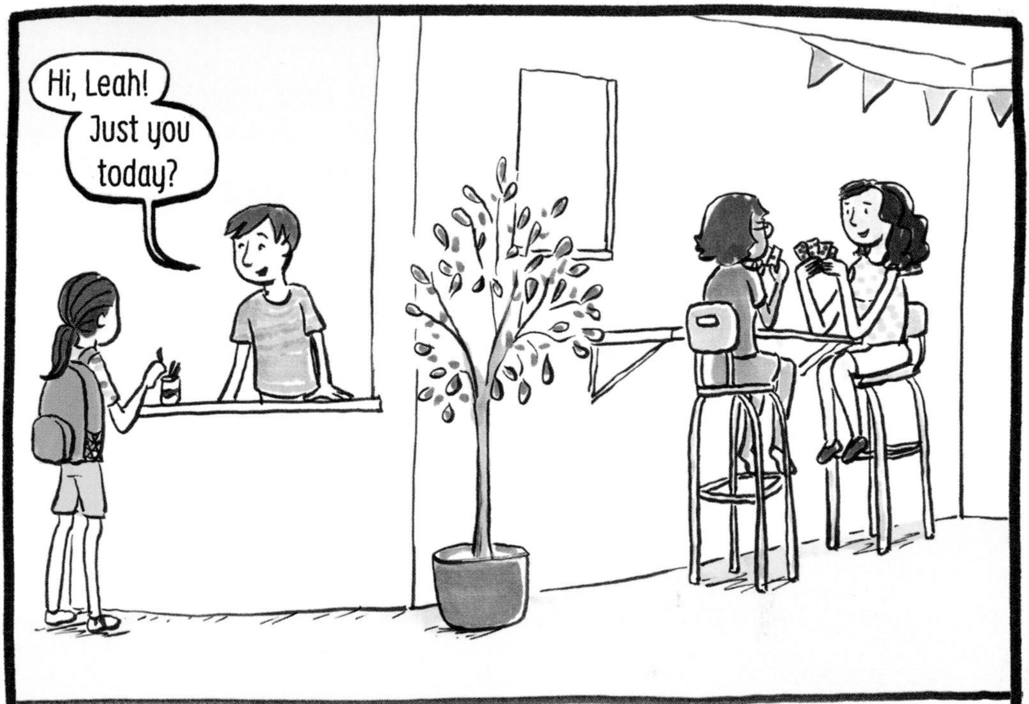
Hi, Leah!
Just you today?

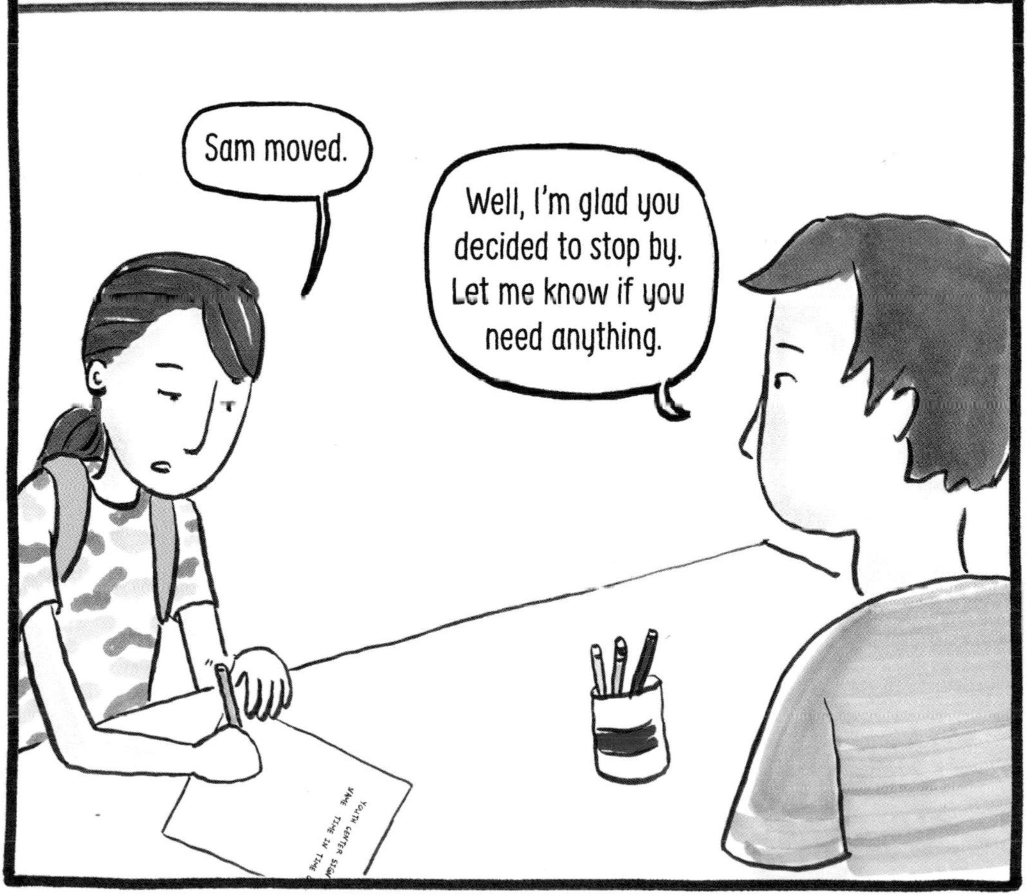
Sam moved.
Well, I'm glad you decided to stop by. Let me know if you need anything.

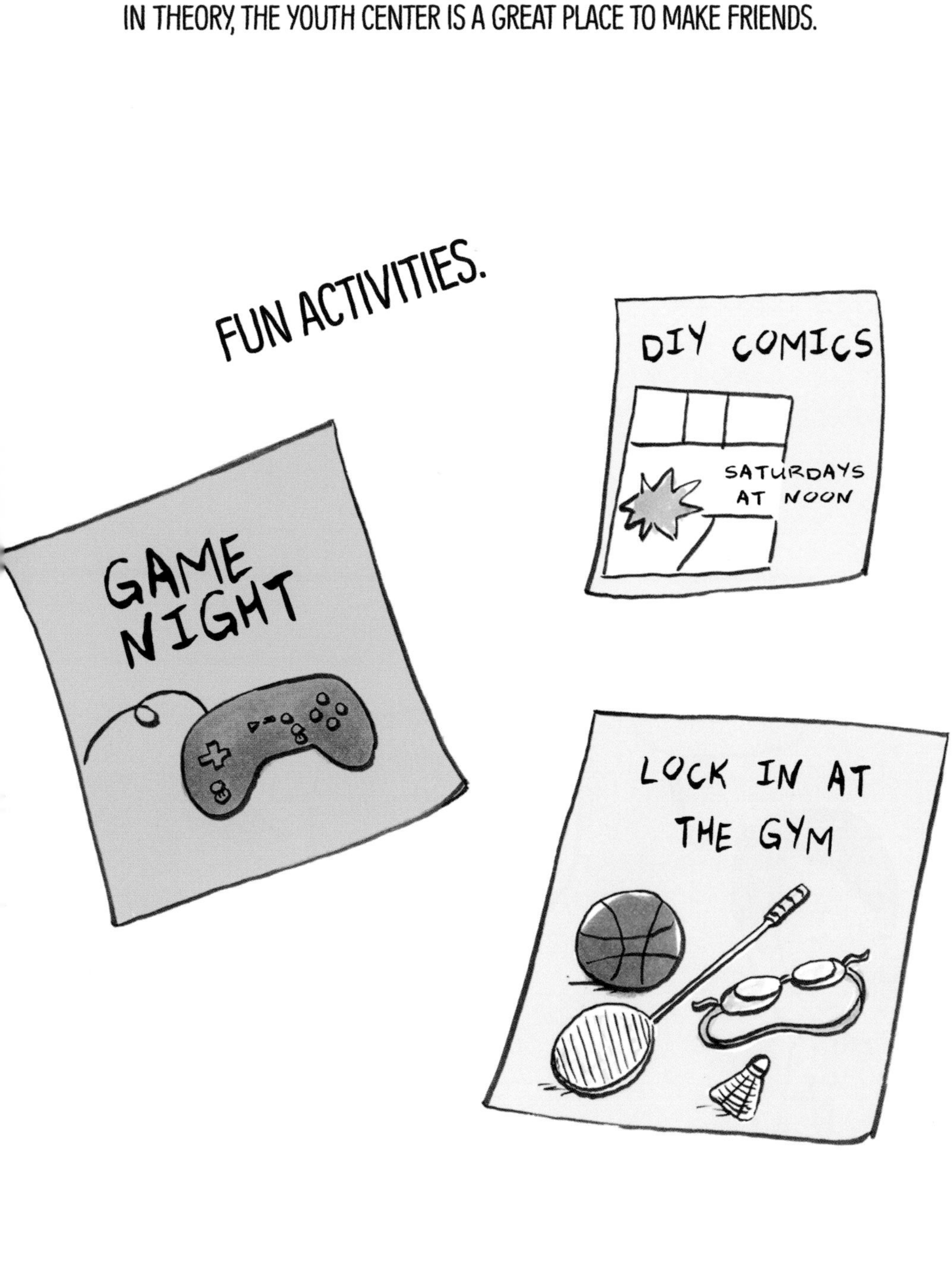
IN THEORY, THE YOUTH CENTER IS A GREAT PLACE TO MAKE FRIENDS.
FUN ACTIVITIES.
DIY COMICS
SATURDAYS AT NOON
GAME NIGHT
LOCK IN AT THE GYM

GOOD COMPANY.

BUT TODAY –

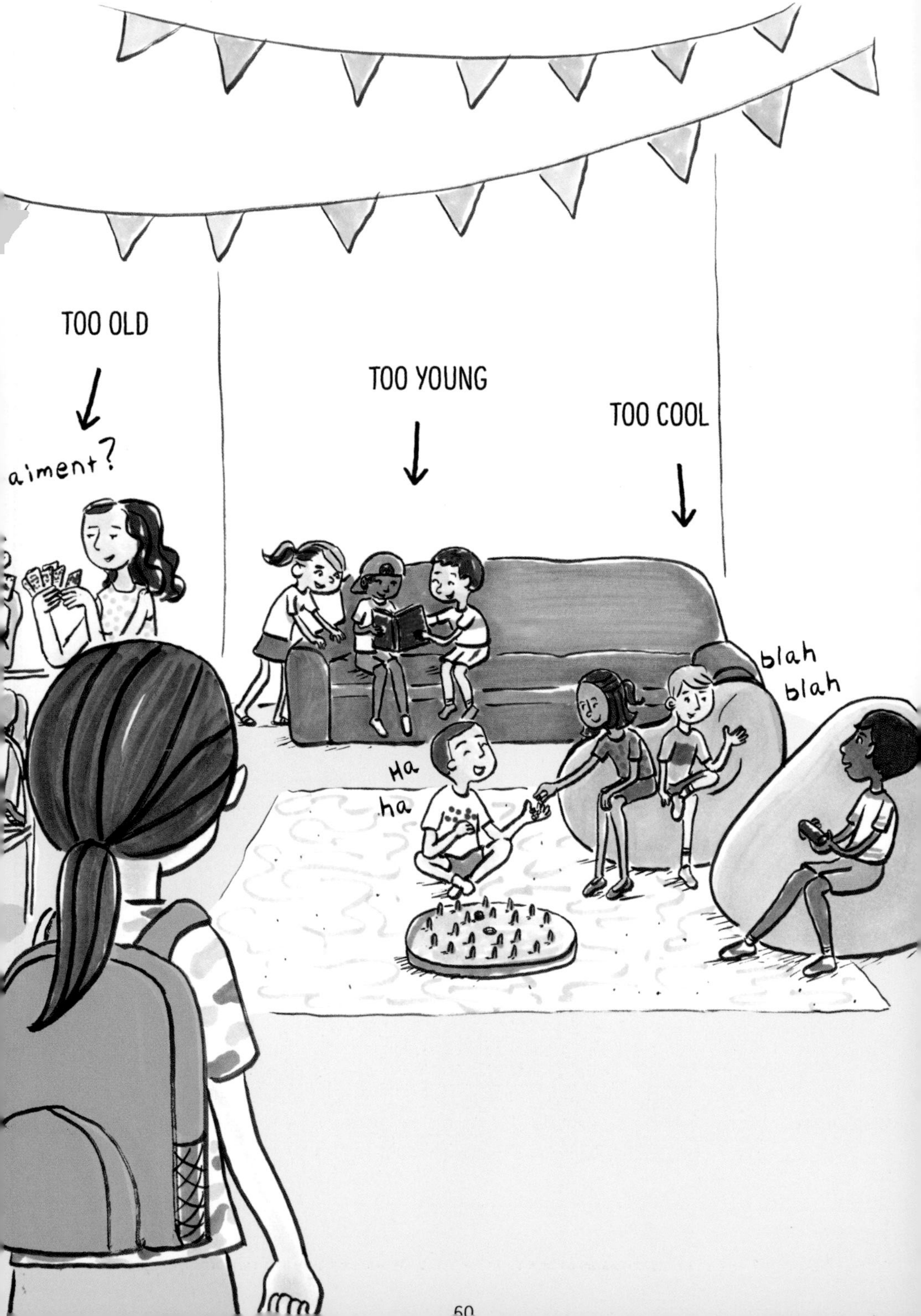
TOO OLD
aiment?
TOO YOUNG
TOO COOL
blah
blah
Ha
ha

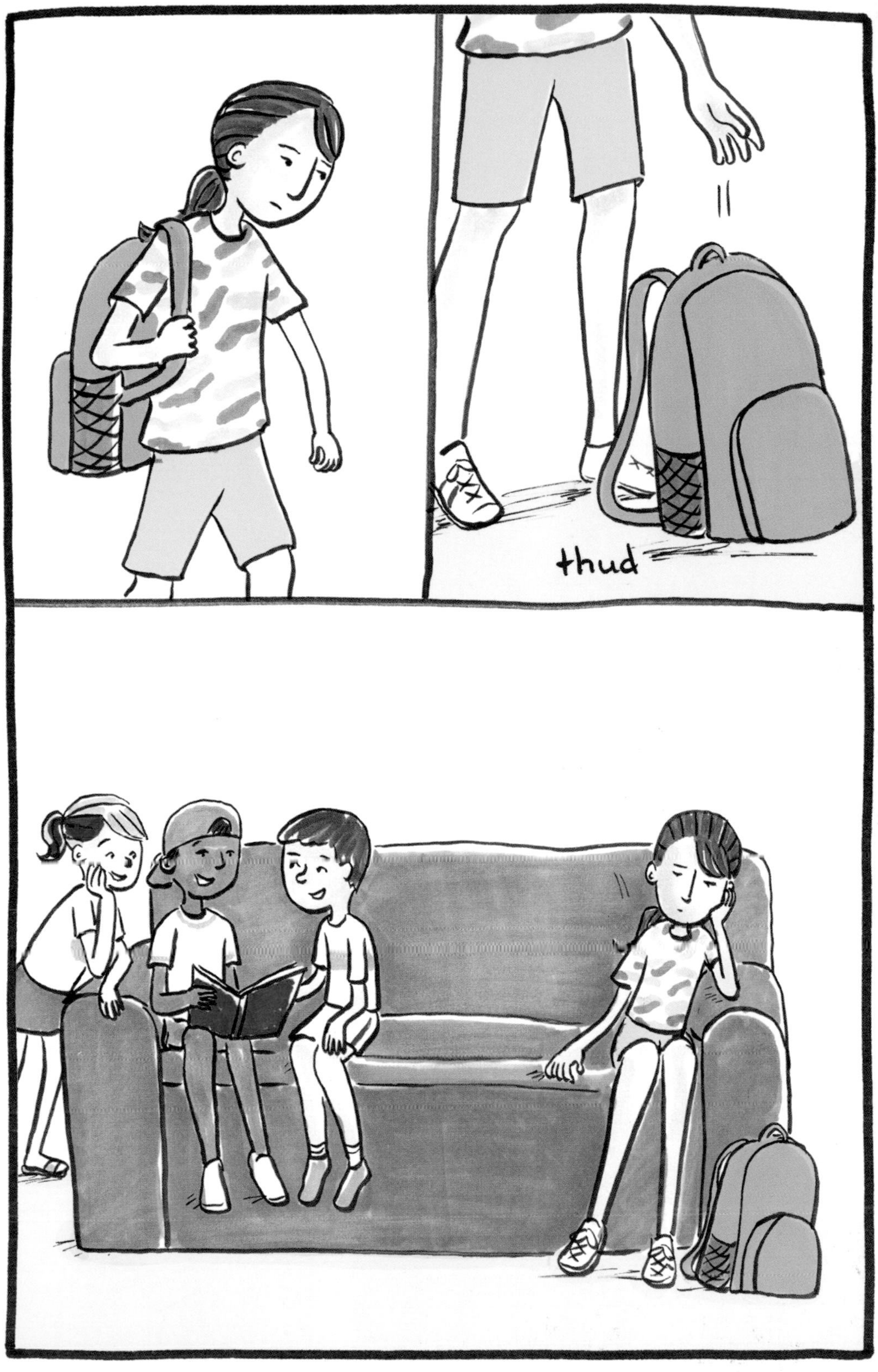
thud

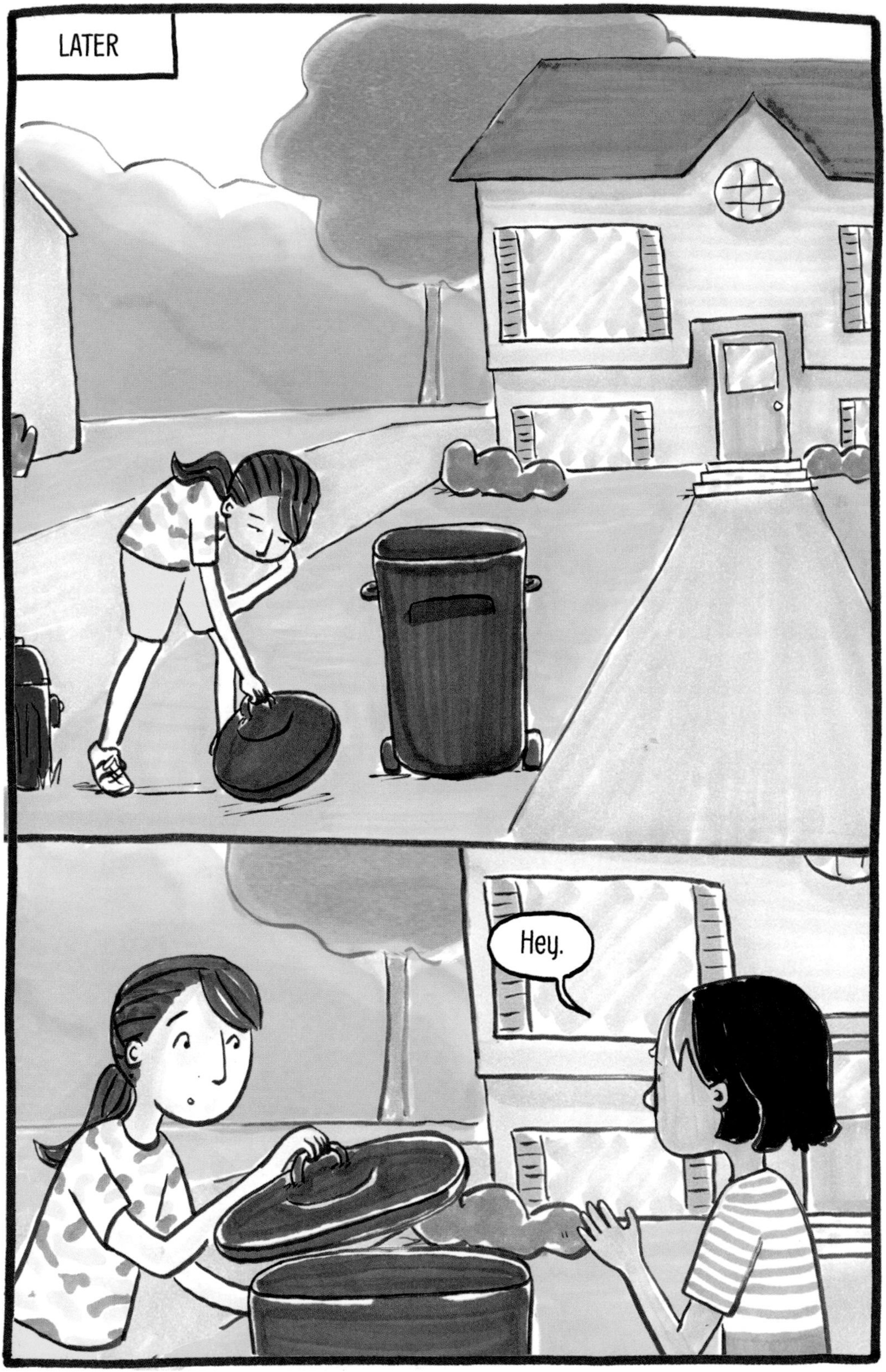
LATER
Hey.

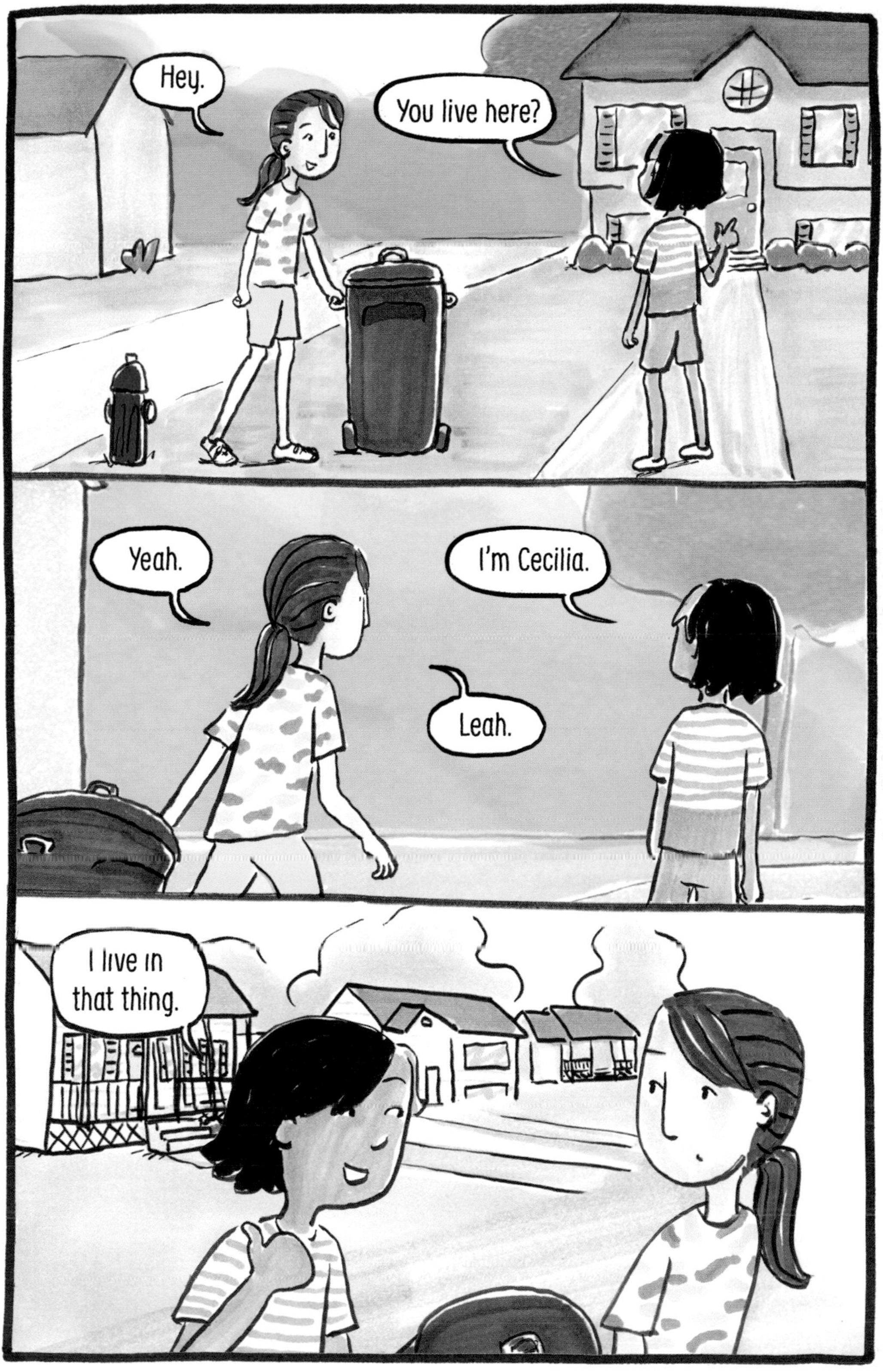
Hey.
You live here?
Yeah.
I'm Cecilia.
Leah.
I live in that thing.

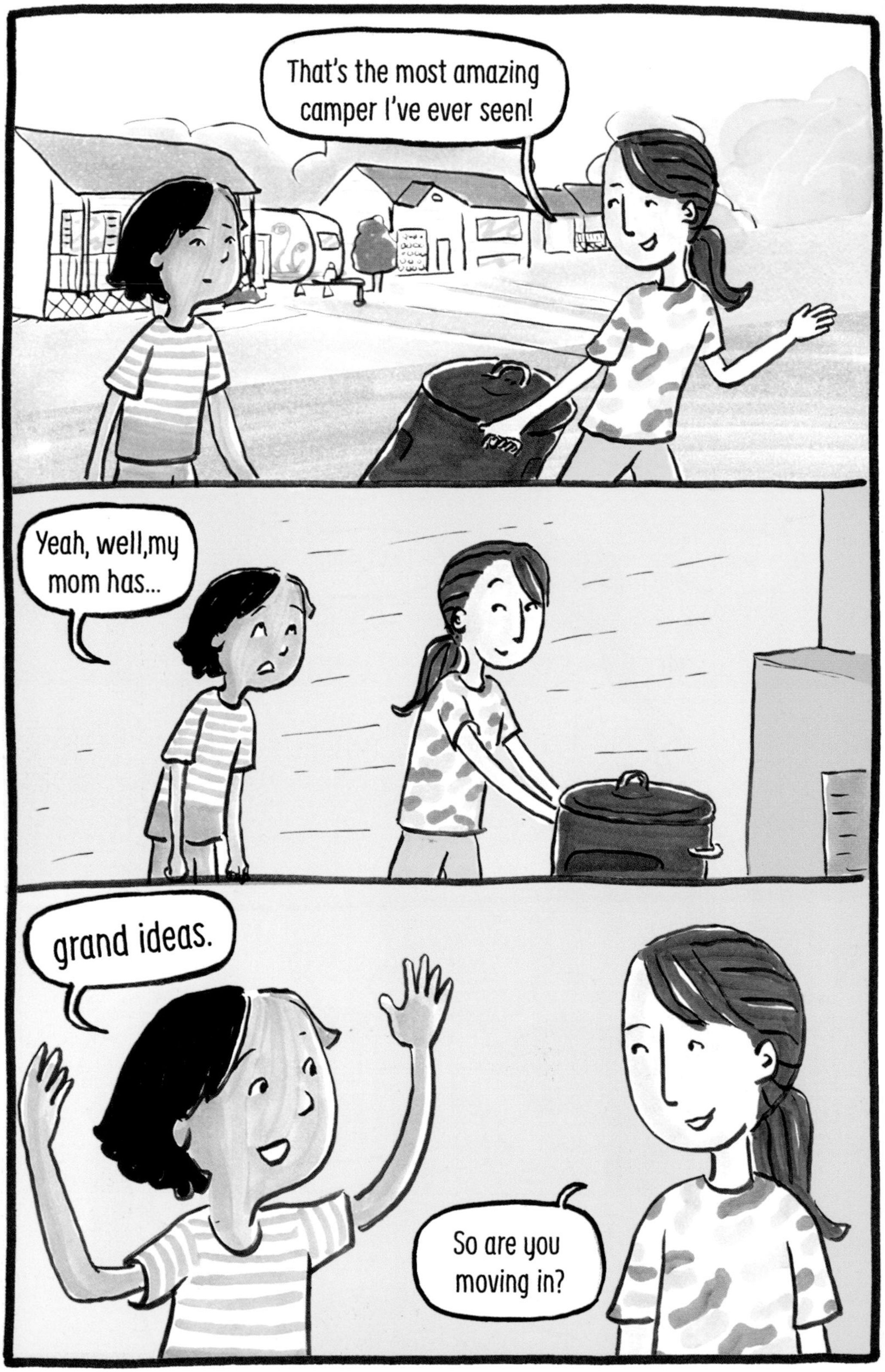
That's the most amazing camper I've ever seen!
Yeah, well,my mom has...
grand ideas.
So are you moving in?

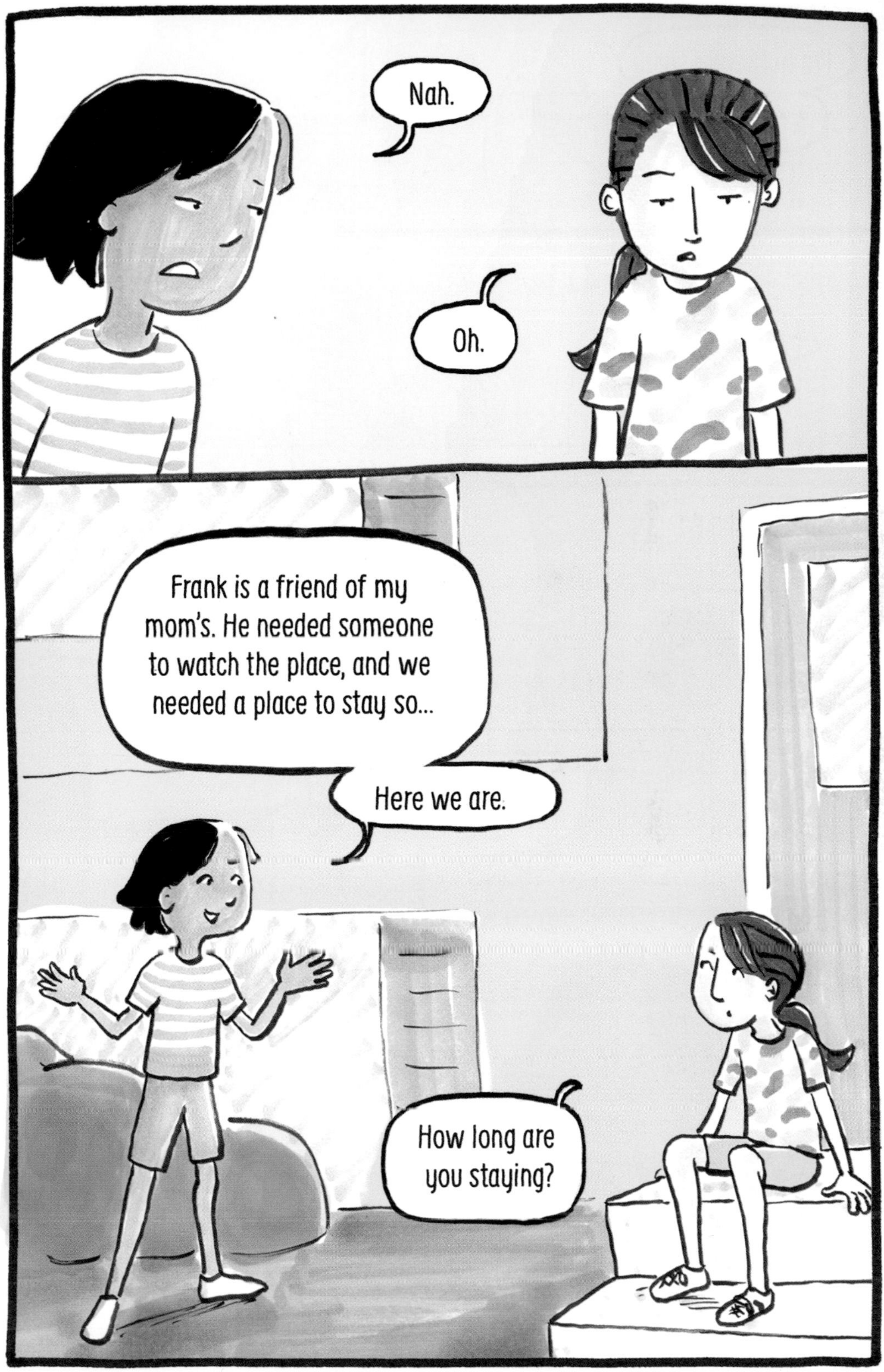
Nah.
Oh.
Frank is a friend of my mom's. He needed someone to watch the place, and we needed a place to stay so...
Here we are.
How long are you staying?

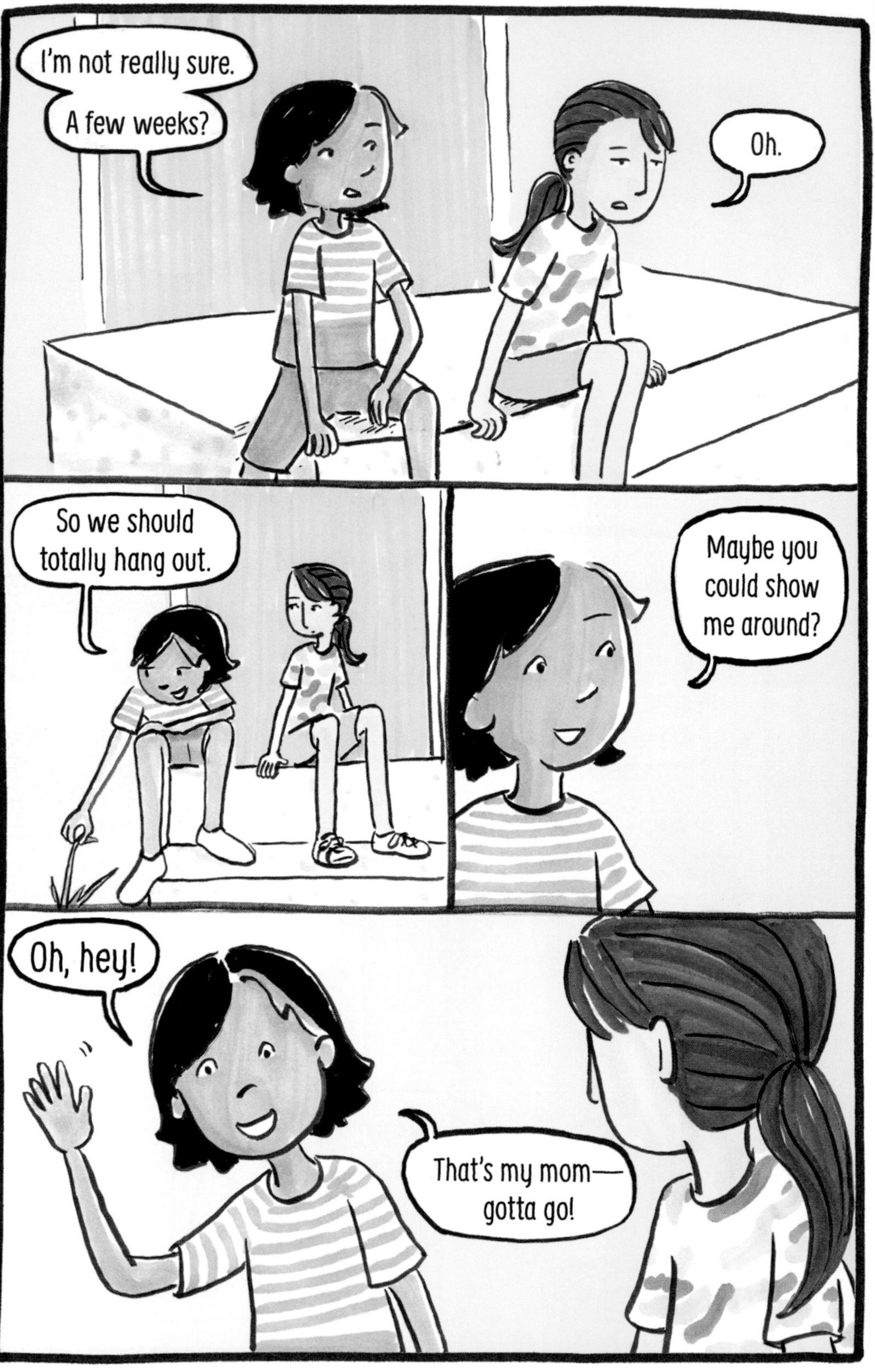
I'm not really sure.
A few weeks?
Oh.
So we should totally hang out.
Maybe you could show me around?
Oh, hey!
That's my mom—gotta go!

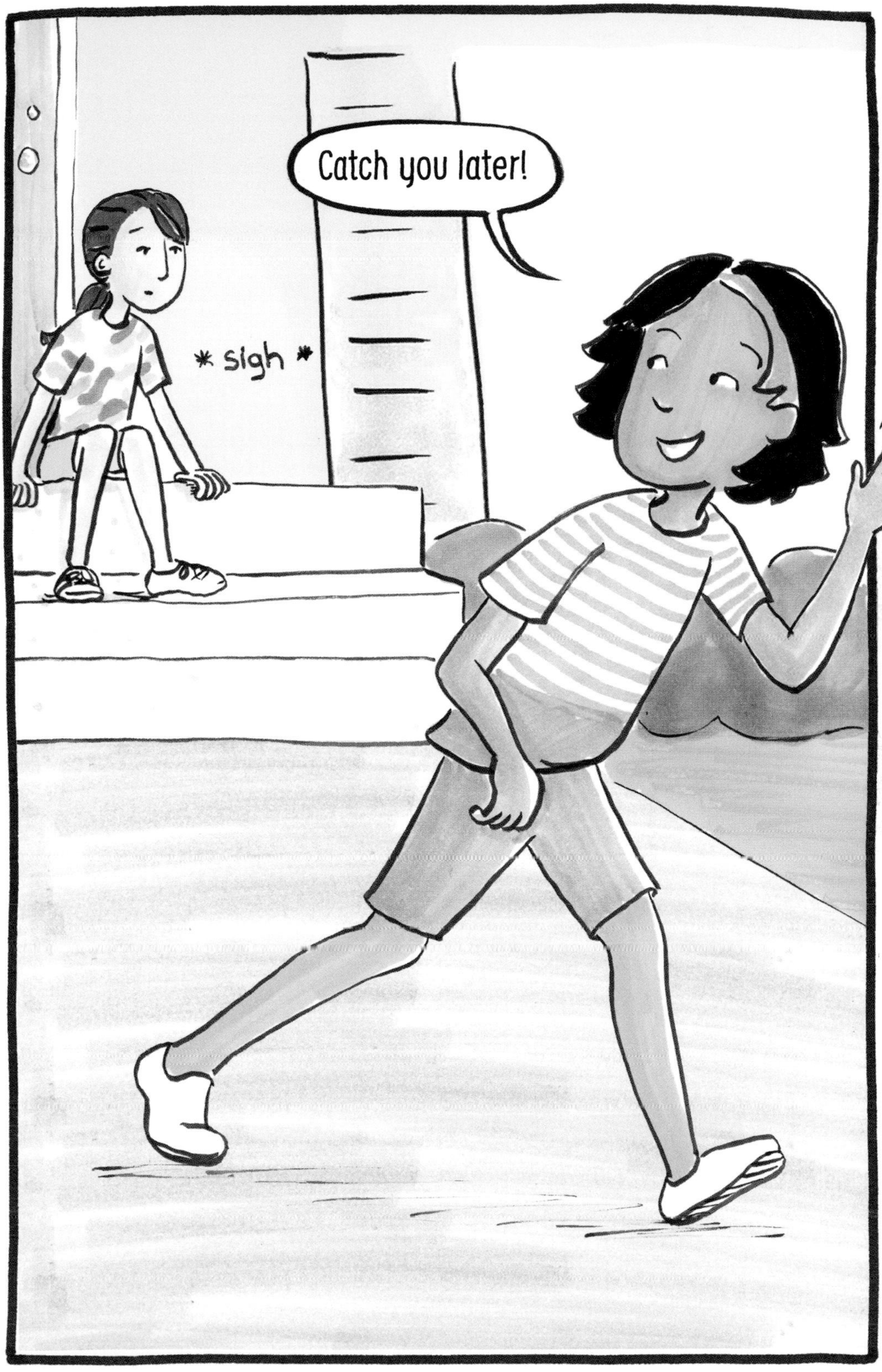
Catch you later!
* sigh *

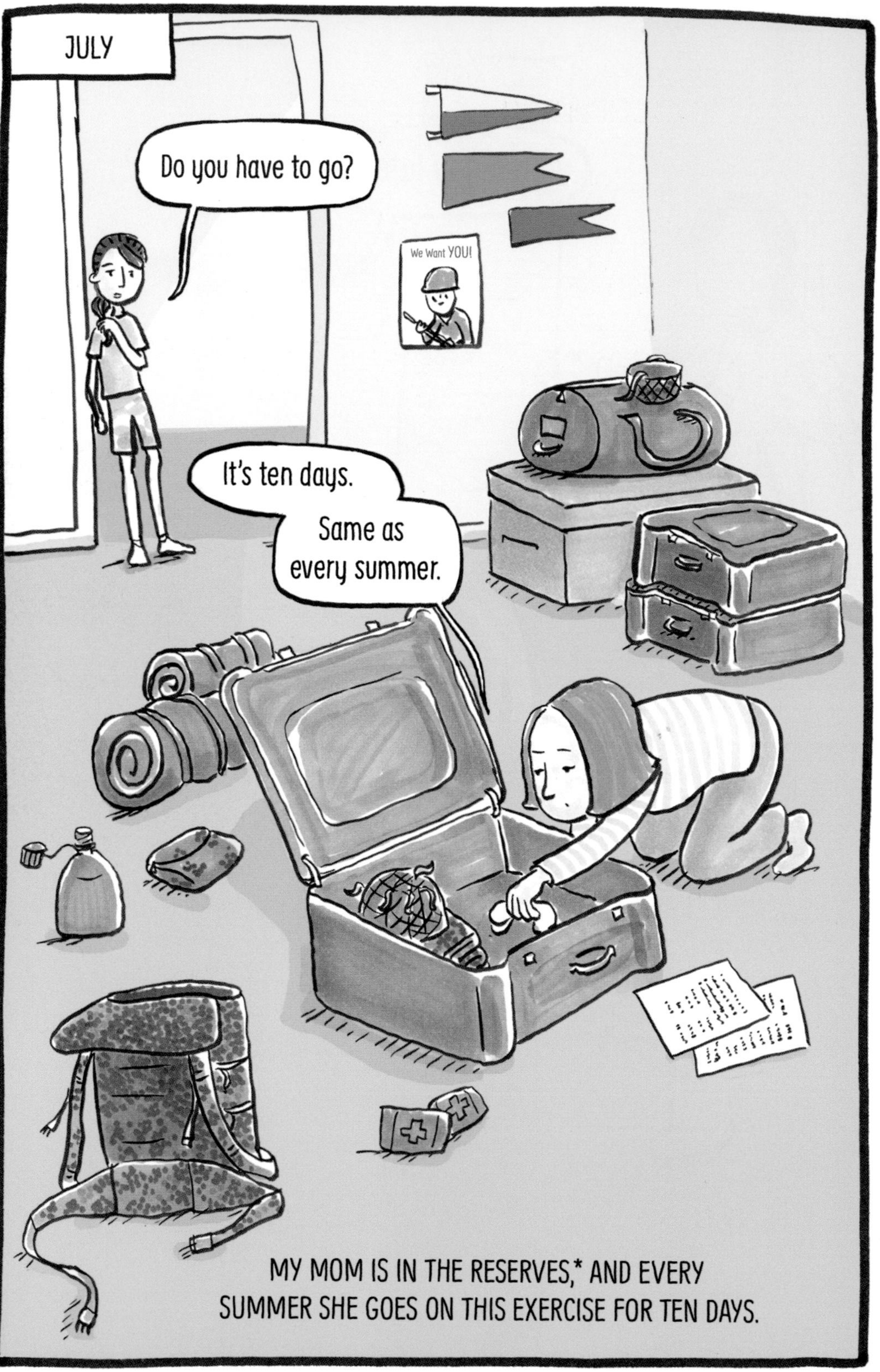
JULY
Do you have to go?
We Want YOU!
It's ten days.
Same as every summer.
MY MOM IS IN THE RESERVES,* AND EVERY SUMMER SHE GOES ON THIS EXERCISE FOR TEN DAYS.

*Army Reserve = military organization of part-time soldiers.

TEN DAYS OF SKILLS AND DRILLS BEFORE GOING BACK TO JUST BEING MY MOM AGAIN.

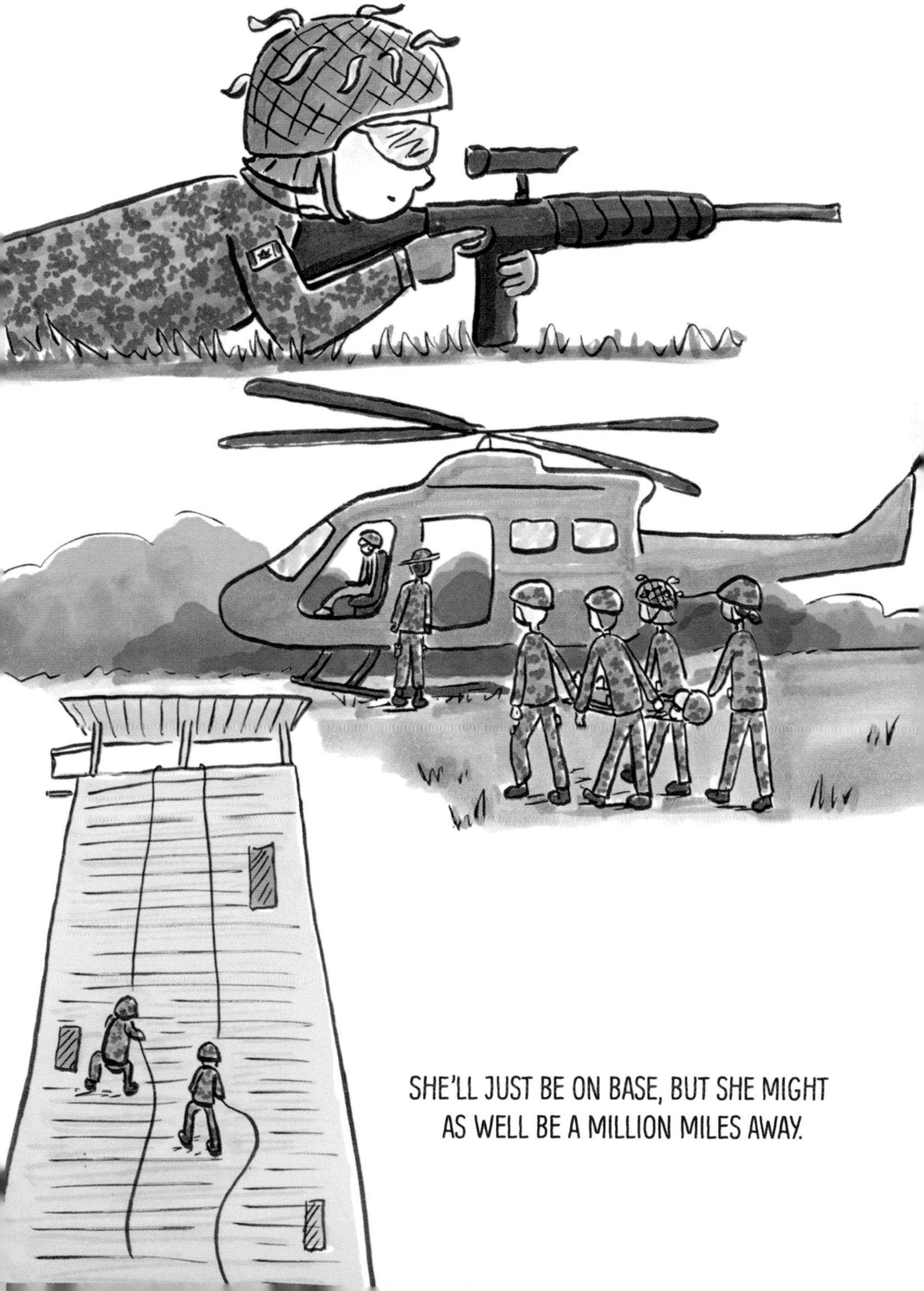
SHE'LL JUST BE ON BASE, BUT SHE MIGHT AS WELL BE A MILLION MILES AWAY.

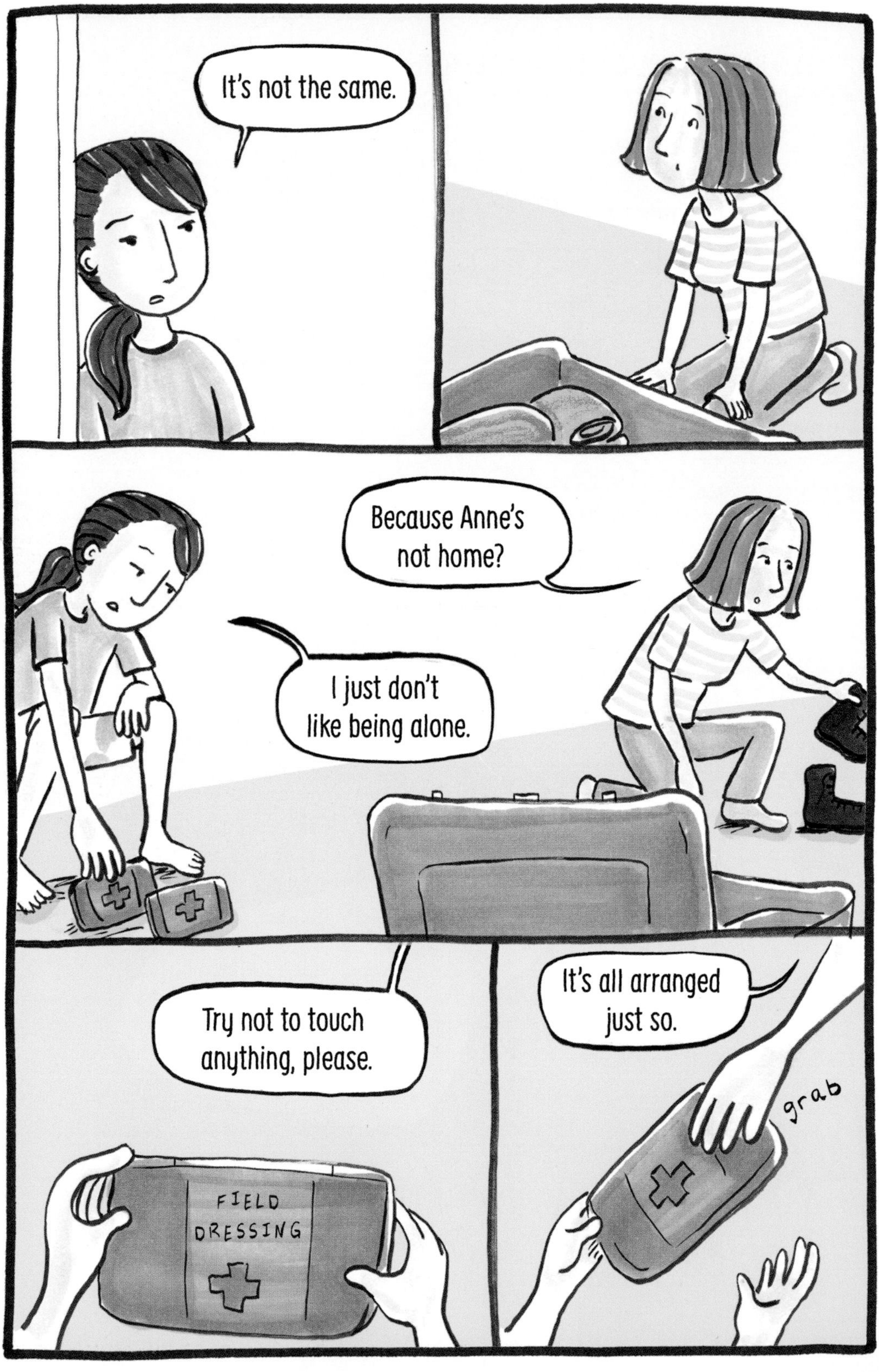
It's not the same.
Because Anne's not home?
I just don't like being alone.
Try not to touch anything, please.
FIELD DRESSING
It's all arranged just so.
grab

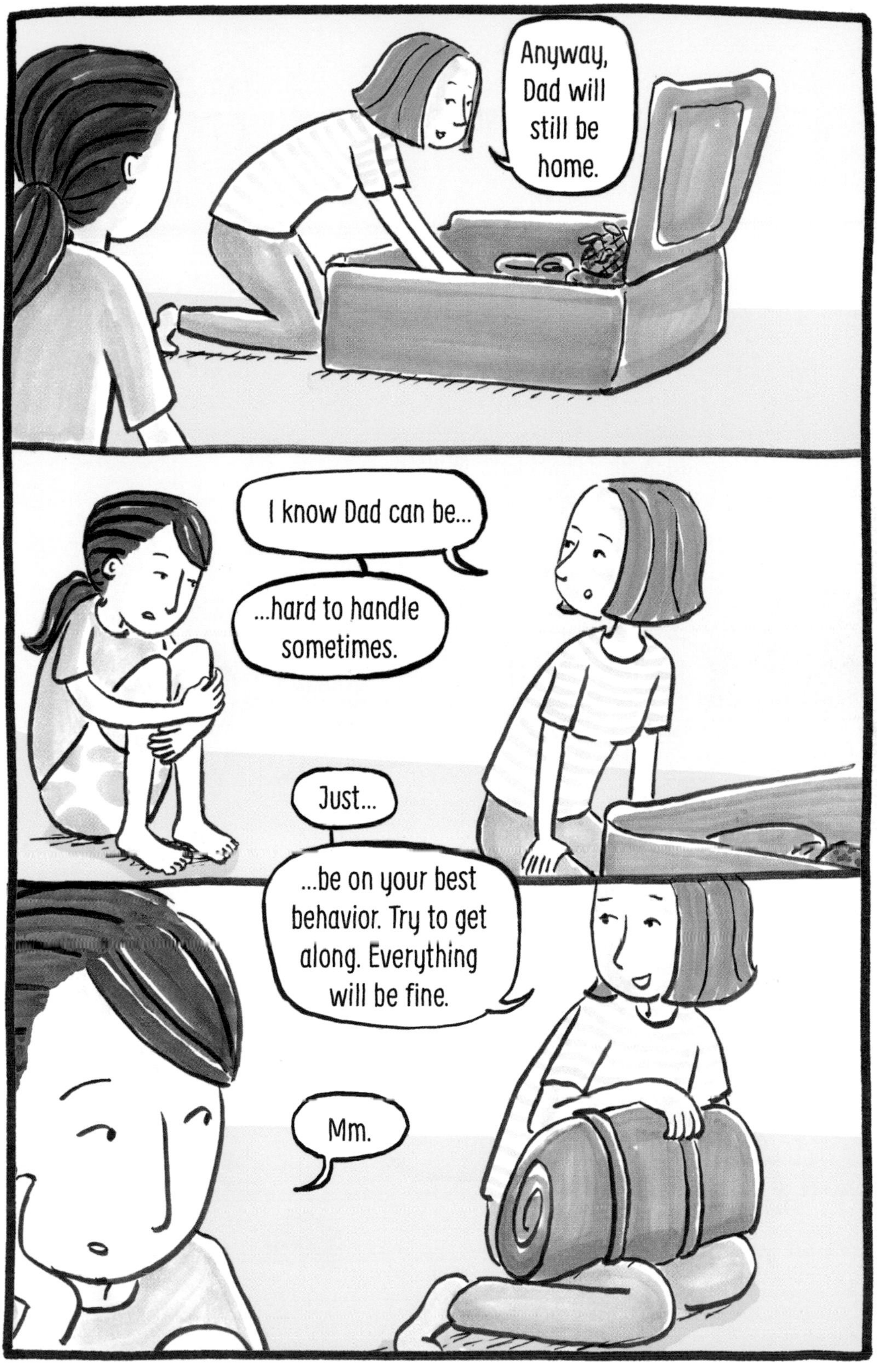
Anyway, Dad will still be home.
I know Dad can be...
...hard to handle sometimes.
Just...
...be on your best behavior. Try to get along. Everything will be fine.
Mm.

"HARD TO HANDLE" IS AN UNDERSTATEMENT.

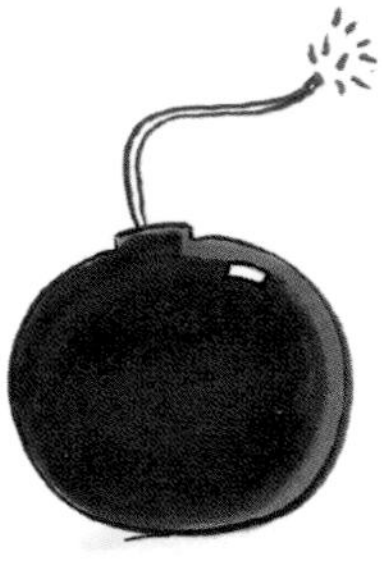

DAD IS LIKE A TICKING TIME BOMB.

SOMETIMES HE'S PERFECTLY NORMAL.

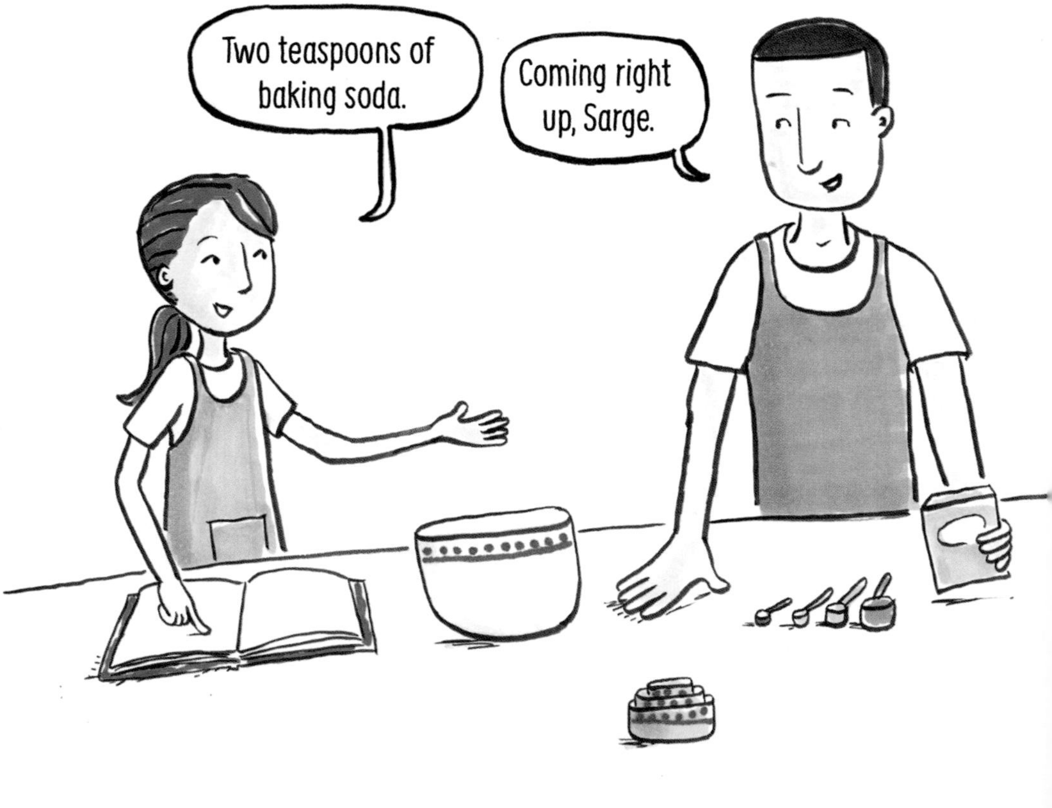
Two teaspoons of baking soda.
Coming right up, Sarge.

SOMETIMES HE WON'T TALK.

OR HIDES OUT IN THE BASEMENT FOR HOURS ON END.

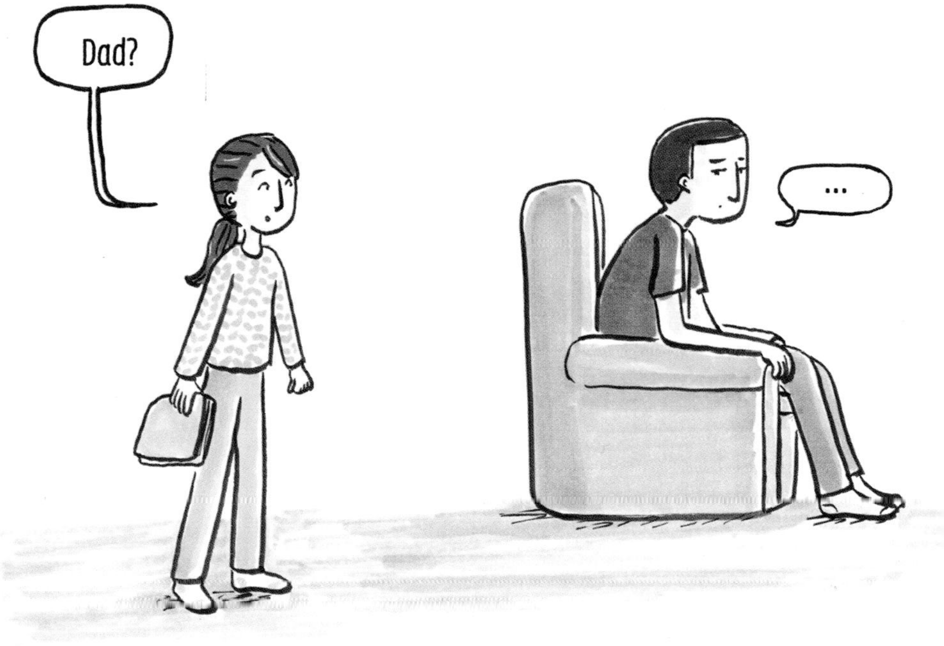
Dad?
...

AND YOU NEVER KNOW WHEN HE MIGHT EXPLODE.

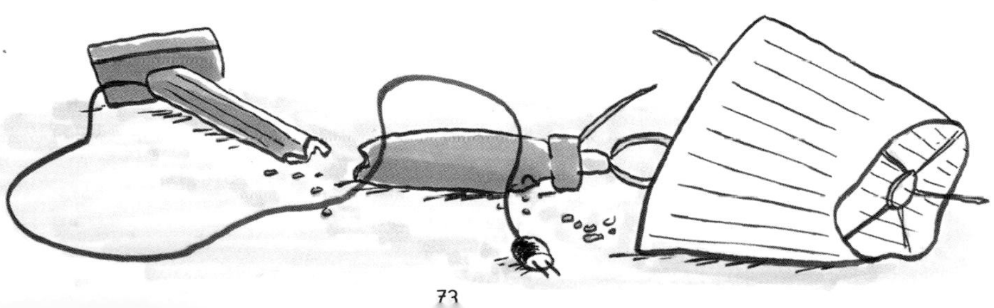

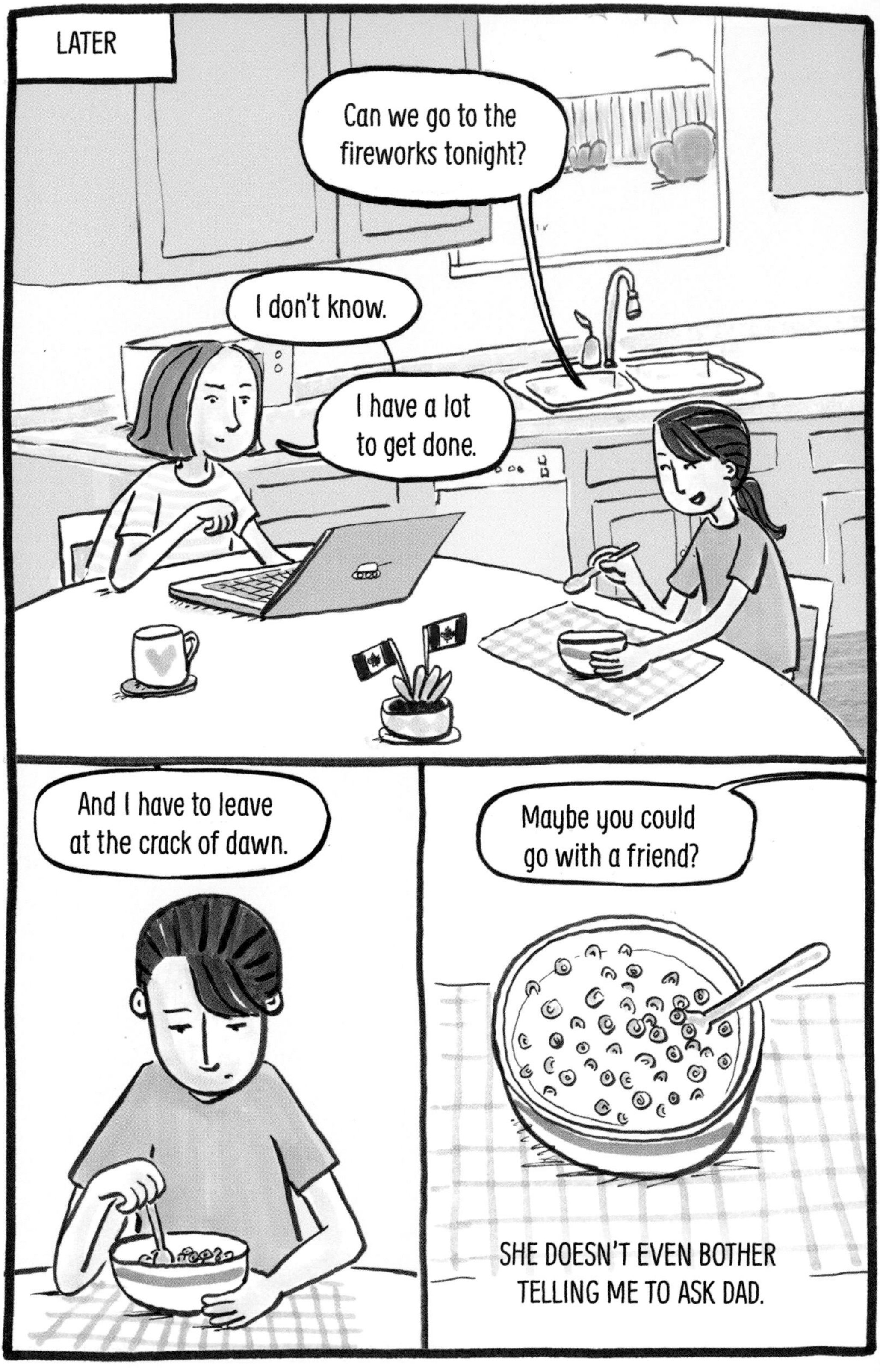
LATER
Can we go to the fireworks tonight?
I don't know.
I have a lot to get done.
And I have to leave at the crack of dawn.
Maybe you could go with a friend?
SHE DOESN'T EVEN BOTHER TELLING ME TO ASK DAD.

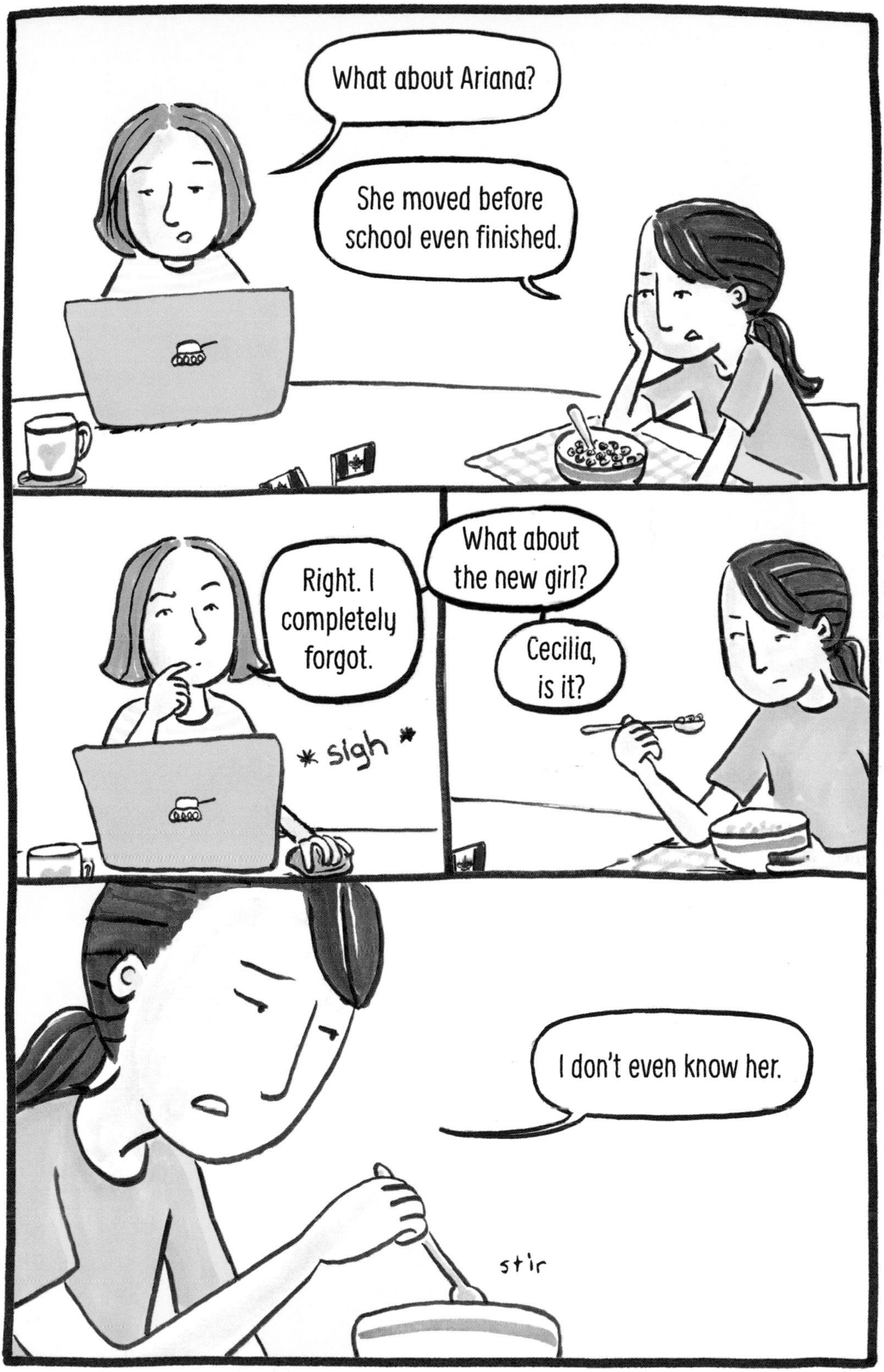
What about Ariana?
She moved before school even finished.
Right. I completely forgot.
sigh
What about the new girl?
Cecilia, is it?
I don't even know her.
stir

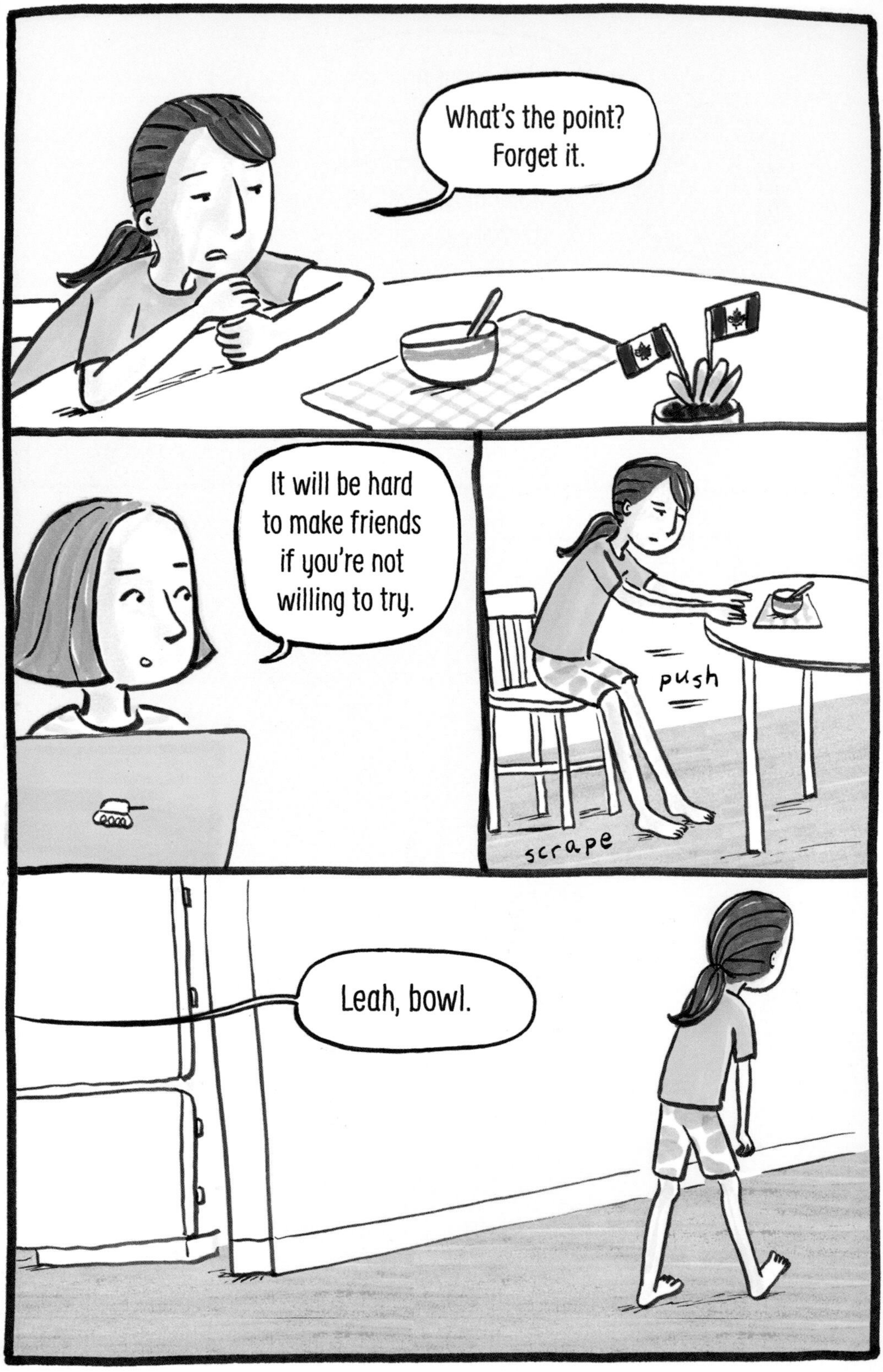
What's the point? Forget it.
It will be hard to make friends if you're not willing to try.
push
scrape
Leah, bowl.

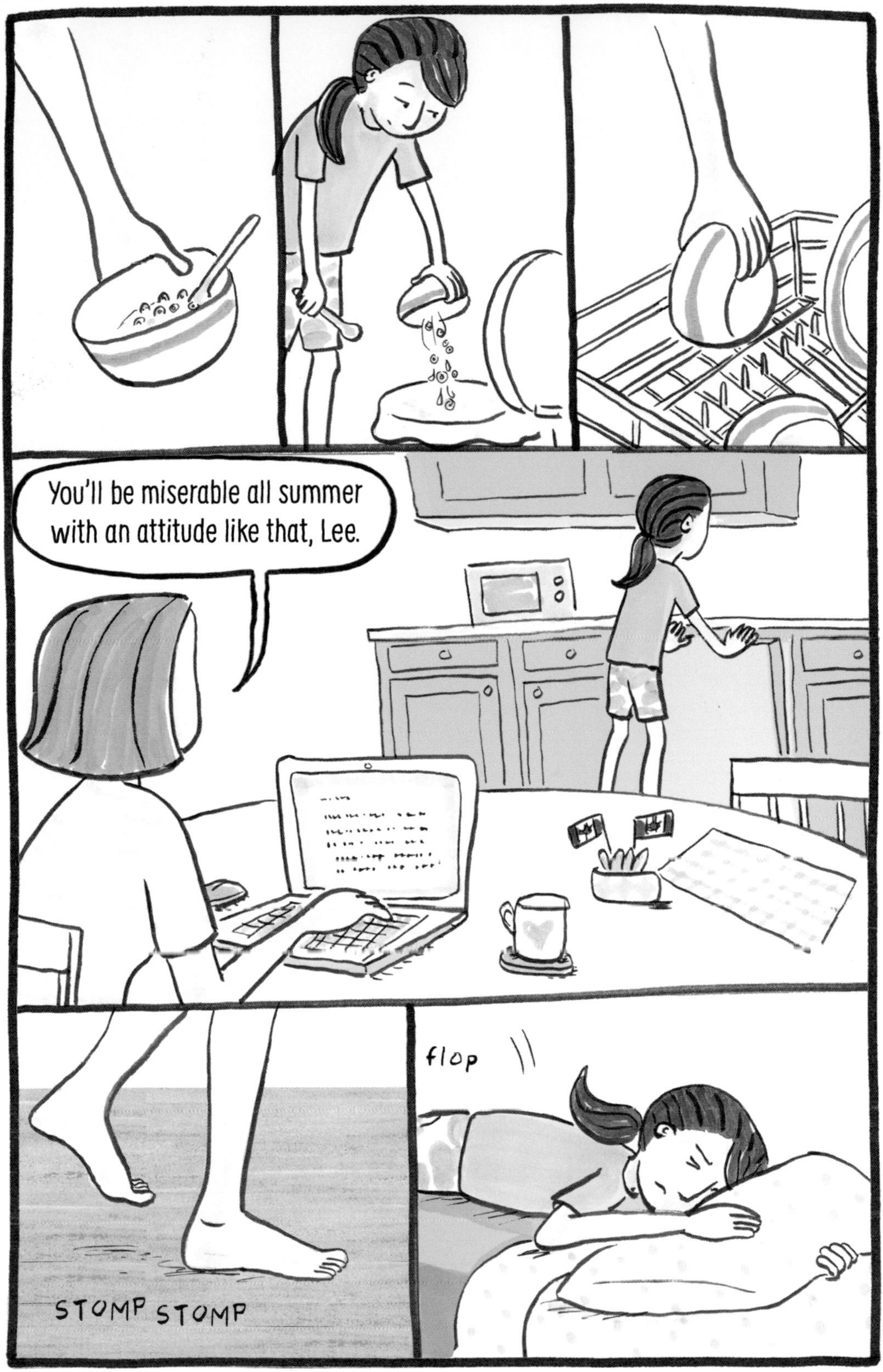
You'll be miserable all summer with an attitude like that, Lee.
STOMP STOMP
flop

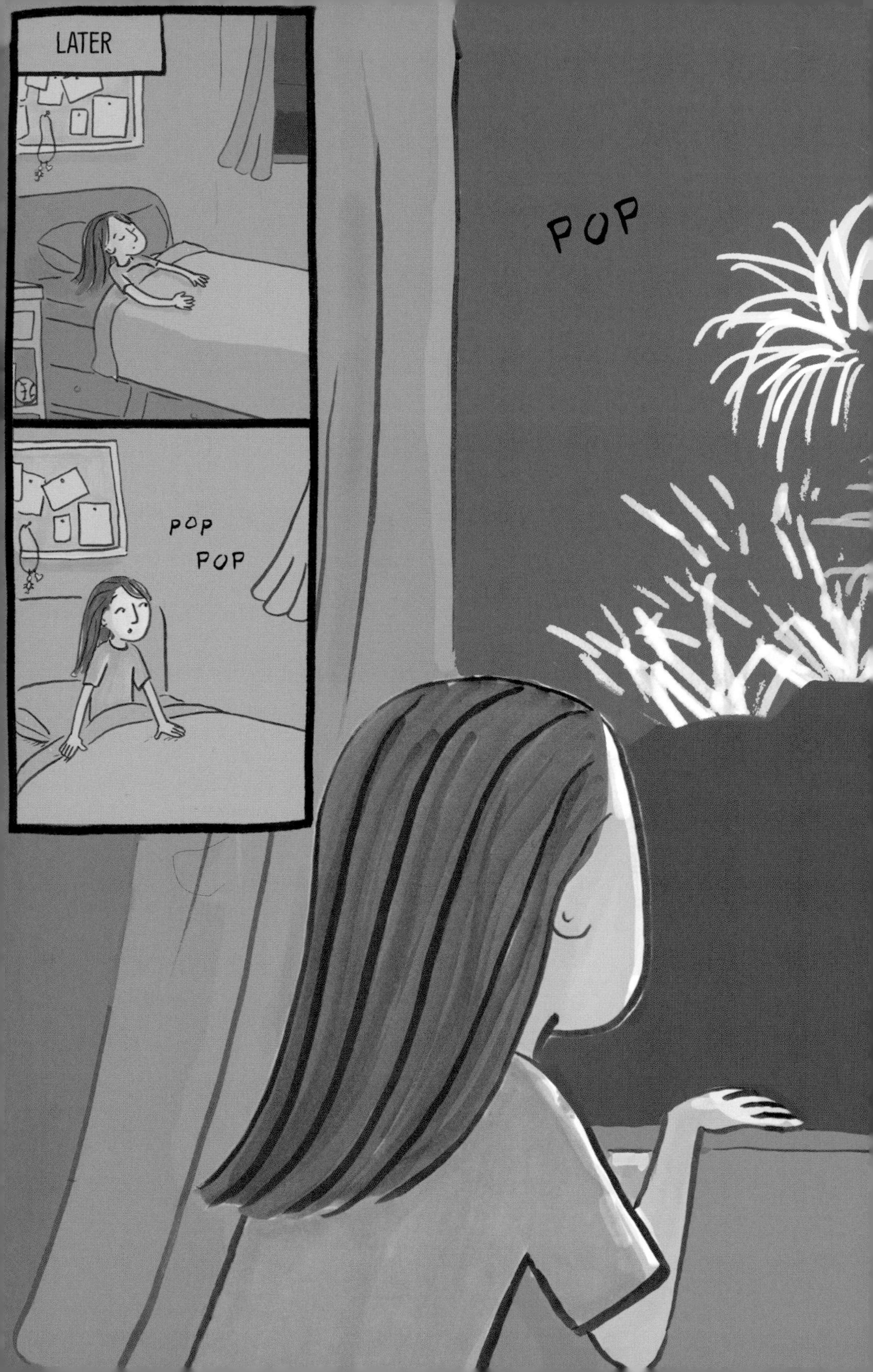
LATER
POP
POP
POP

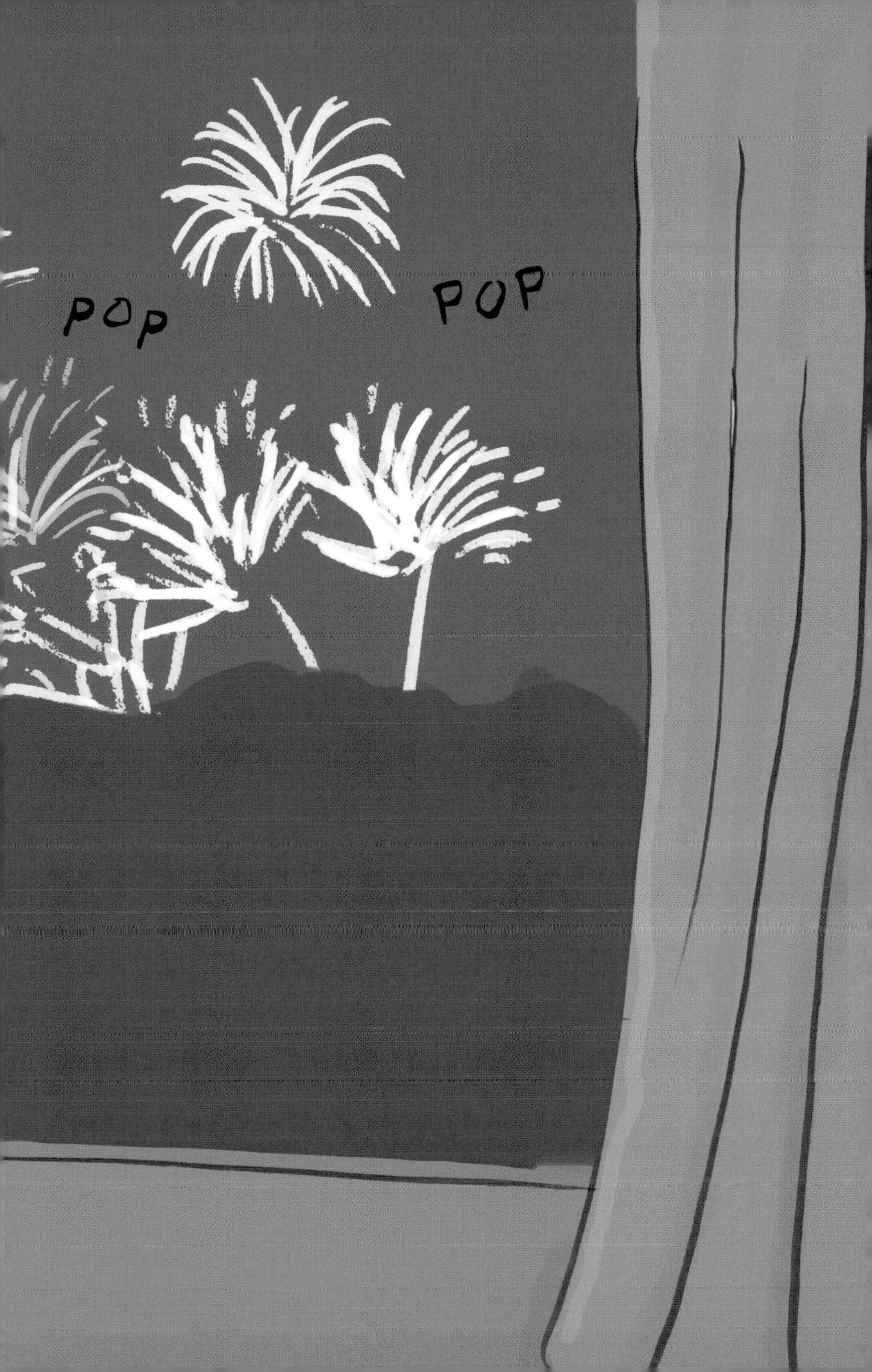
POP
POP

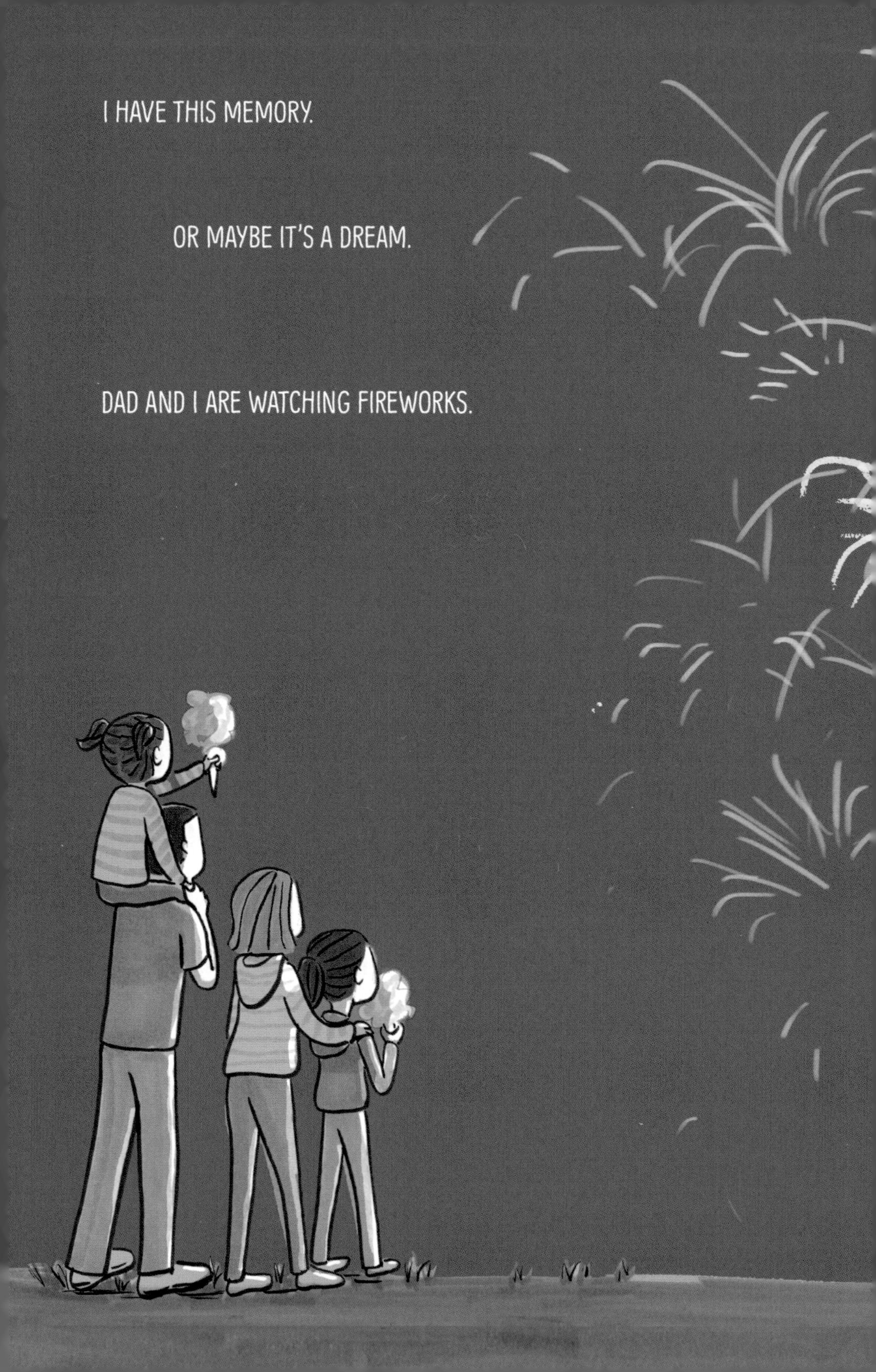
I HAVE THIS MEMORY.
OR MAYBE IT'S A DREAM.
DAD AND I ARE WATCHING FIREWORKS.

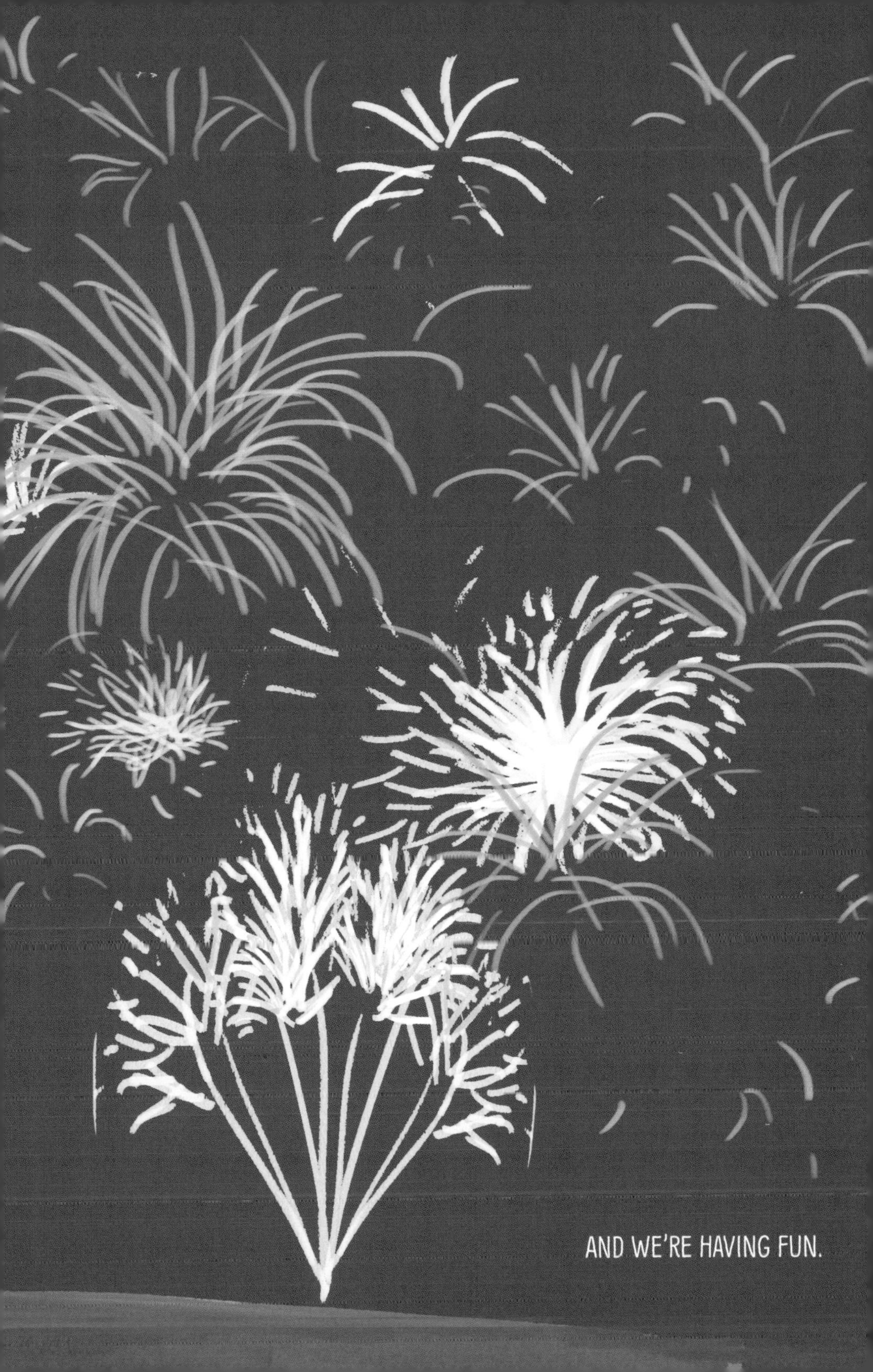

AND WE'RE HAVING FUN.

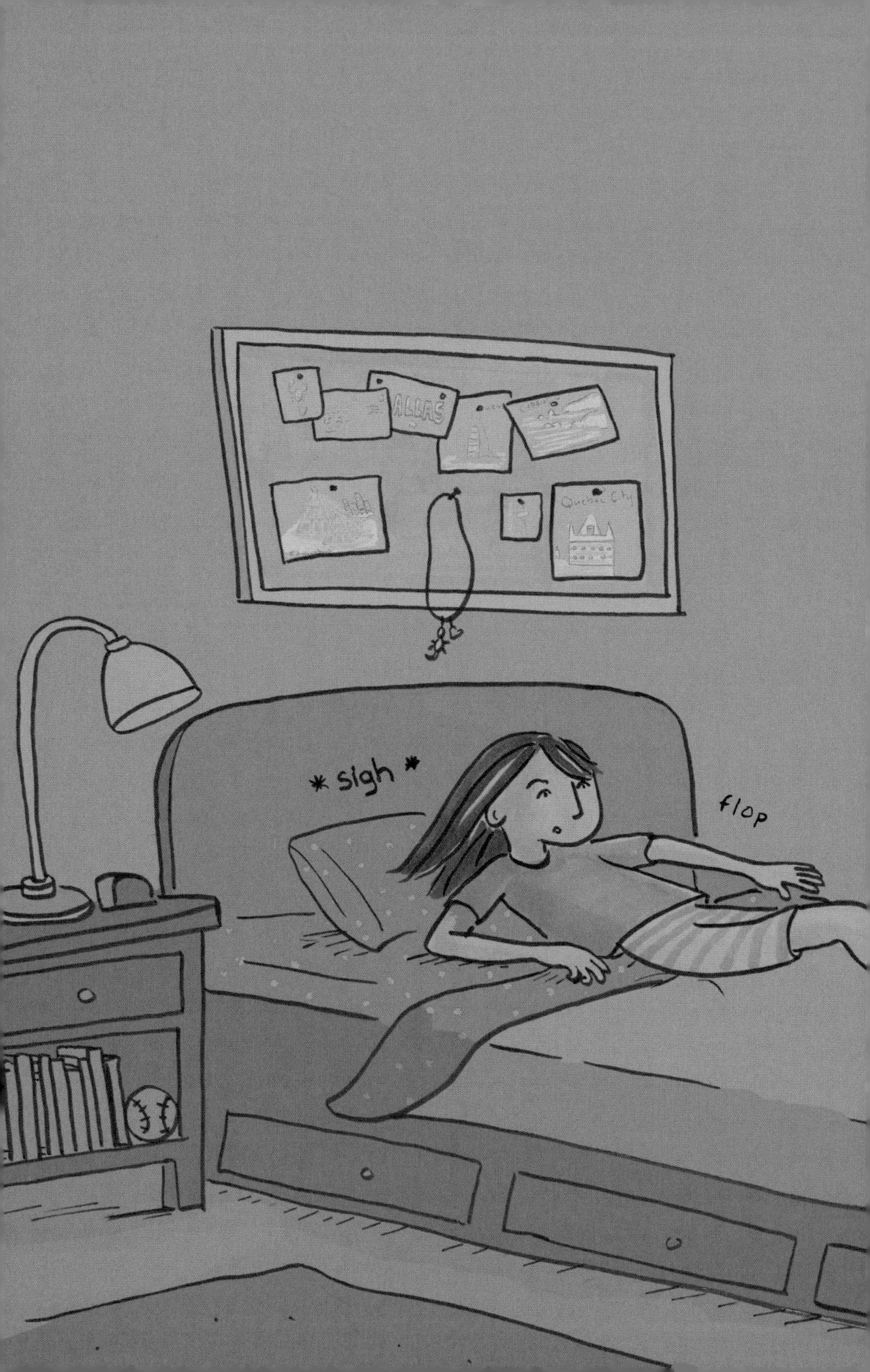
sigh
flop

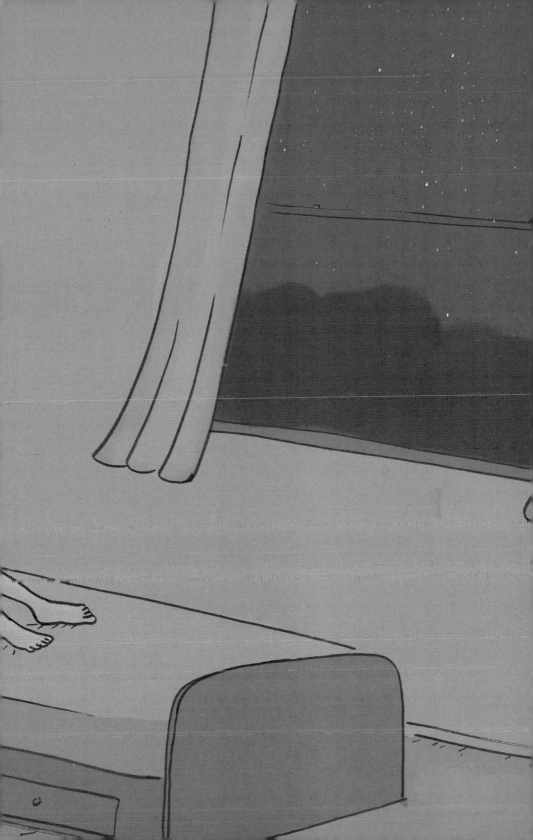

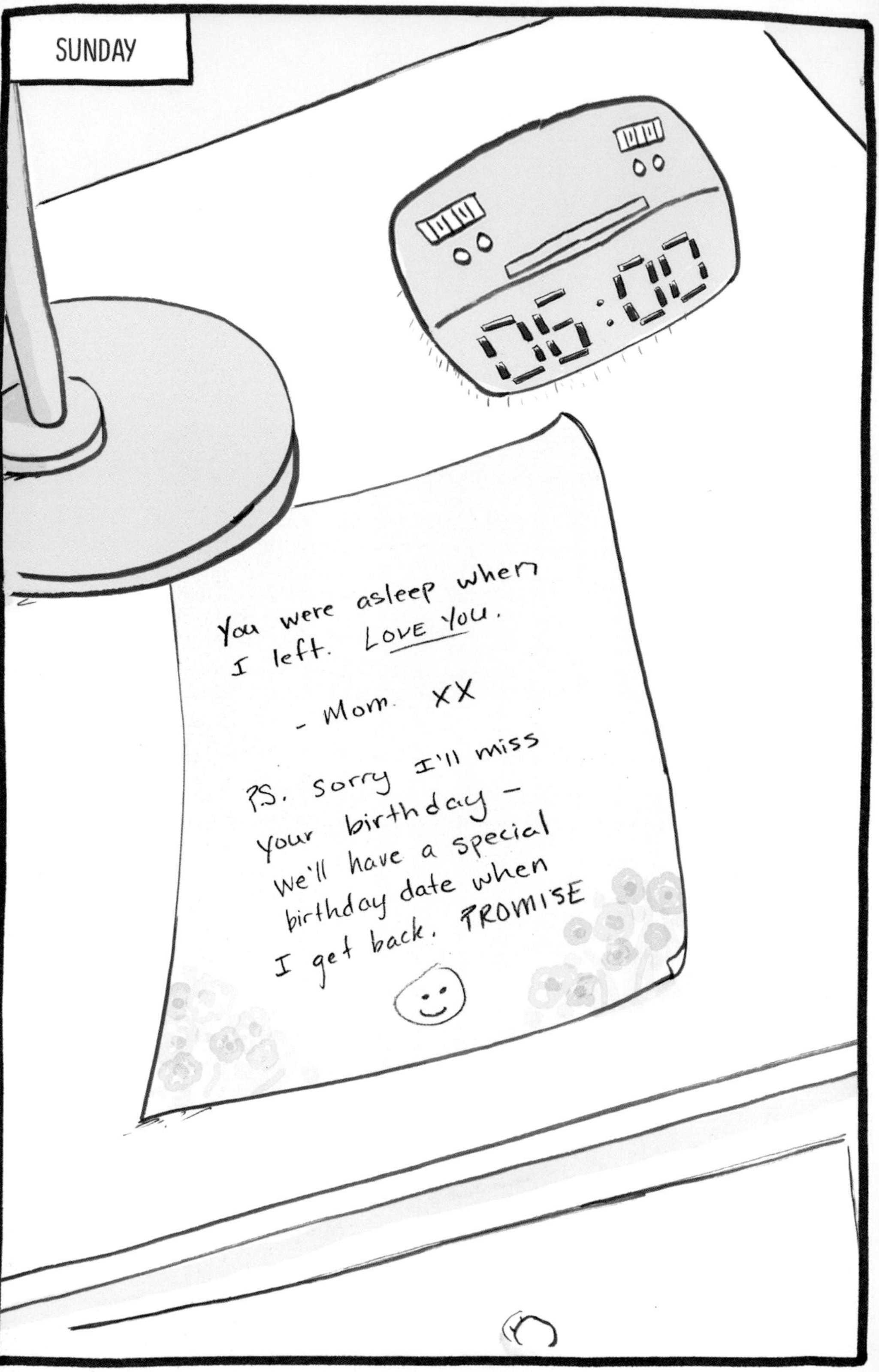
SUNDAY
05:00
You were asleep when I left. LOVE YOU.
- Mom. XX
P.S. Sorry I'll miss your birthday - We'll have a special birthday date when I get back. PROMISE

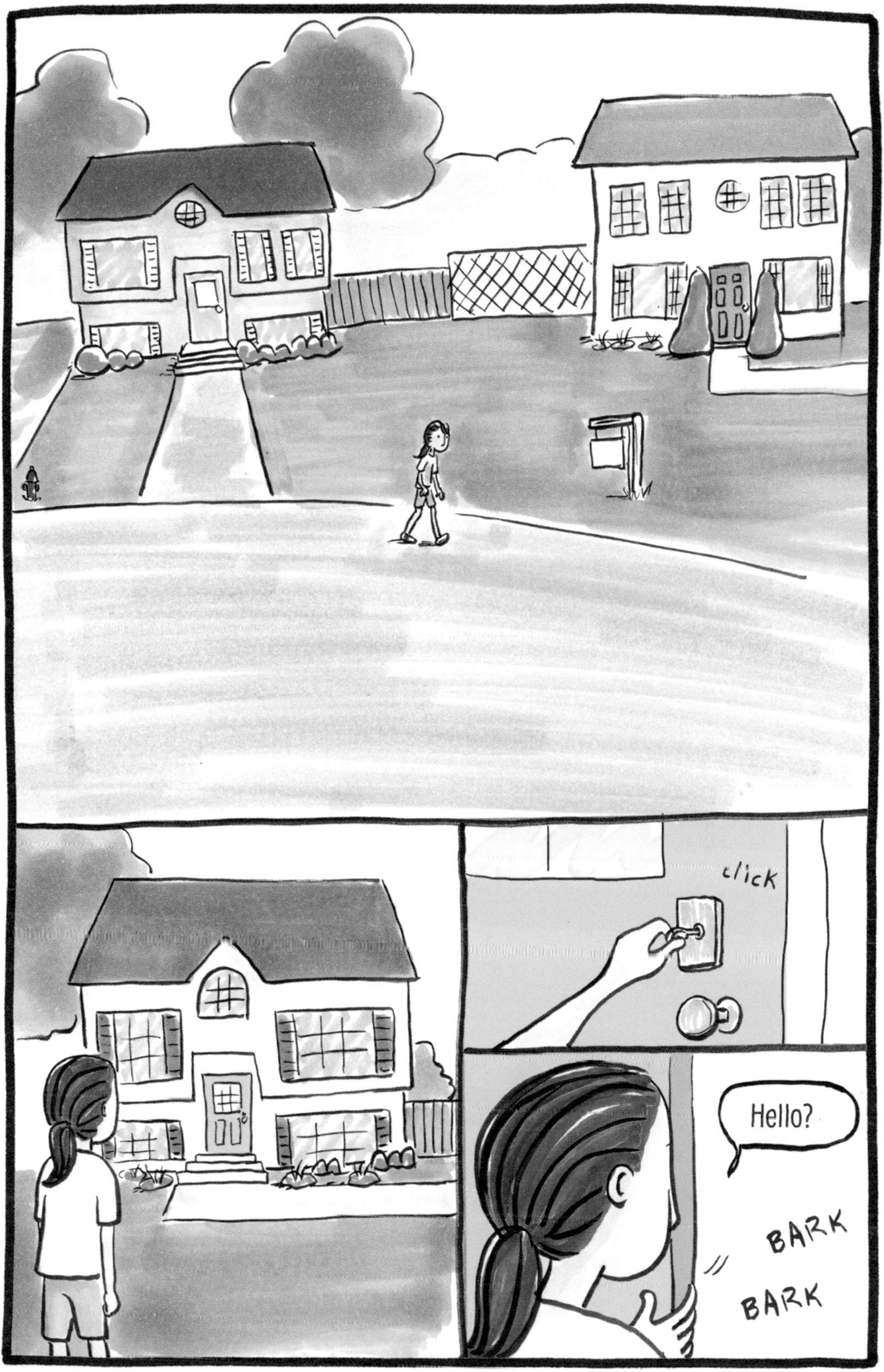
click
Hello?
BARK
BARK

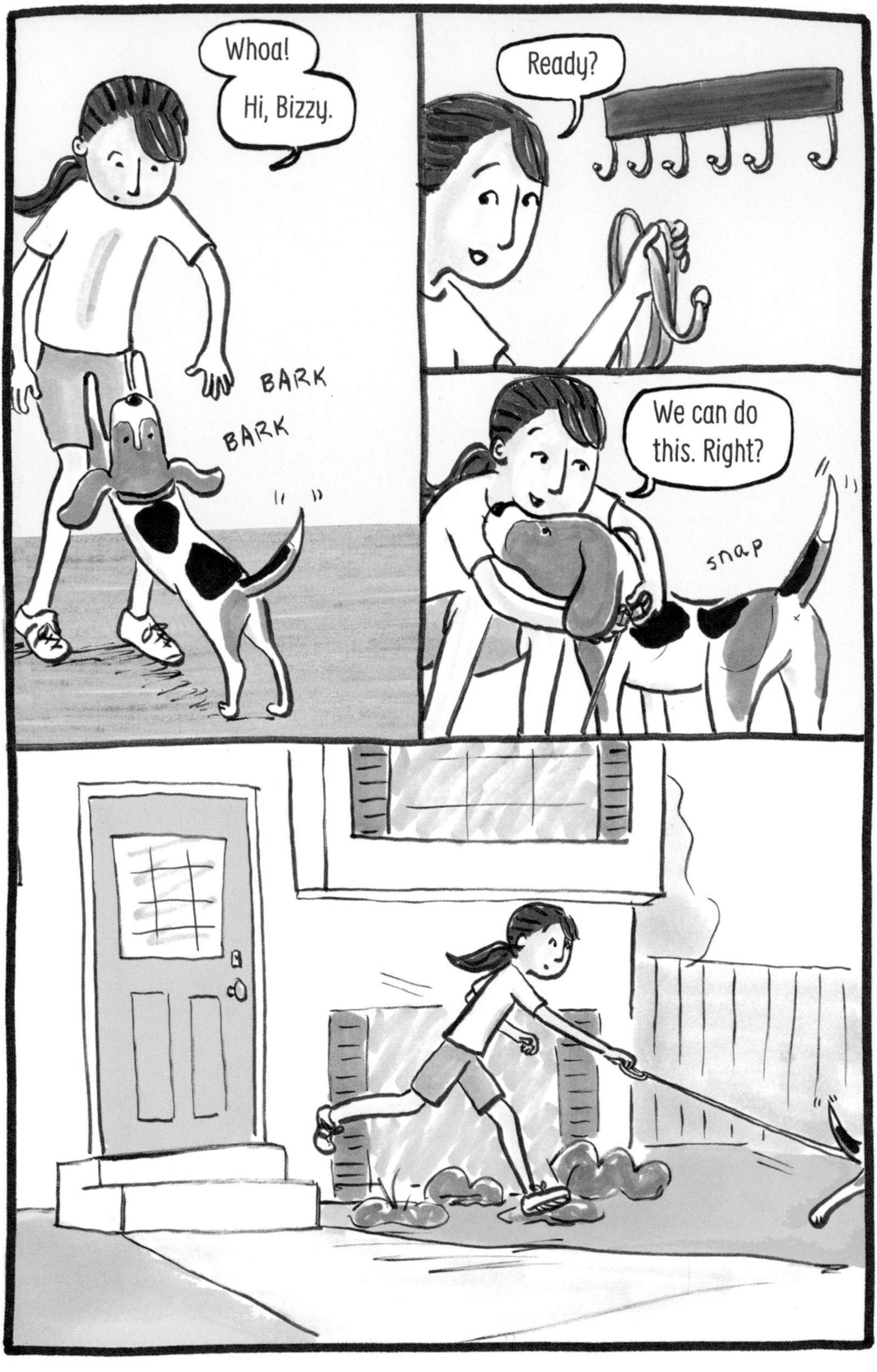
Whoa!
Hi, Bizzy.
BARK
BARK
Ready?
We can do this. Right?
snap

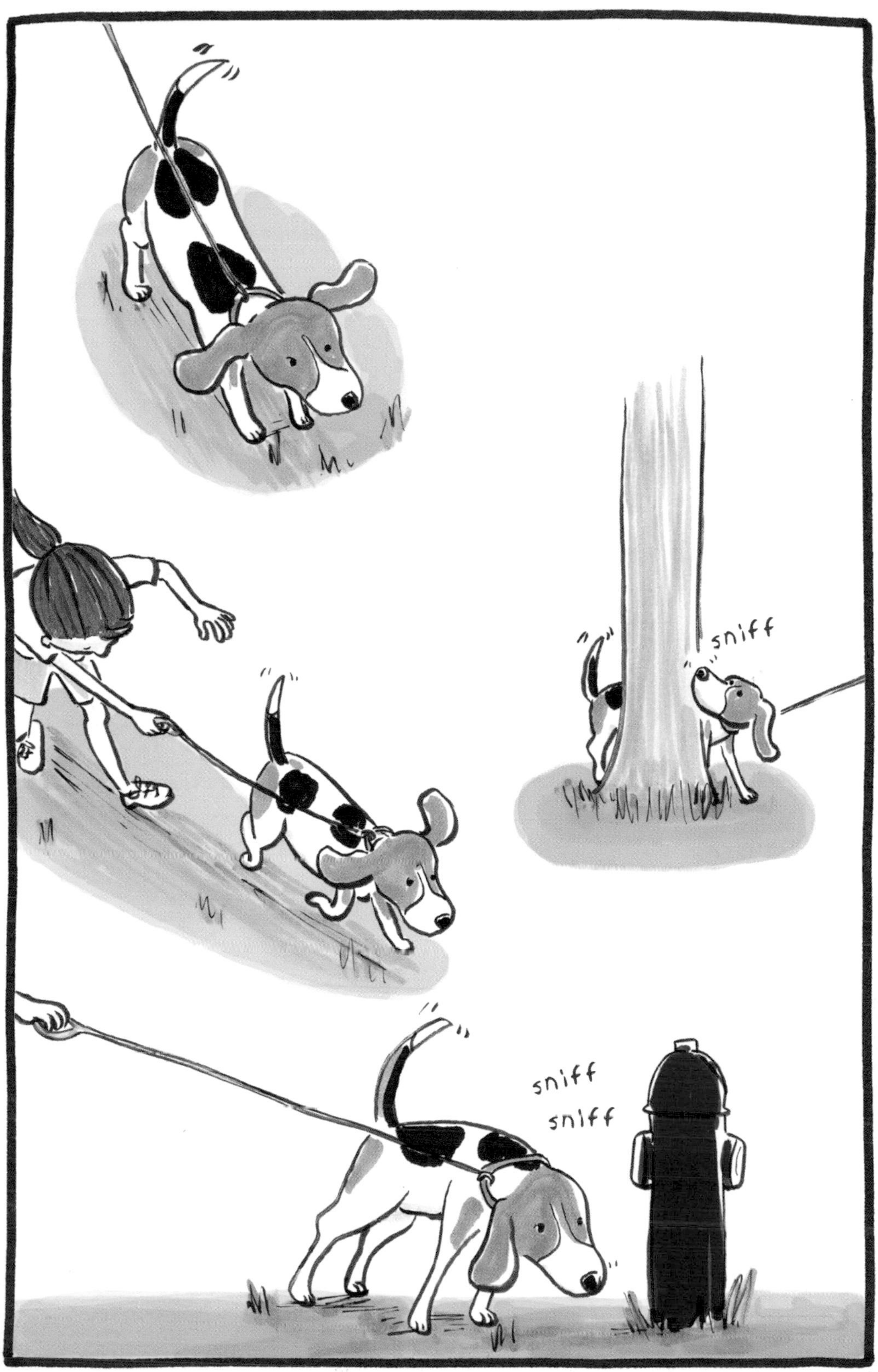
sniff
sniff
sniff

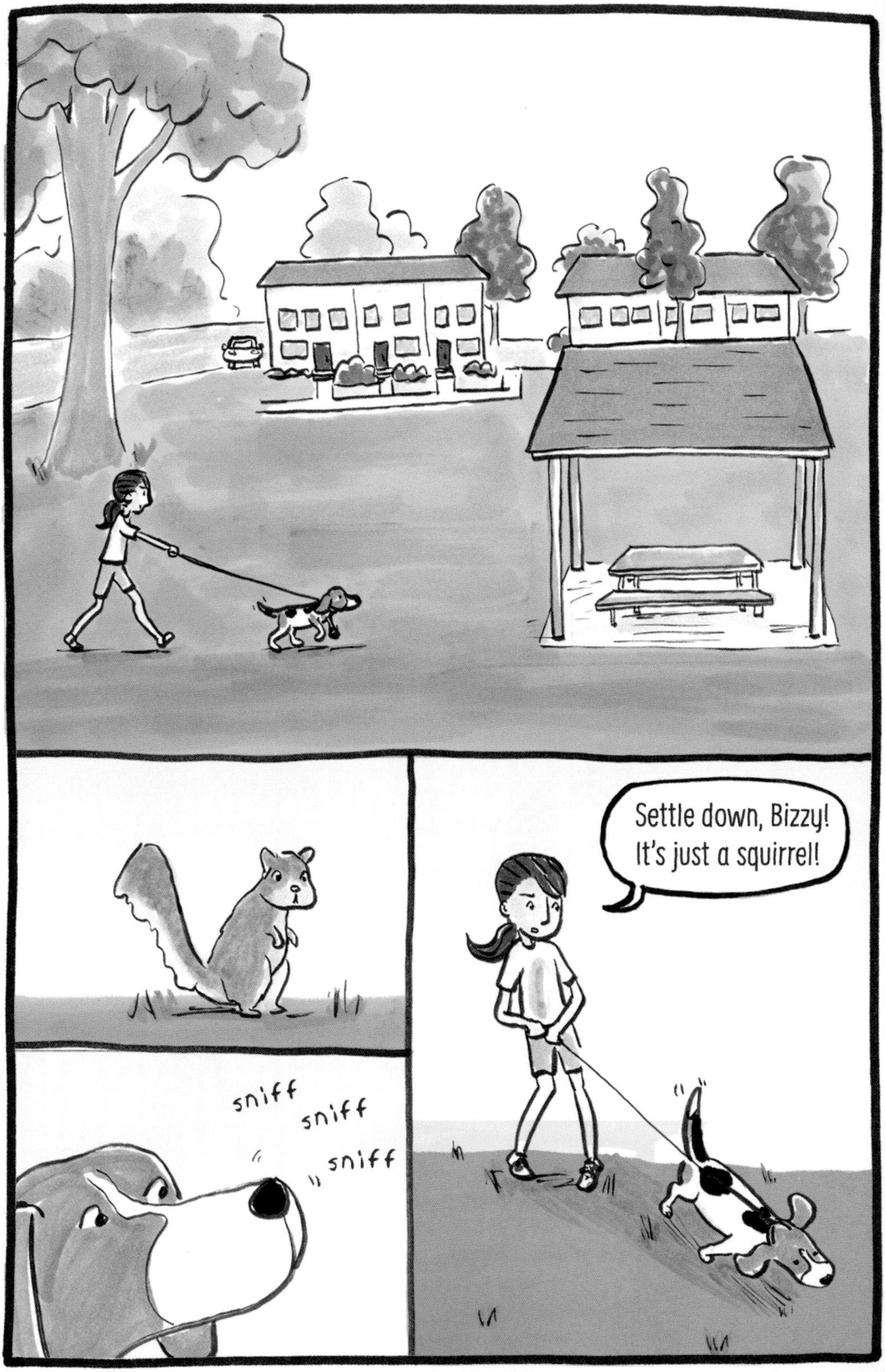
Settle down, Bizzy!
It's just a squirrel!
sniff
sniff
sniff

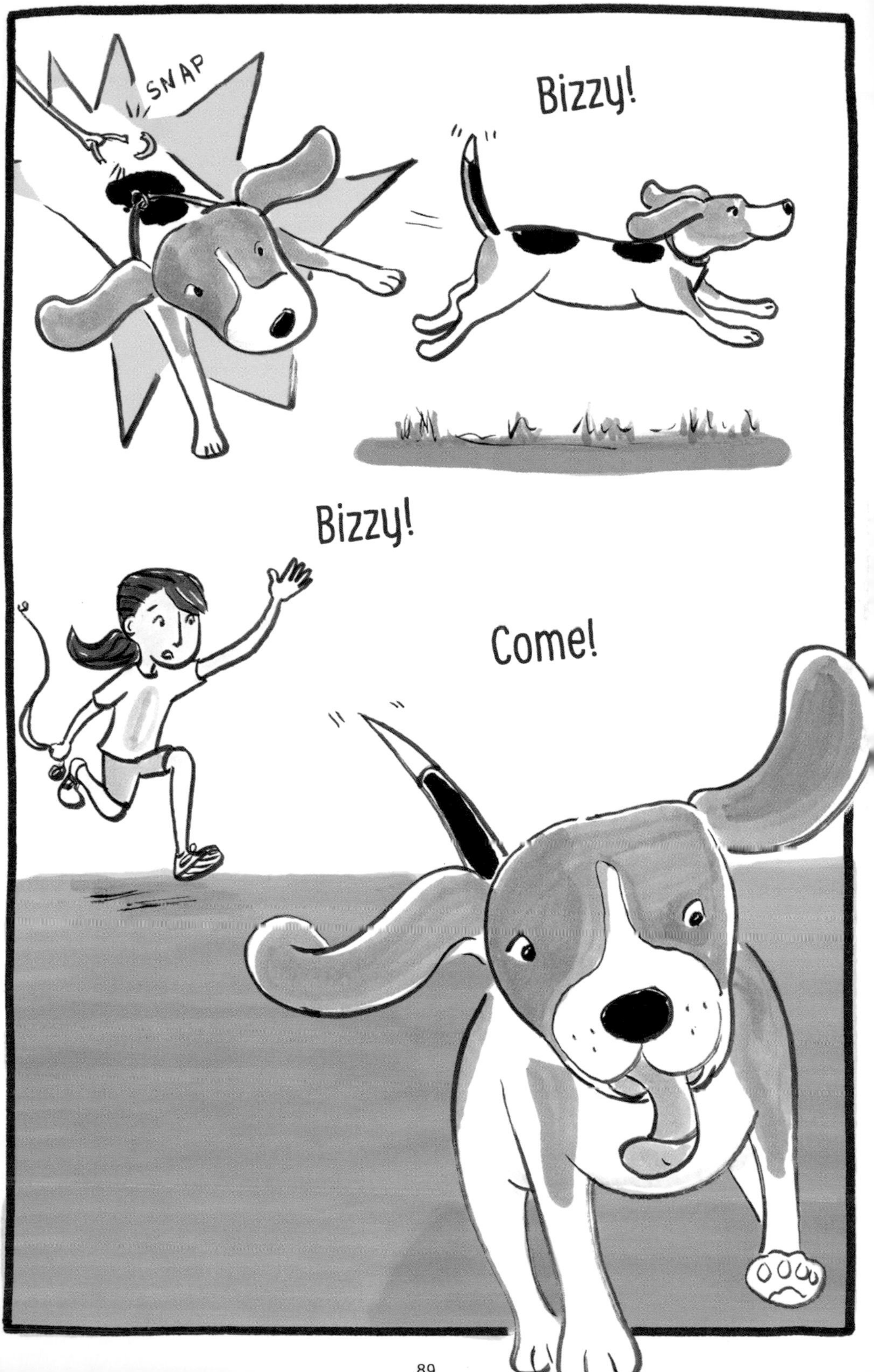
SNAP
Bizzy!
Bizzy!
Come!

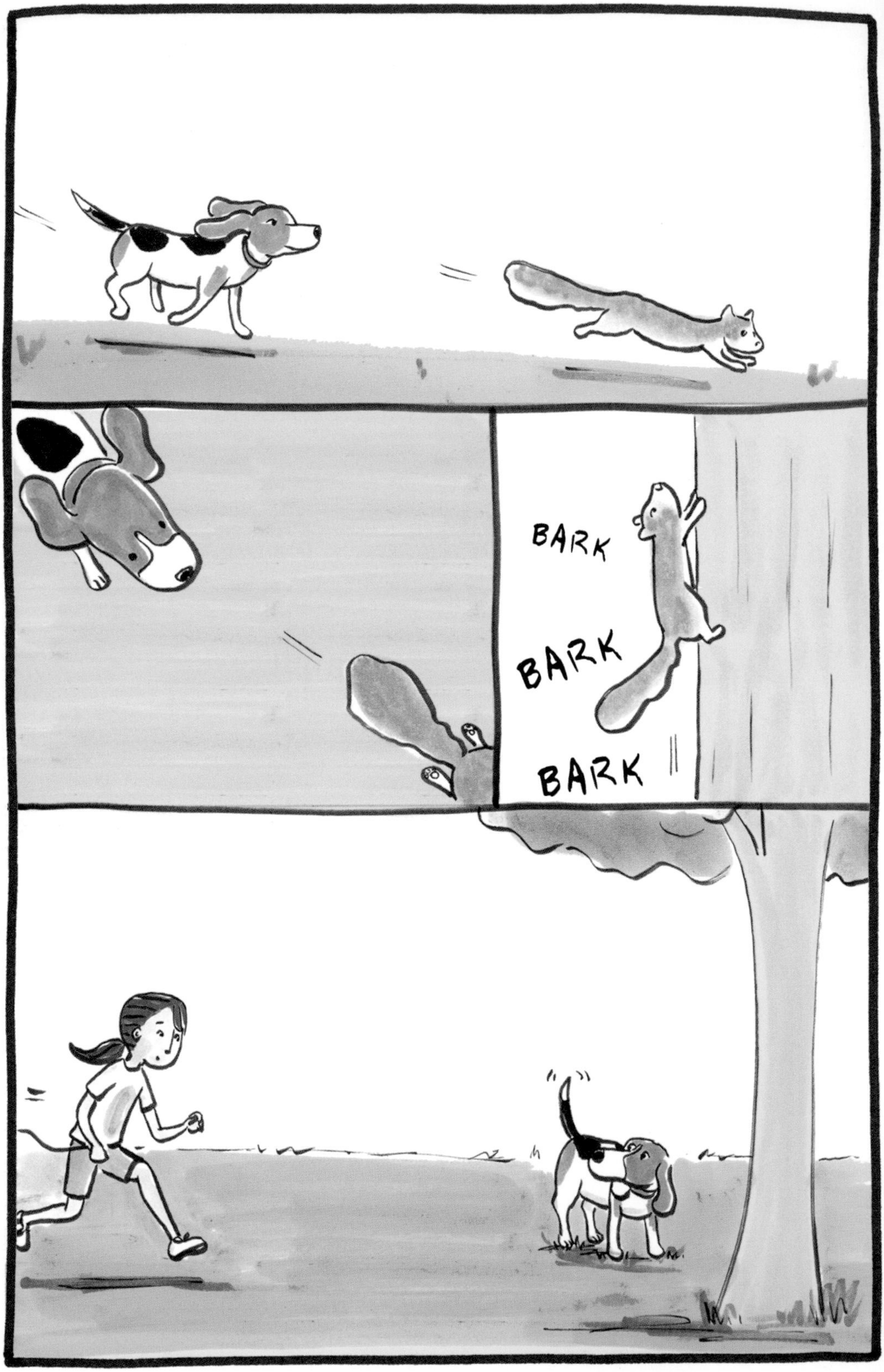
BARK
BARK
BARK

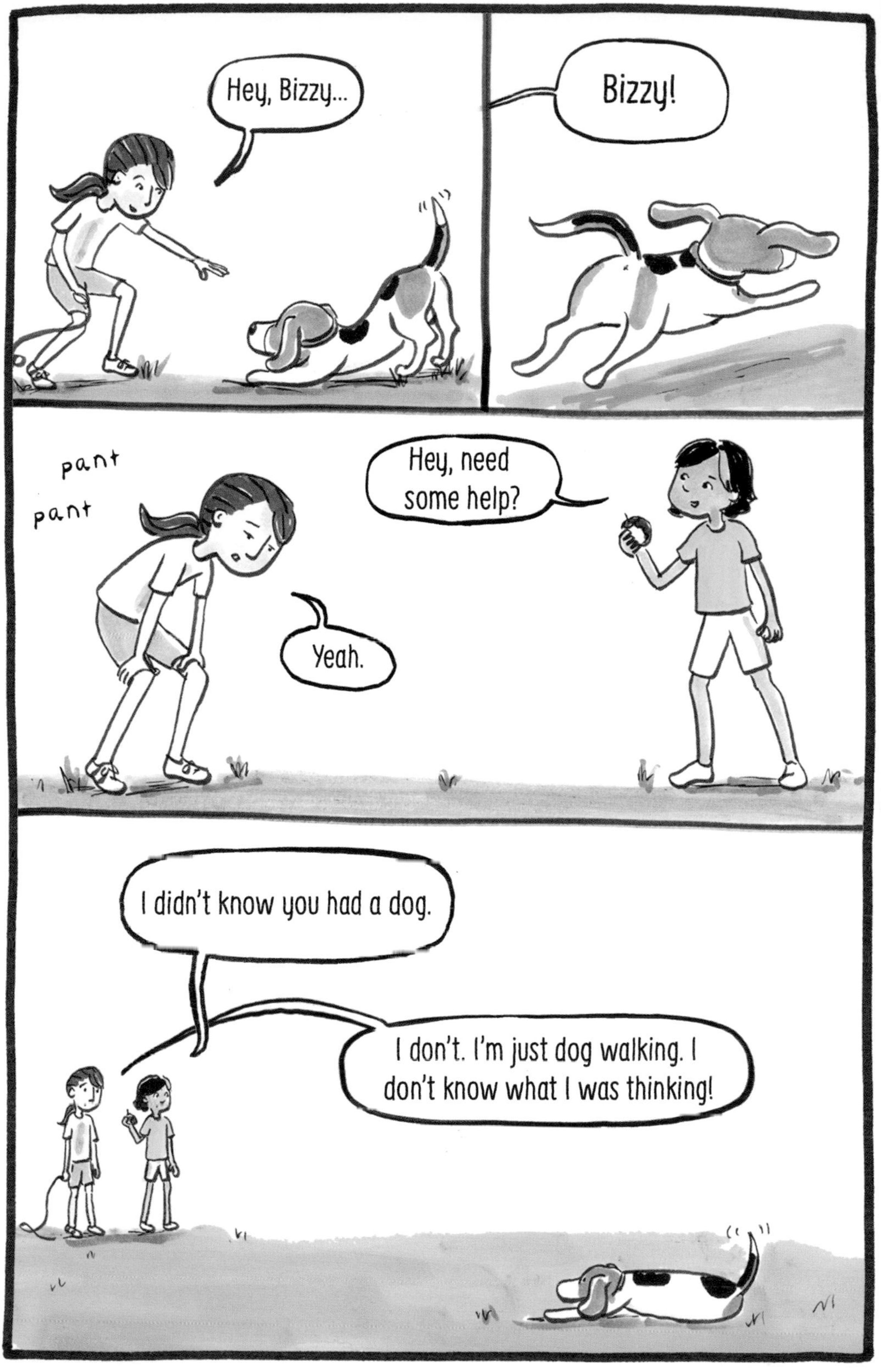
Hey, Bizzy...
Bizzy!
pant
pant
Hey, need some help?
Yeah.
I didn't know you had a dog.
I don't. I'm just dog walking. I don't know what I was thinking!

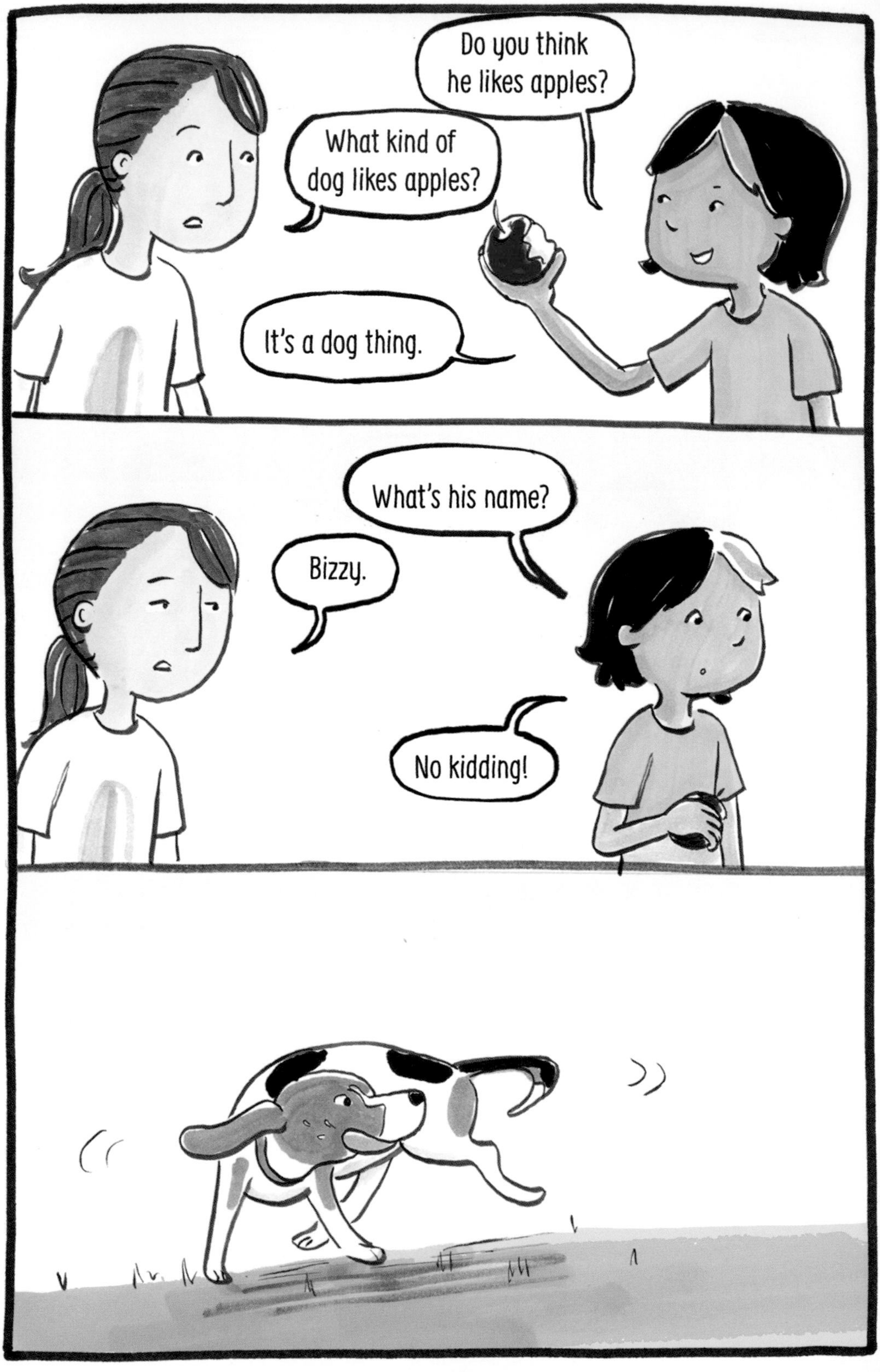
Do you think he likes apples?
What kind of dog likes apples?
It's a dog thing.
What's his name?
Bizzy.
No kidding!

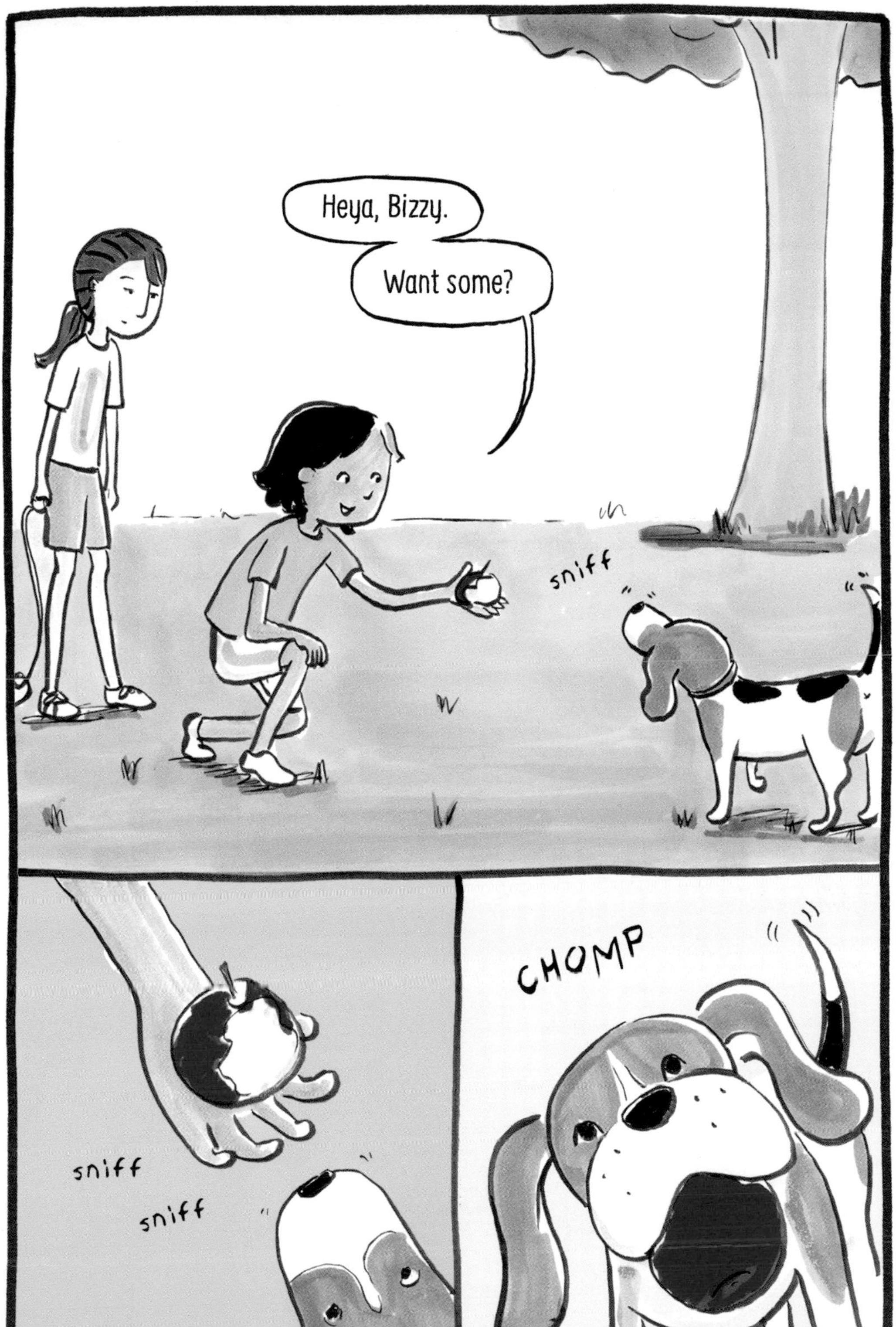
Heya, Bizzy.
Want some?
sniff
sniff
sniff
CHOMP

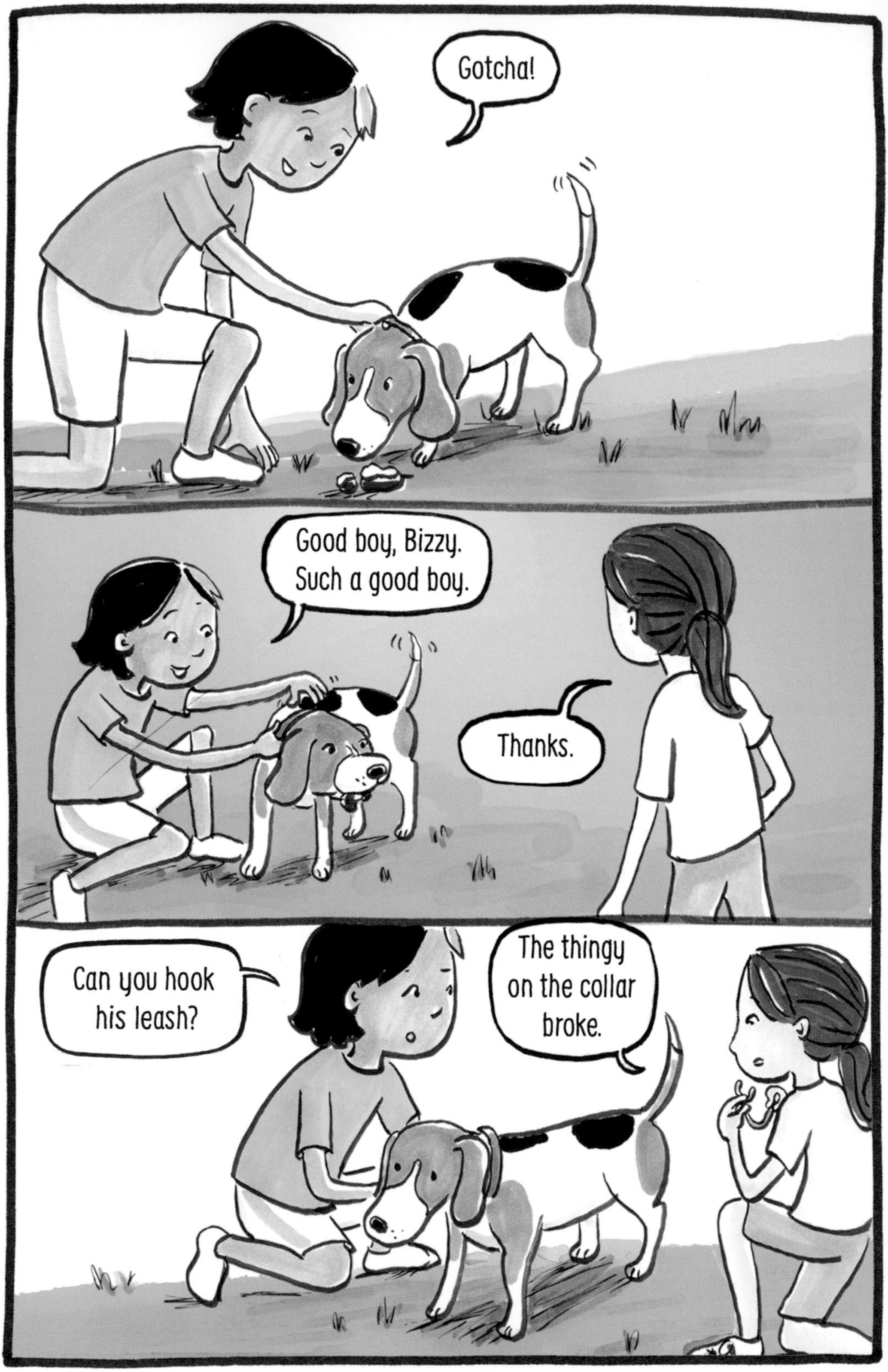
Gotcha!
Good boy, Bizzy. Such a good boy.
Thanks.
Can you hook his leash?
The thingy on the collar broke.

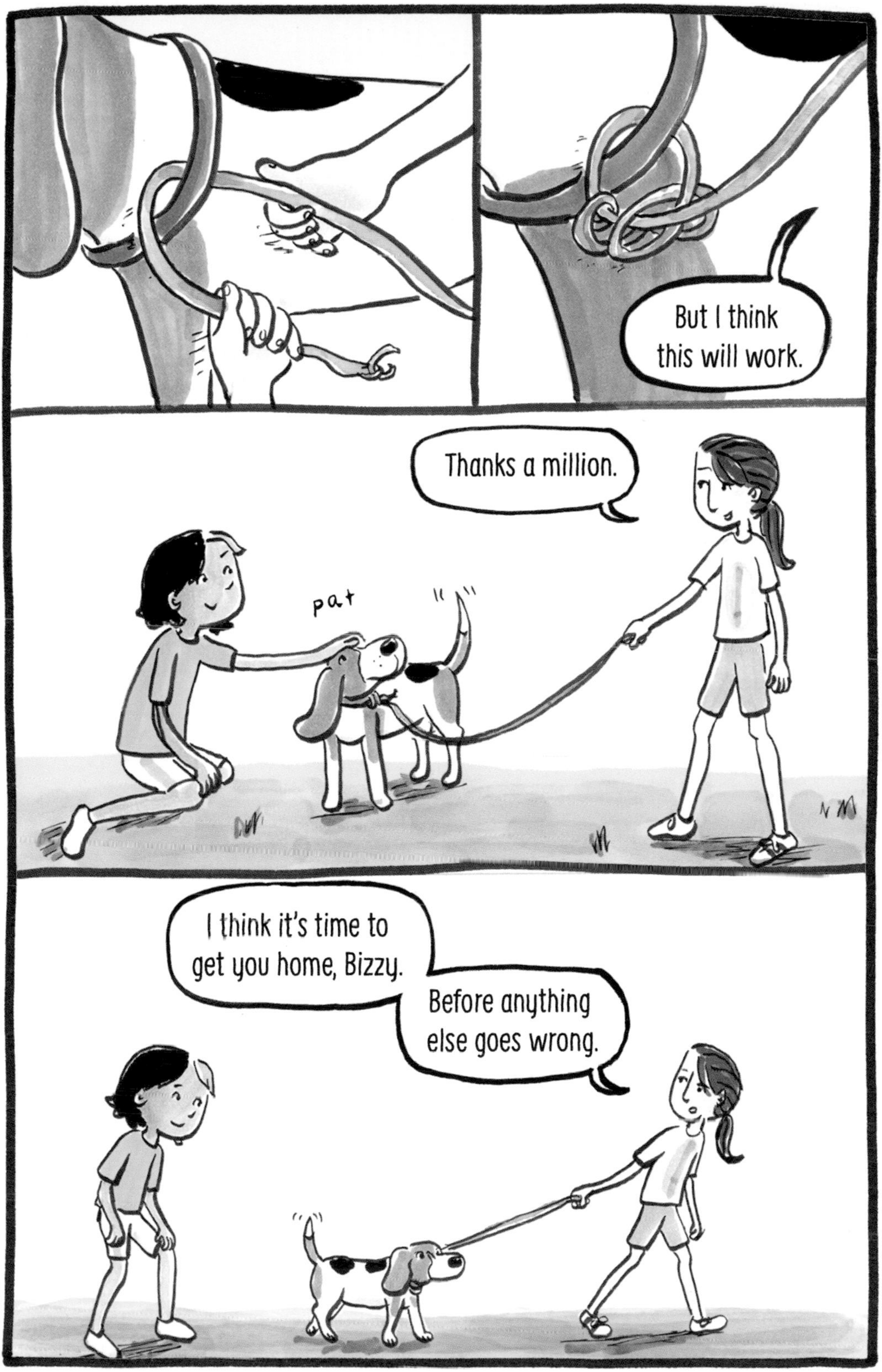
But I think this will work.
Thanks a million.
pat
I think it's time to get you home, Bizzy.
Before anything else goes wrong.

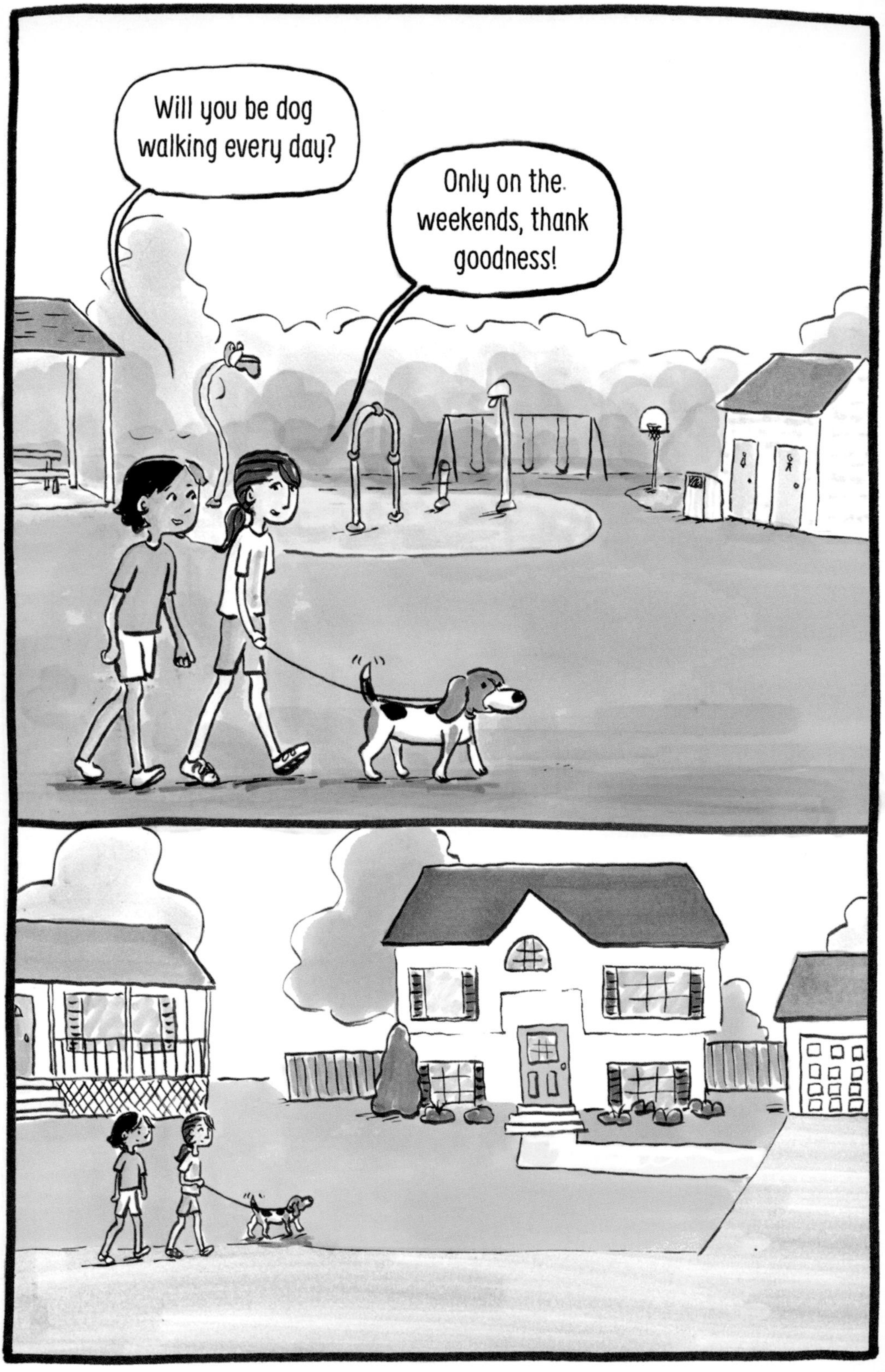
Will you be dog walking every day?
Only on the weekends, thank goodness!

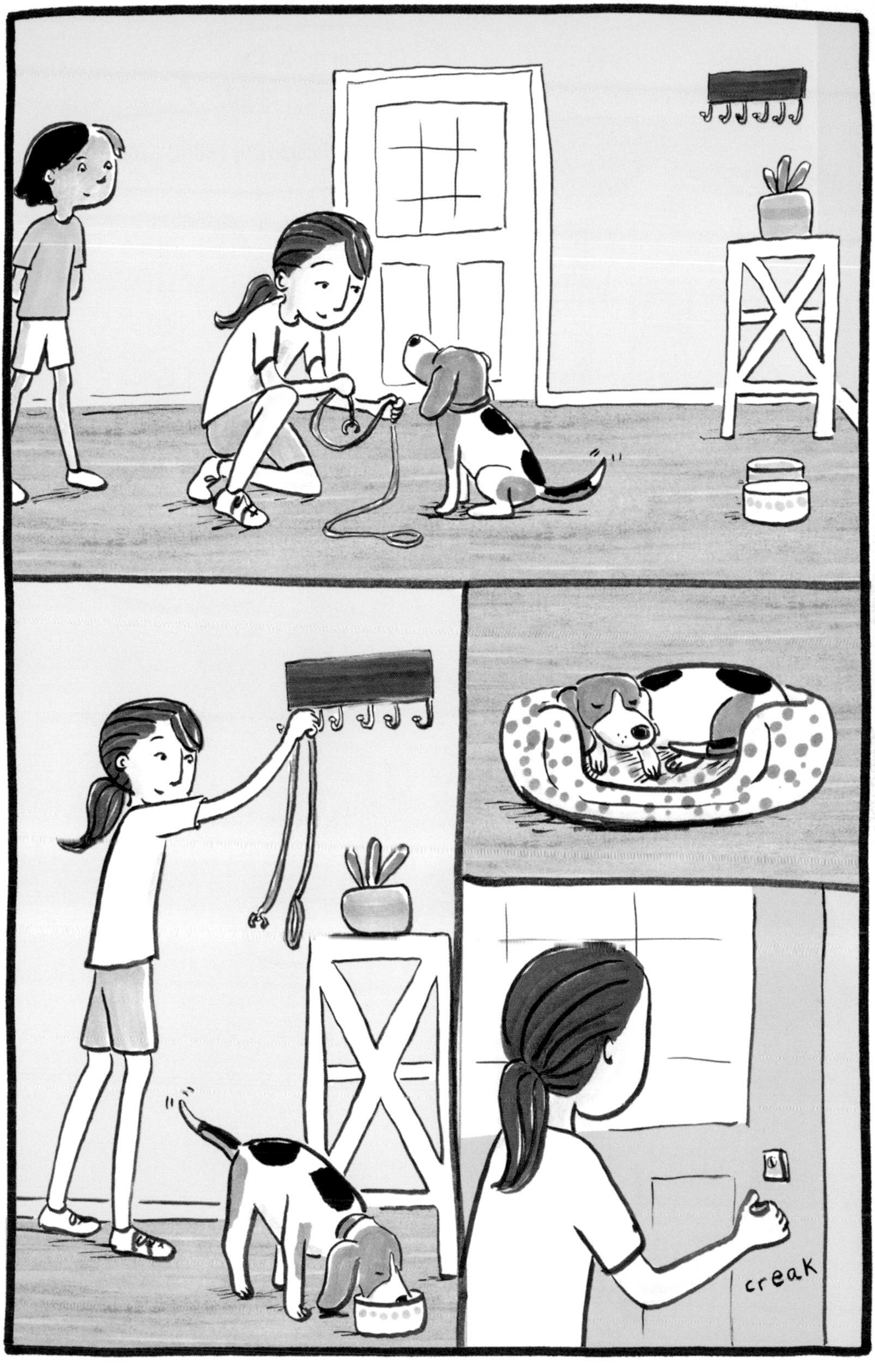
creak

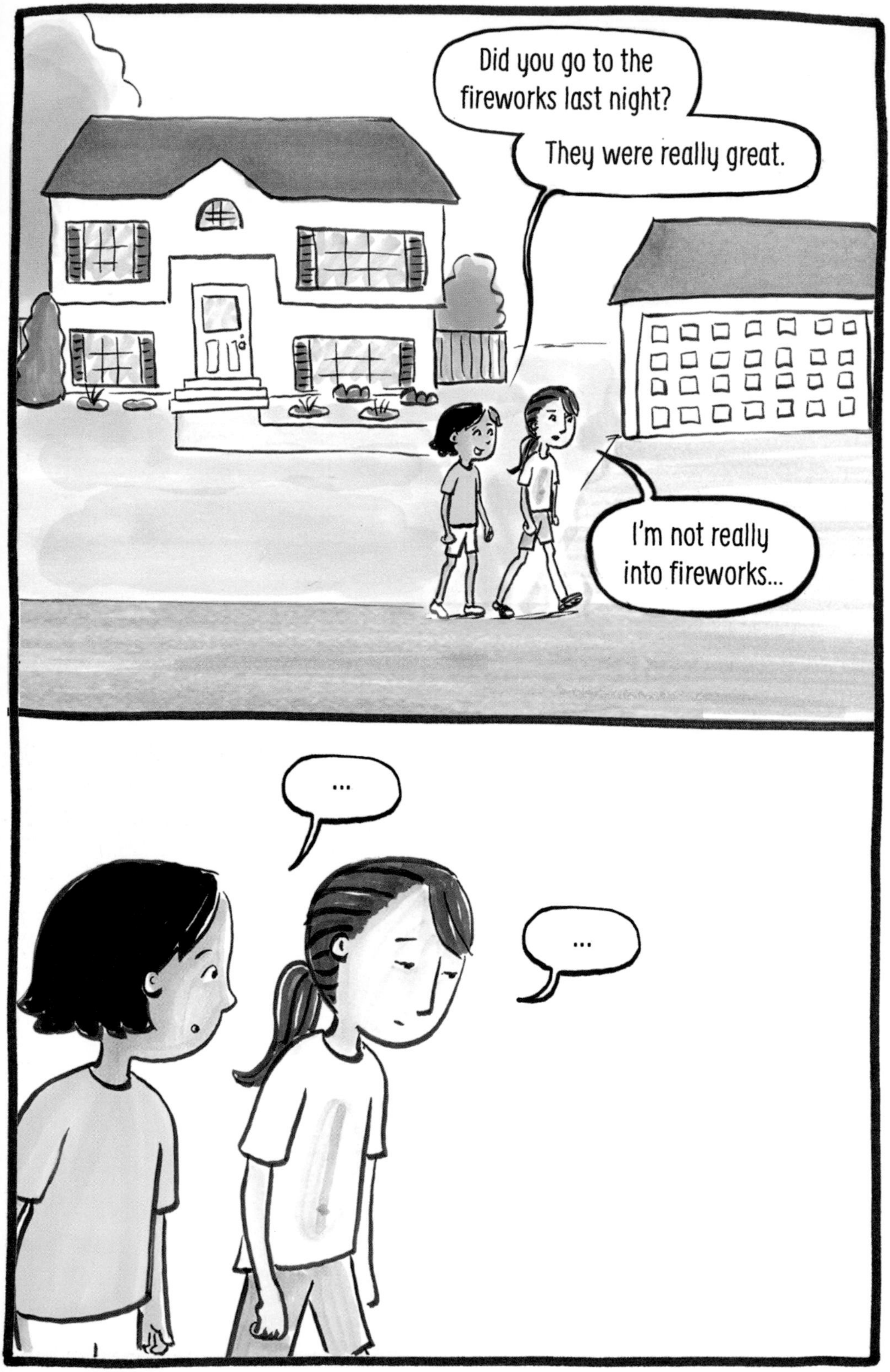
Did you go to the fireworks last night?
They were really great.
I'm not really into fireworks...
...
...

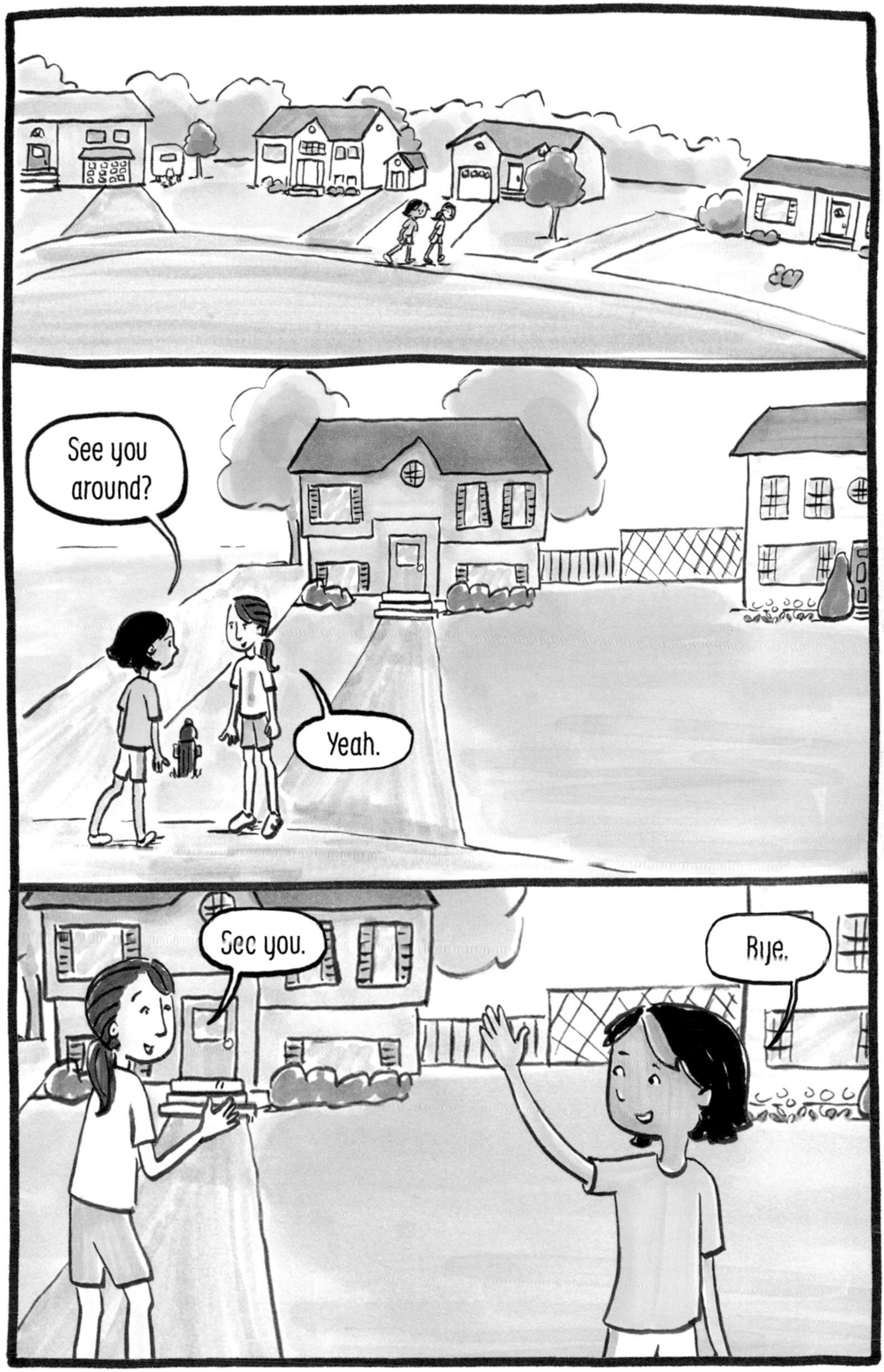
See you around?
Yeah.
See you.
Bye.

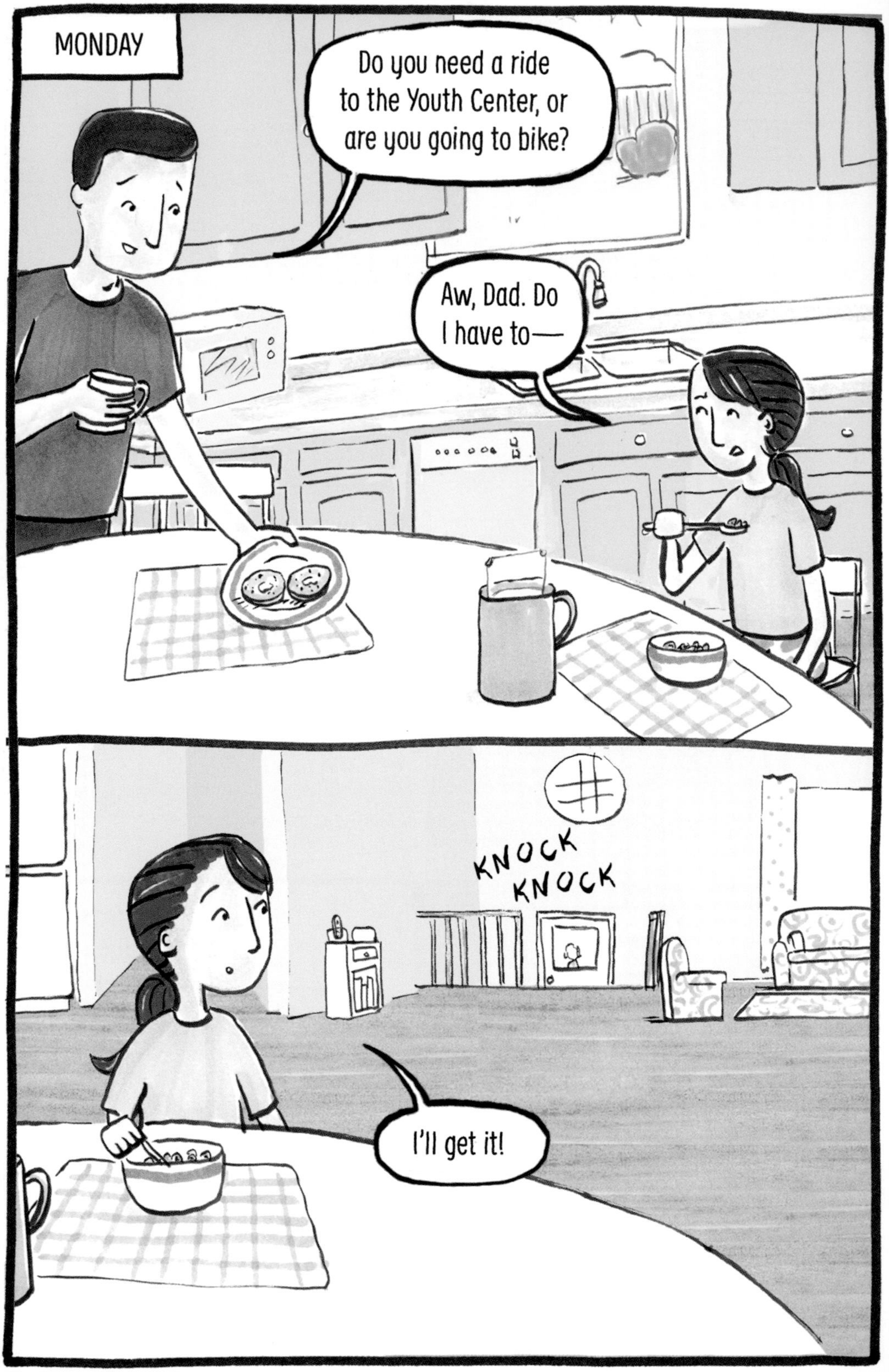
MONDAY
Do you need a ride to the Youth Center, or are you going to bike?
Aw, Dad. Do I have to—
KNOCK KNOCK
I'll get it!

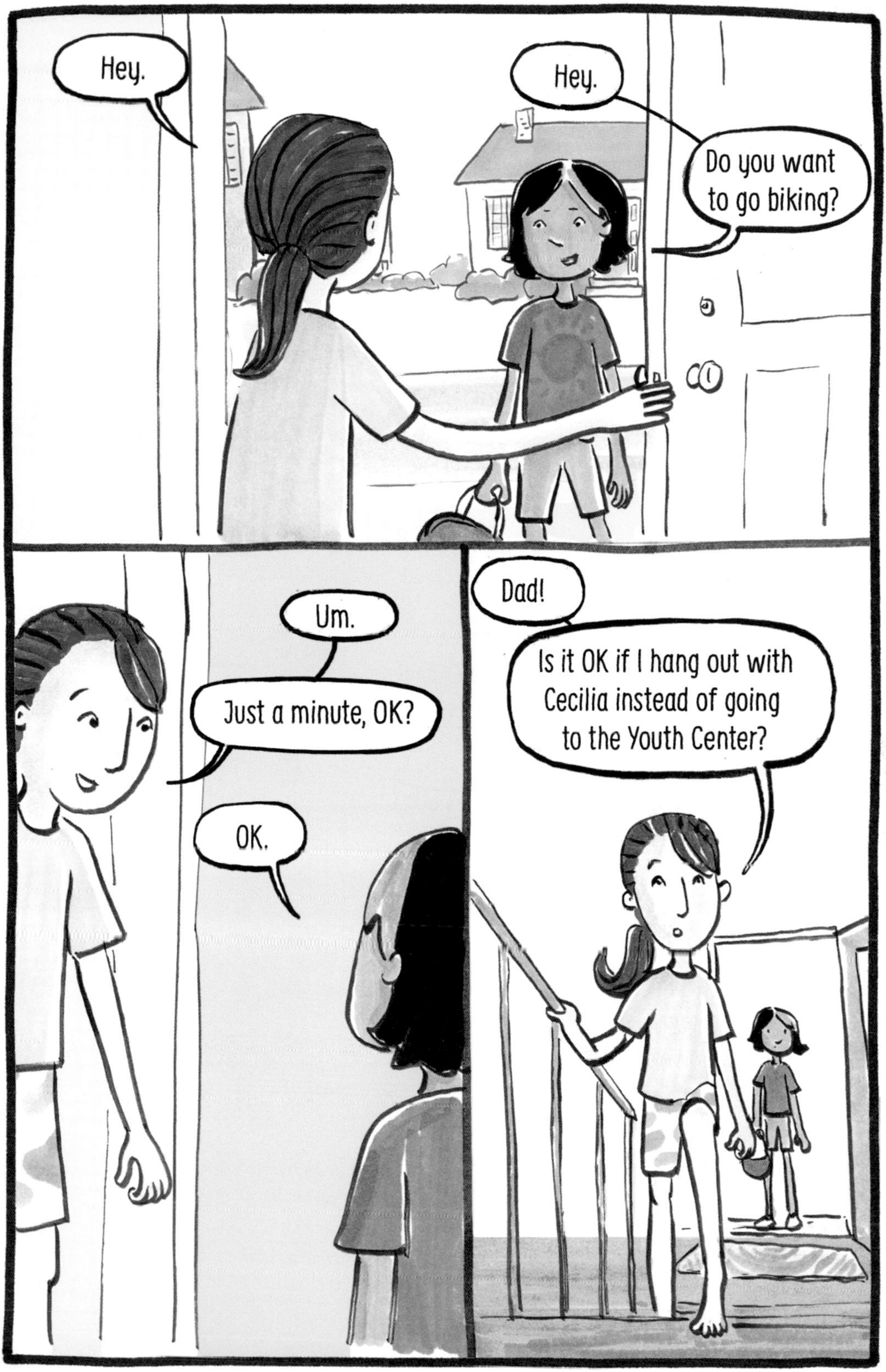
Hey.
Hey.
Do you want to go biking?
Um.
Just a minute, OK?
OK.
Dad!
Is it OK if I hang out with Cecilia instead of going to the Youth Center?

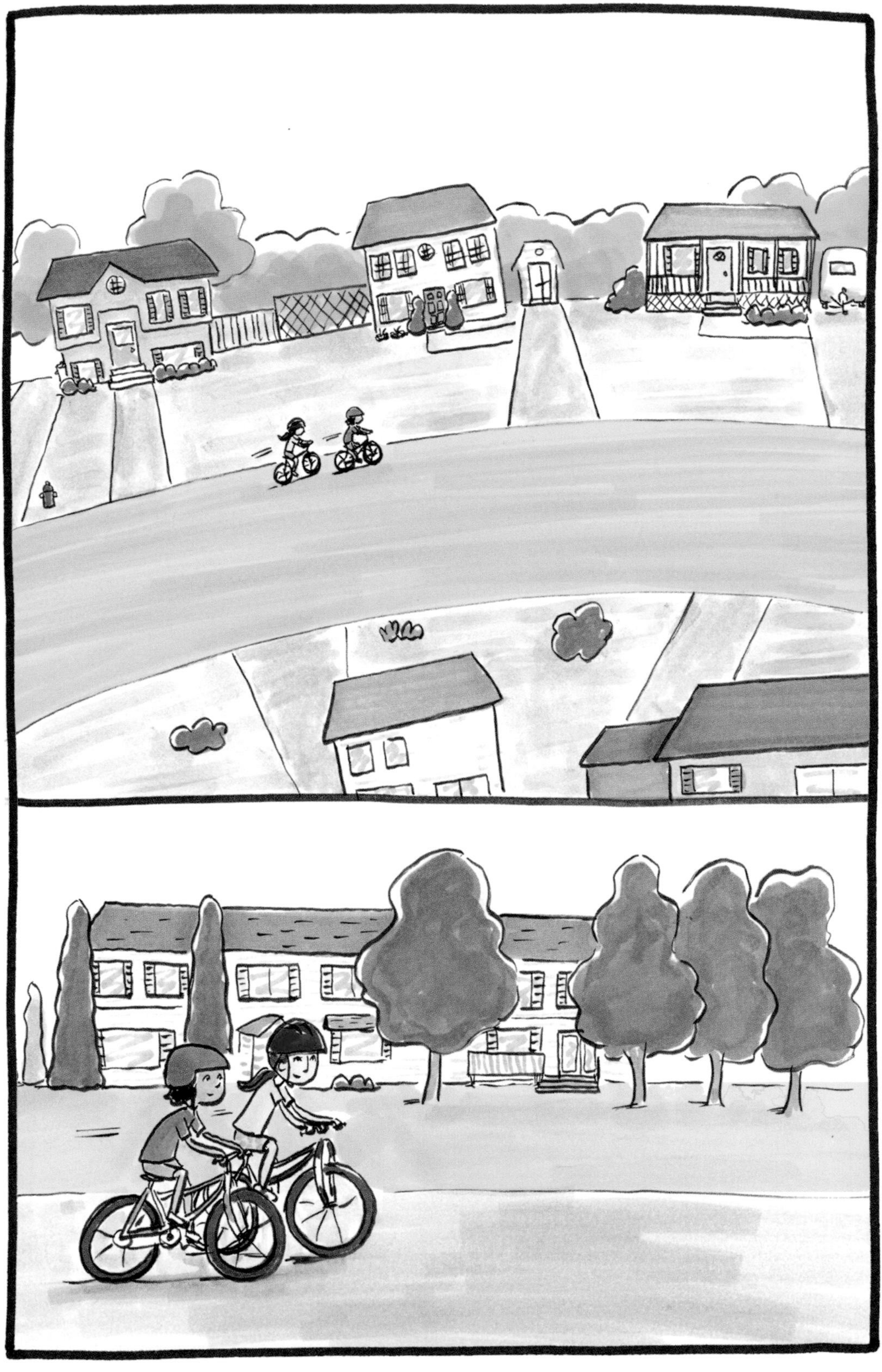

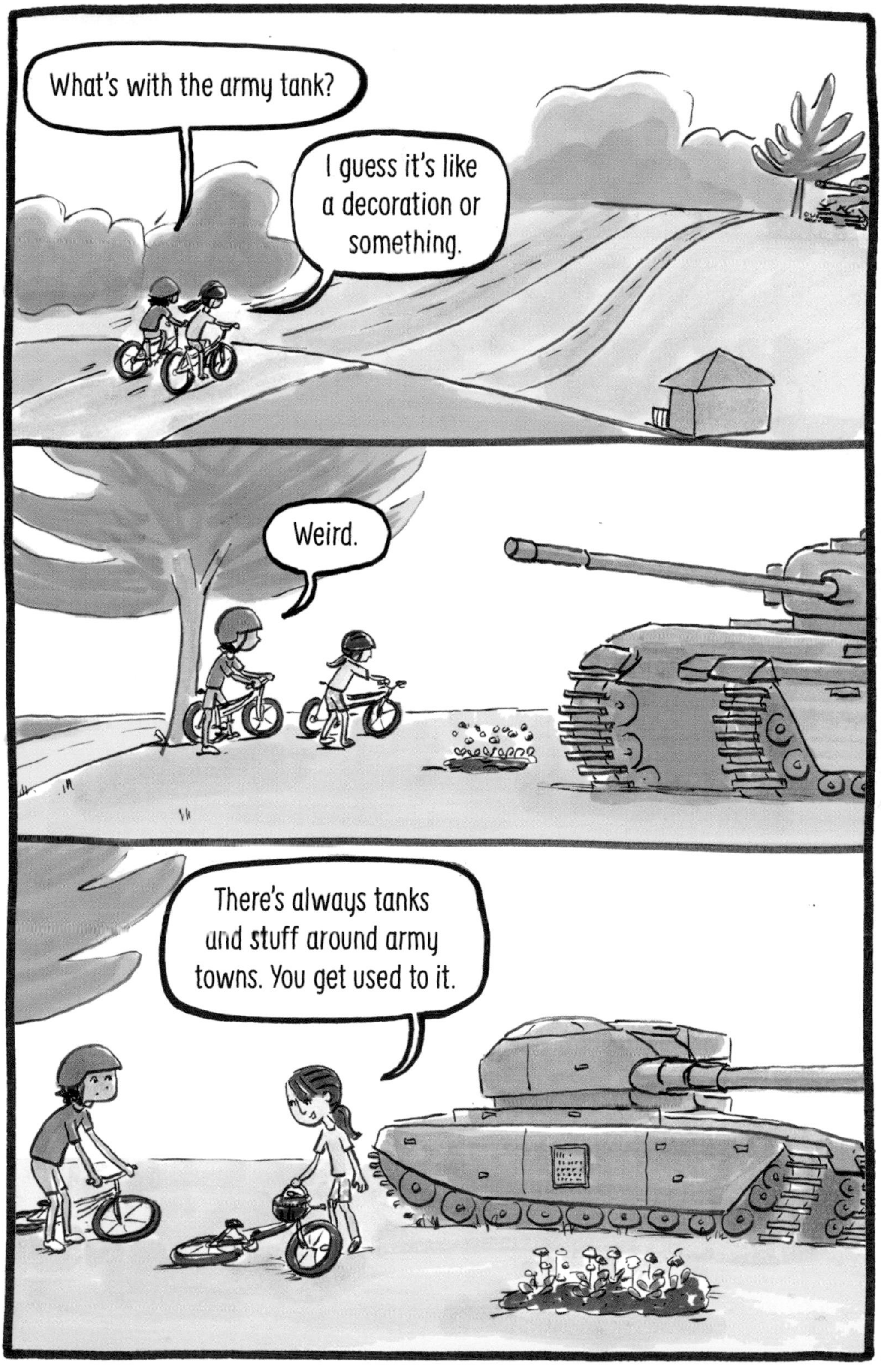
What's with the army tank?
I guess it's like a decoration or something.
Weird.
There's always tanks and stuff around army towns. You get used to it.

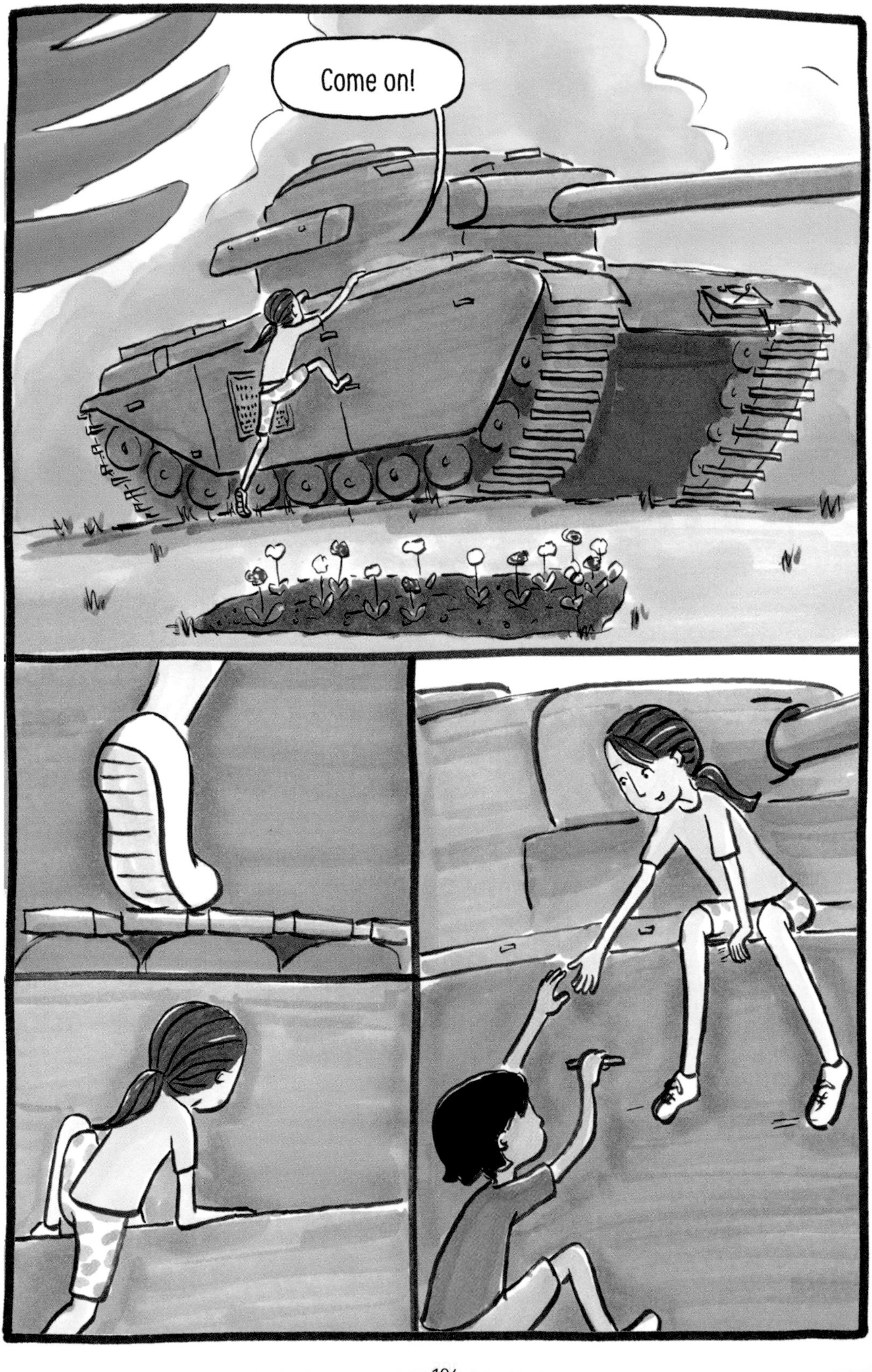
Come on!

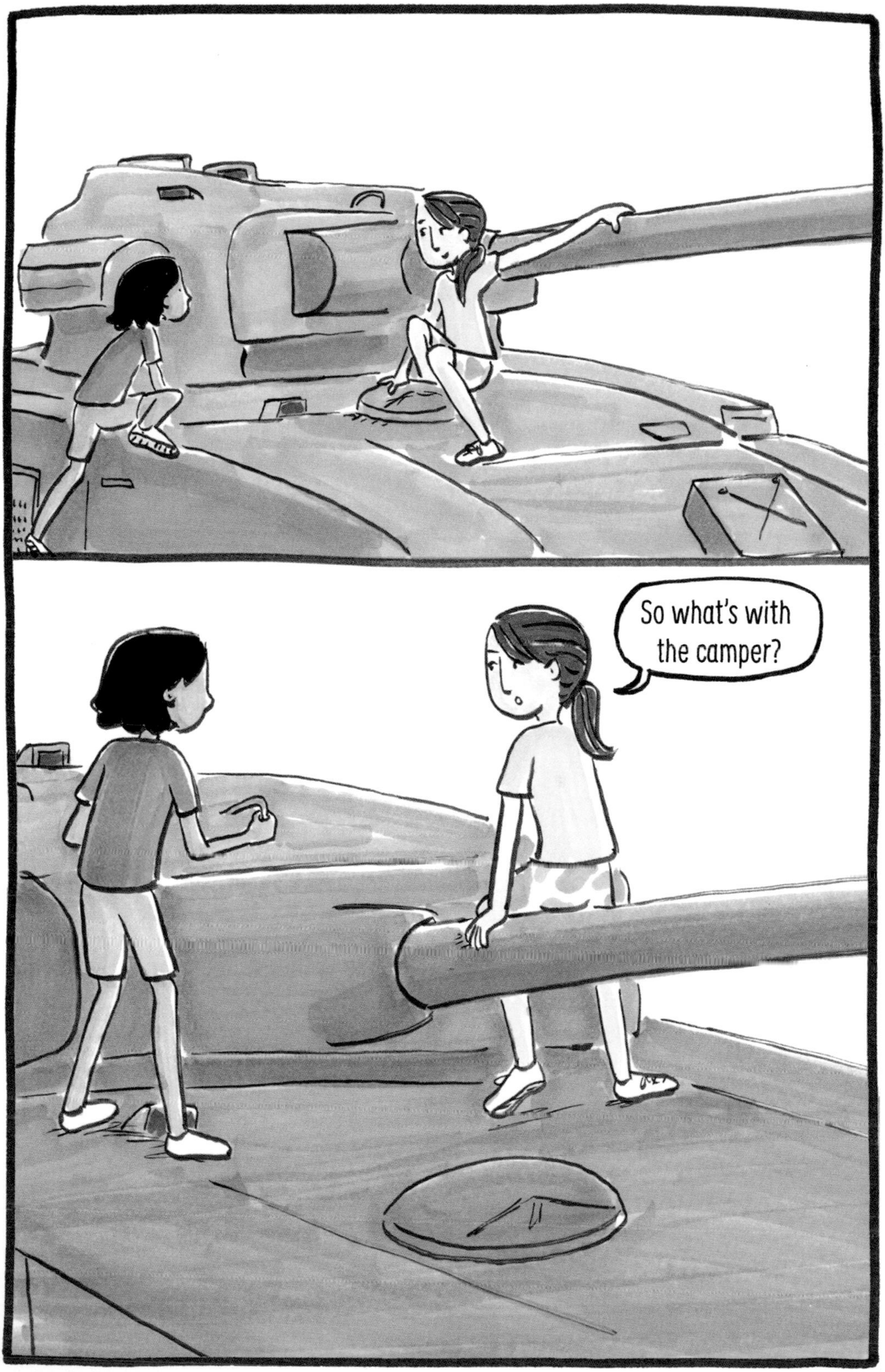
So what's with the camper?

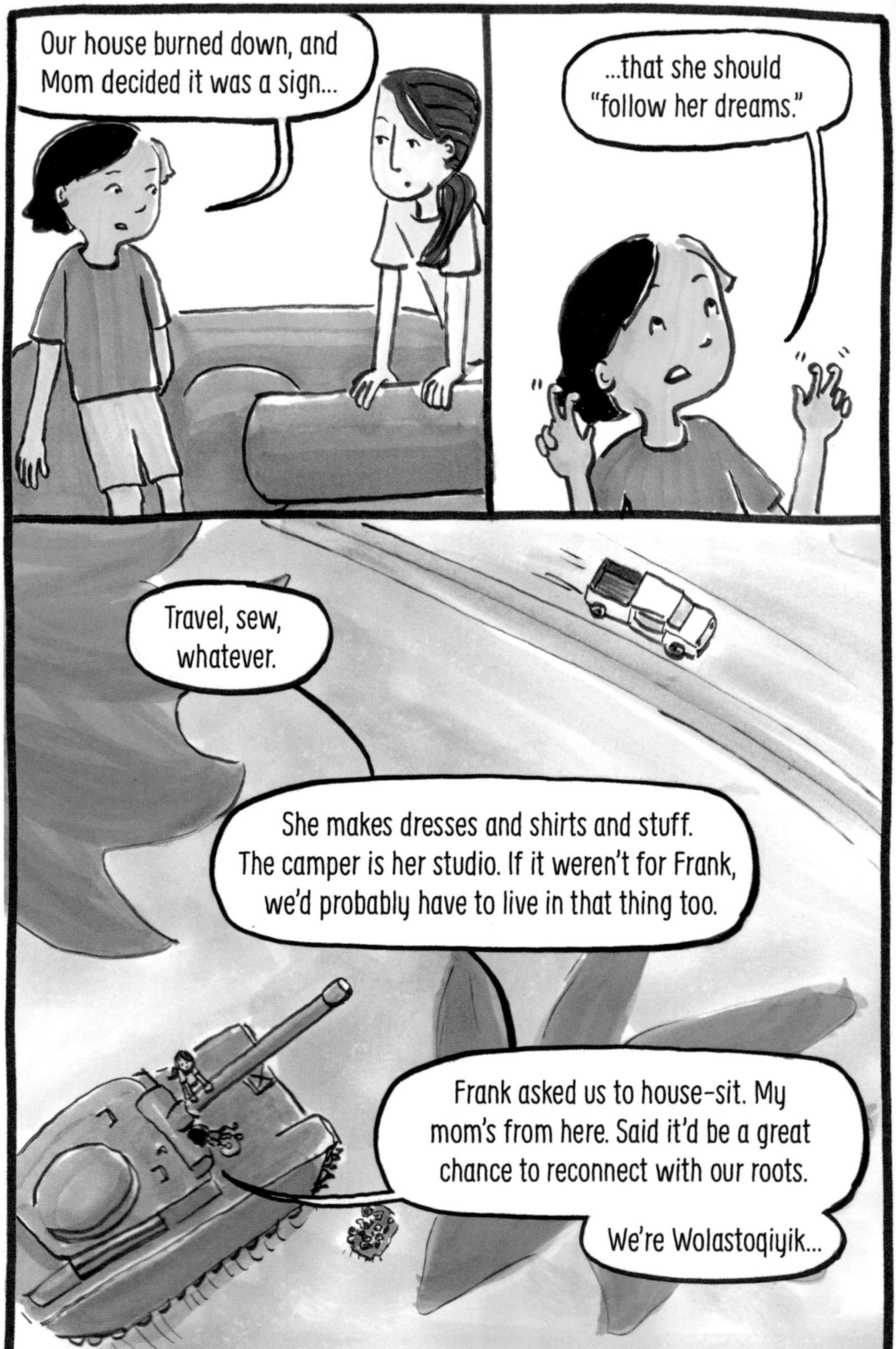
Our house burned down, and Mom decided it was a sign...
...that she should "follow her dreams."
Travel, sew, whatever.
She makes dresses and shirts and stuff. The camper is her studio. If it weren't for Frank, we'd probably have to live in that thing too.
Frank asked us to house-sit. My mom's from here. Said it'd be a great chance to reconnect with our roots.
We're Wolastoqiyik...

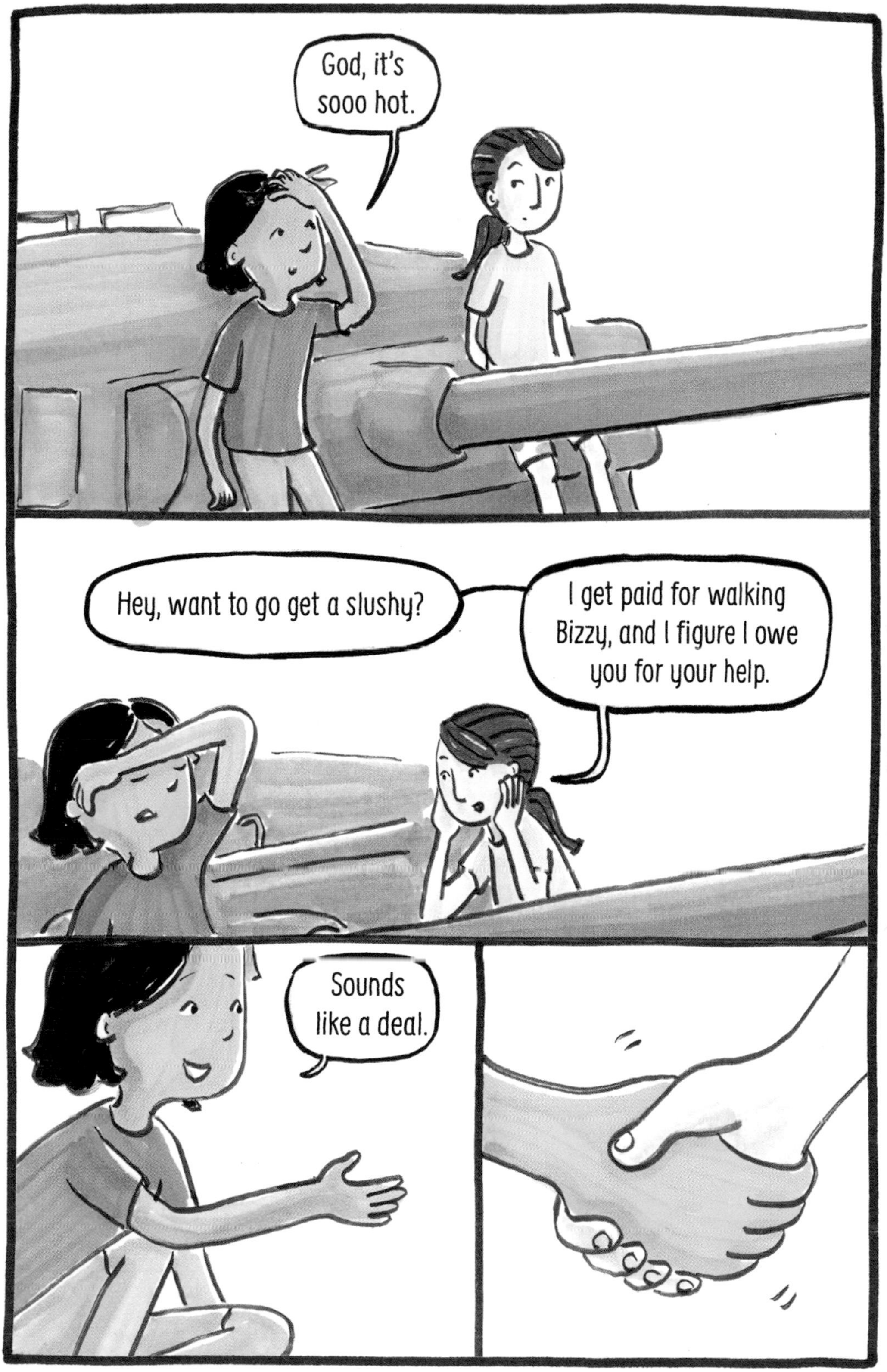
God, it's sooo hot.
Hey, want to go get a slushy?
I get paid for walking Bizzy, and I figure I owe you for your help.
Sounds like a deal.

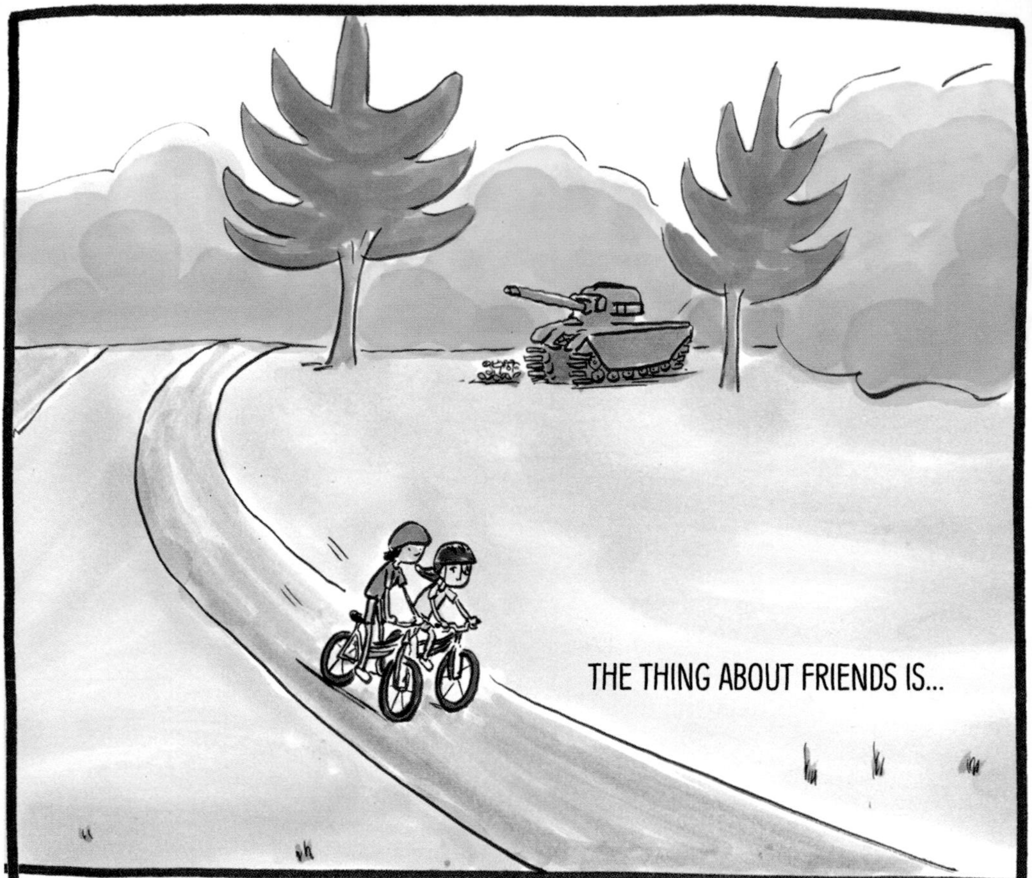
THE THING ABOUT FRIENDS IS...

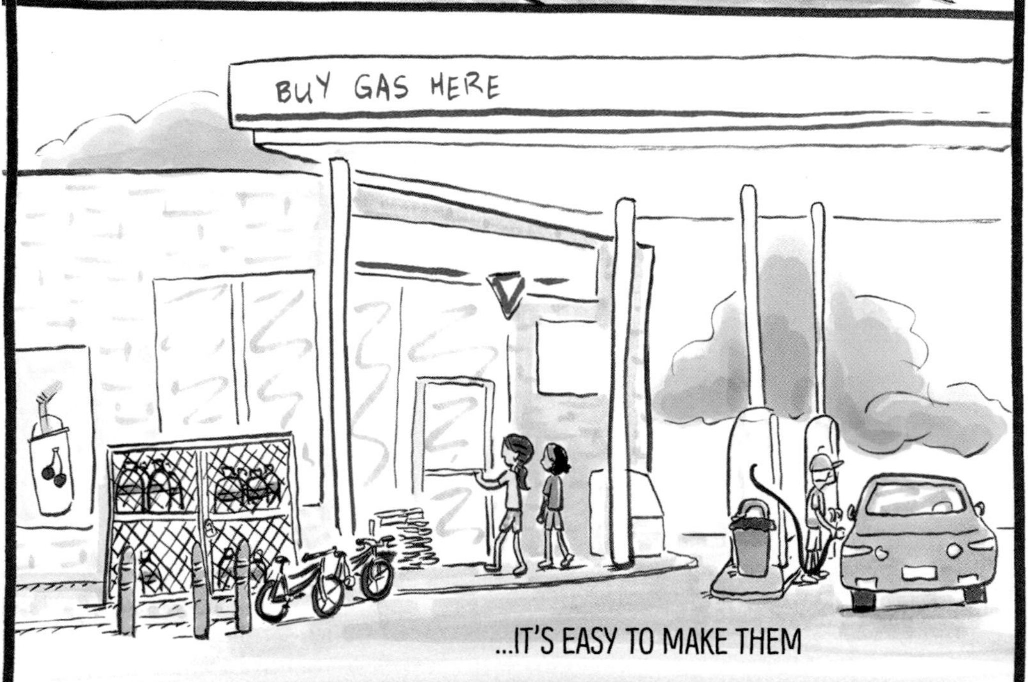
BUY GAS HERE
...IT'S EASY TO MAKE THEM

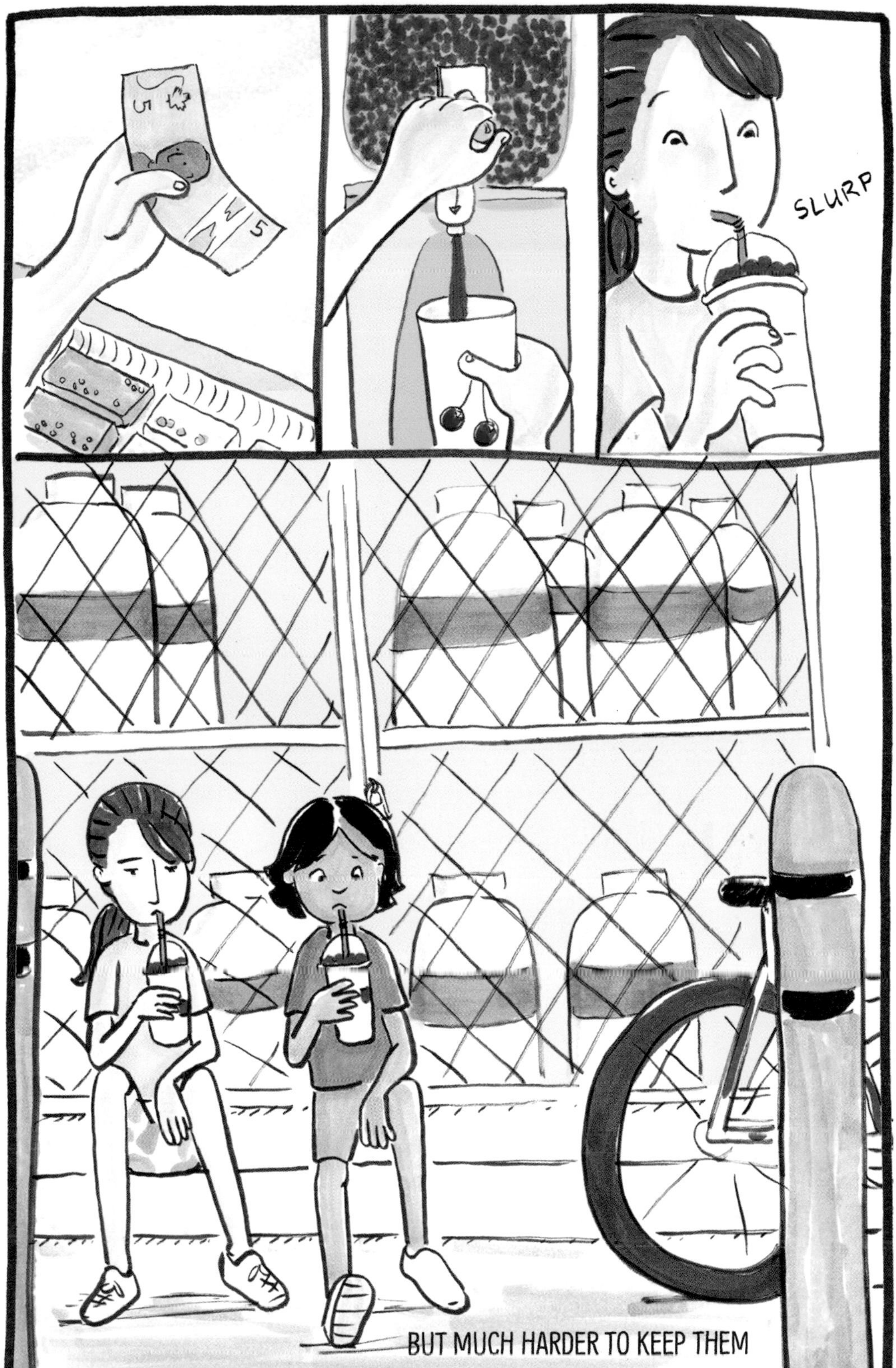
SLURP
BUT MUCH HARDER TO KEEP THEM

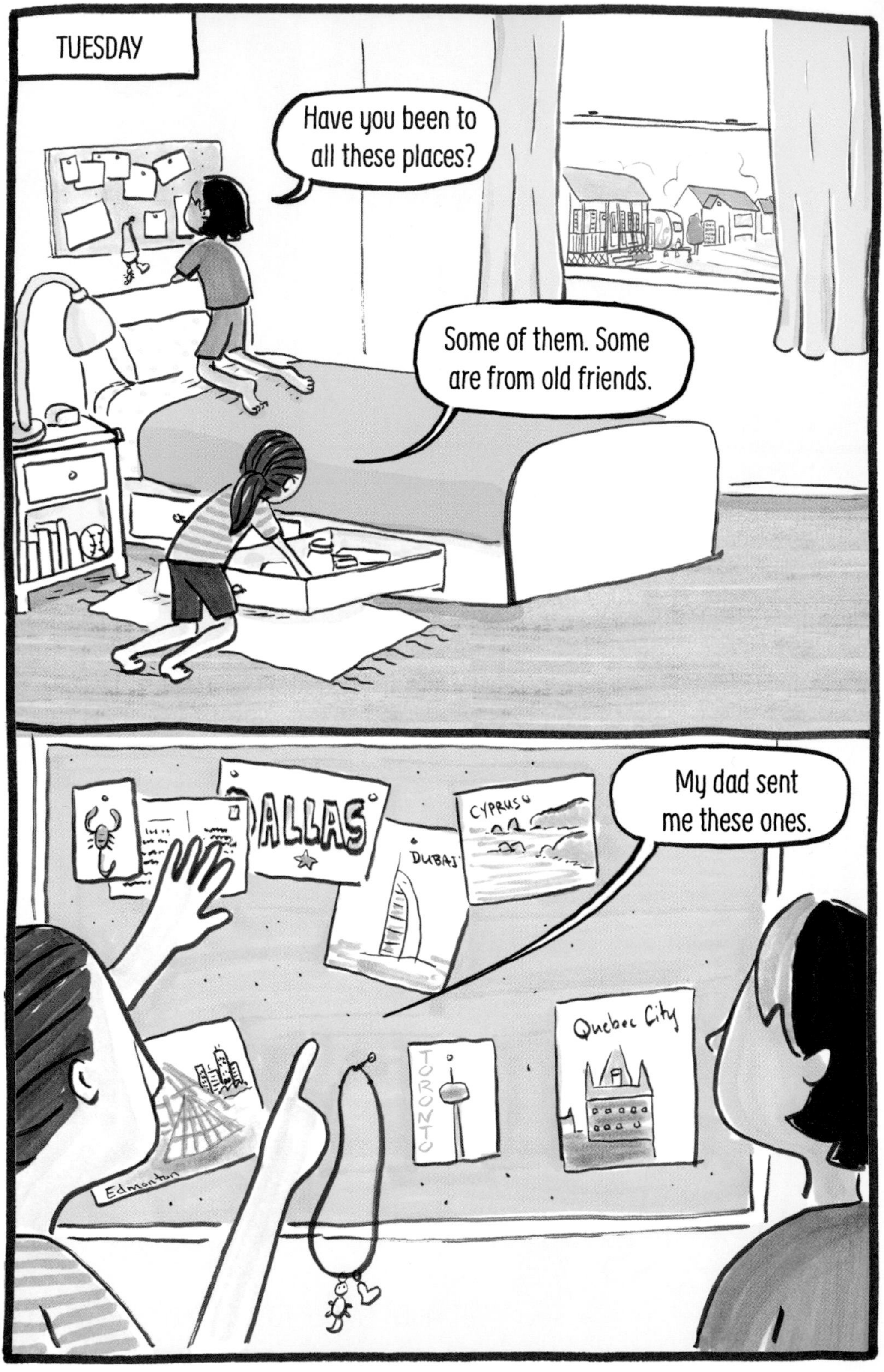
TUESDAY
Have you been to all these places?
Some of them. Some are from old friends.
DALLAS
CYPRUS
DUBAI
My dad sent me these ones.
Quebec City
TORONTO
Edmonton

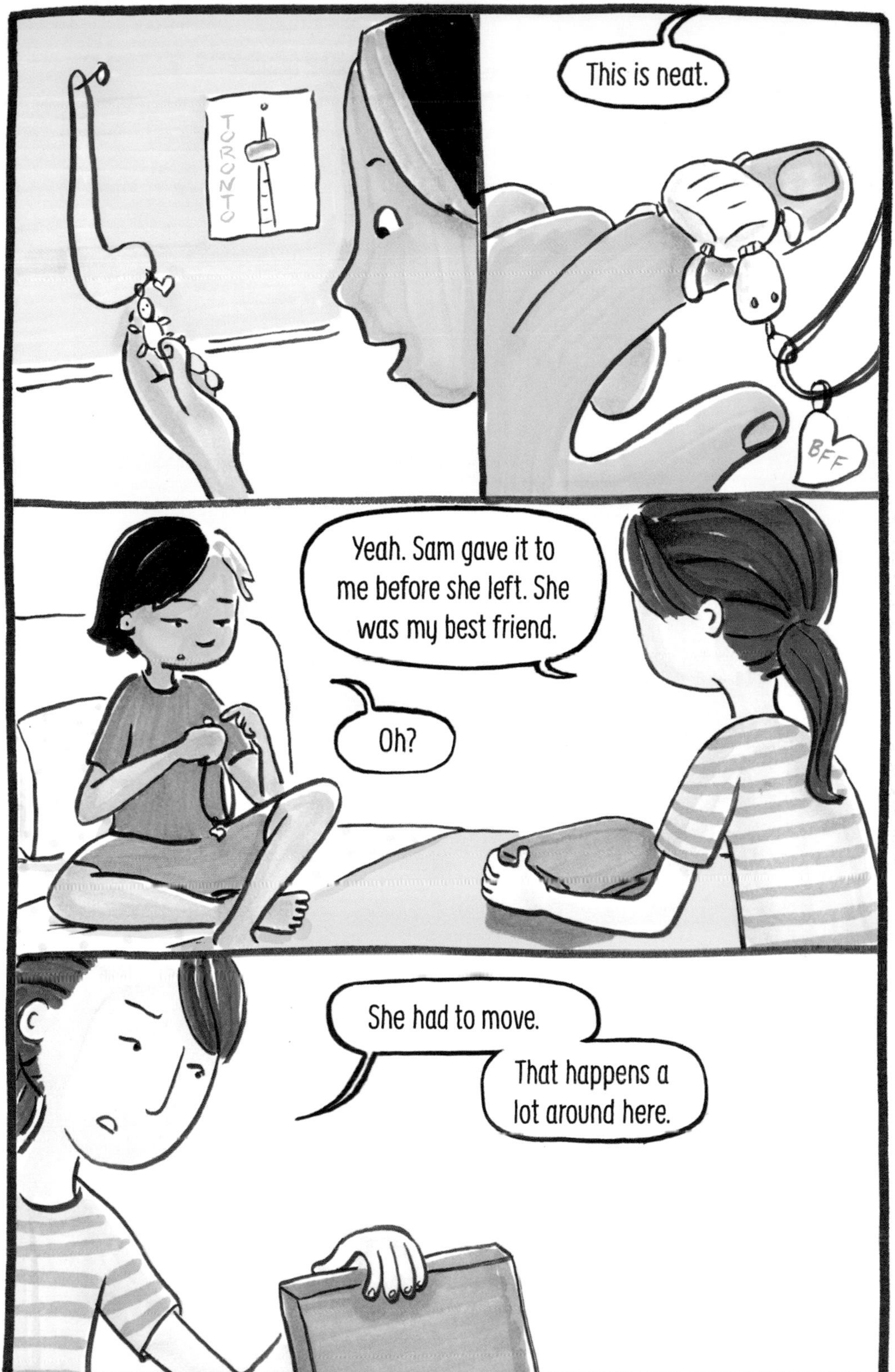
TORONTO
This is neat.
BFF
Yeah. Sam gave it to me before she left. She was my best friend.
Oh?
She had to move.
That happens a lot around here.

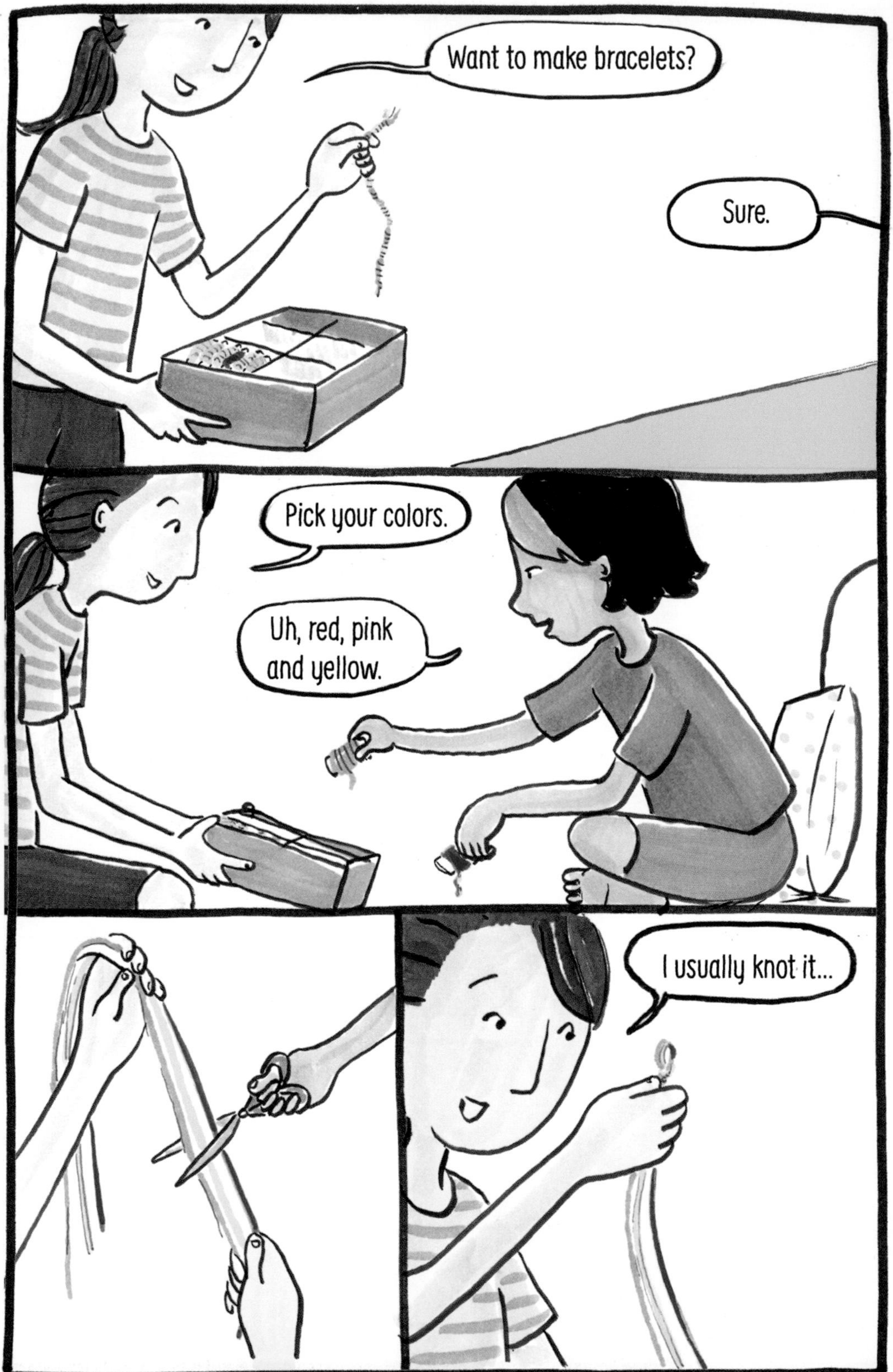
Want to make bracelets?
Sure.
Pick your colors.
Uh, red, pink and yellow.
I usually knot it...

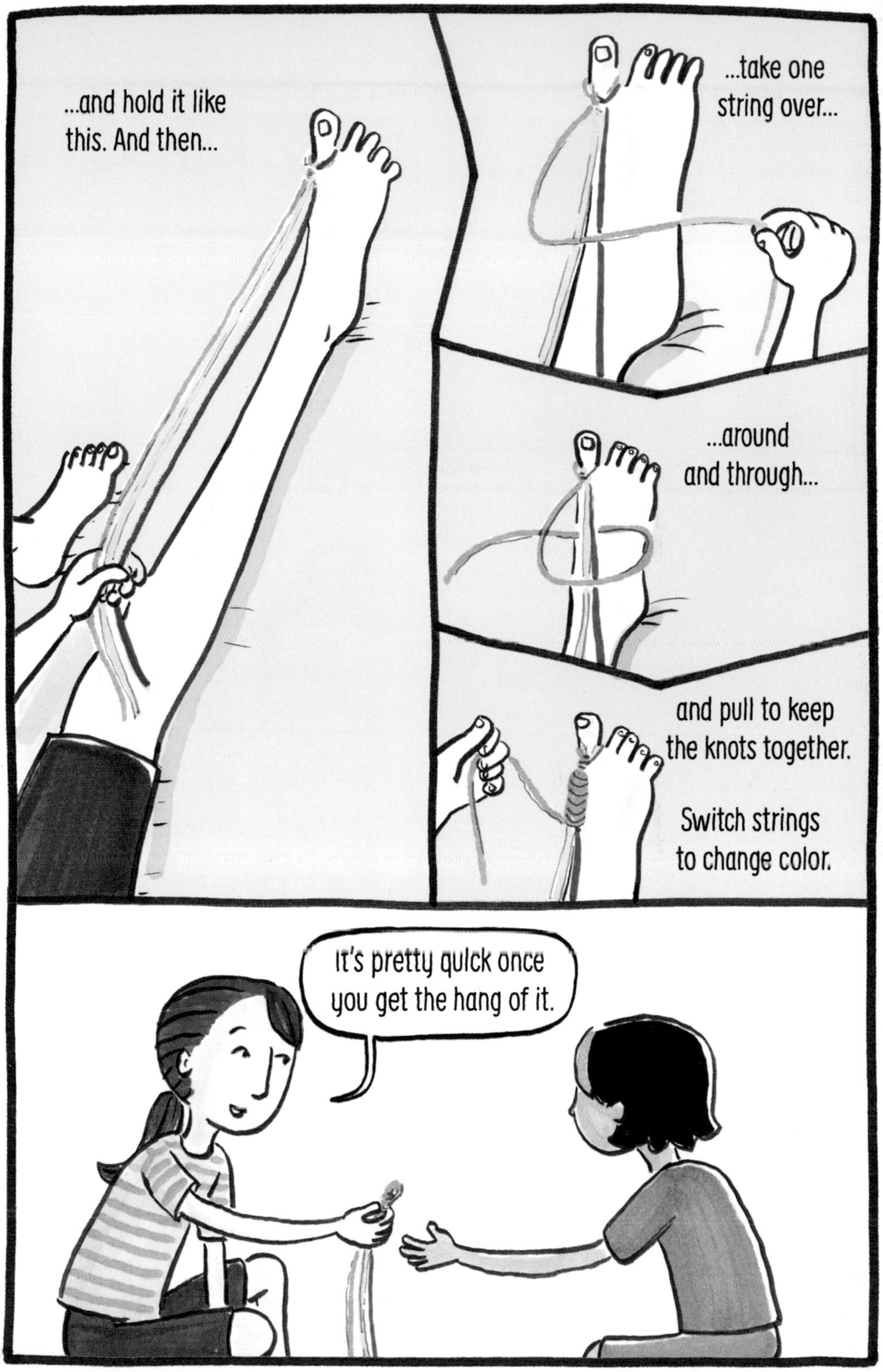
...and hold it like this. And then...
...take one string over...
...around and through...
and pull to keep the knots together.
Switch strings to change color.
It's pretty quick once you get the hang of it.

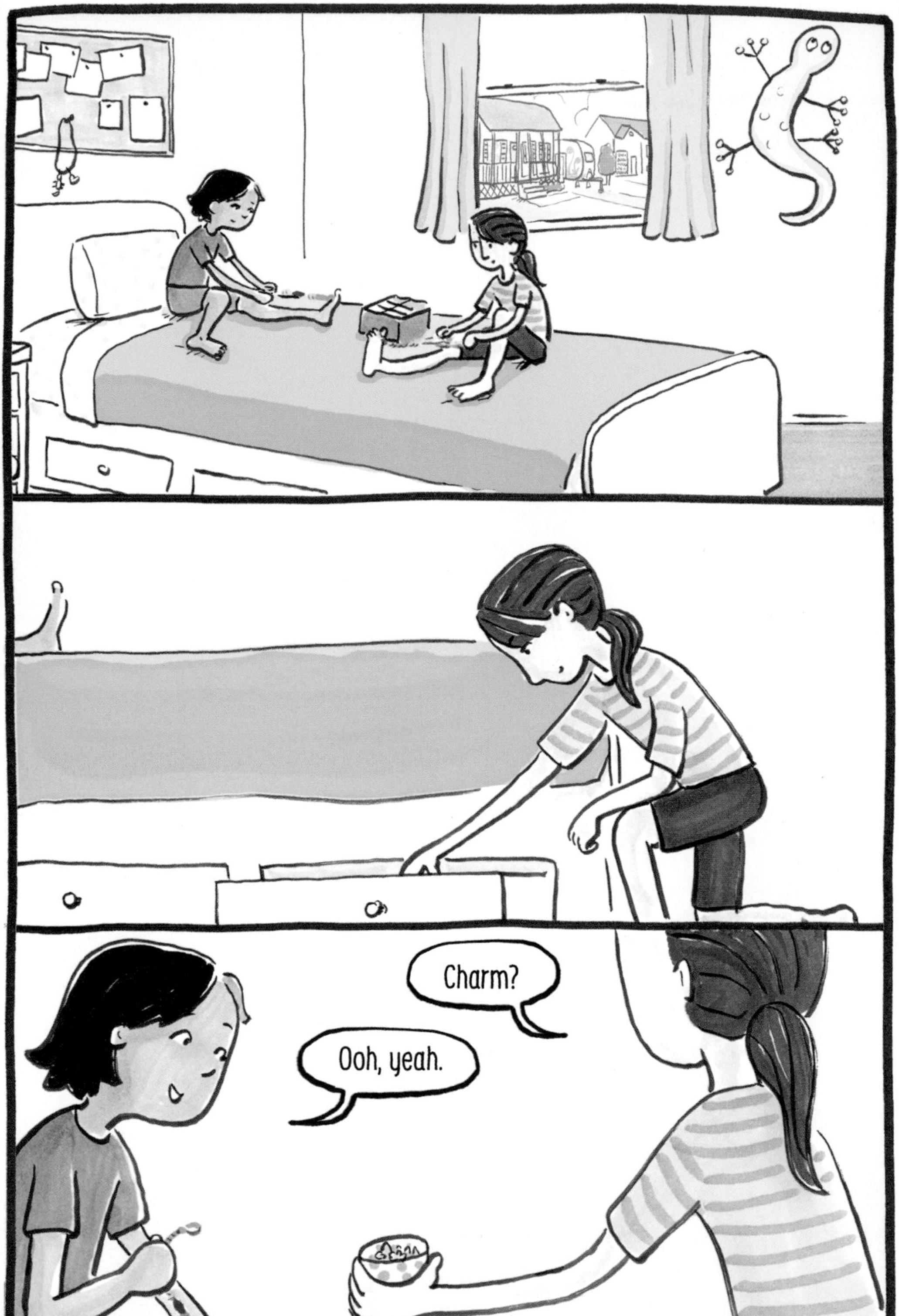
Charm?
Ooh, yeah.

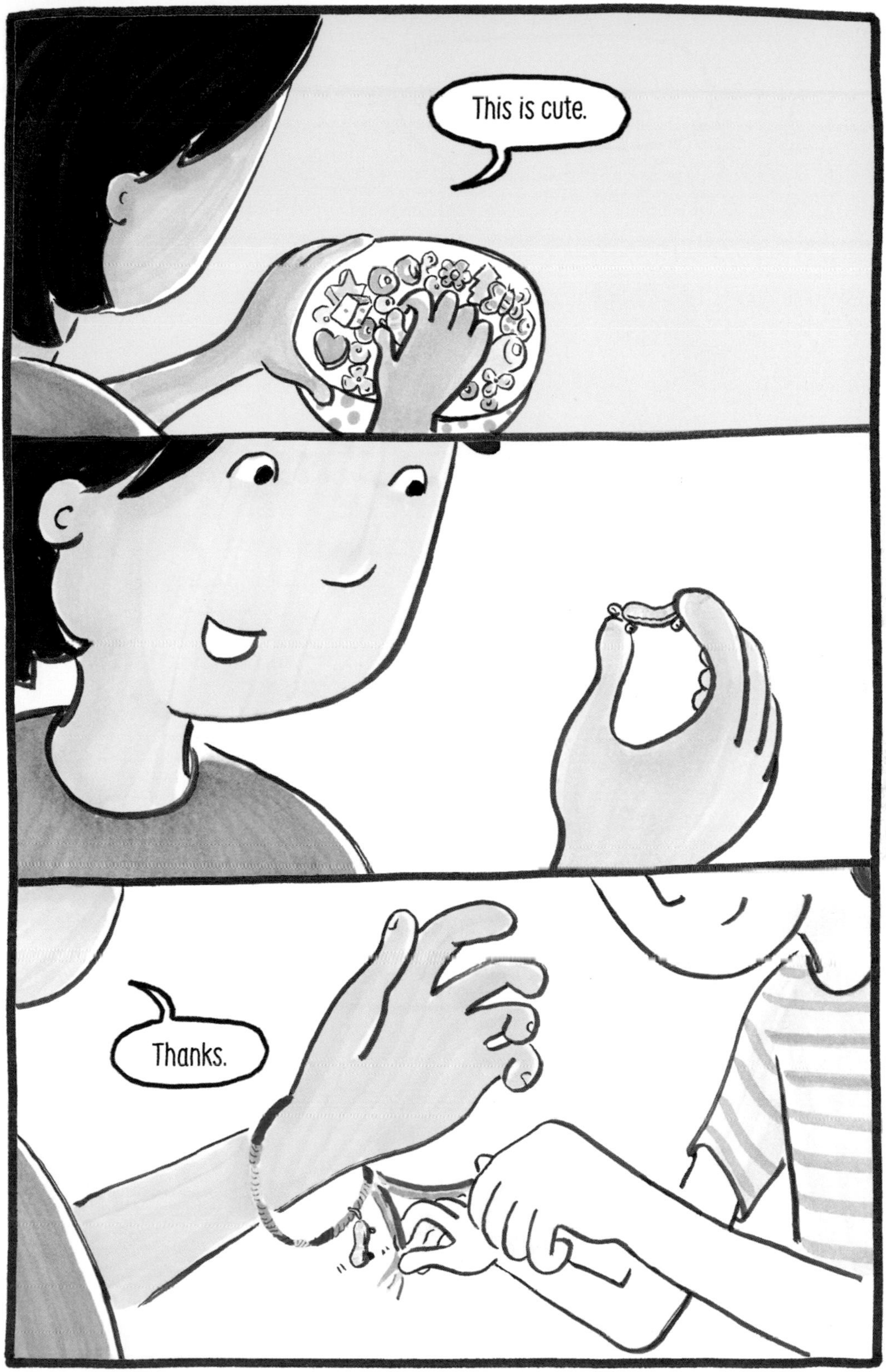
This is cute.
Thanks.

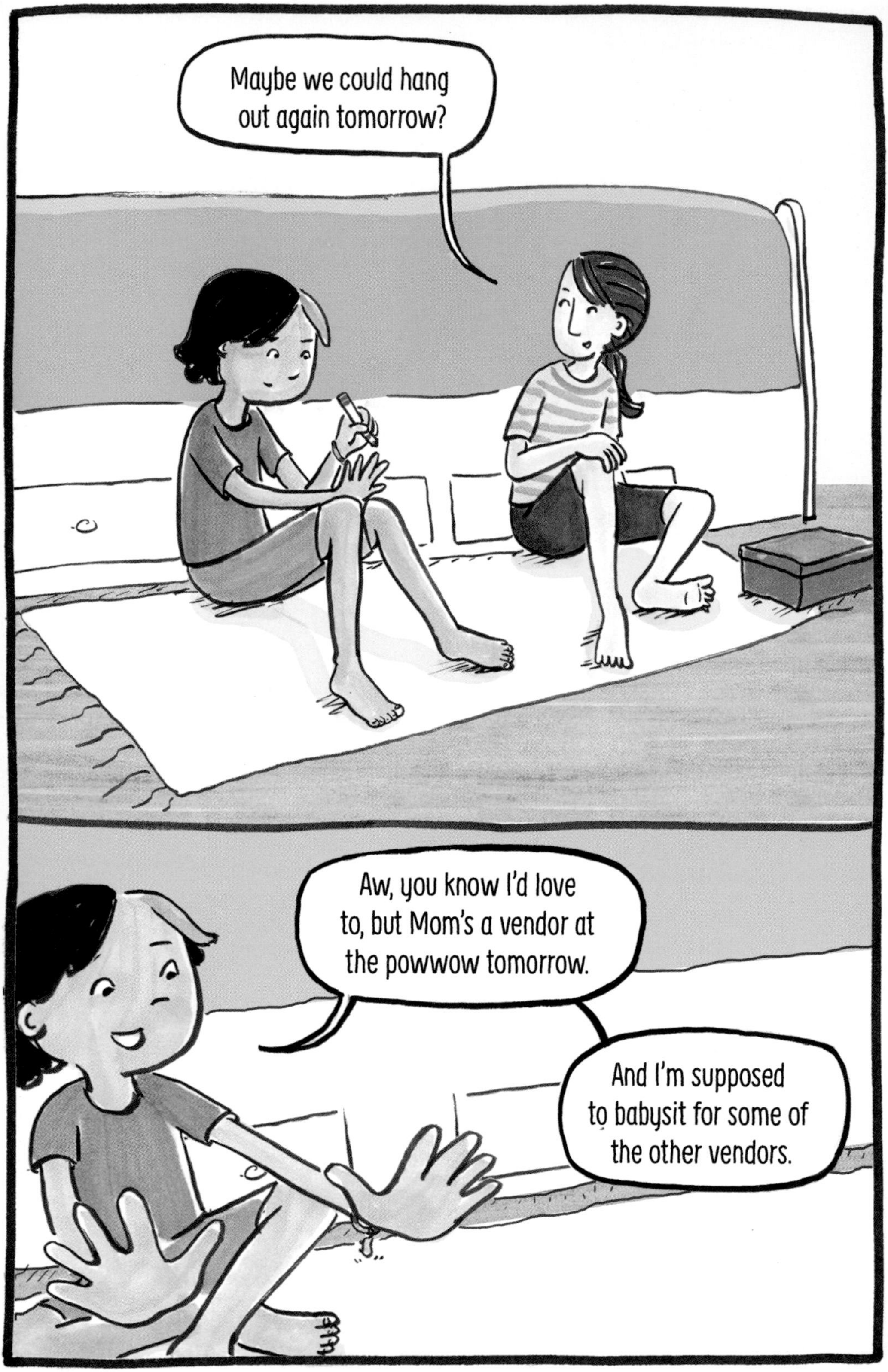
Maybe we could hang out again tomorrow?
Aw, you know I'd love to, but Mom's a vendor at the powwow tomorrow.
And I'm supposed to babysit for some of the other vendors.

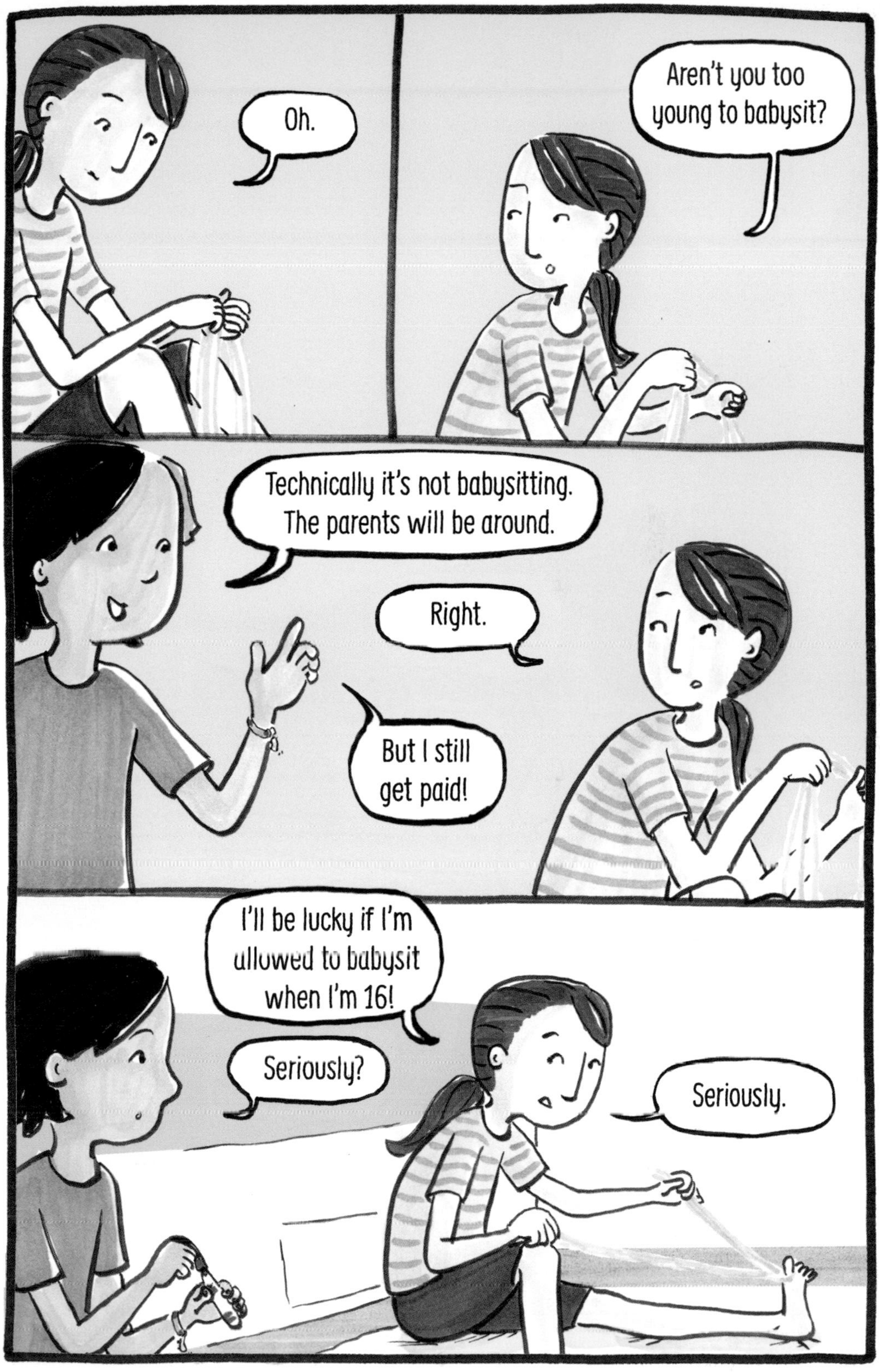
Oh.
Aren't you too young to babysit?
Technically it's not babysitting. The parents will be around.
Right.
But I still get paid!
I'll be lucky if I'm allowed to babysit when I'm 16!
Seriously?
Seriously.

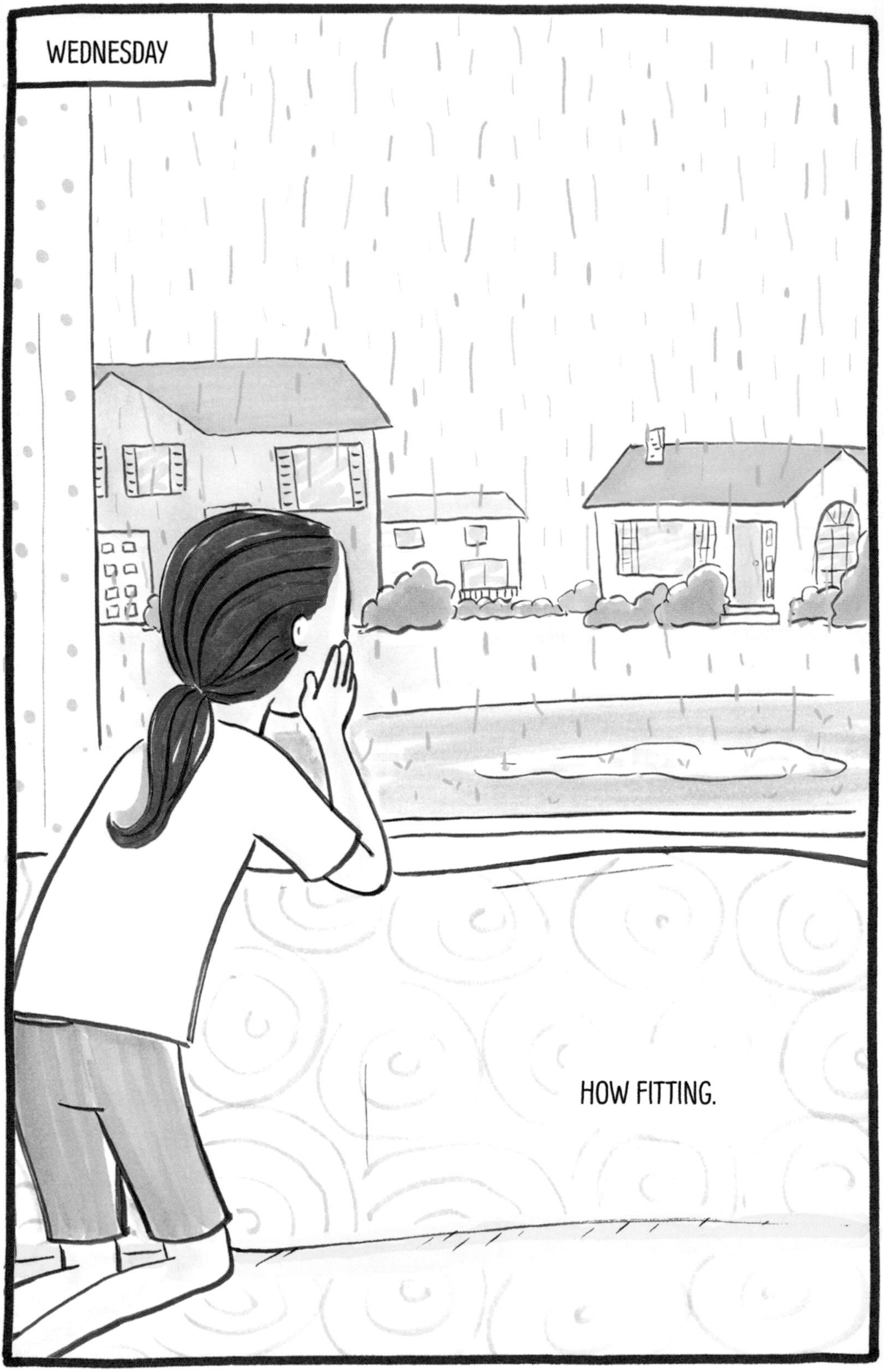
WEDNESDAY
HOW FITTING.

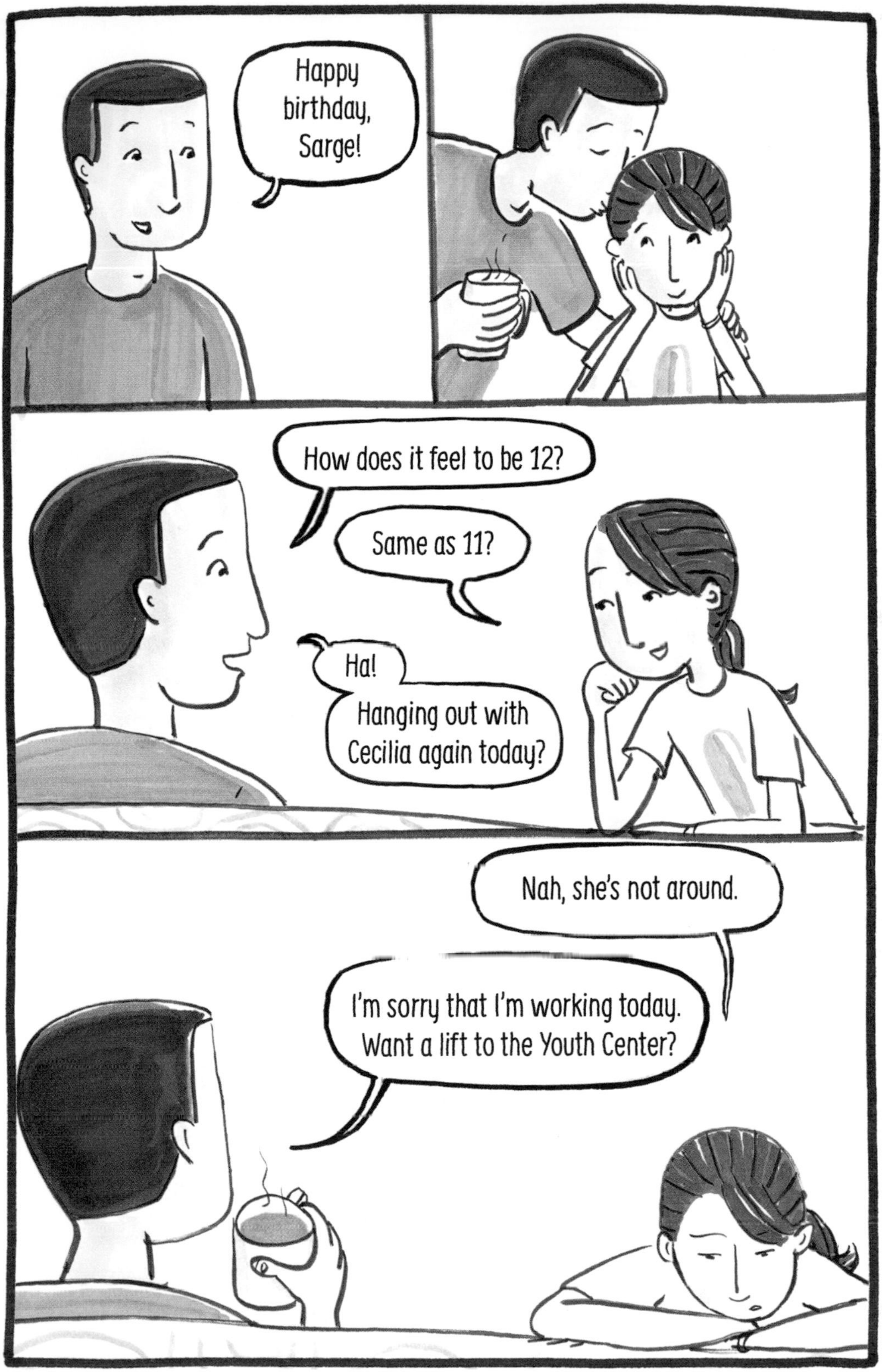
Happy birthday, Sarge!
How does it feel to be 12?
Same as 11?
Ha!
Hanging out with Cecilia again today?
Nah, she's not around.
I'm sorry that I'm working today. Want a lift to the Youth Center?

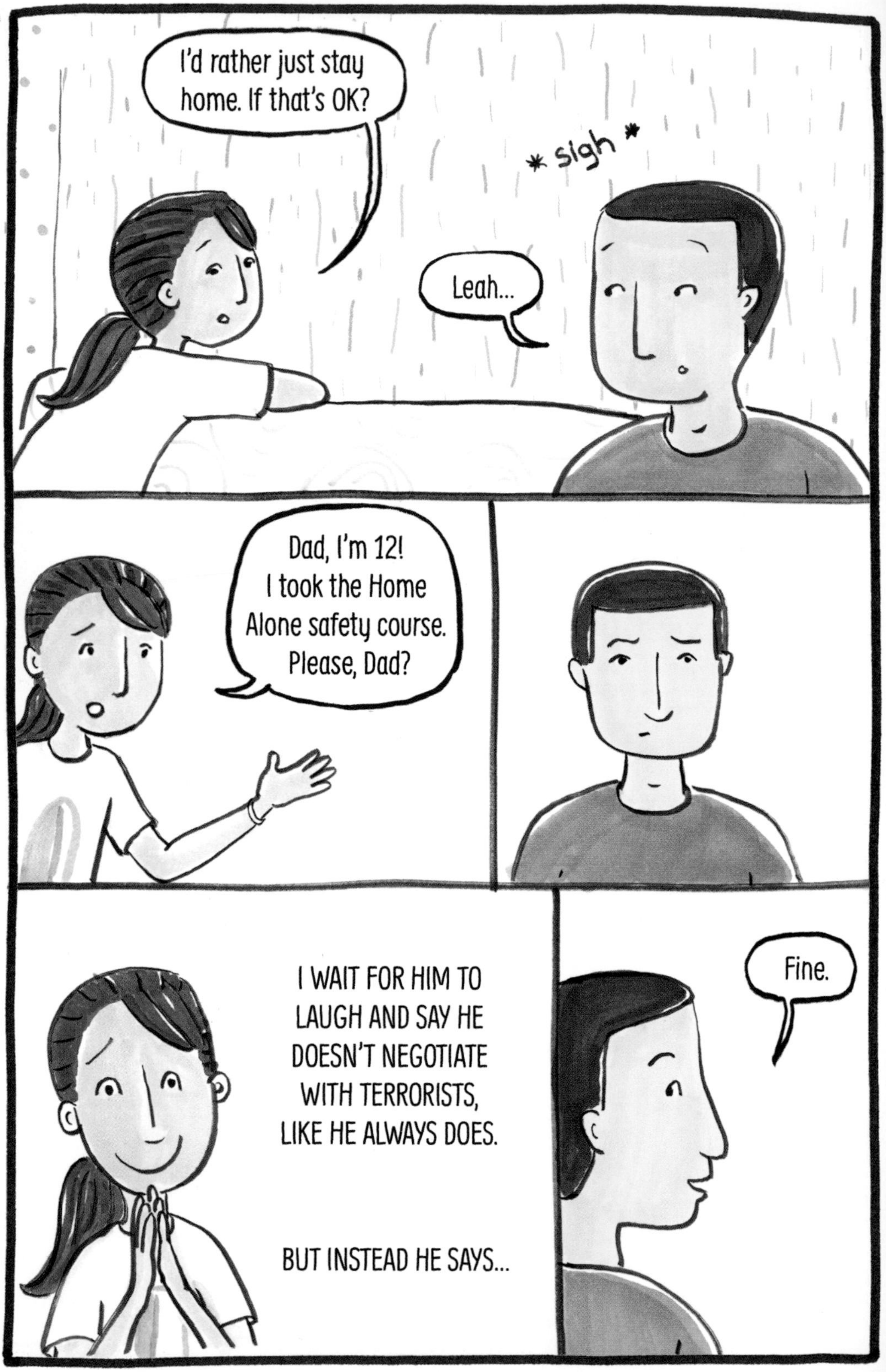
I'd rather just stay home. If that's OK?
sigh
Leah...
Dad, I'm 12! I took the Home Alone safety course. Please, Dad?
I WAIT FOR HIM TO LAUGH AND SAY HE DOESN'T NEGOTIATE WITH TERRORISTS, LIKE HE ALWAYS DOES.
BUT INSTEAD HE SAYS...
Fine.

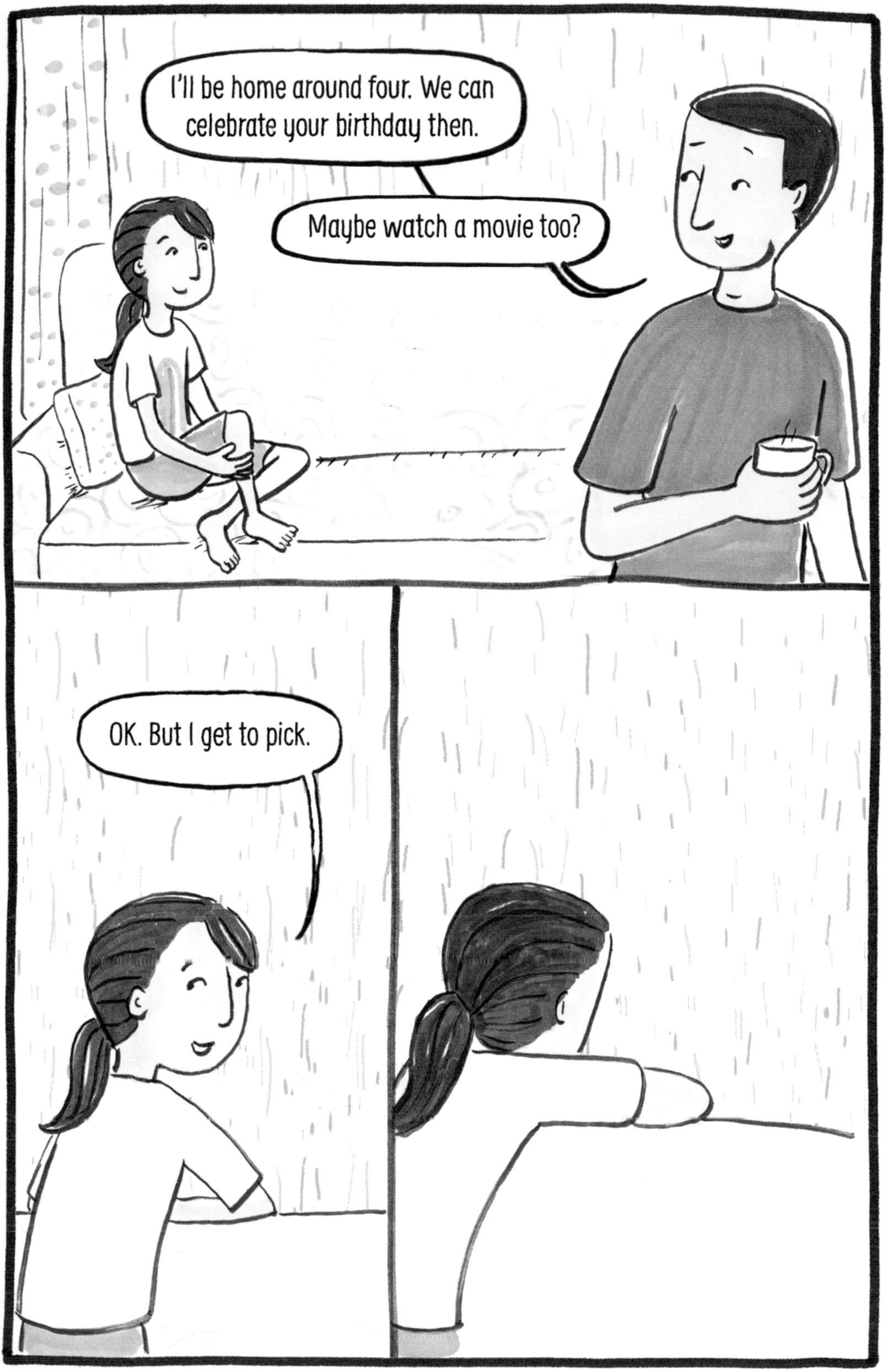
I'll be home around four. We can celebrate your birthday then.
Maybe watch a movie too?
OK. But I get to pick.

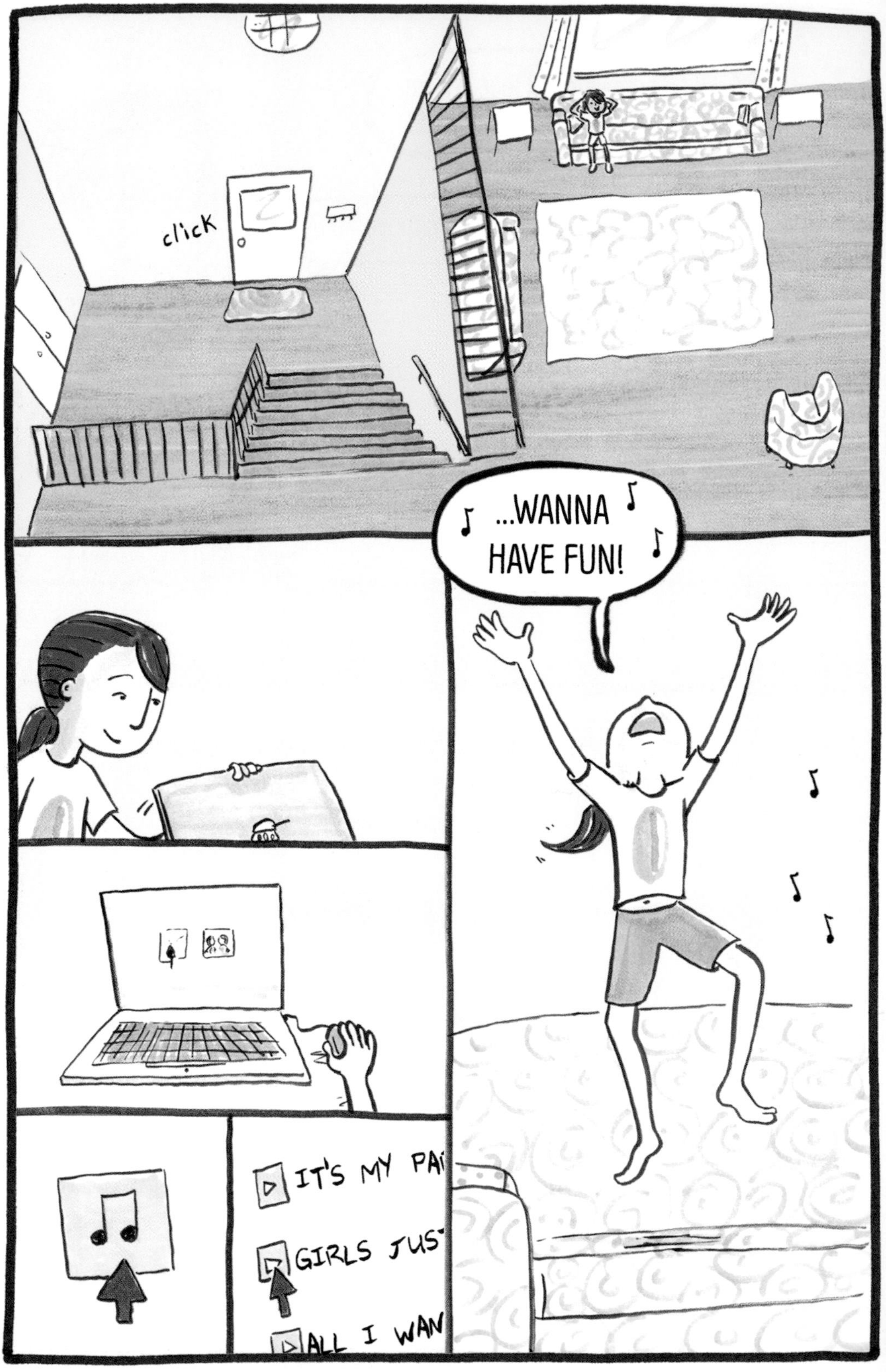
click
...WANNA HAVE FUN!
IT'S MY PA
GIRLS JUS
ALL I WAN

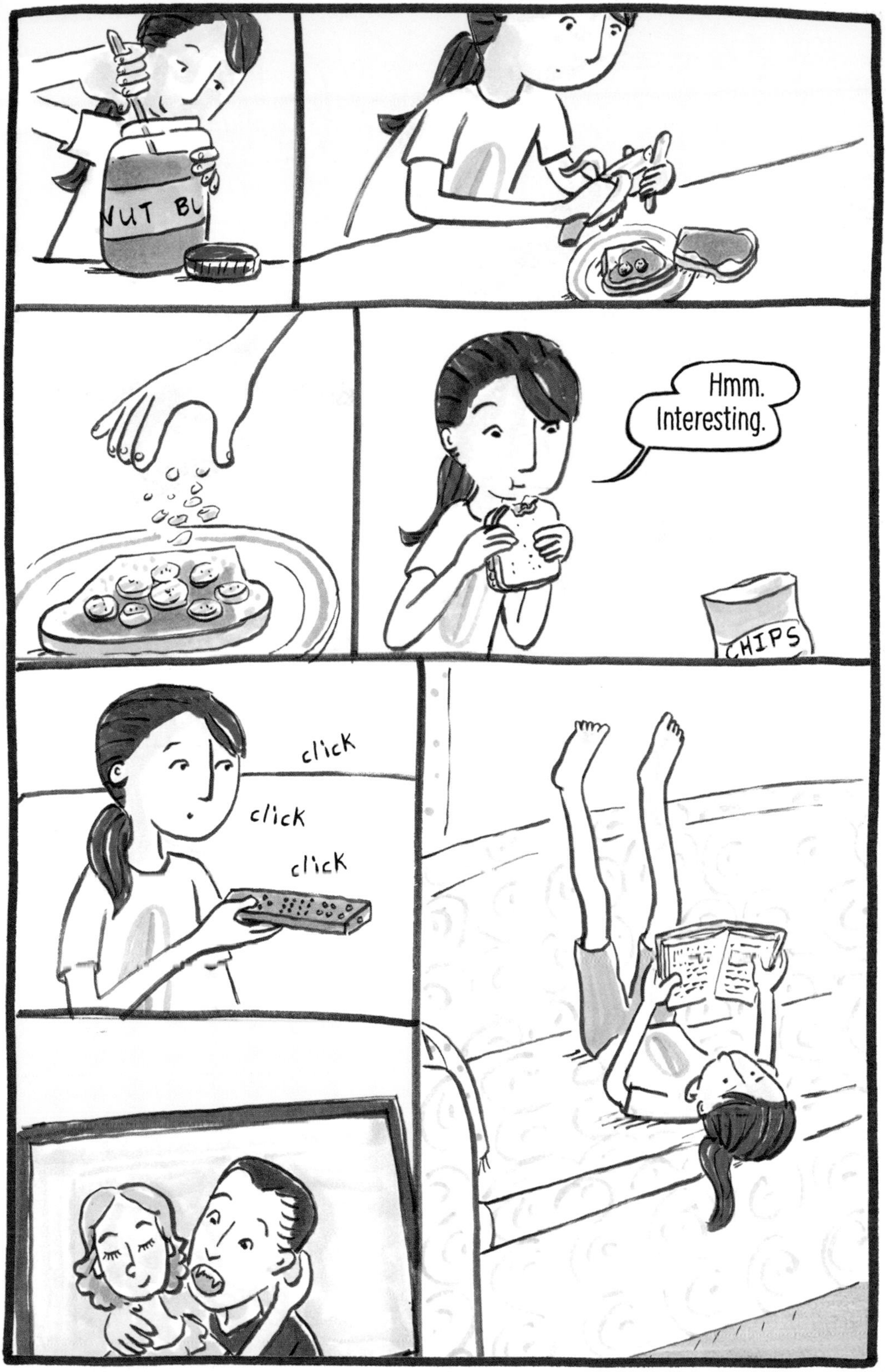
NUT BU
Hmm.
Interesting.
CHIPS
click
click
click

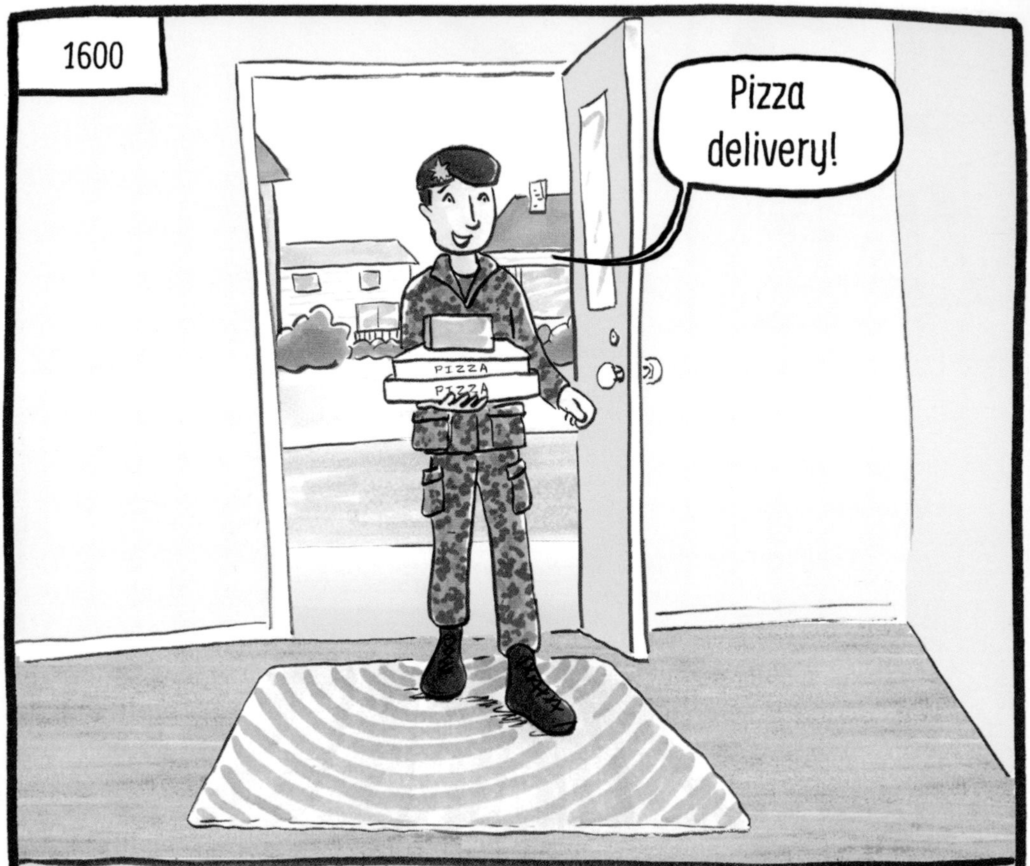
1600
Pizza delivery!
PIZZA
PIZZA

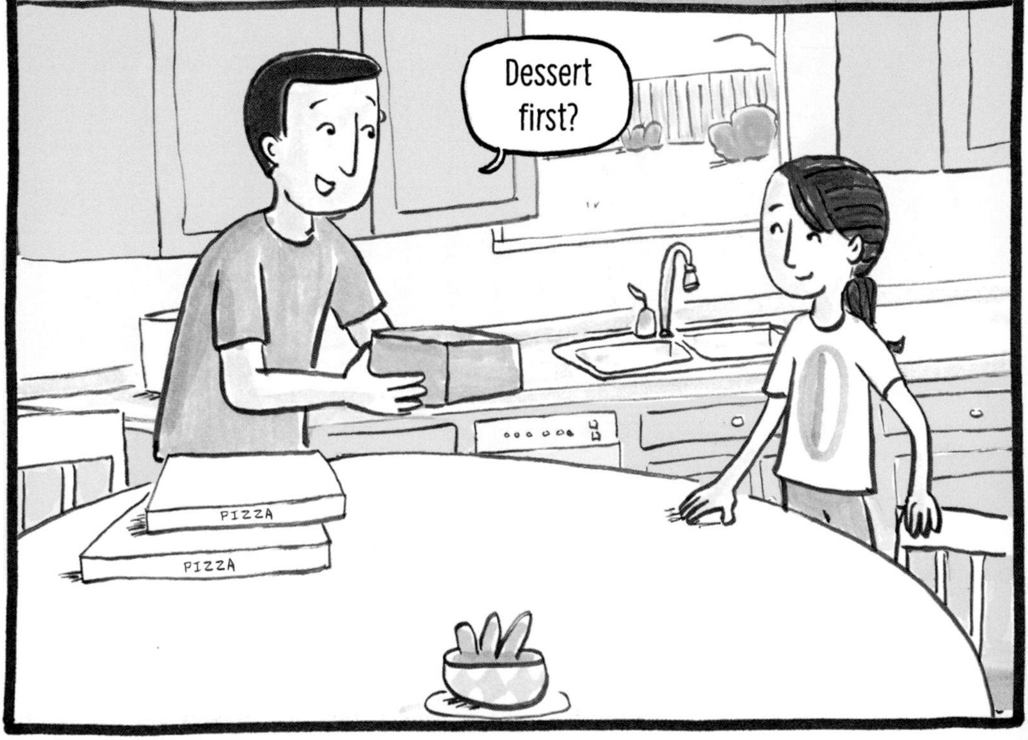
Dessert first?
PIZZA
PIZZA

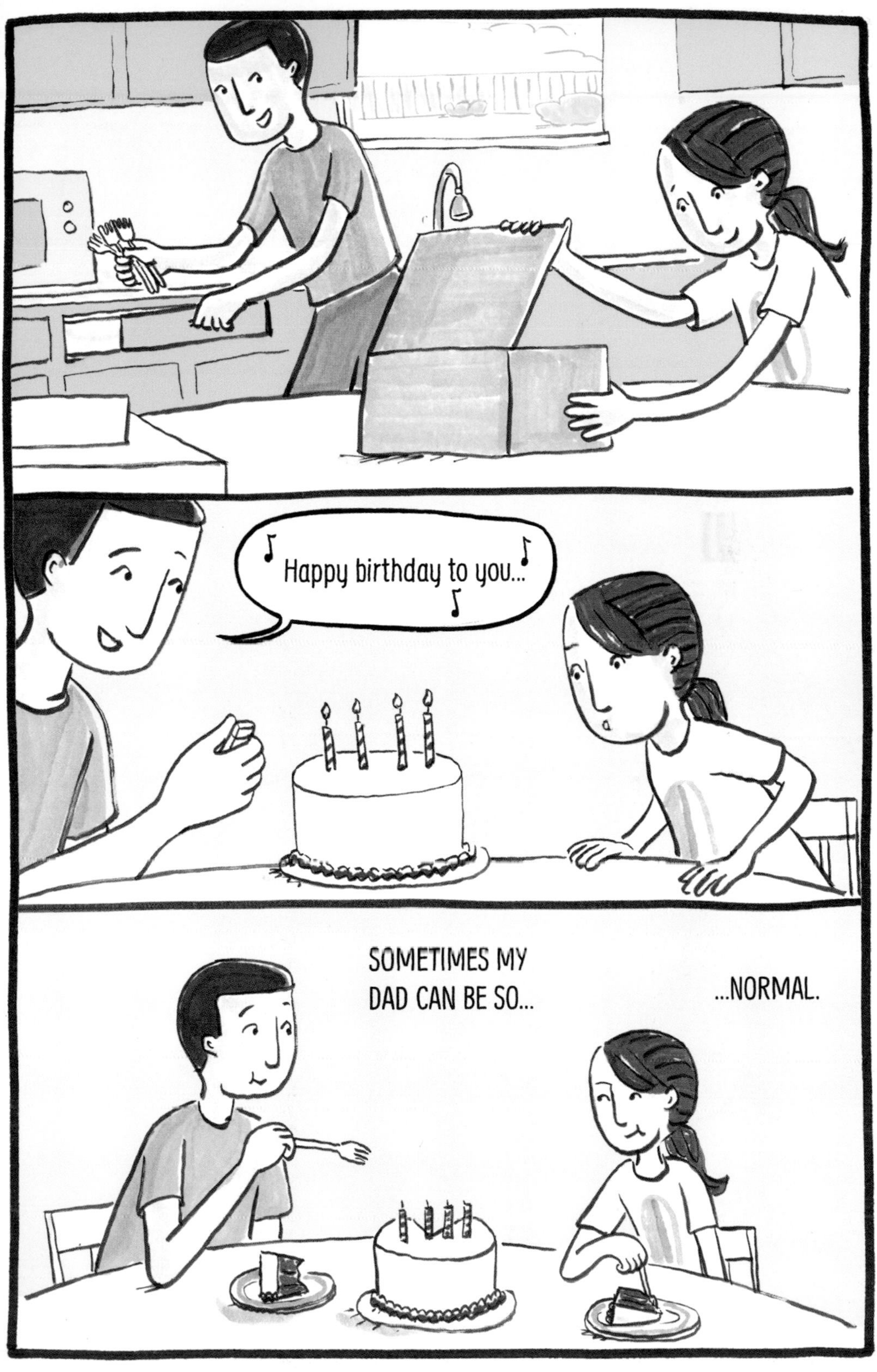
Happy birthday to you...
SOMETIMES MY DAD CAN BE SO...
...NORMAL.

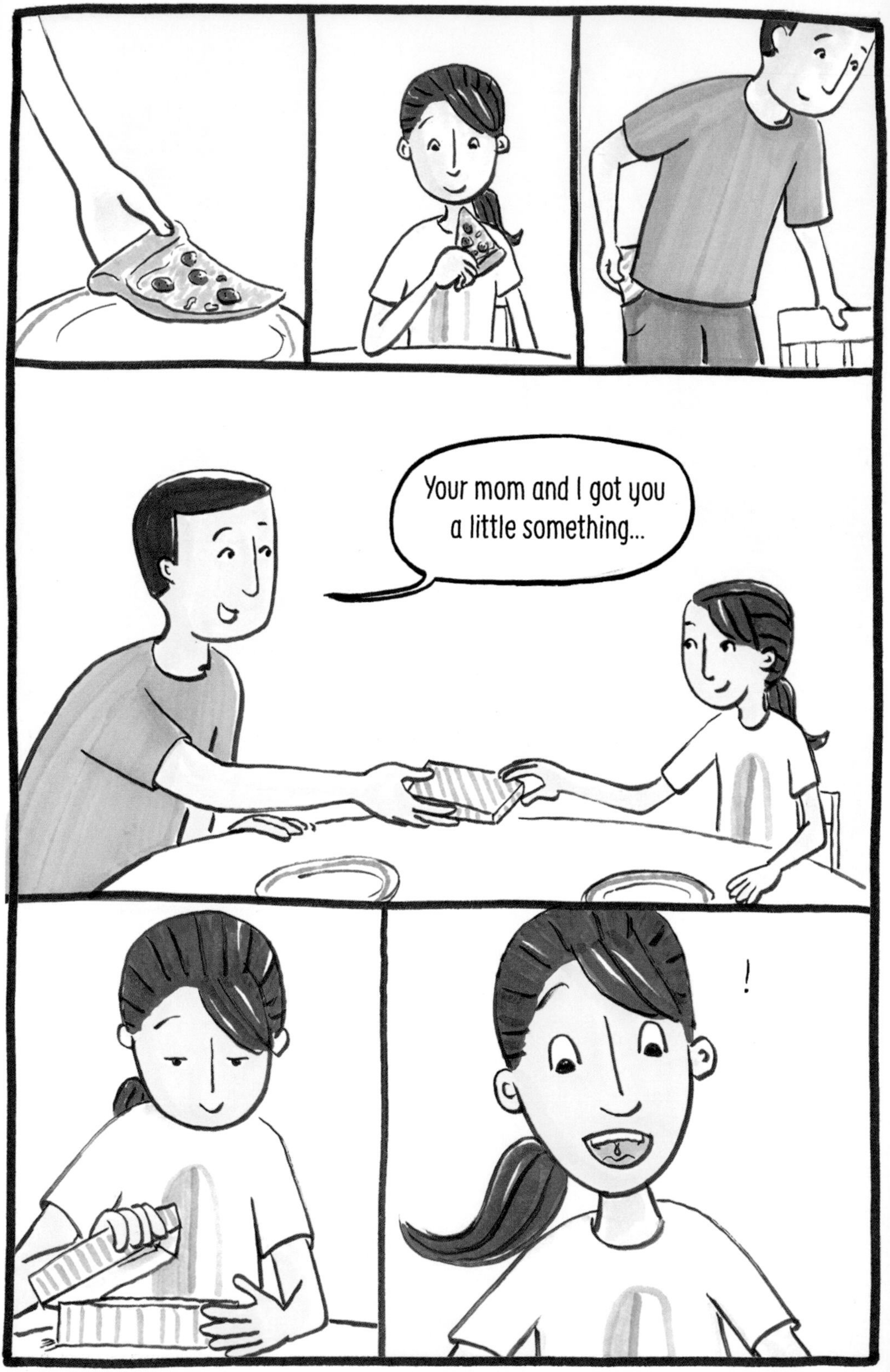
Your mom and I got you a little something...
!

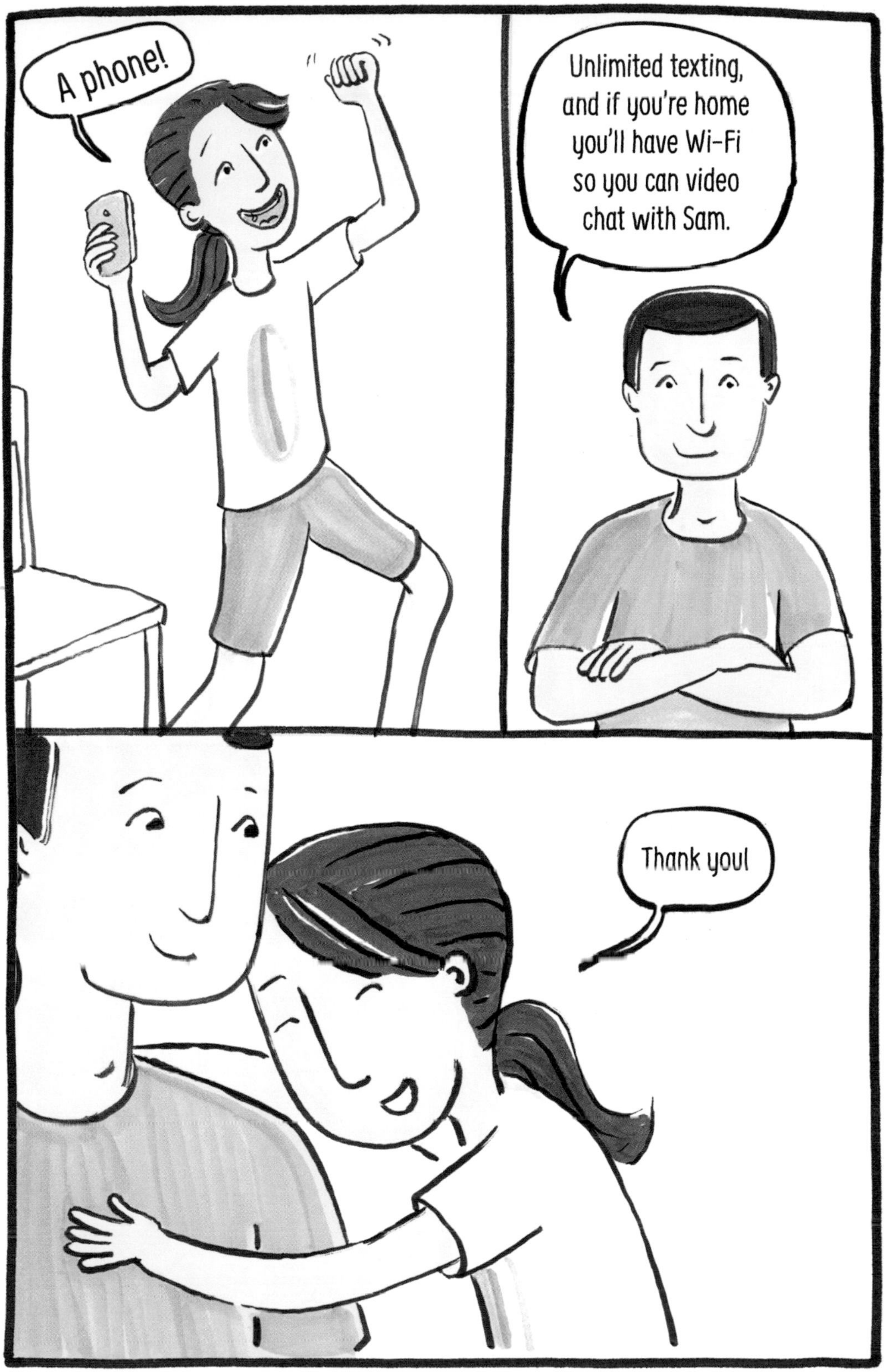
A phone!
Unlimited texting, and if you're home you'll have Wi-Fi so you can video chat with Sam.
Thank you!

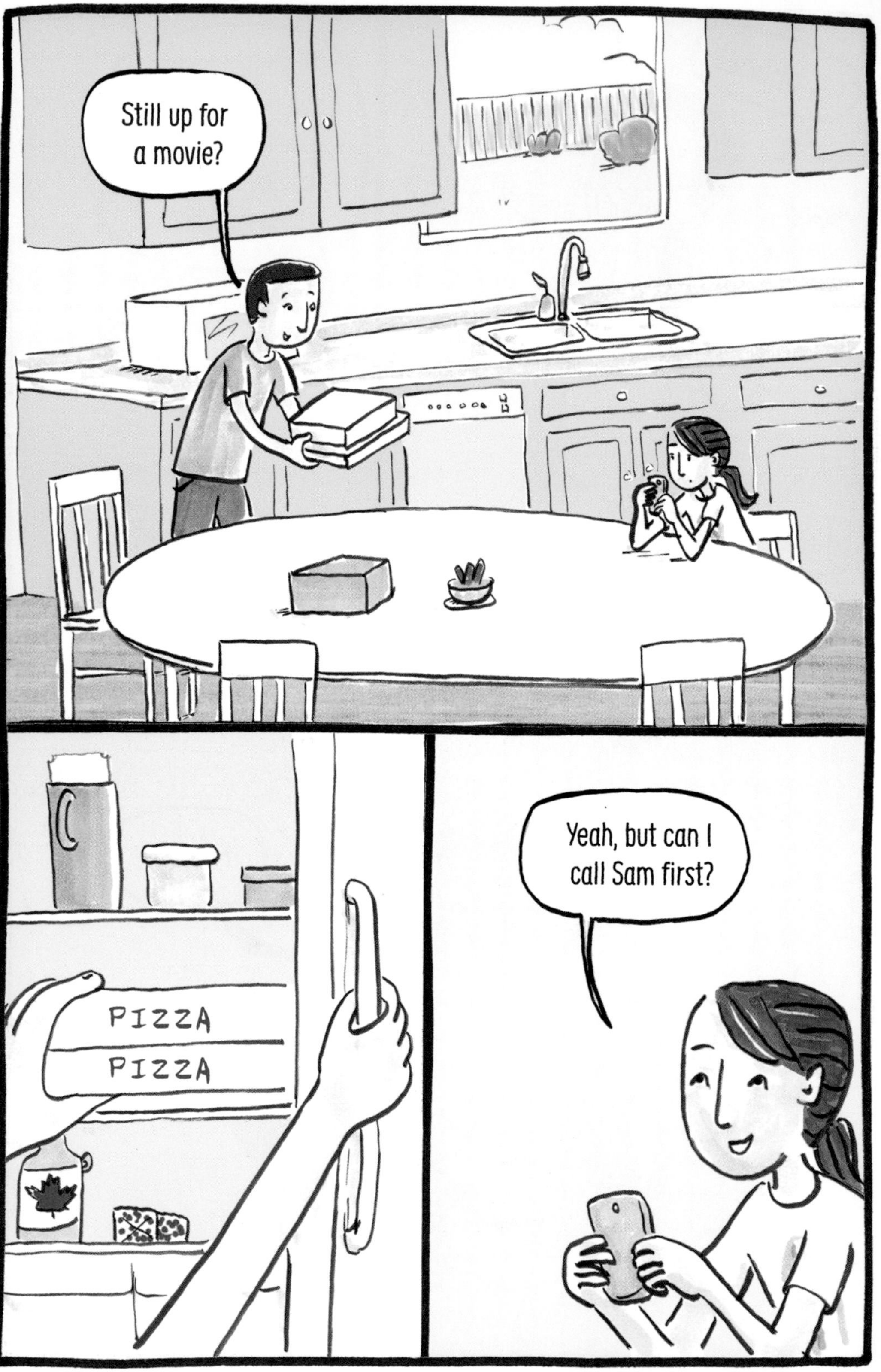
Still up for a movie?
PIZZA
PIZZA
Yeah, but can I call Sam first?

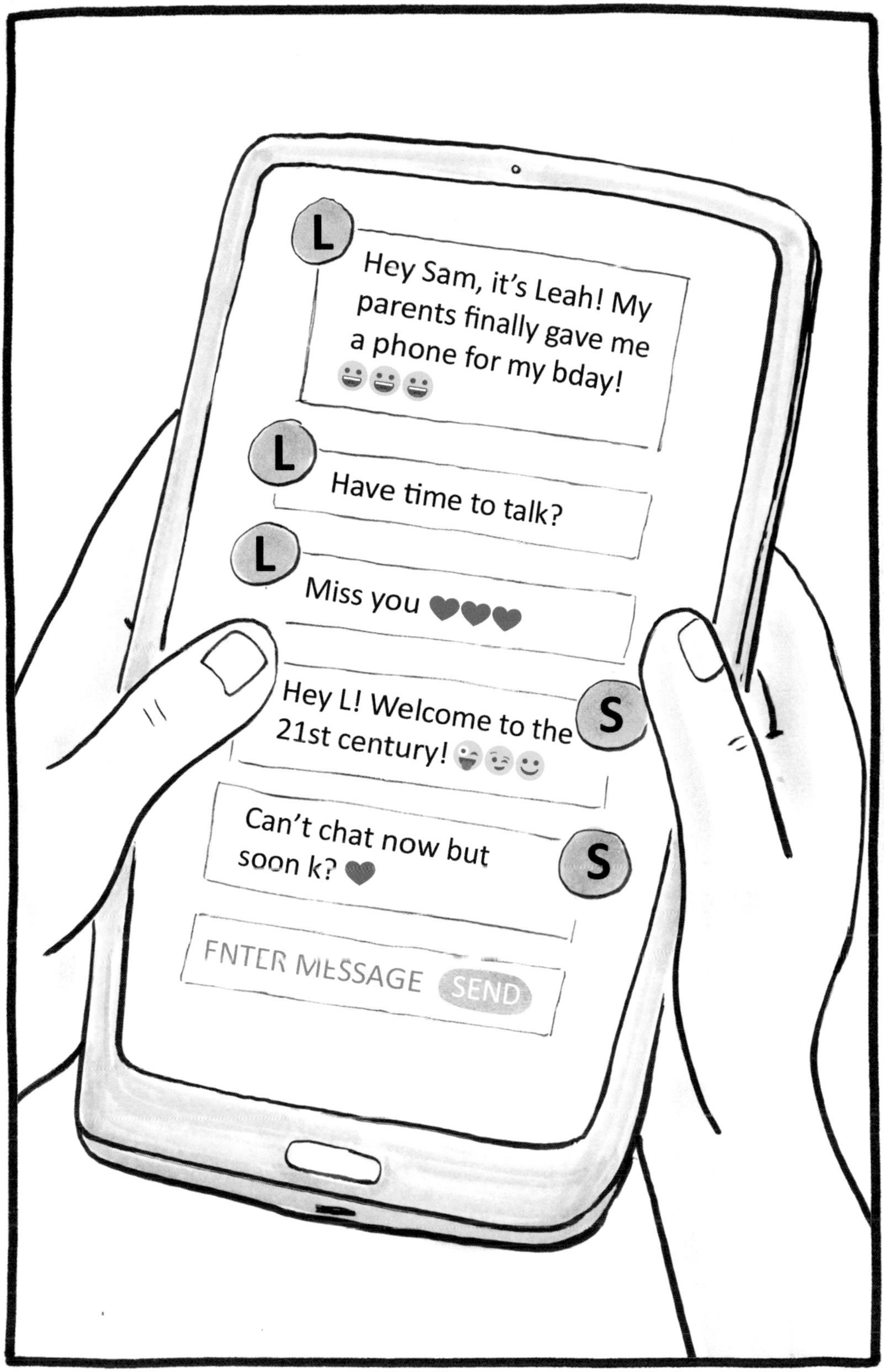
L
Hey Sam, it's Leah! My parents finally gave me a phone for my bday!
L
Have time to talk?
L
Miss you
S
Hey L! Welcome to the 21st century!
S
Can't chat now but soon k?
ENTER MESSAGE
SEND

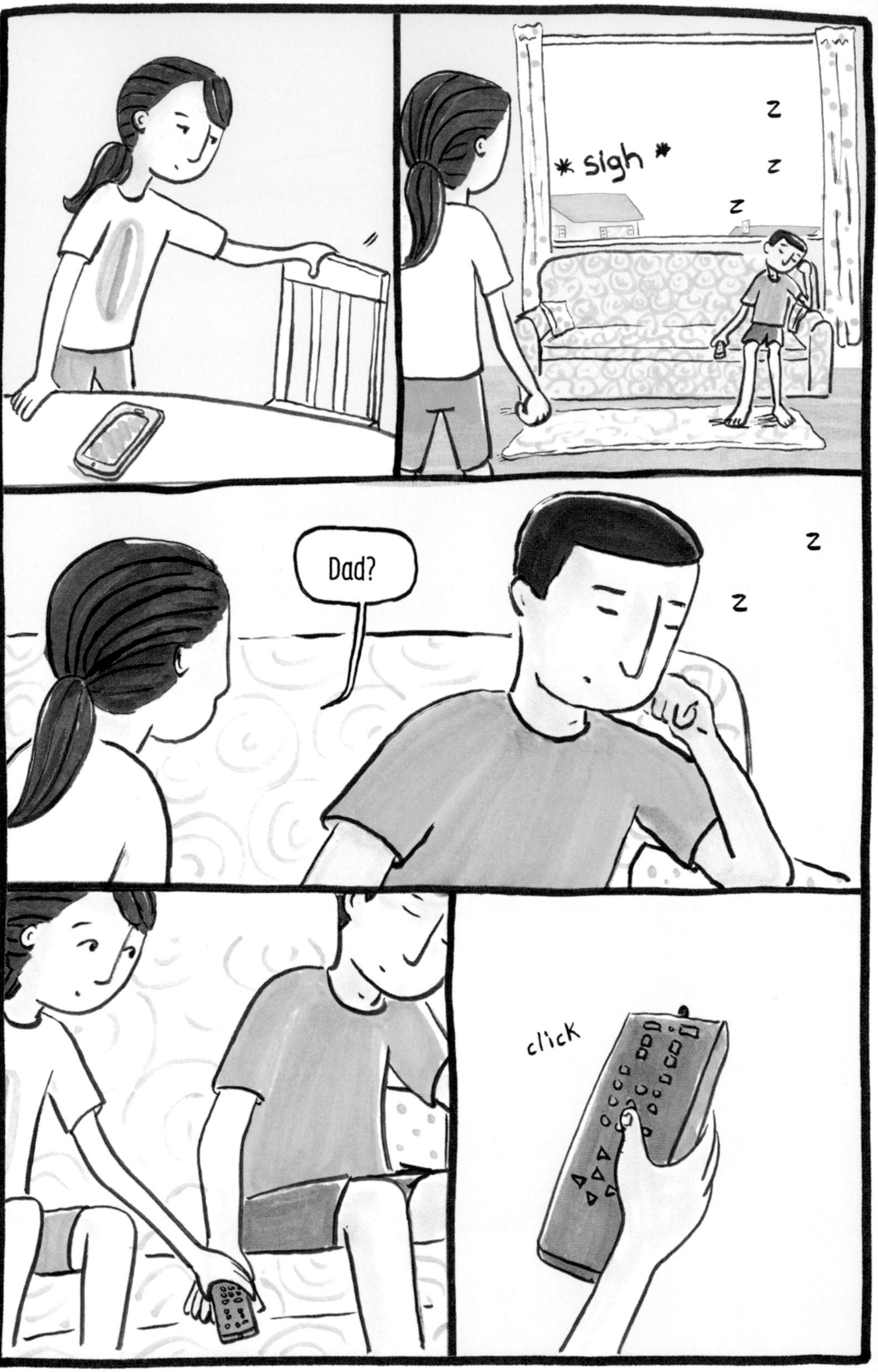
sigh
Z
Z
Z
Dad?
Z
Z
click

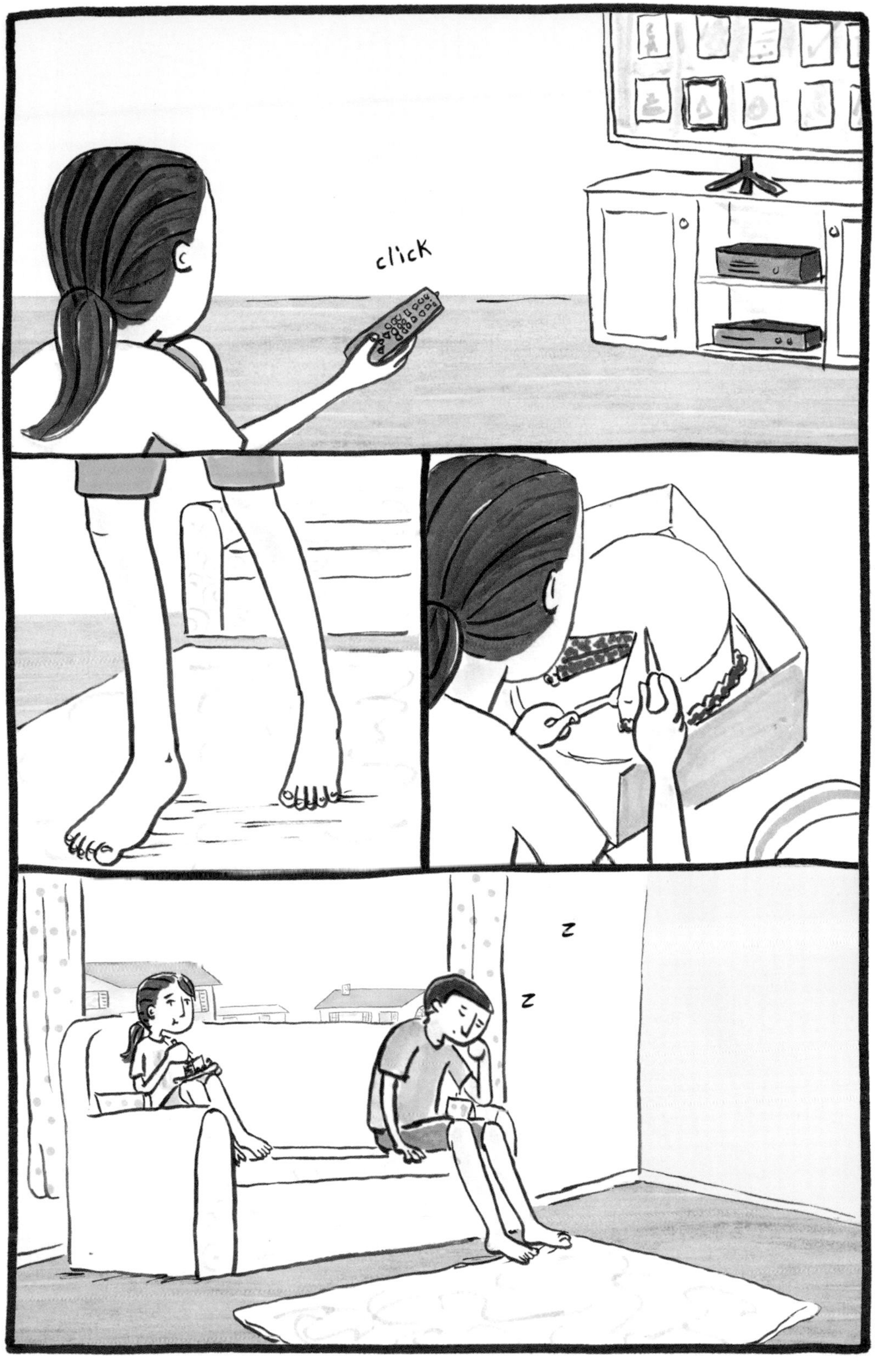
click
z
z

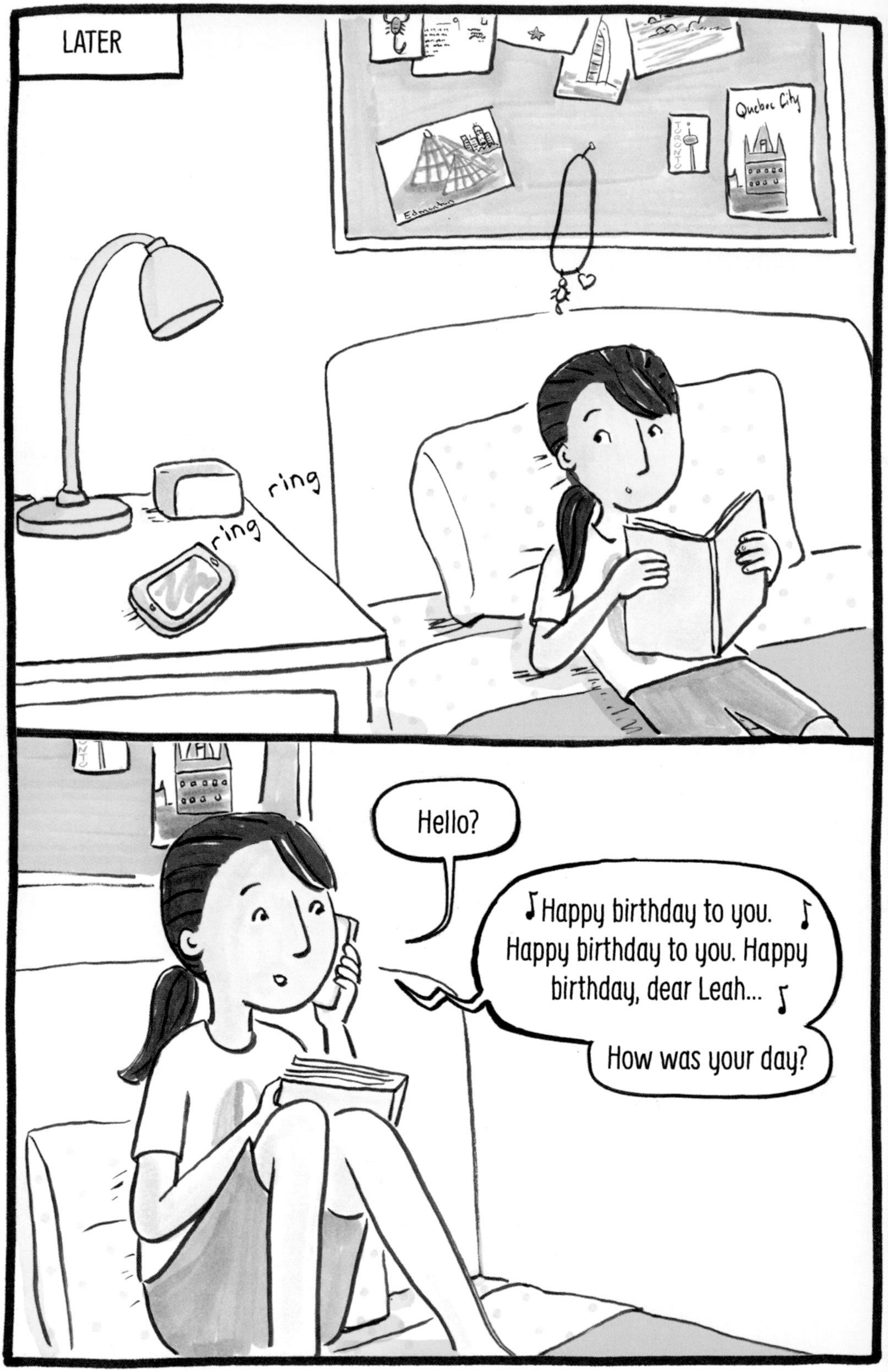
LATER
Edmonton
TORONTO
Quebec City
ring
ring
Hello?
♪ Happy birthday to you. ♪ Happy birthday to you. Happy birthday, dear Leah... ♪
How was your day?

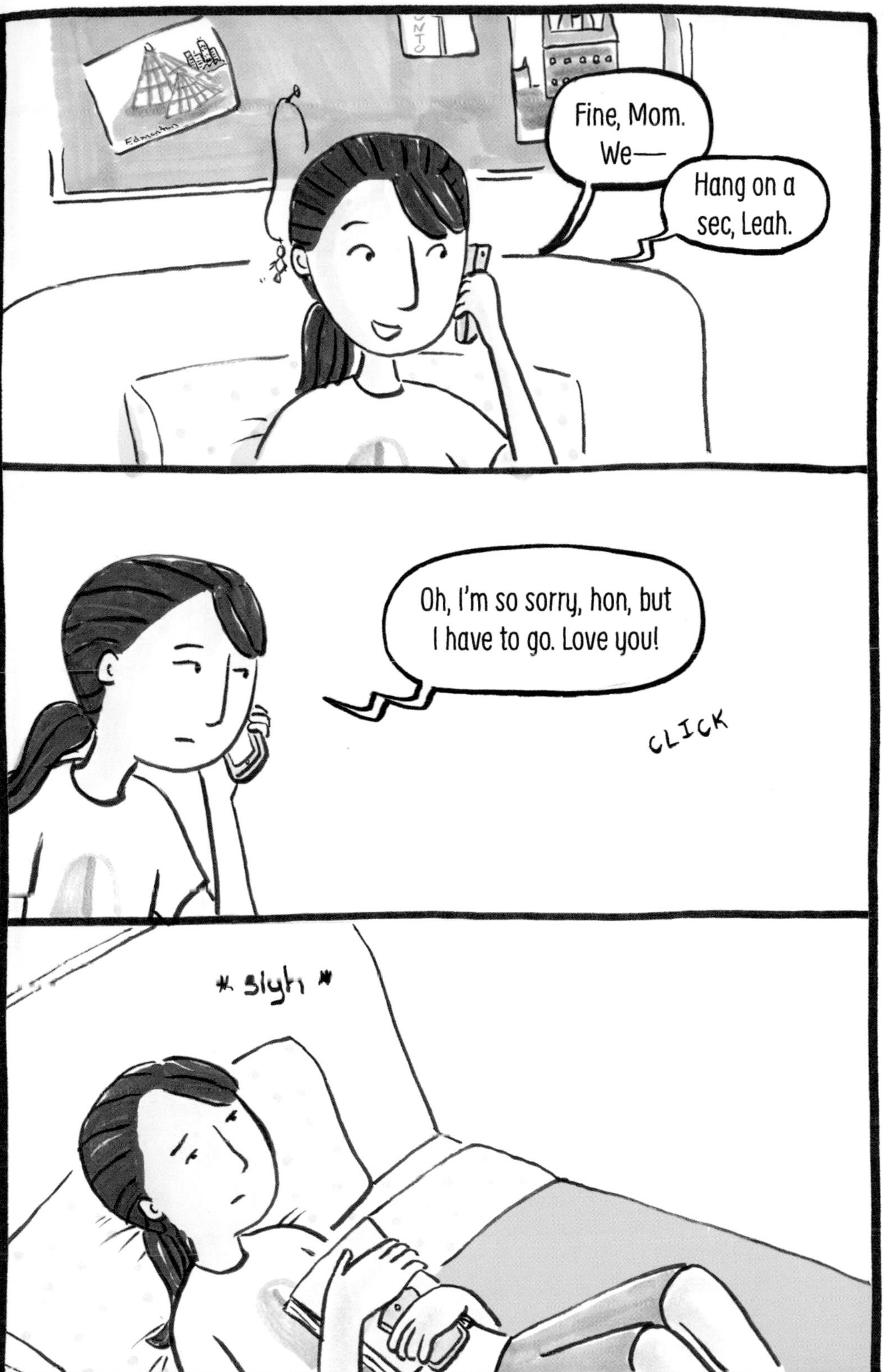
Fine, Mom. We—
Hang on a sec, Leah.
Oh, I'm so sorry, hon, but I have to go. Love you!
CLICK
sigh

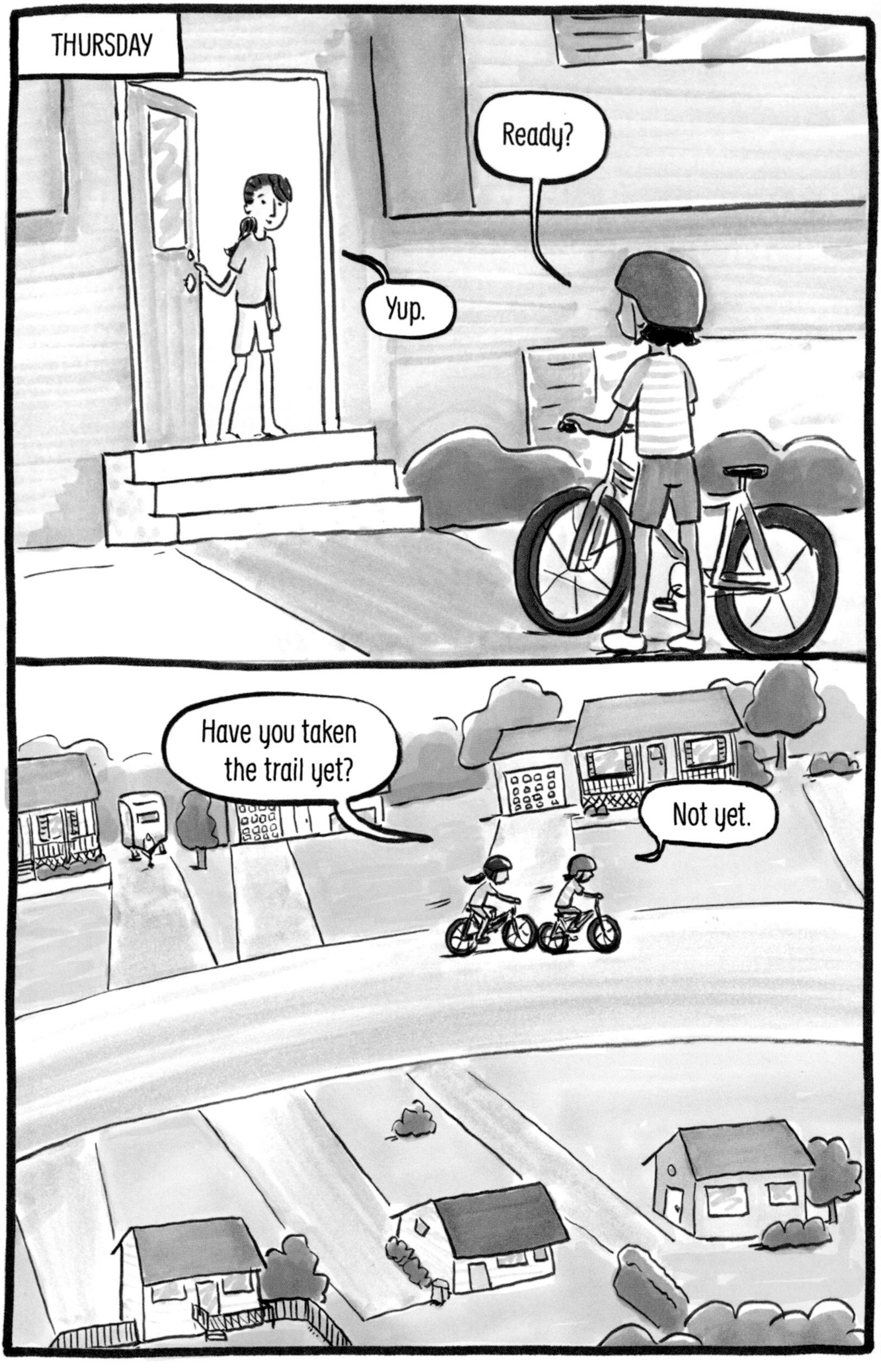
THURSDAY
Ready?
Yup.
Have you taken the trail yet?
Not yet.

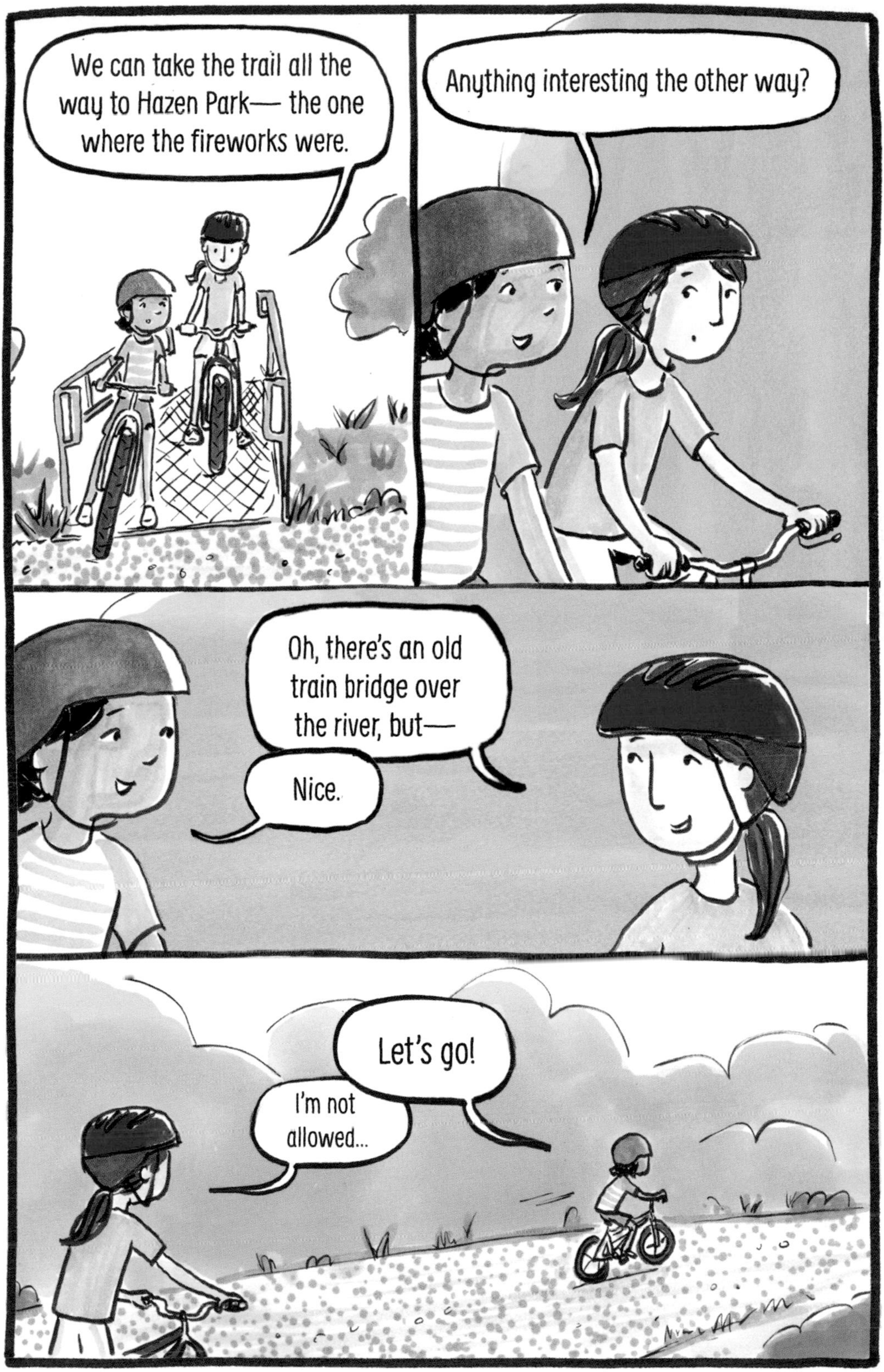
We can take the trail all the way to Hazen Park— the one where the fireworks were.
Anything interesting the other way?
Oh, there's an old train bridge over the river, but—
Nice.
Let's go!
I'm not allowed...

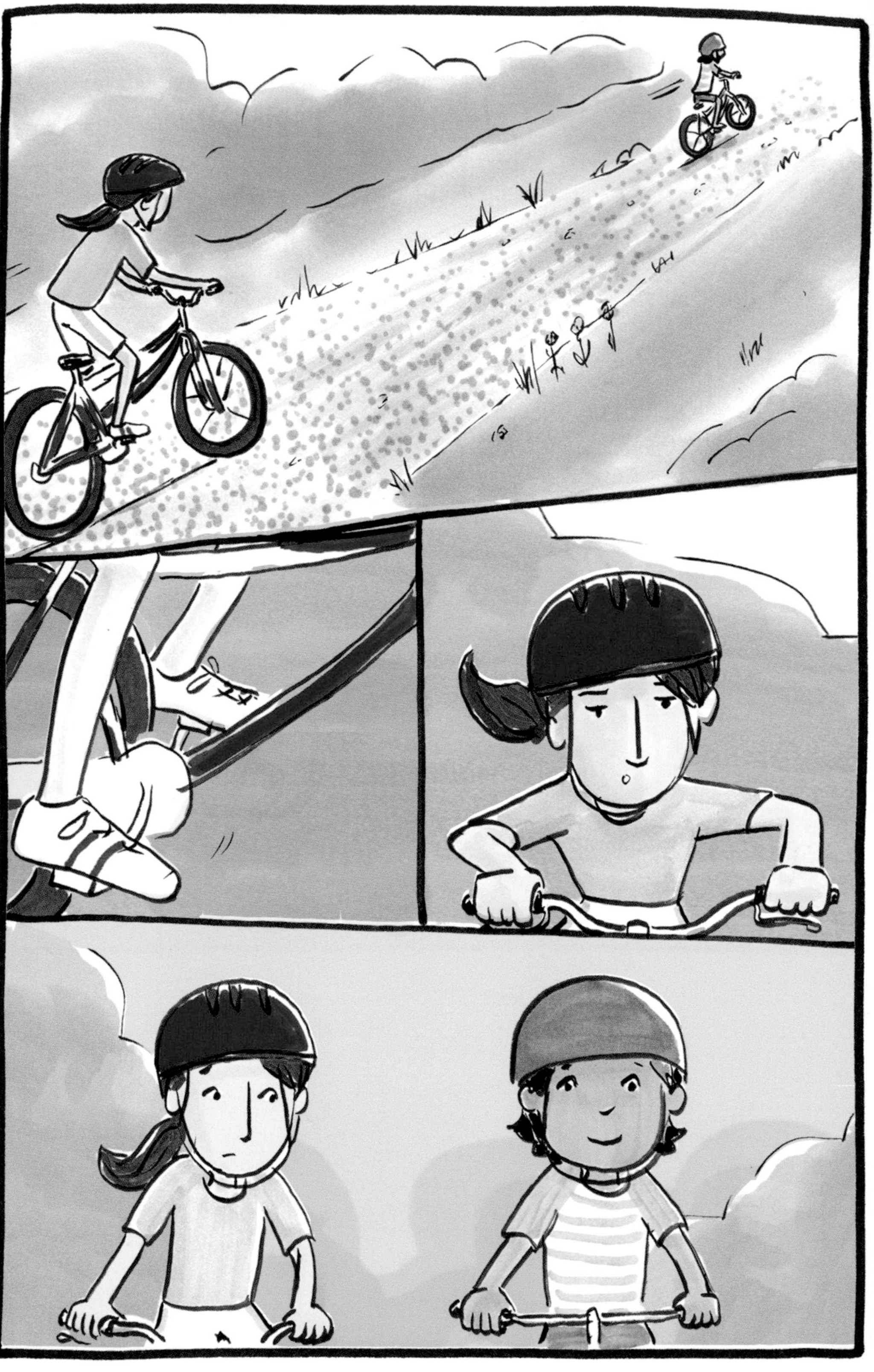

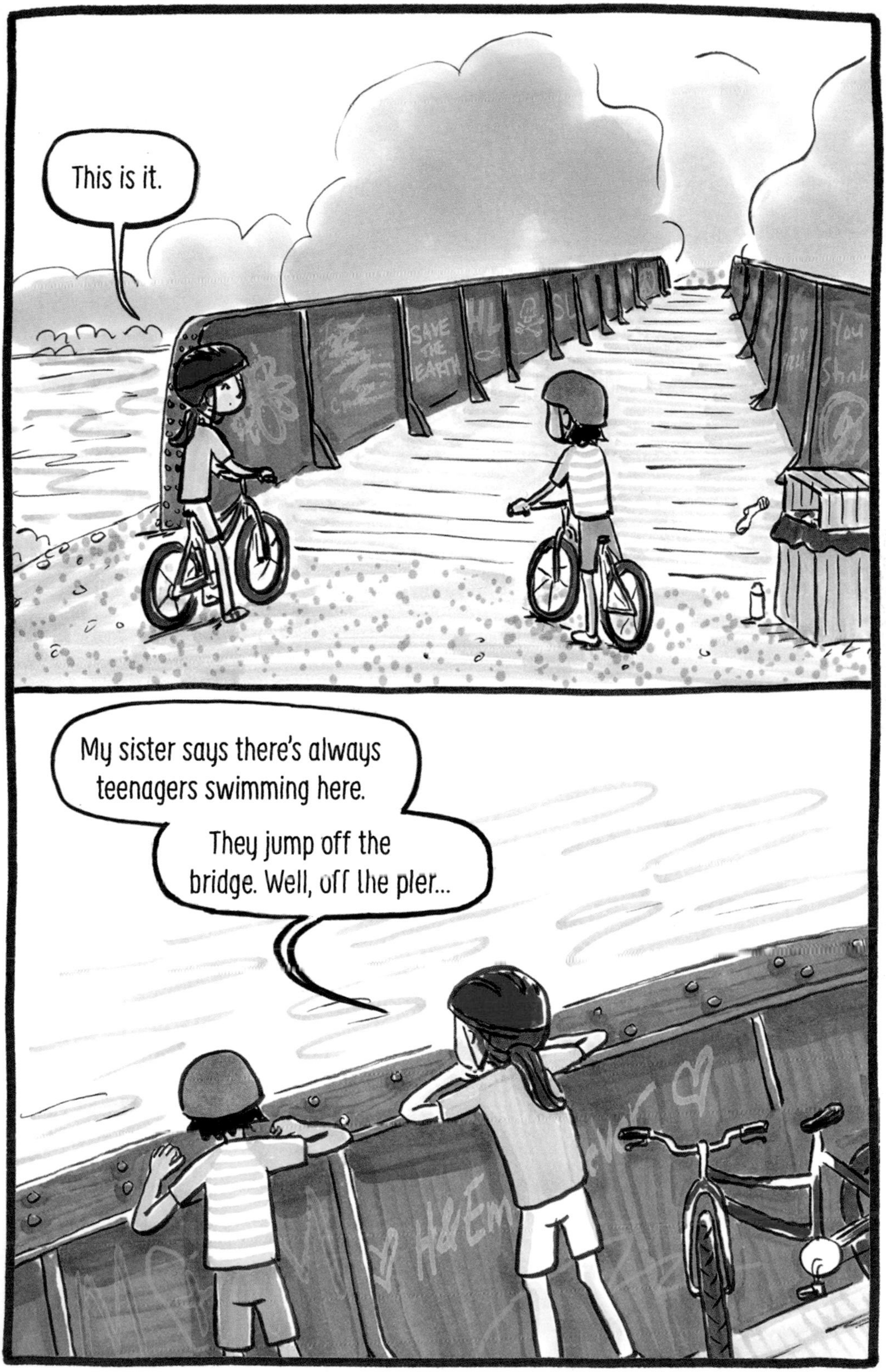
This is it.
SAVE THE EARTH
My sister says there's always teenagers swimming here.
They jump off the bridge. Well, off the pier...

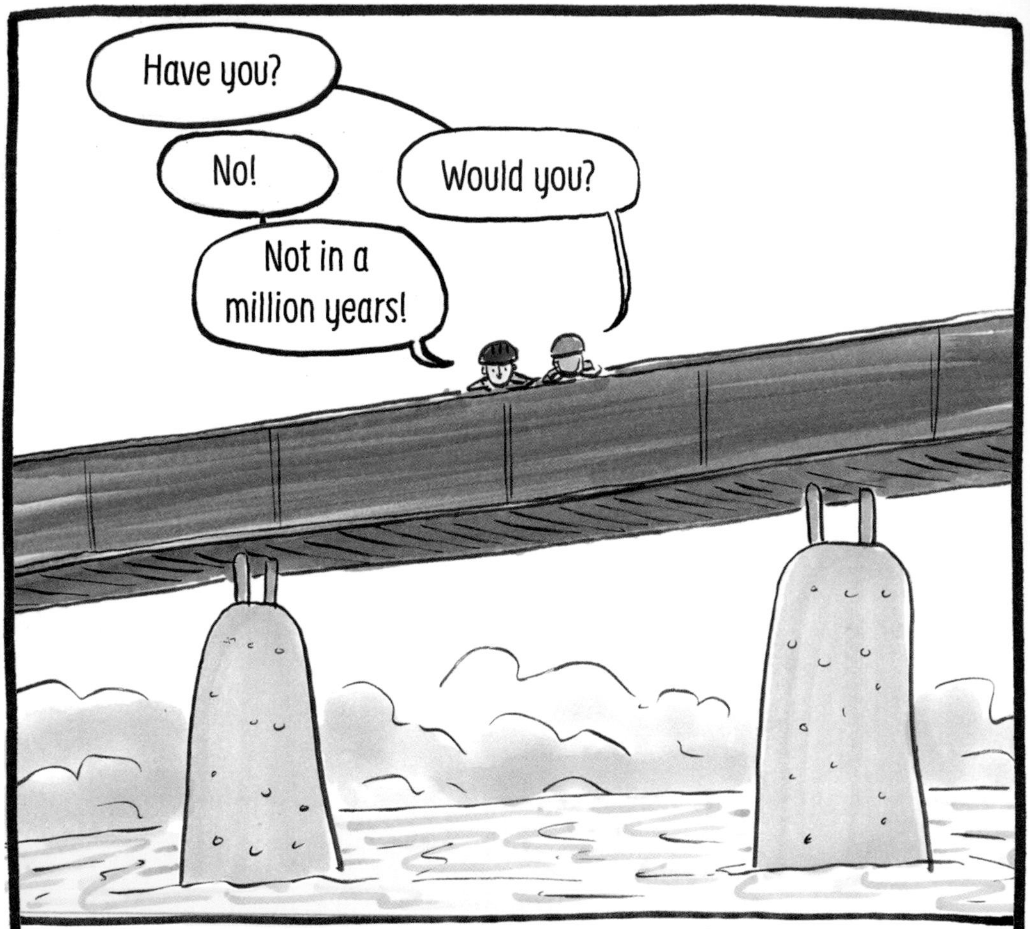
Have you?
No!
Would you?
Not in a million years!

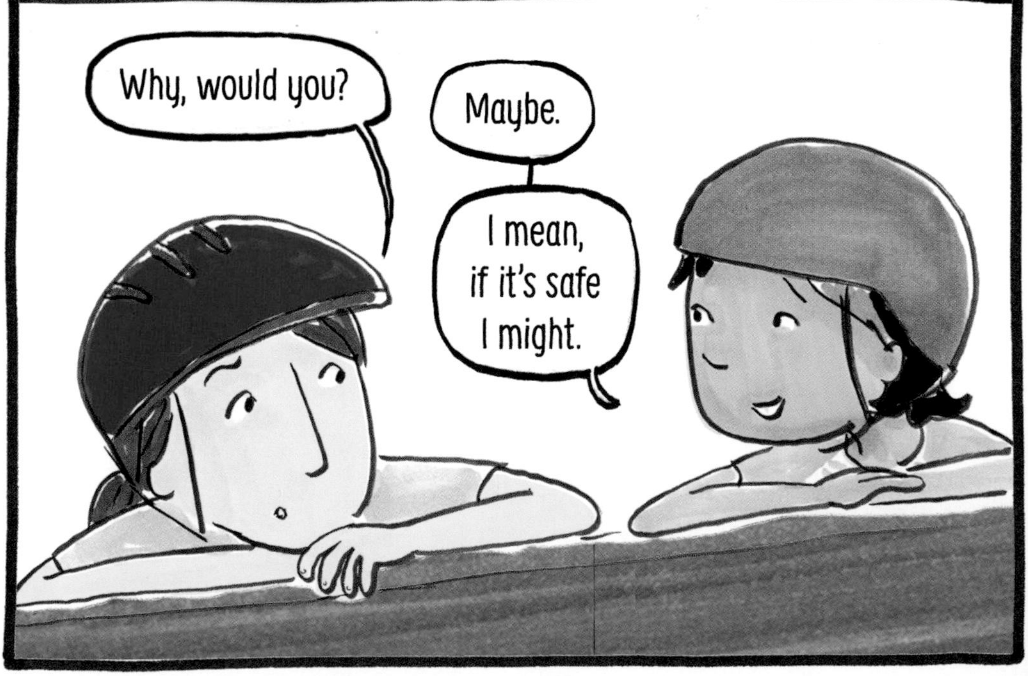
Why, would you?
Maybe.
I mean, if it's safe I might.

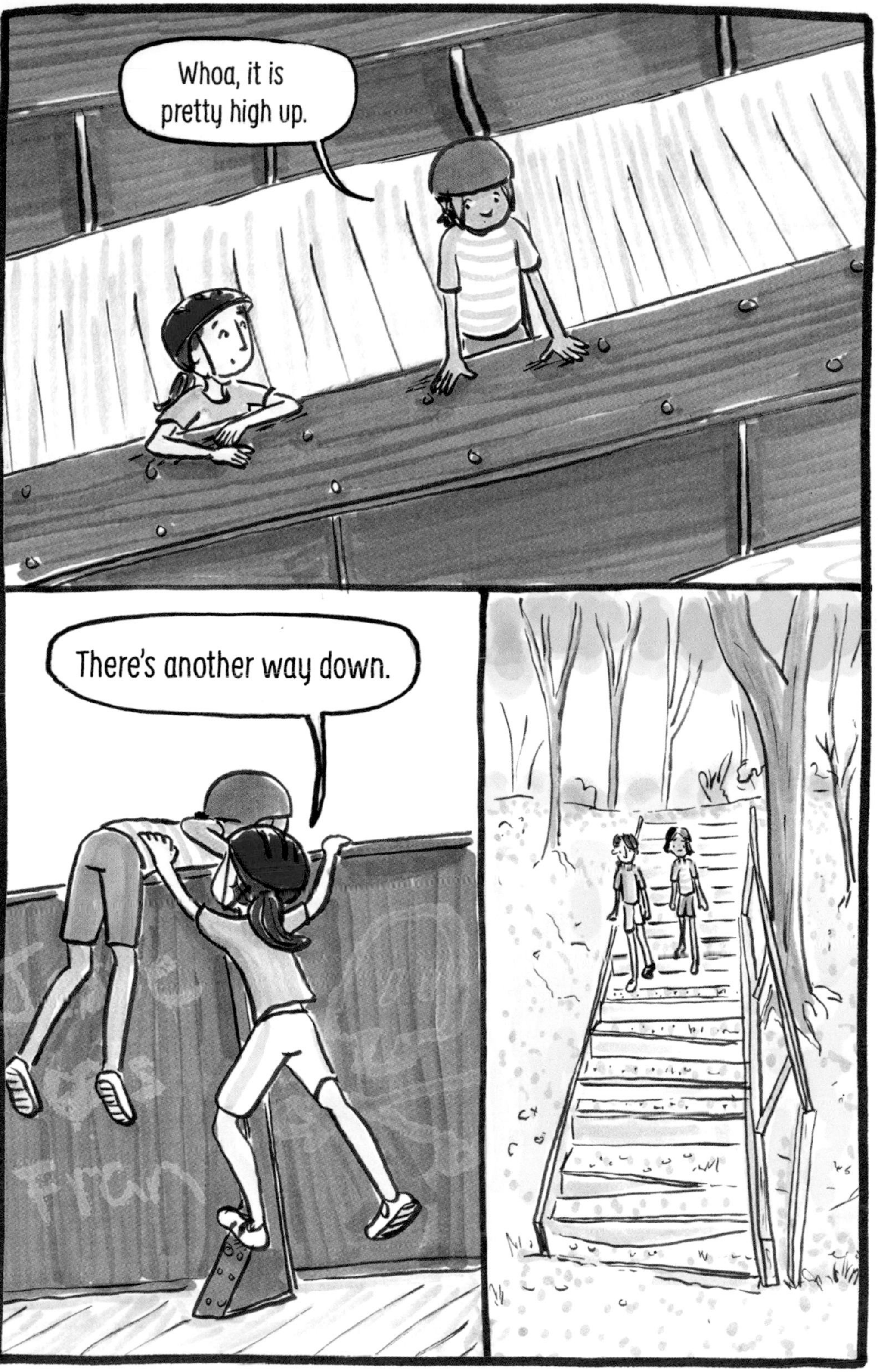
Whoa, it is
pretty high up.
There's another way down.
Fran

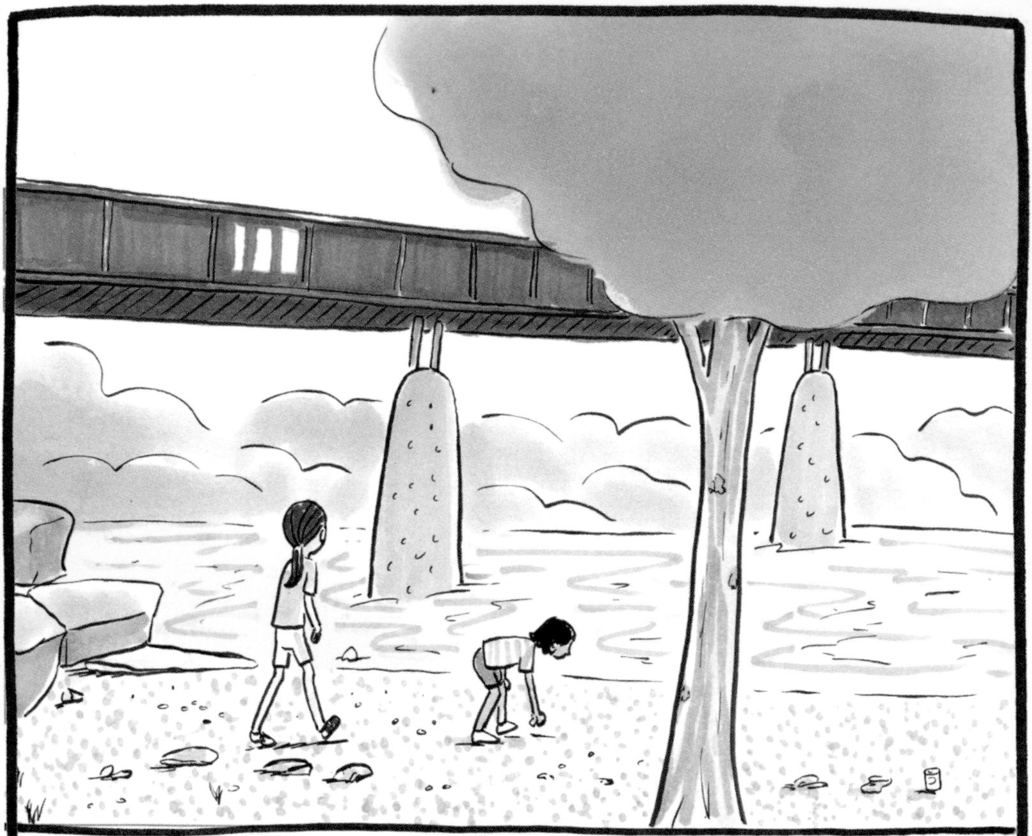

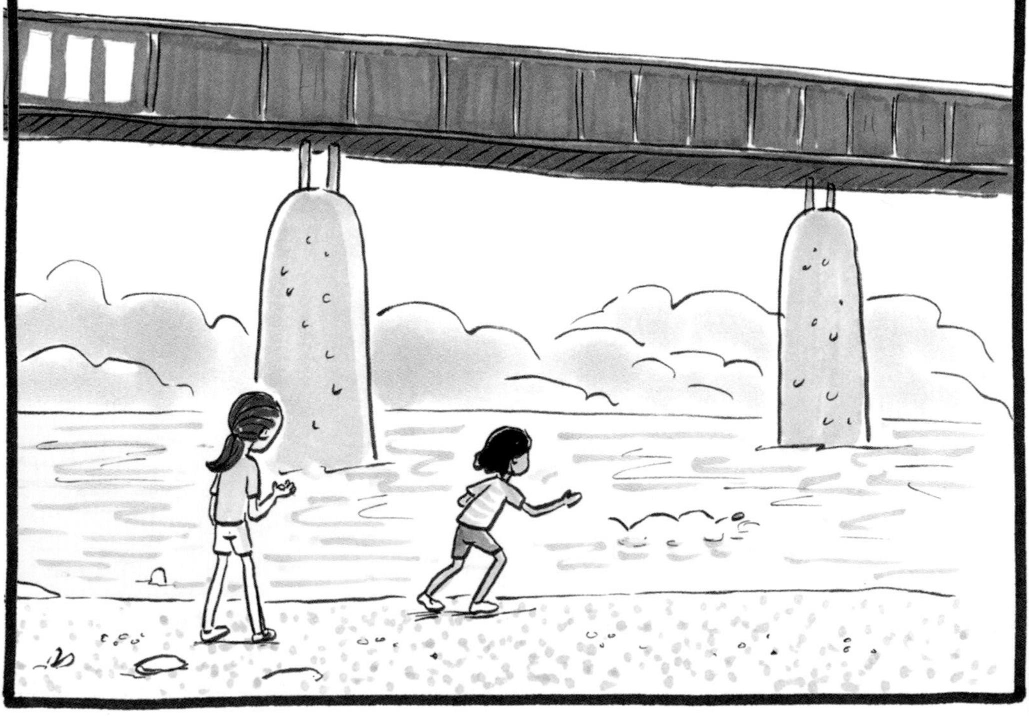

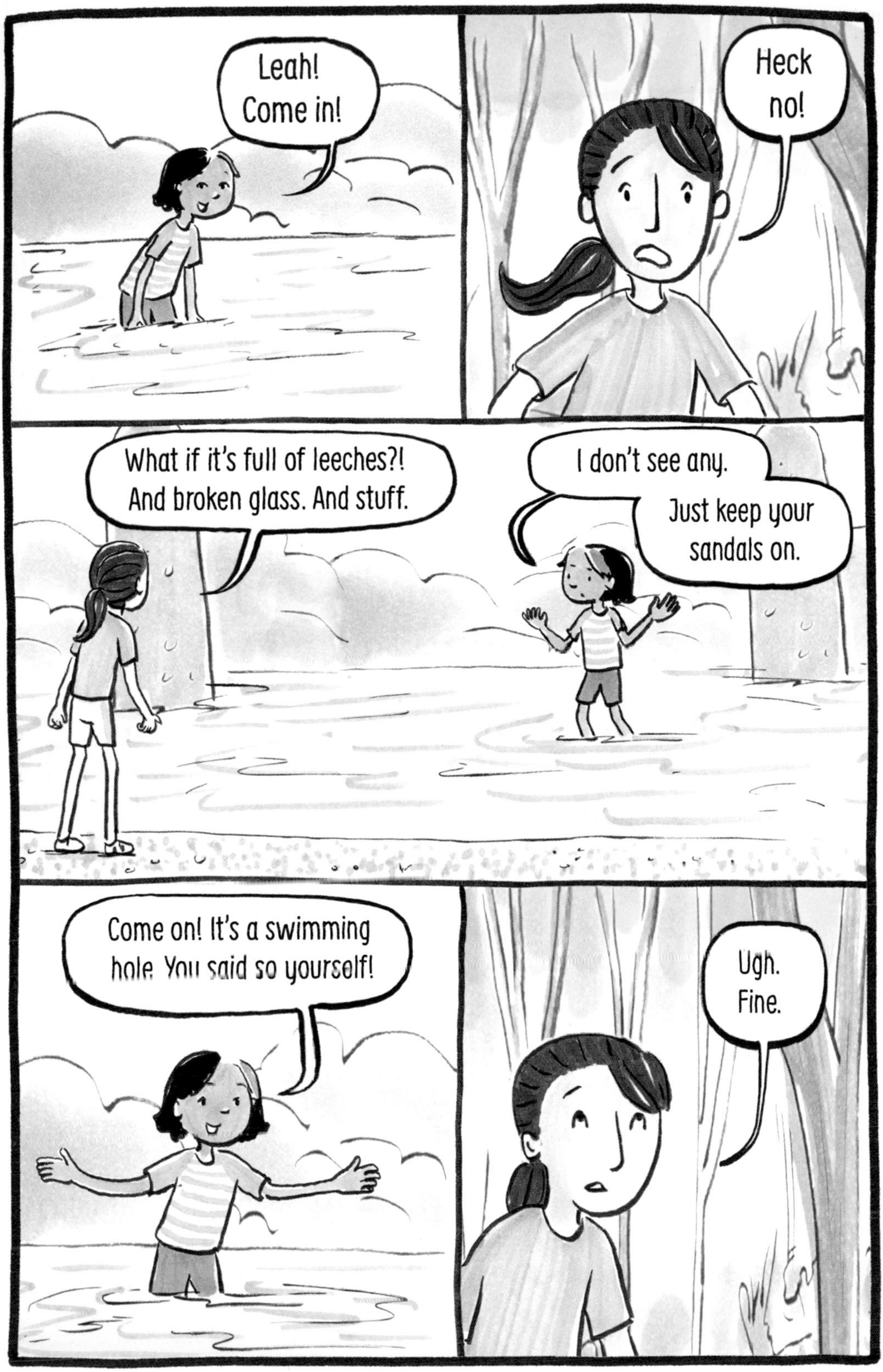
Leah! Come in!
Heck no!
What if it's full of leeches?! And broken glass. And stuff.
I don't see any.
Just keep your sandals on.
Come on! It's a swimming hole. You said so yourself!
Ugh. Fine.

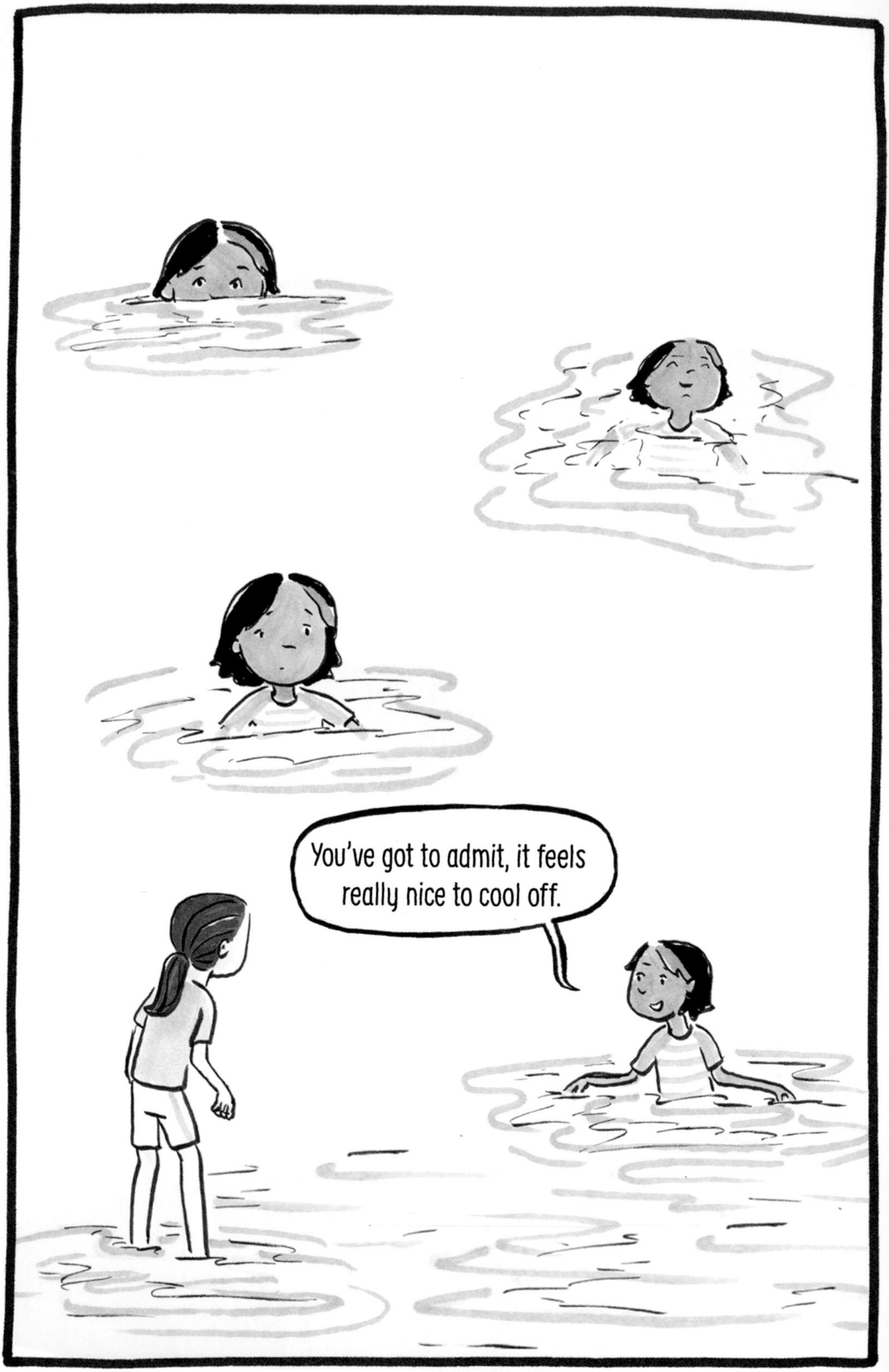
You've got to admit, it feels really nice to cool off.

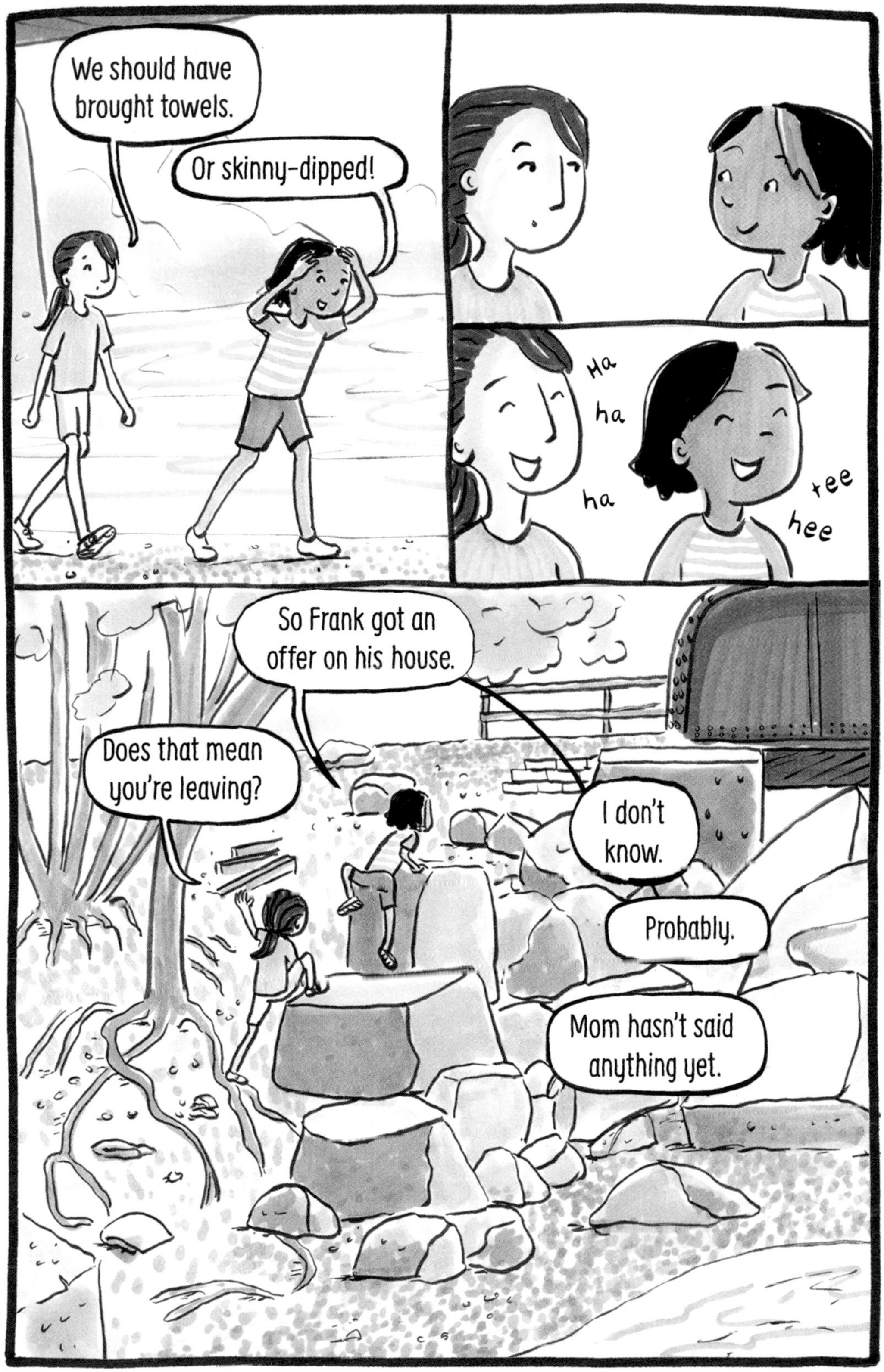
We should have brought towels.
Or skinny-dipped!
Ha
ha
ha
tee
hee
So Frank got an offer on his house.
Does that mean you're leaving?
I don't know.
Probably.
Mom hasn't said anything yet.

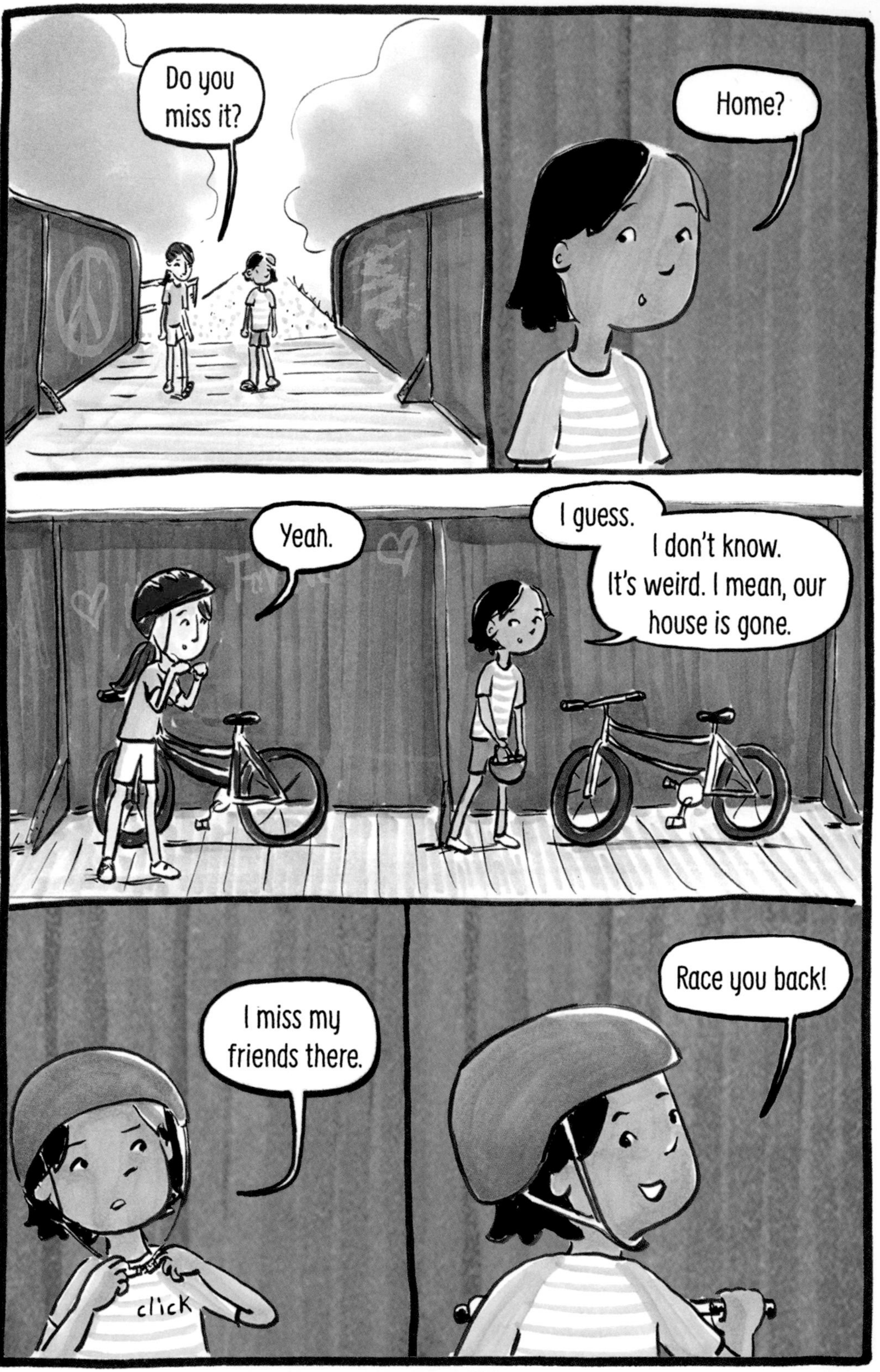
Do you miss it?
Home?
Yeah.
I guess.
I don't know.
It's weird. I mean, our house is gone.
I miss my friends there.
click
Race you back!

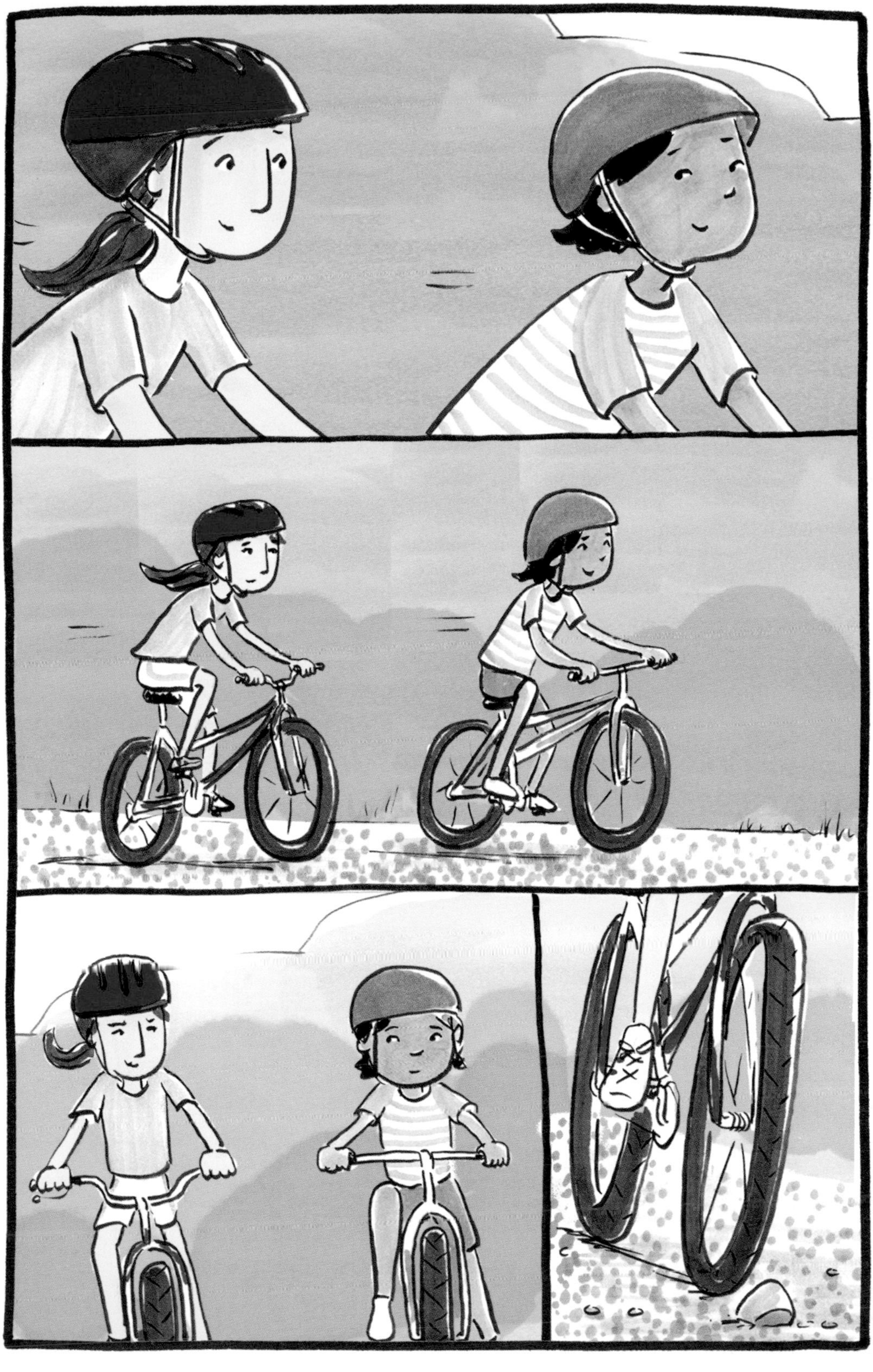

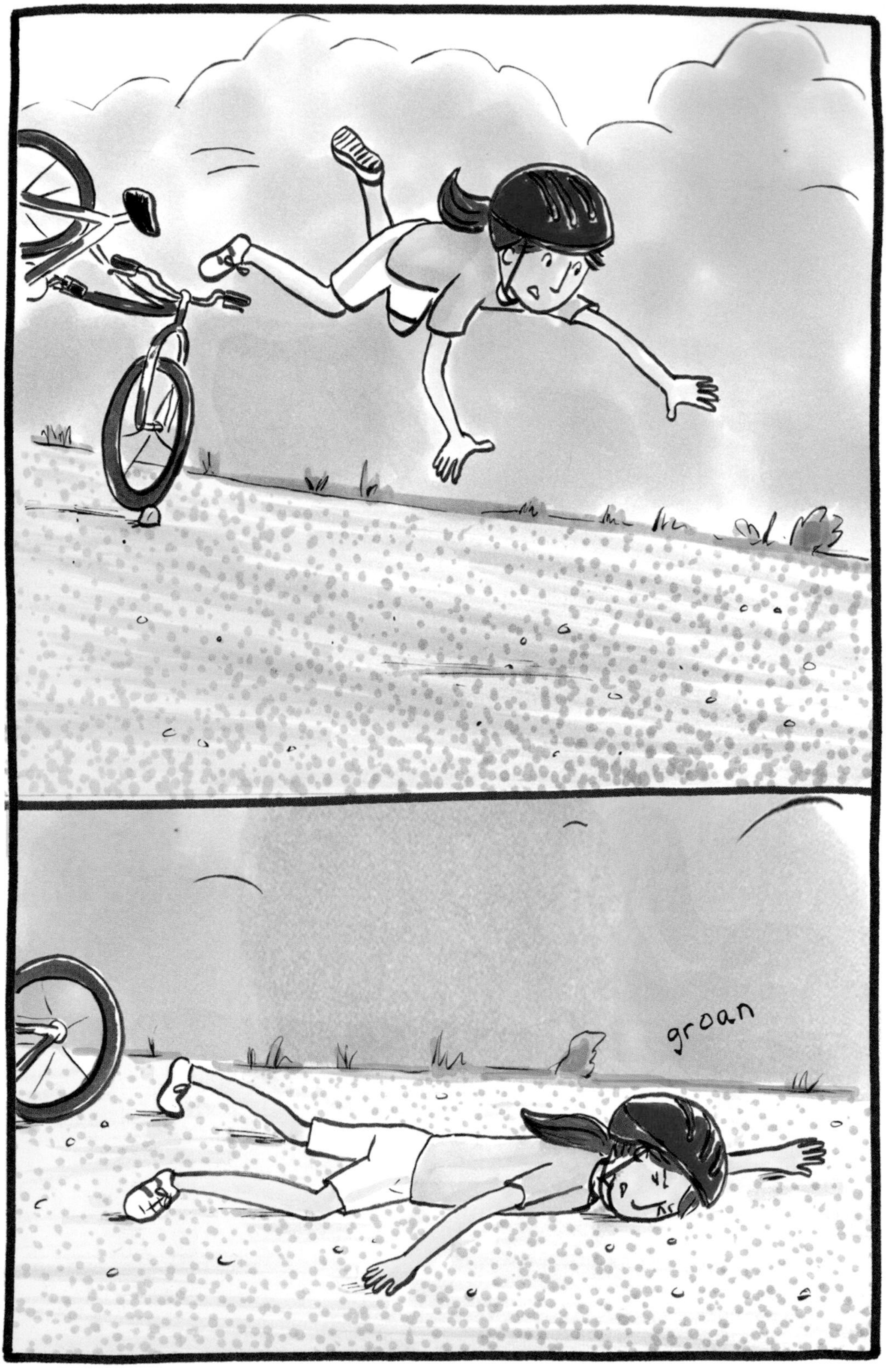
groan

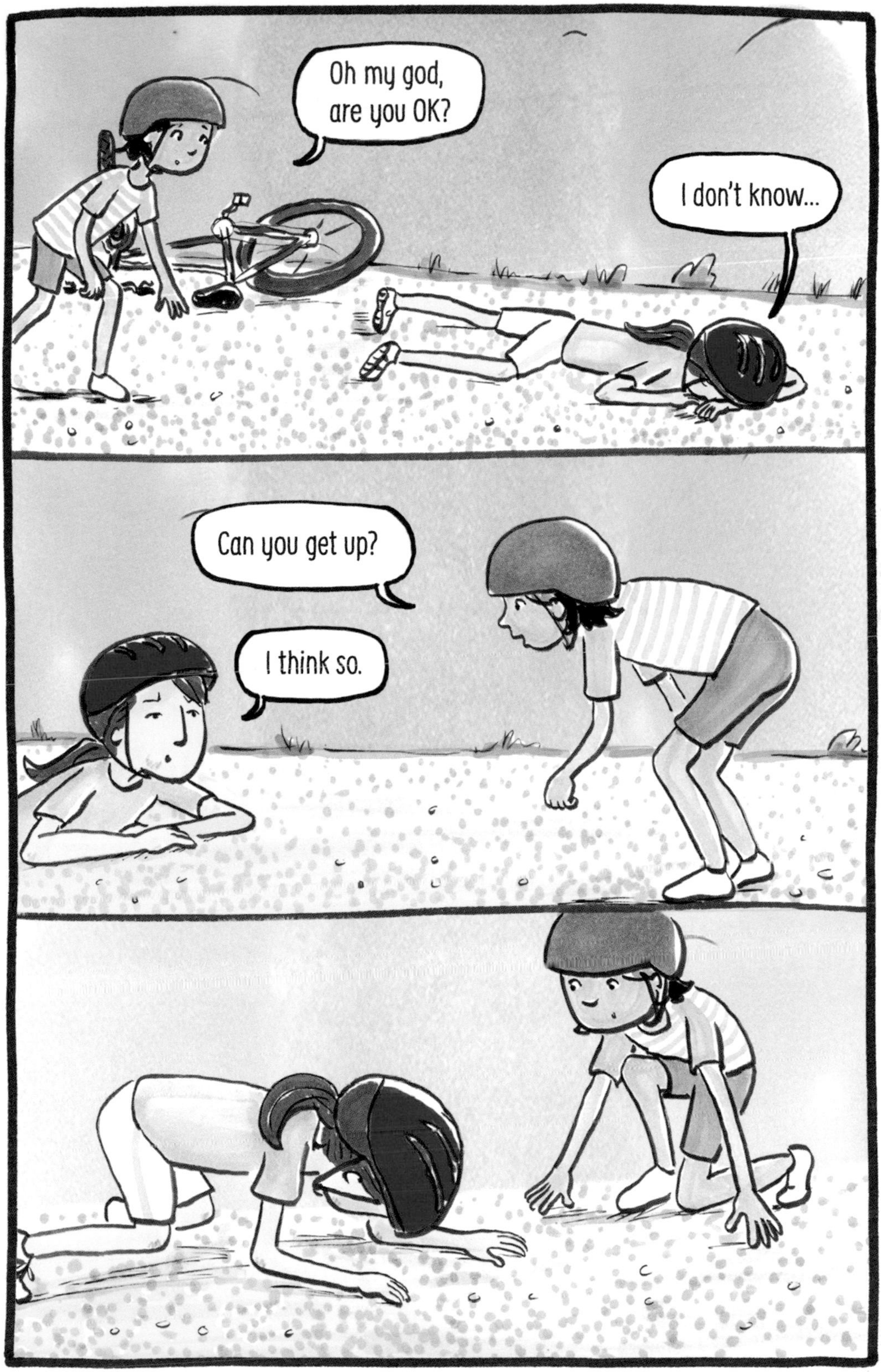
Oh my god, are you OK?
I don't know...
Can you get up?
I think so.

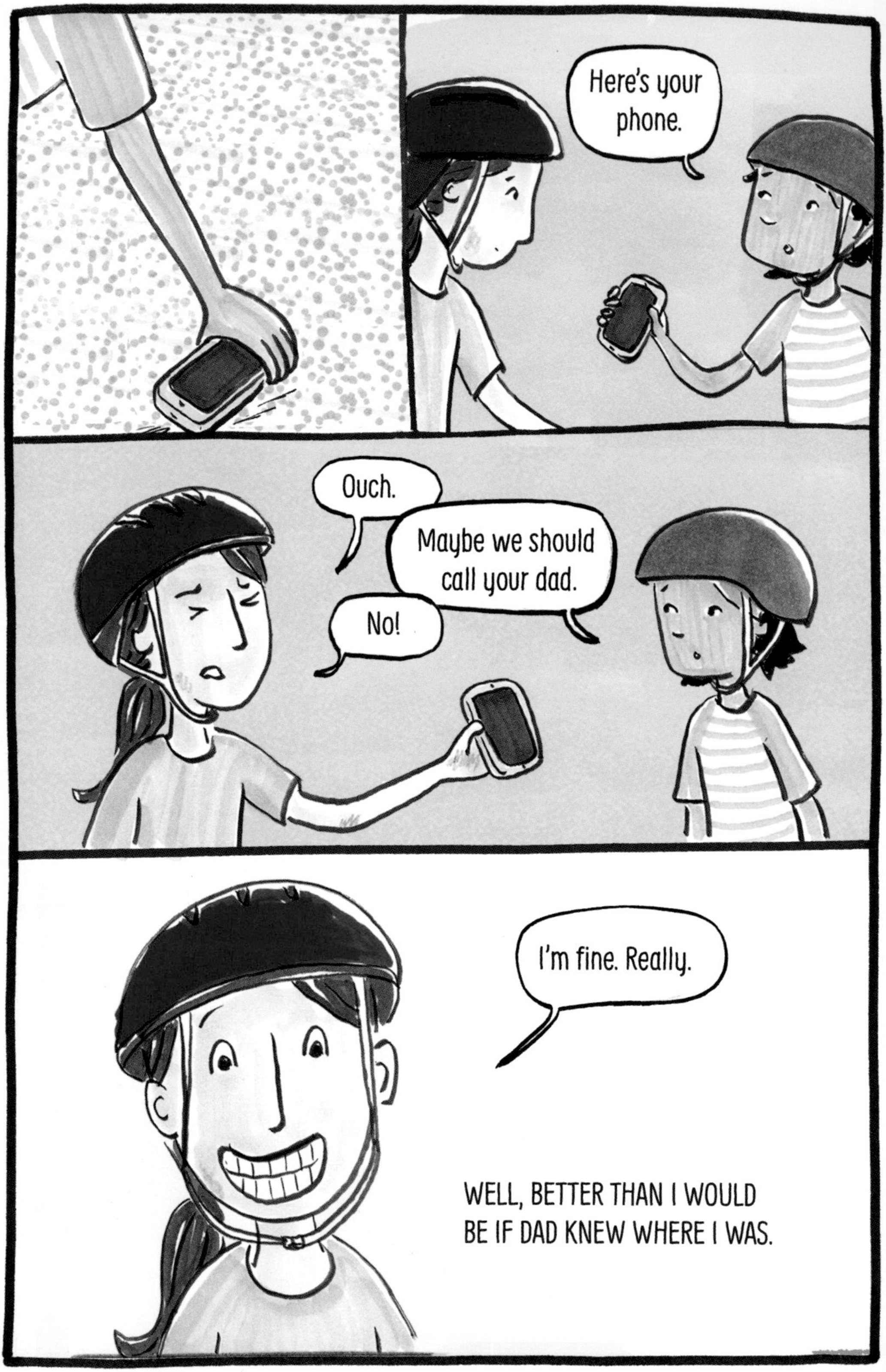
Here's your phone.
Ouch.
Maybe we should call your dad.
No!
I'm fine. Really.
WELL, BETTER THAN I WOULD BE IF DAD KNEW WHERE I WAS.

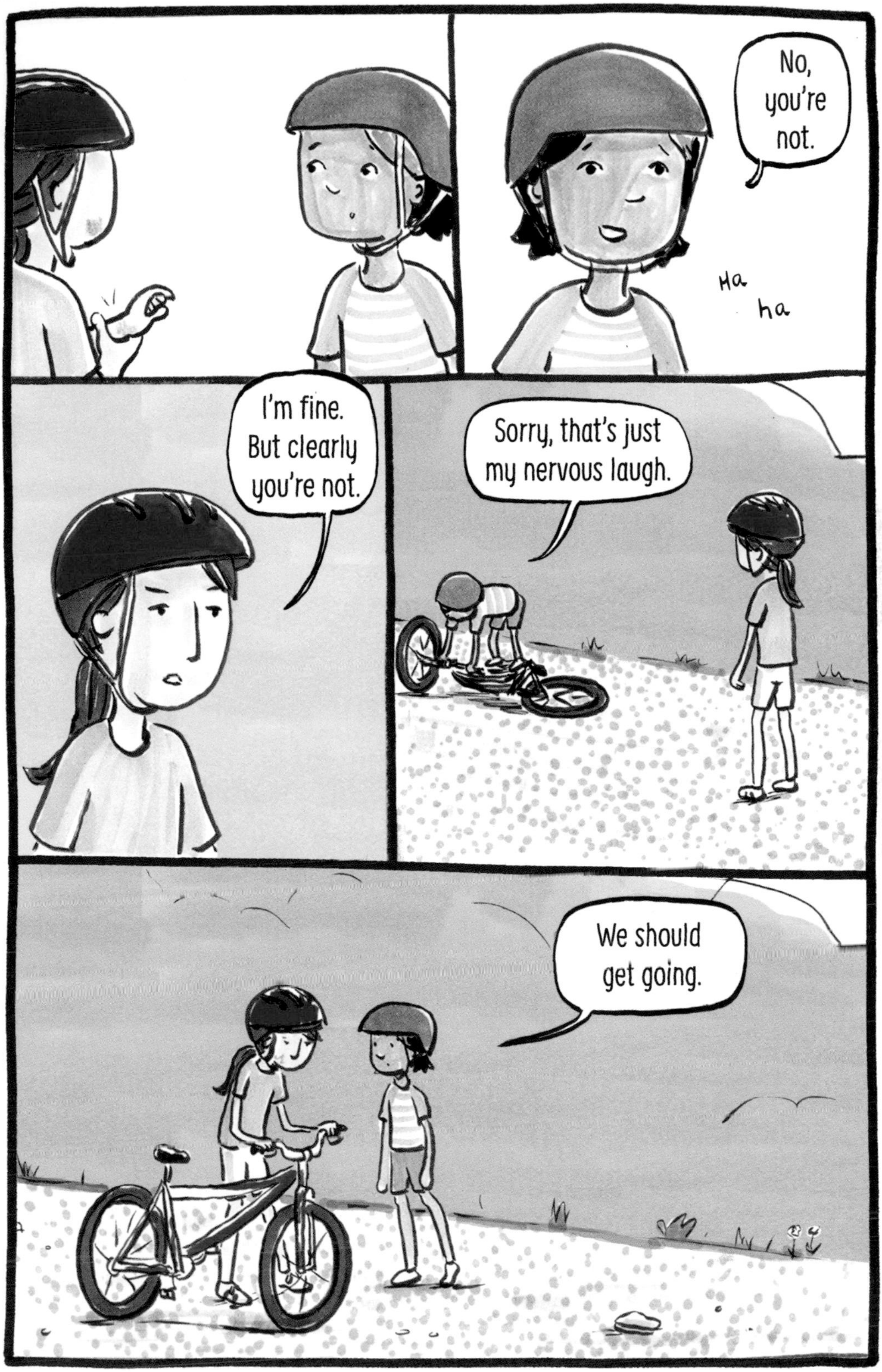
No, you're not.
Ha ha
I'm fine. But clearly you're not.
Sorry, that's just my nervous laugh.
We should get going.

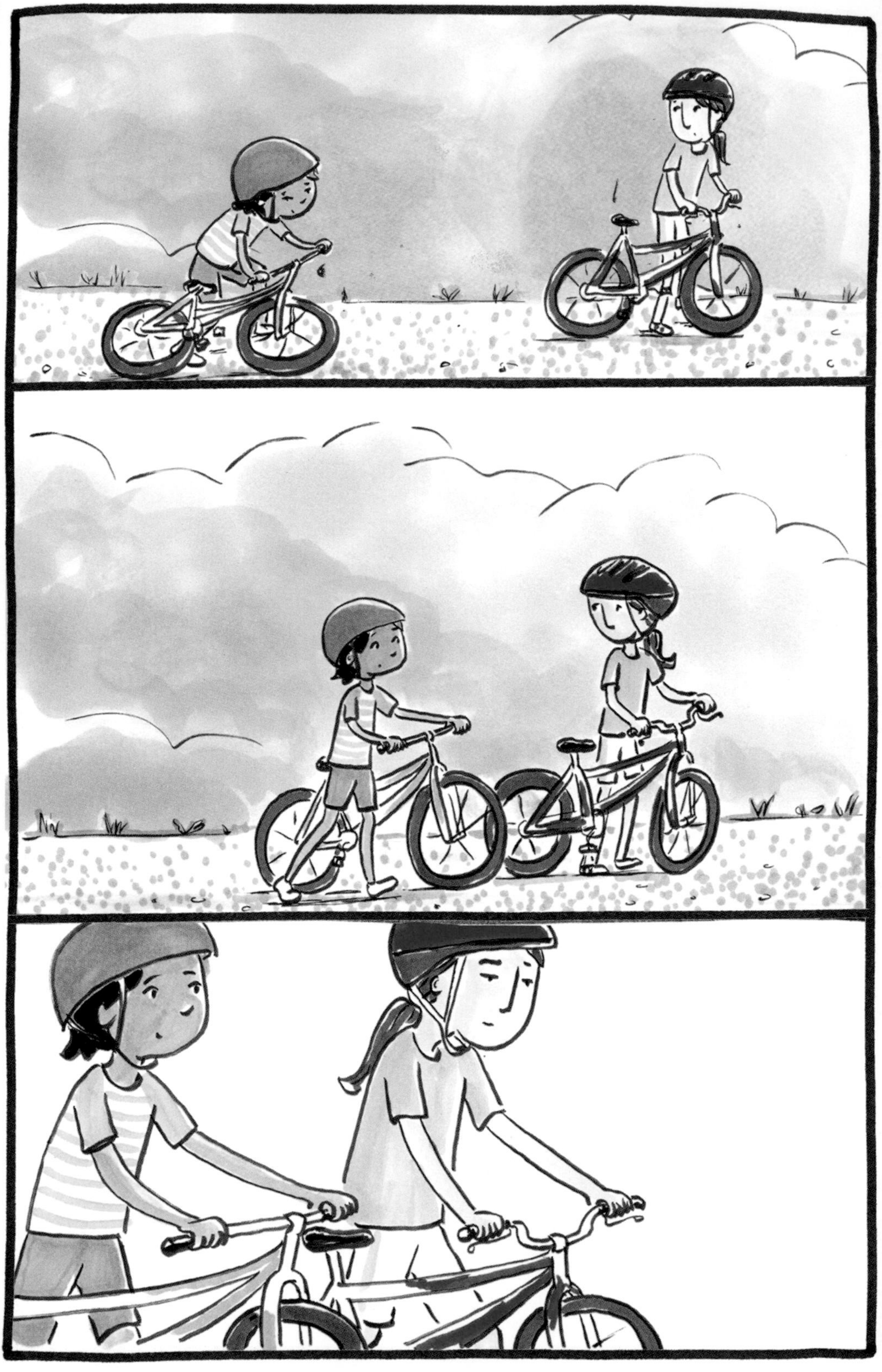

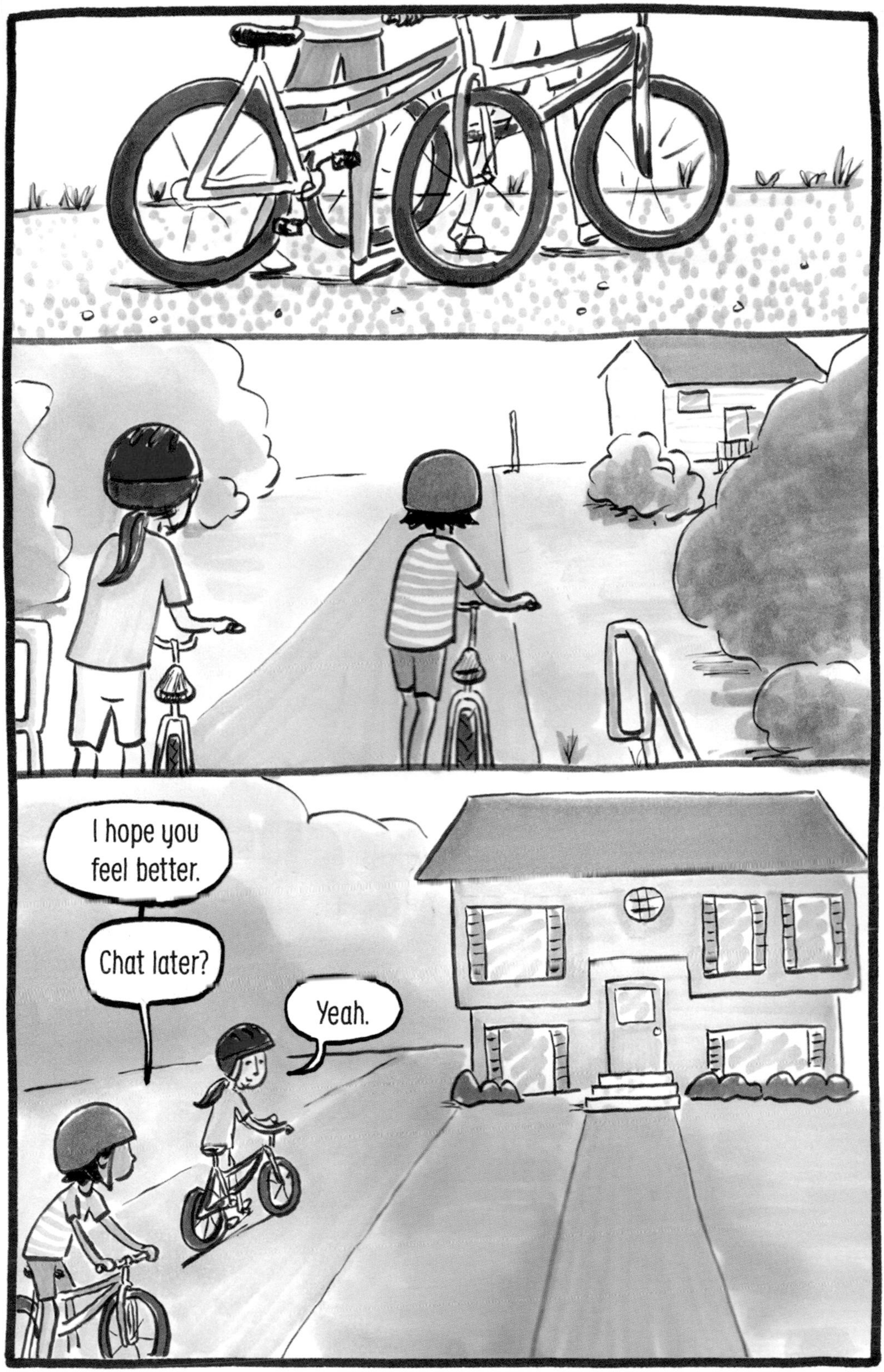
I hope you feel better.
Chat later?
Yeah.

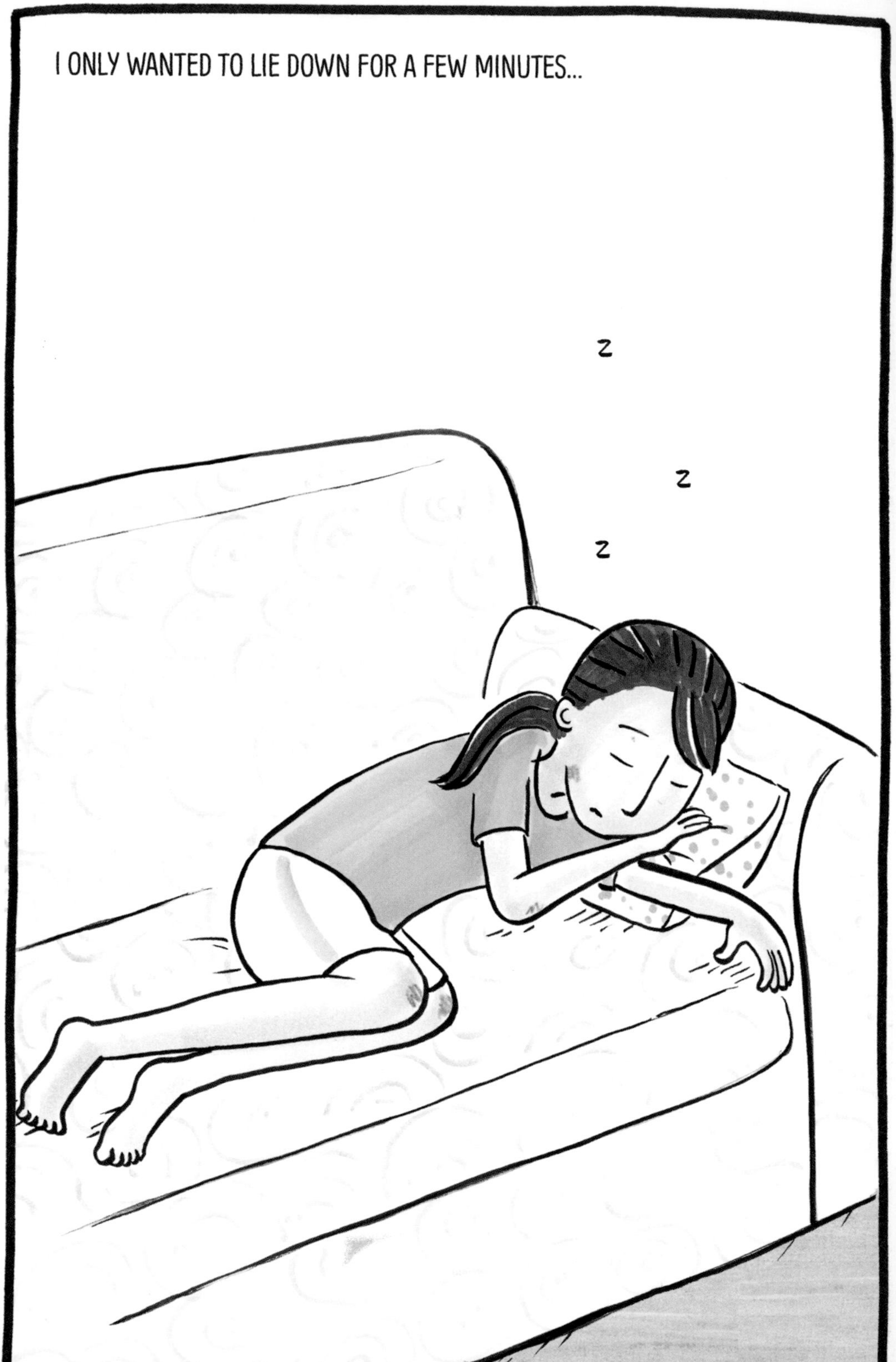
I ONLY WANTED TO LIE DOWN FOR A FEW MINUTES...
Z
Z
Z

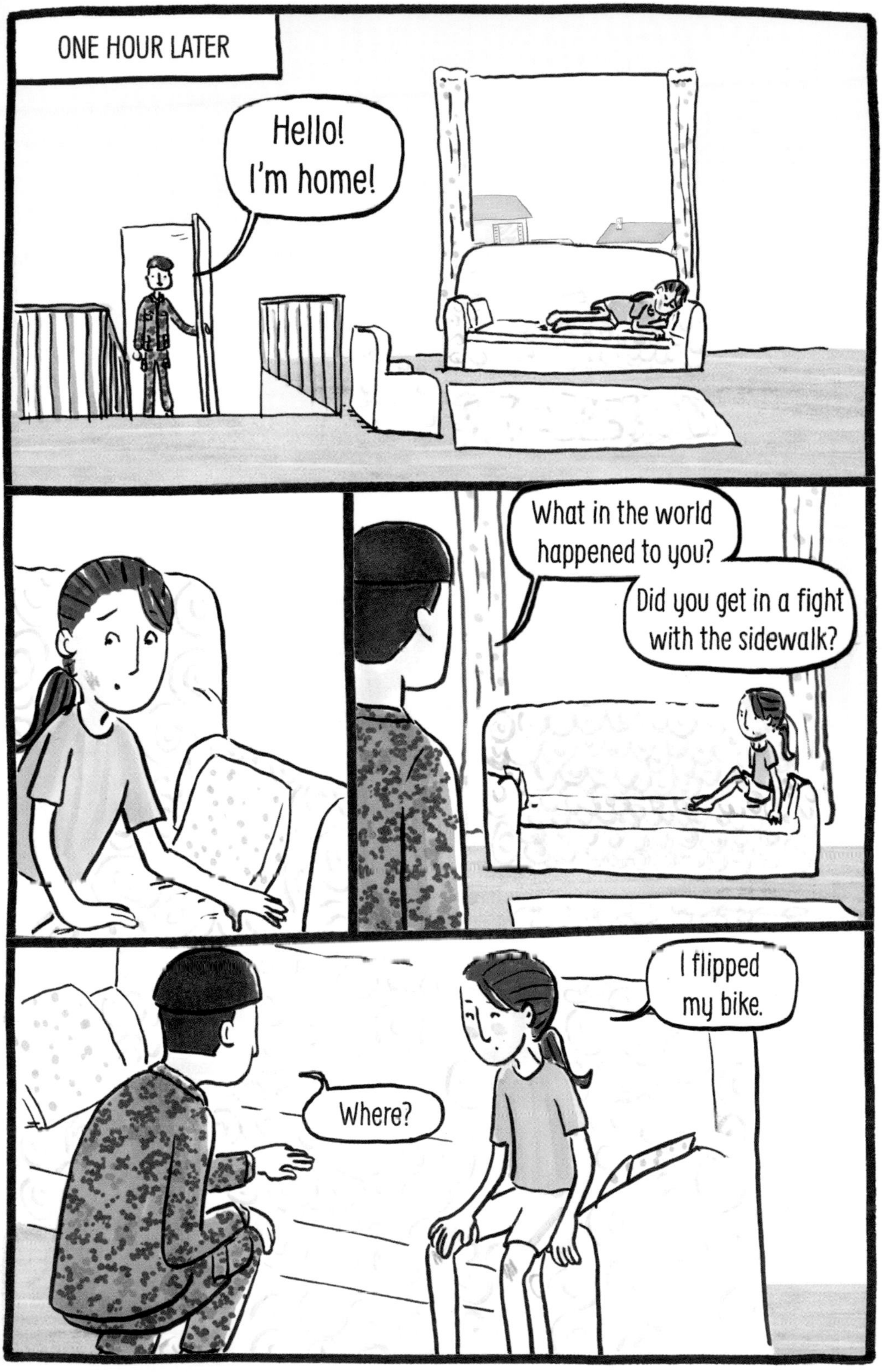
ONE HOUR LATER
Hello! I'm home!
What in the world happened to you?
Did you get in a fight with the sidewalk?
I flipped my bike.
Where?

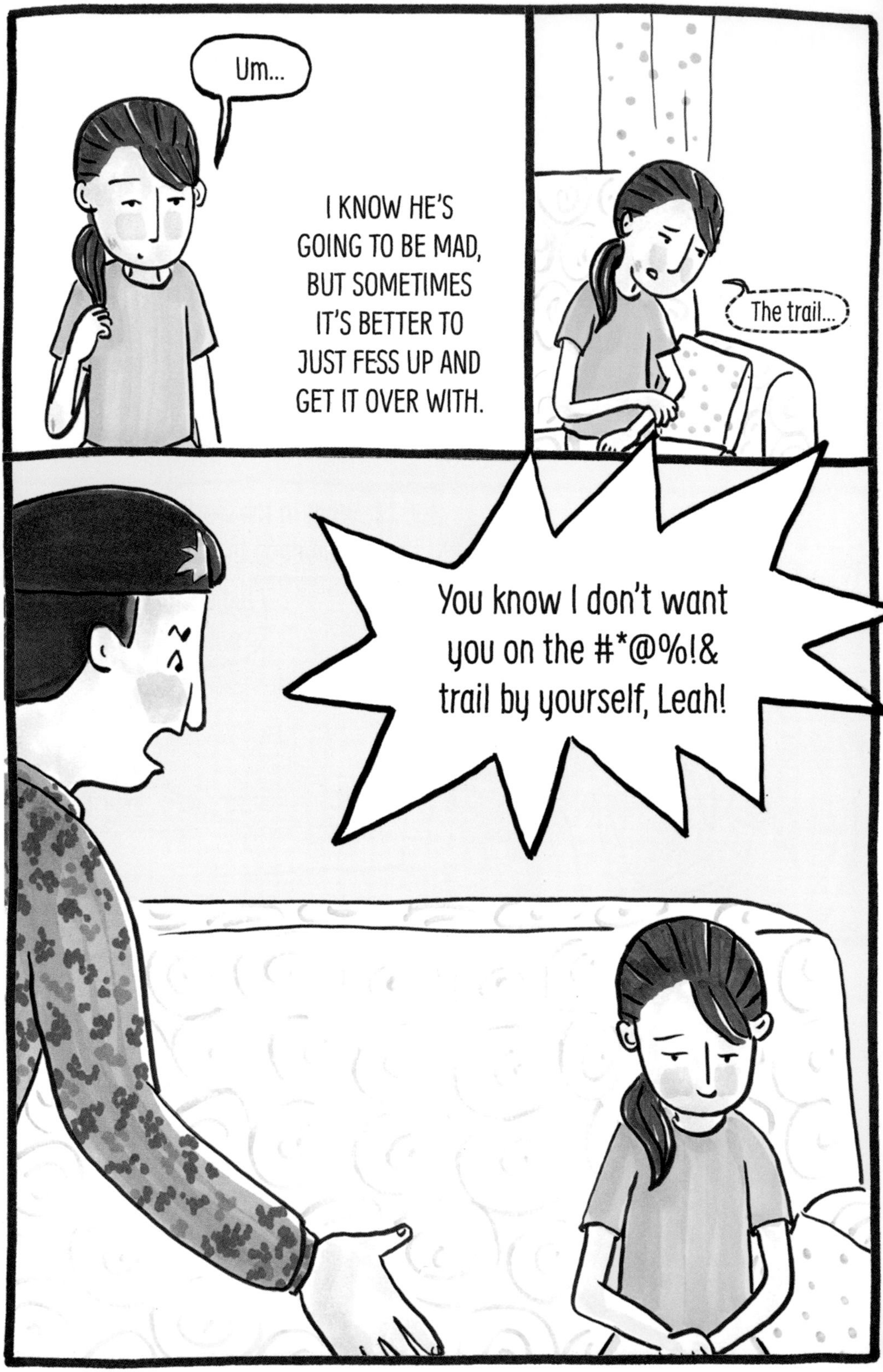
Um...
I KNOW HE'S GOING TO BE MAD, BUT SOMETIMES IT'S BETTER TO JUST FESS UP AND GET IT OVER WITH.
The trail...
You know I don't want you on the #*@%!& trail by yourself, Leah!

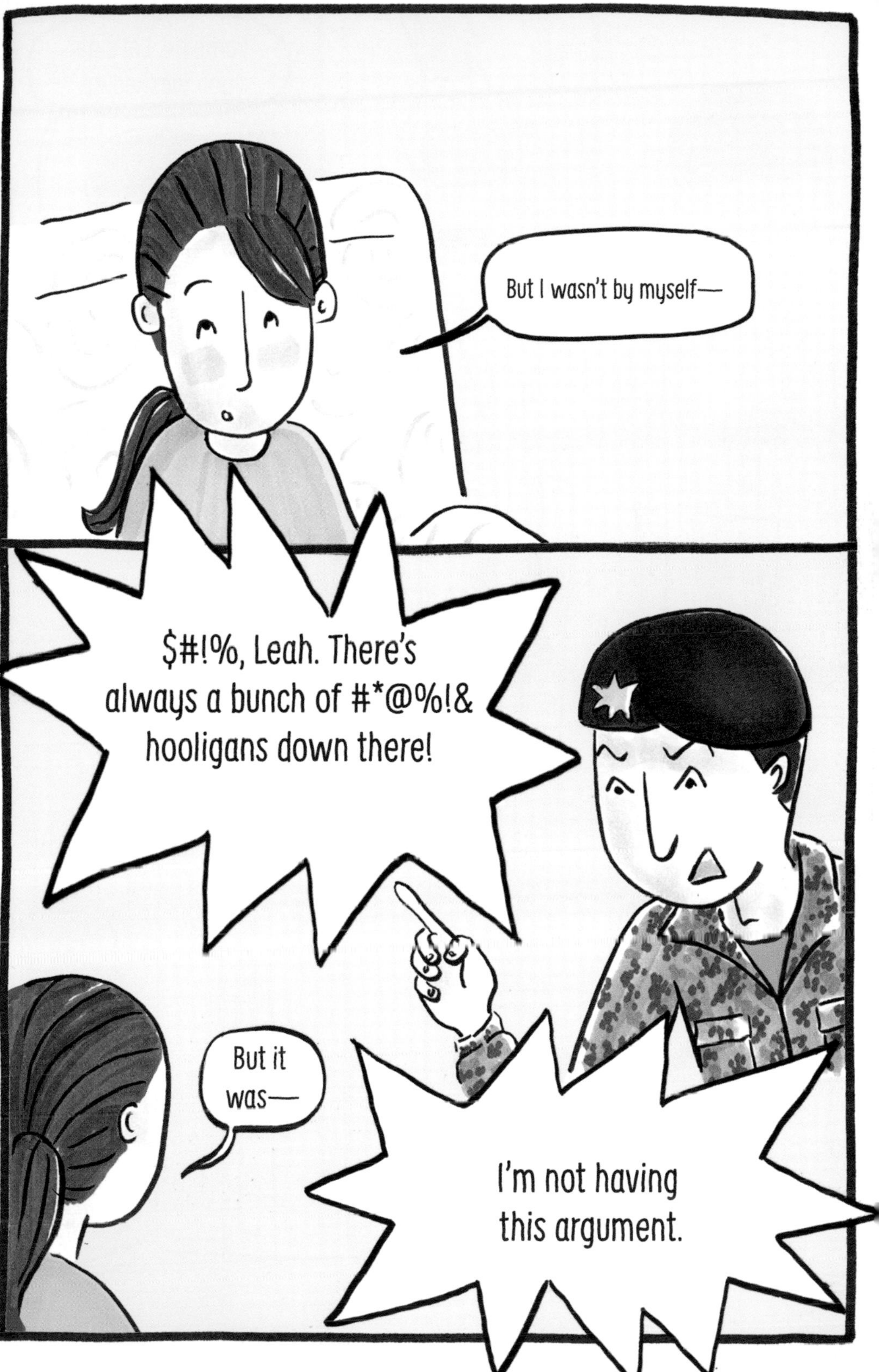
But I wasn't by myself—
$#!%, Leah. There's always a bunch of #*@%!& hooligans down there!
But it was—
I'm not having this argument.

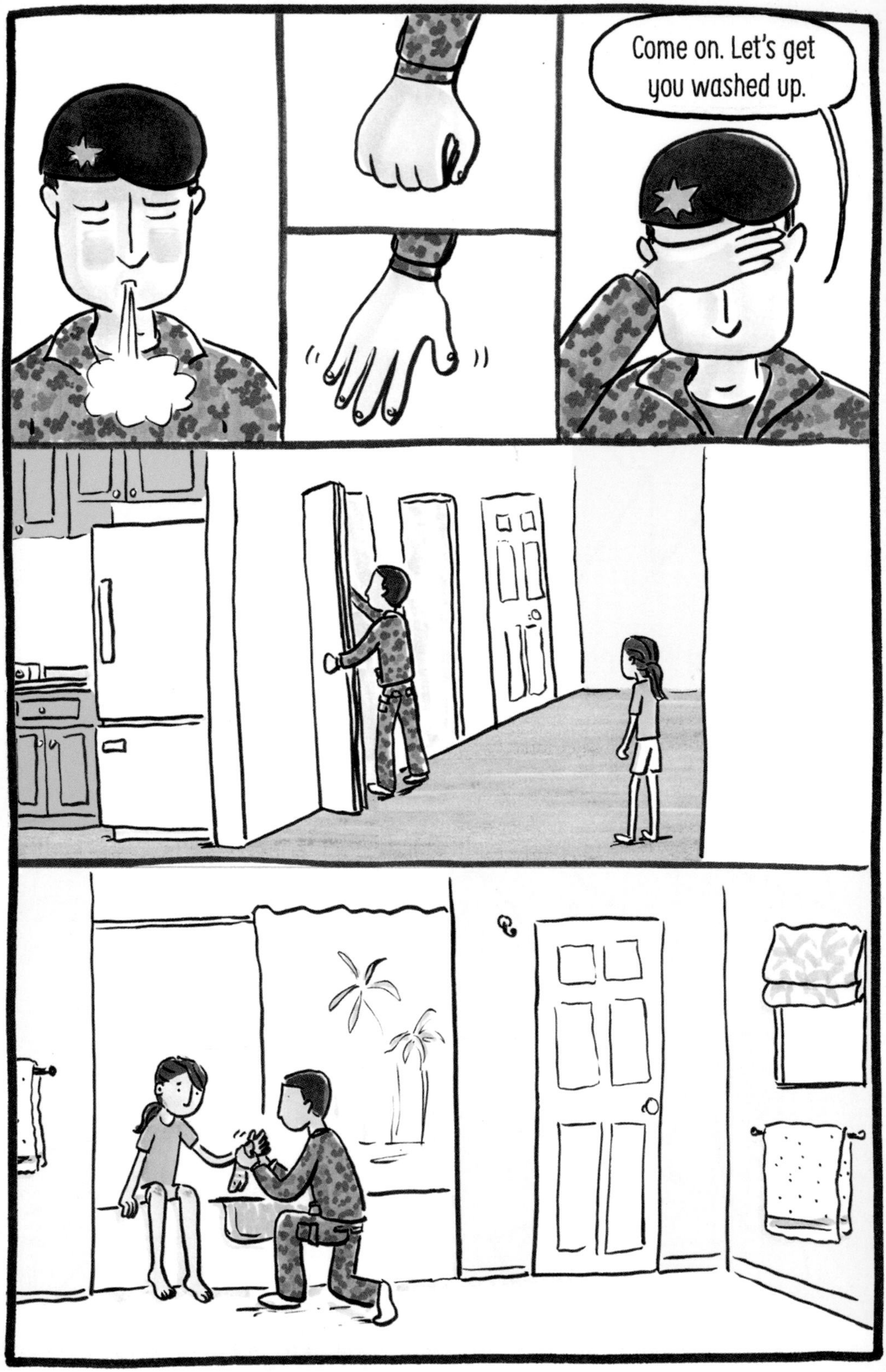
Come on. Let's get you washed up.

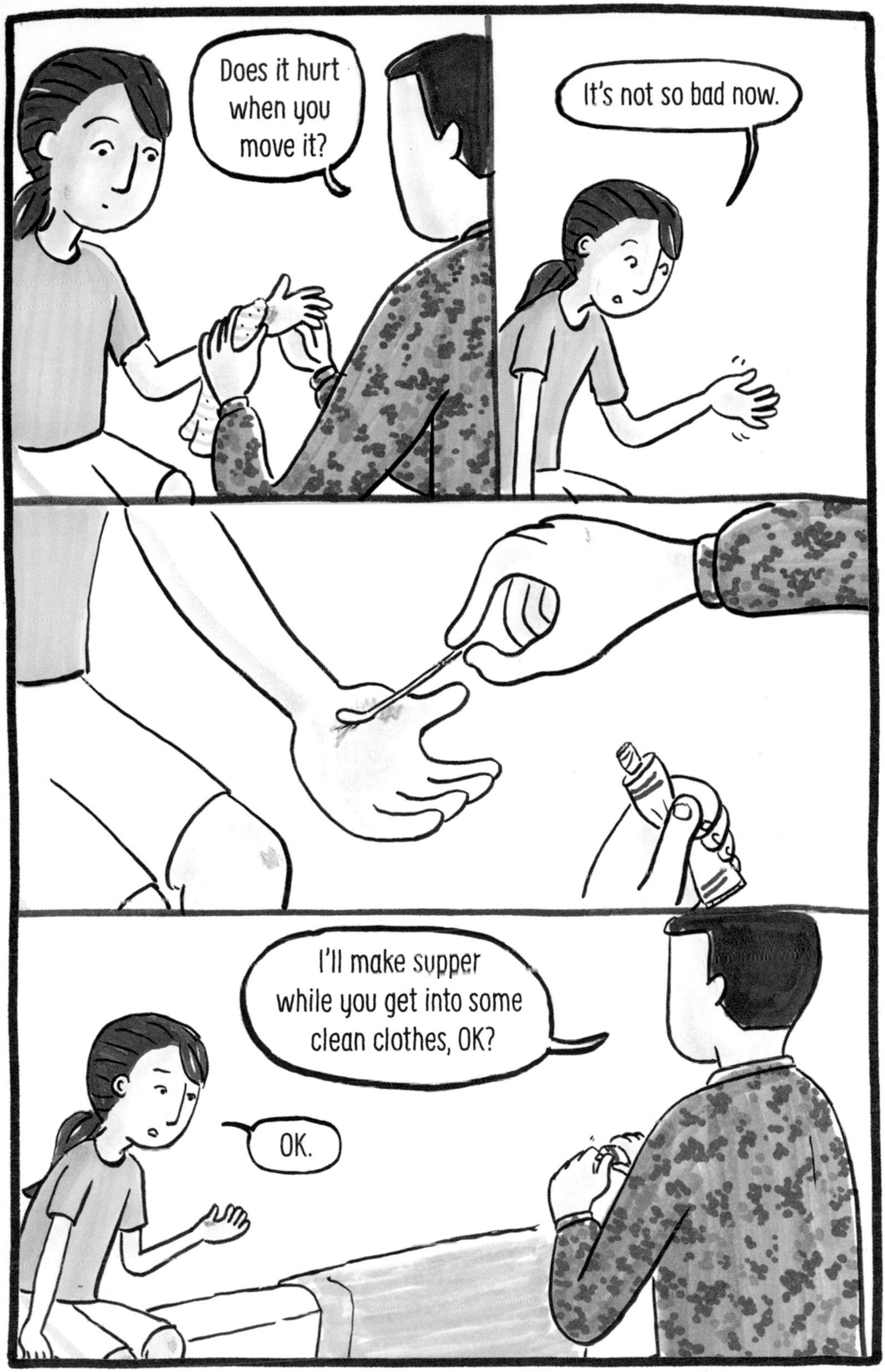
Does it hurt when you move it?
It's not so bad now.
I'll make supper while you get into some clean clothes, OK?
OK.

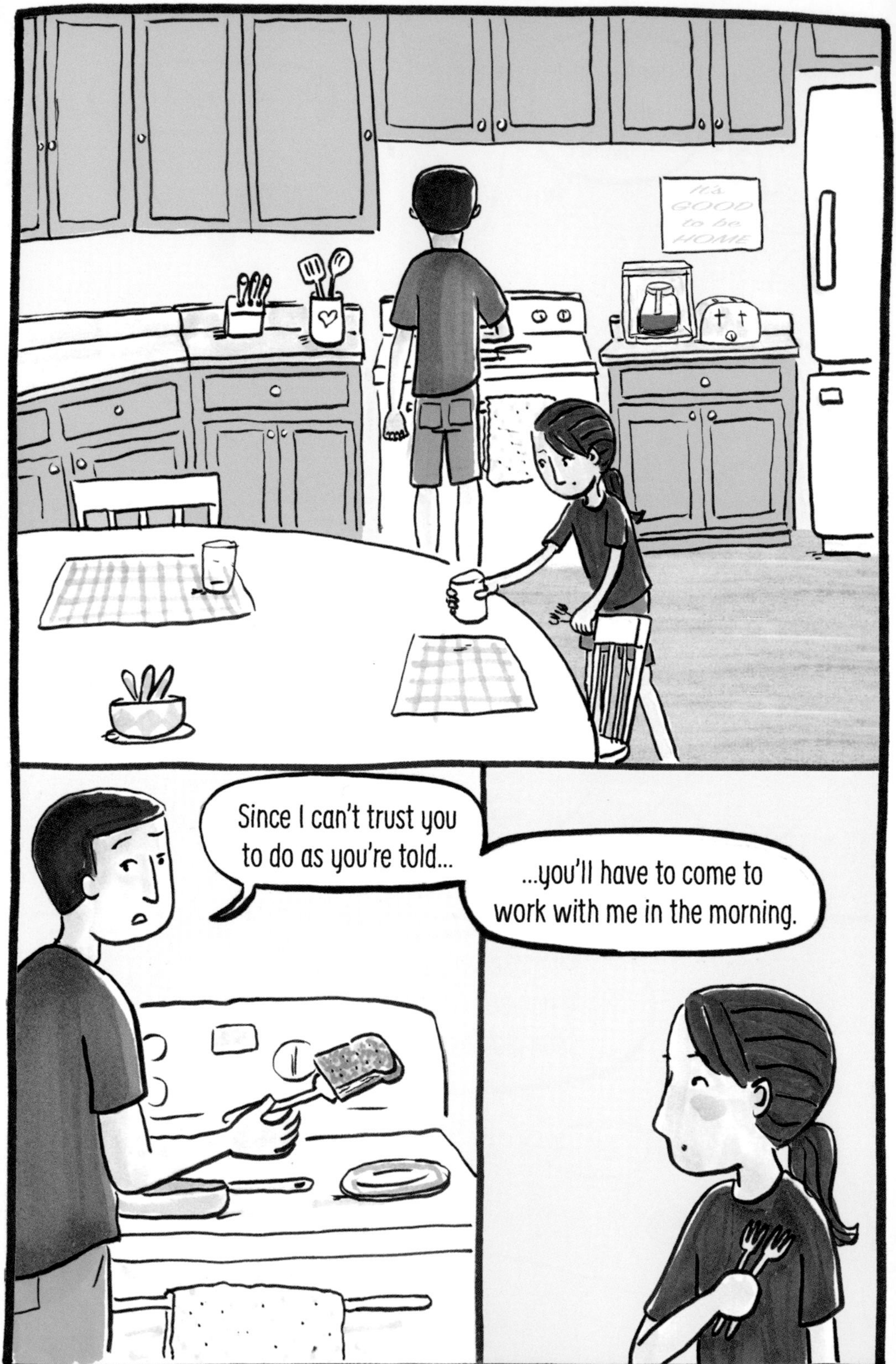
It's GOOD to be HOME
Since I can't trust you to do as you're told...
...you'll have to come to work with me in the morning.

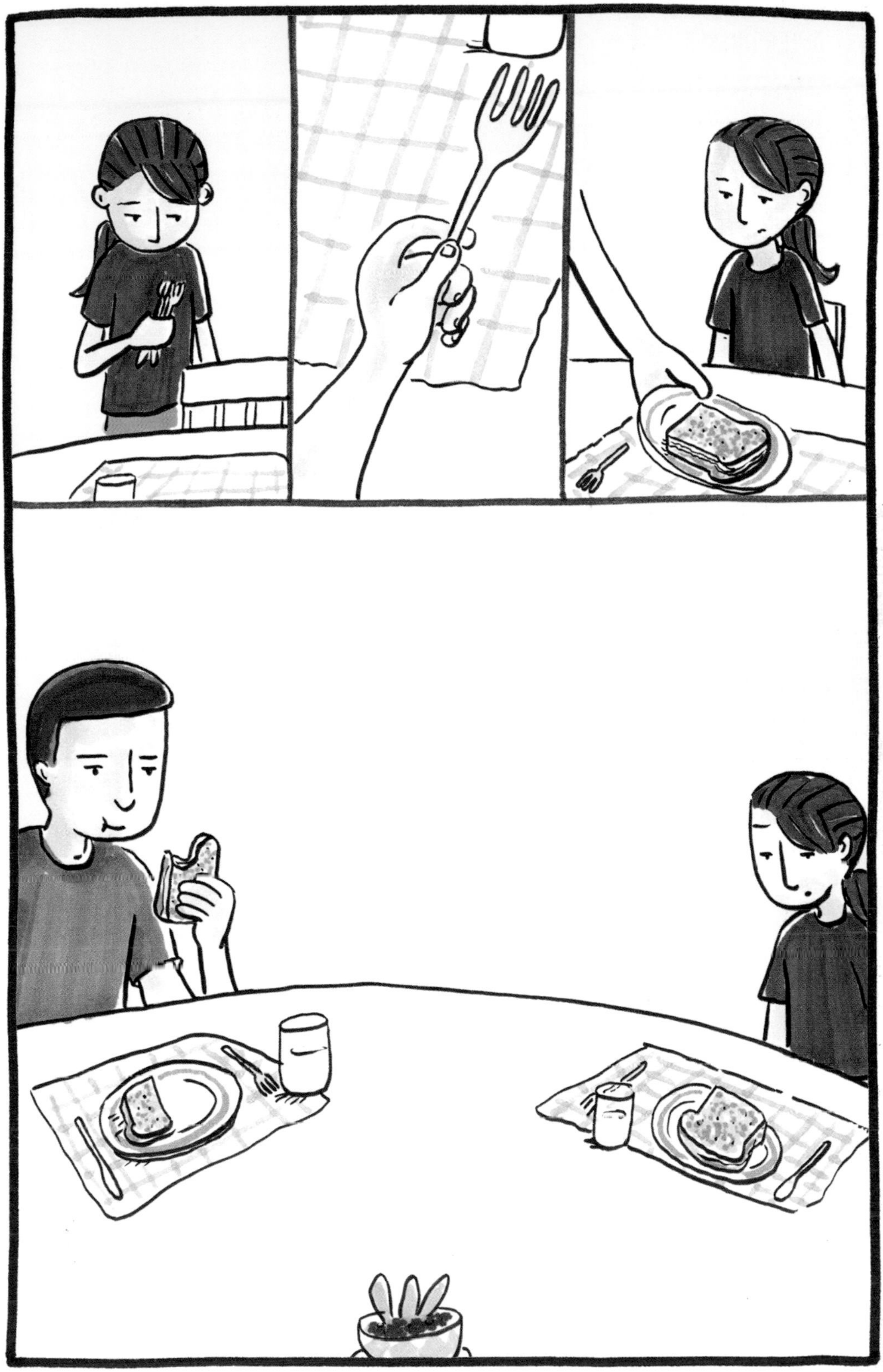

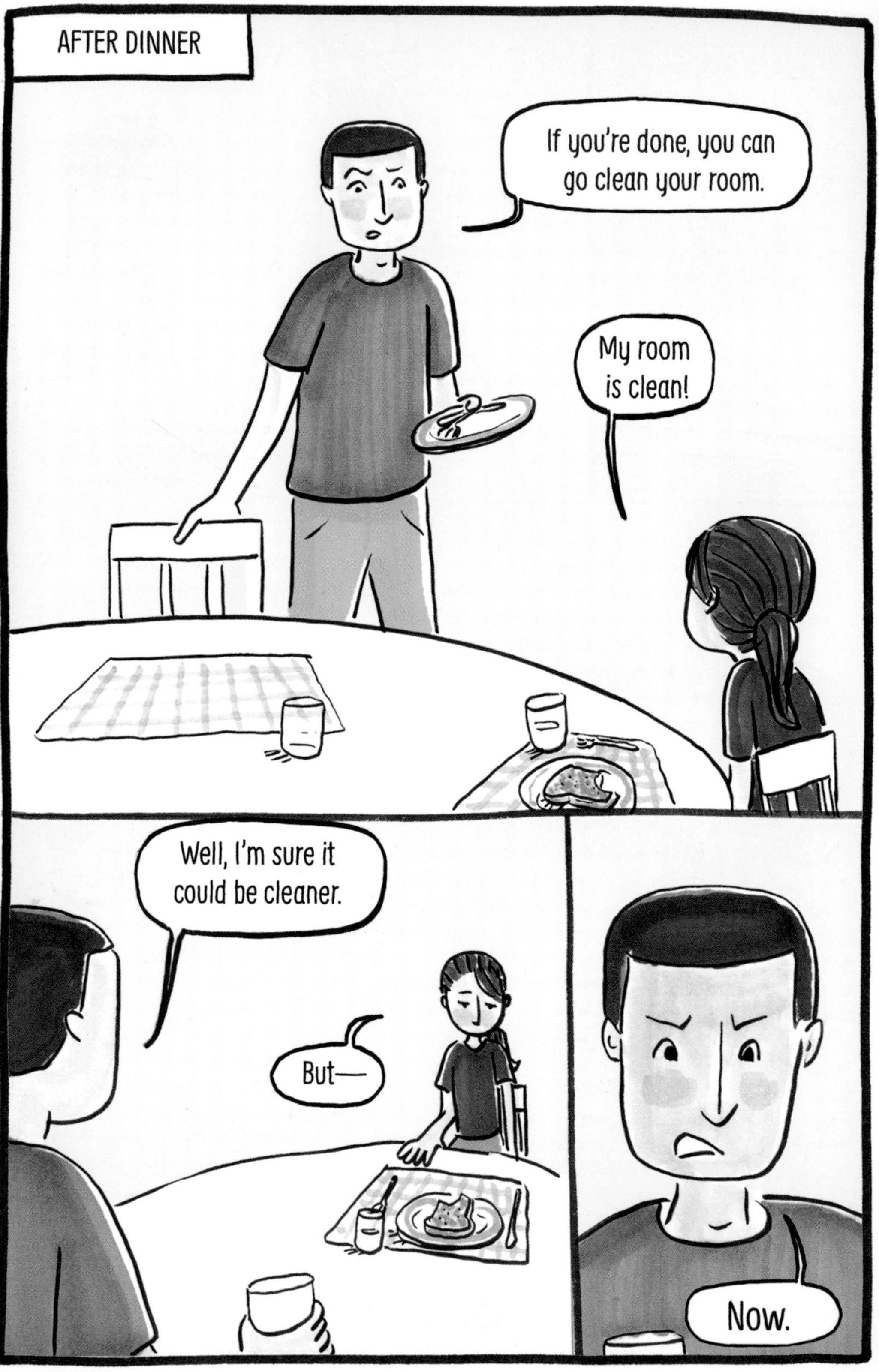
AFTER DINNER
If you're done, you can go clean your room.
My room is clean!
Well, I'm sure it could be cleaner.
But—
Now.

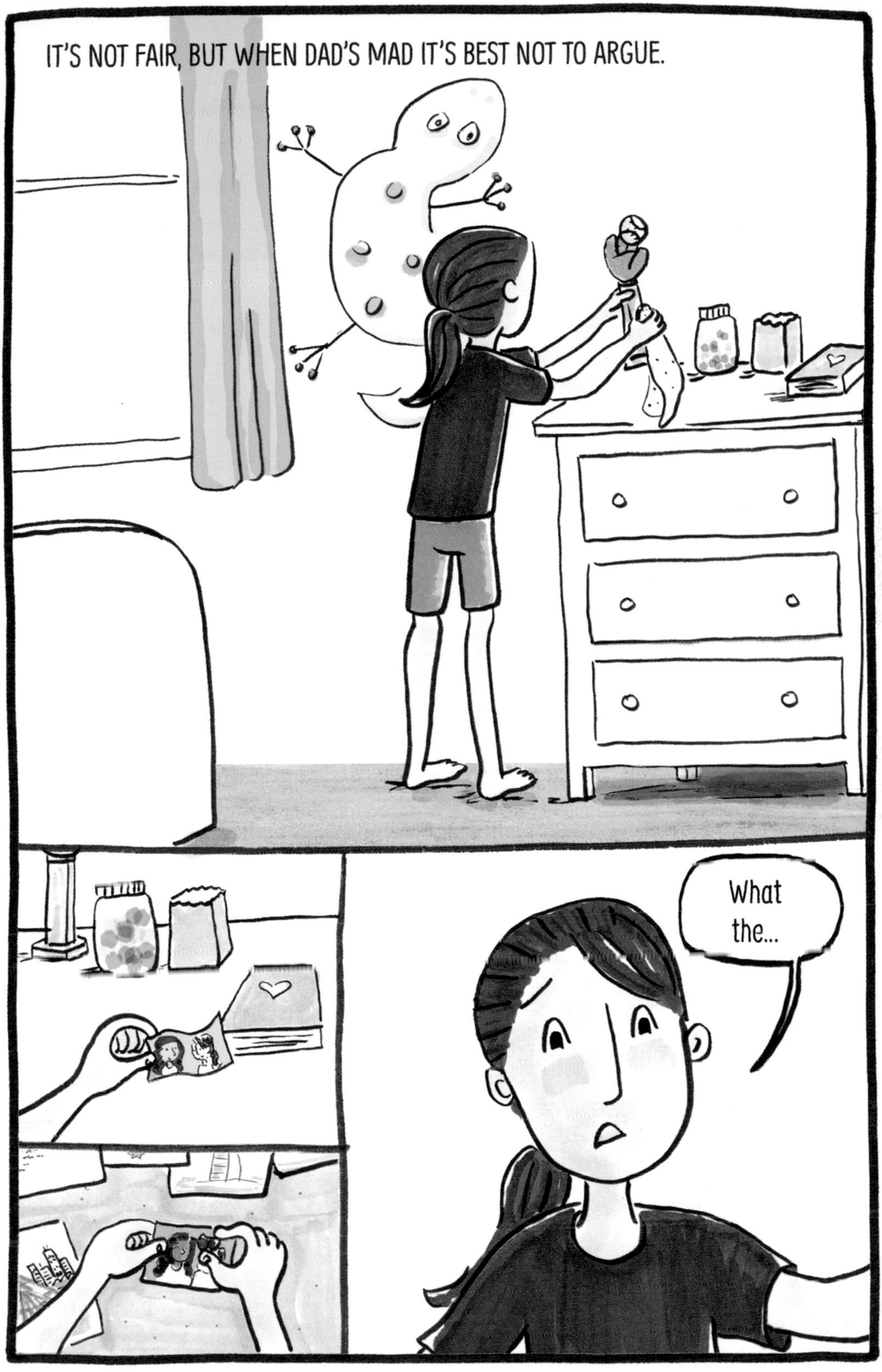
IT'S NOT FAIR, BUT WHEN DAD'S MAD IT'S BEST NOT TO ARGUE.
What the...

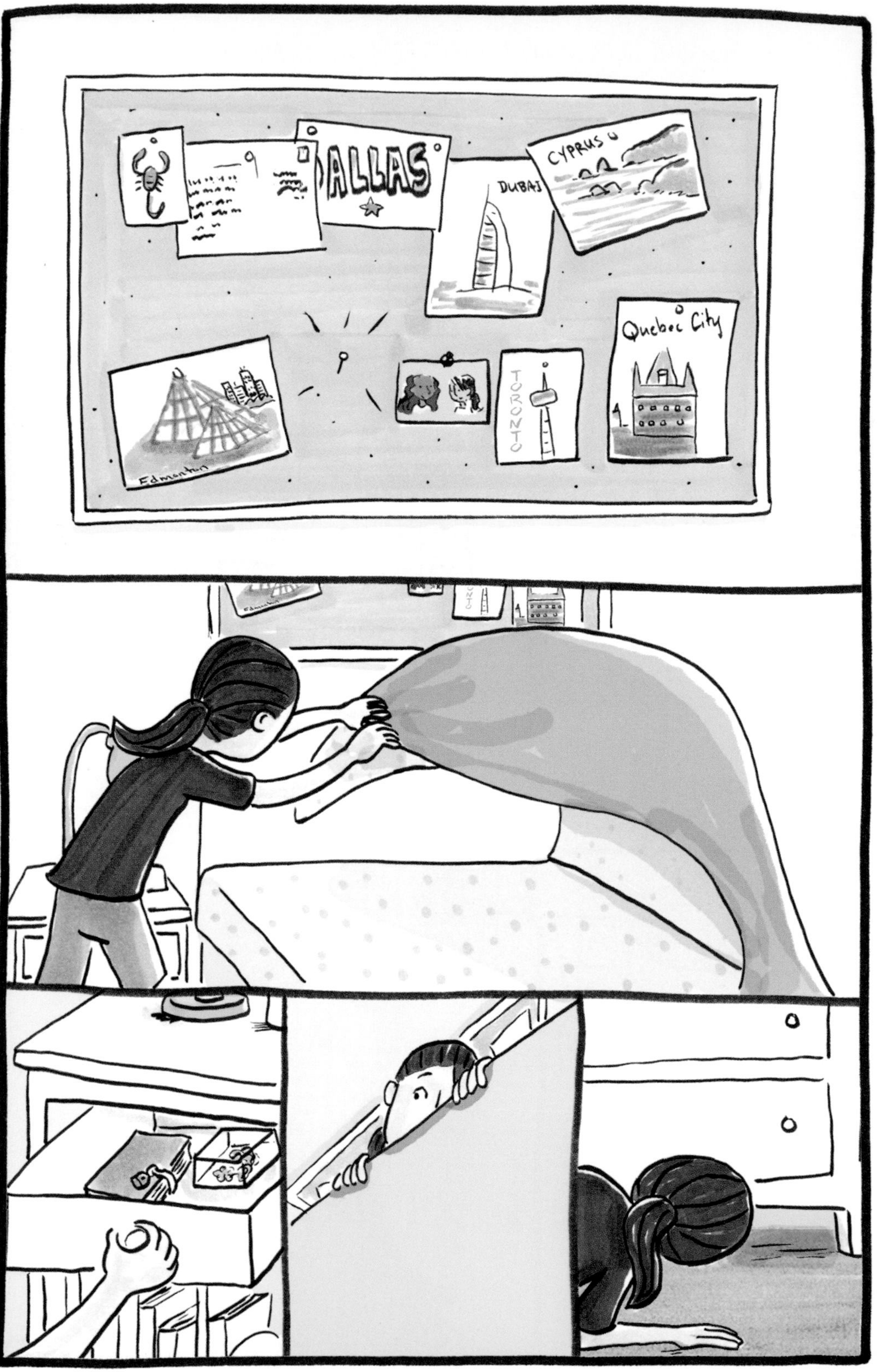
ALLAS
DUBAI
CYPRUS
Quebec City
Edmonton
TORONTO

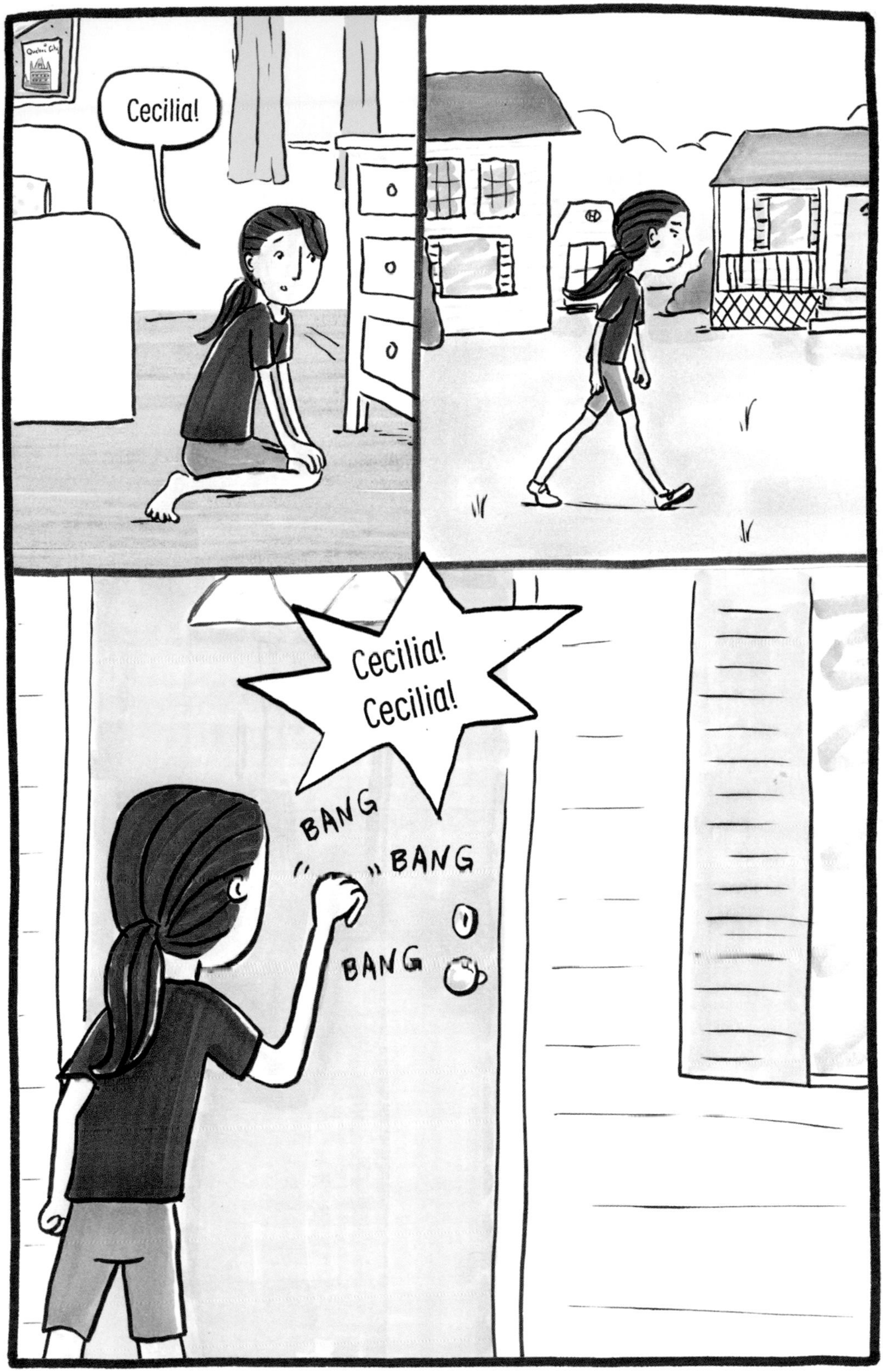
Cecilia!
Cecilia!
Cecilia!
BANG
BANG
BANG

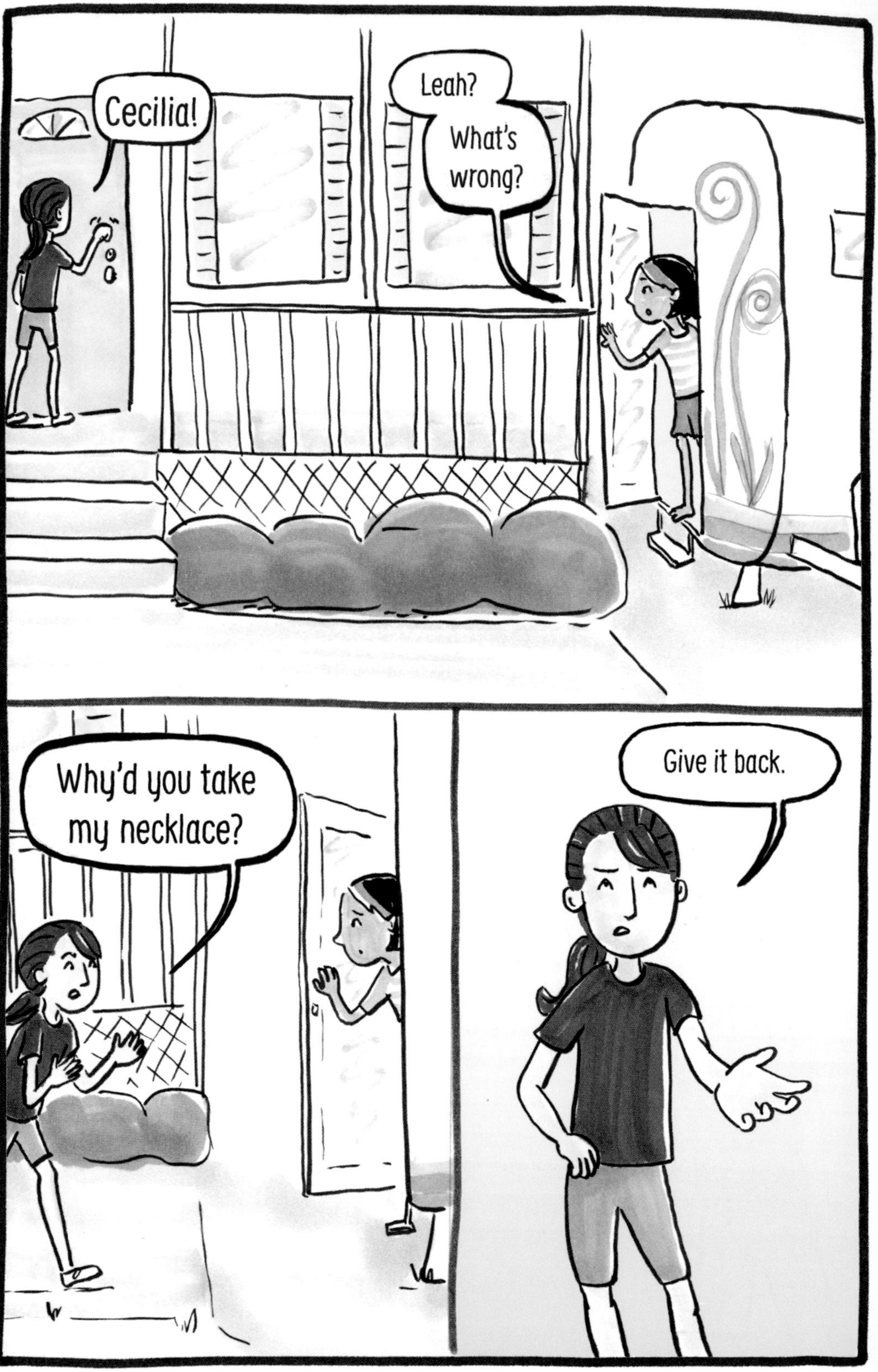
Cecilia!
Leah?
What's wrong?
Why'd you take my necklace?
Give it back.

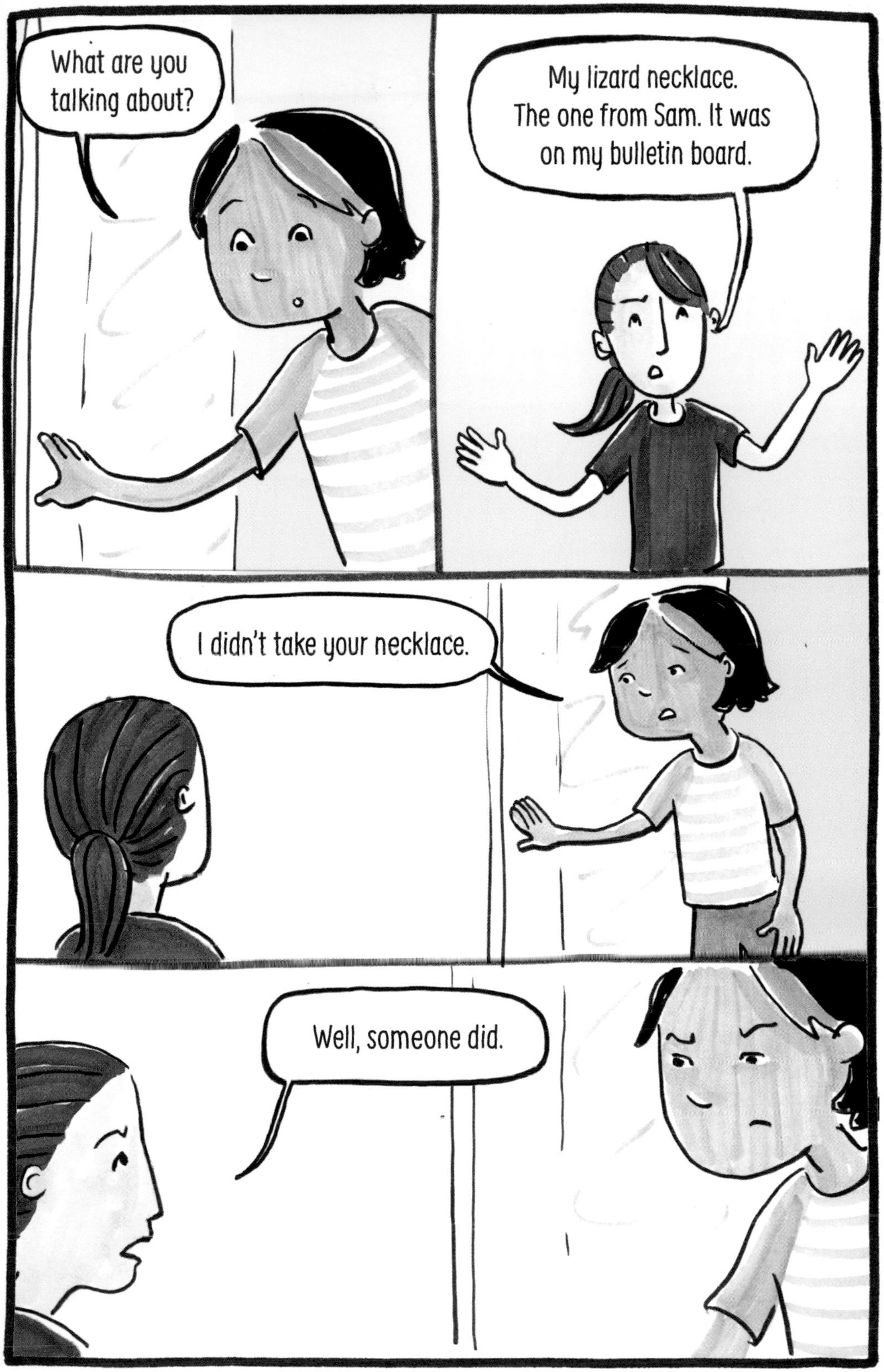
What are you talking about?
My lizard necklace. The one from Sam. It was on my bulletin board.
I didn't take your necklace.
Well, someone did.

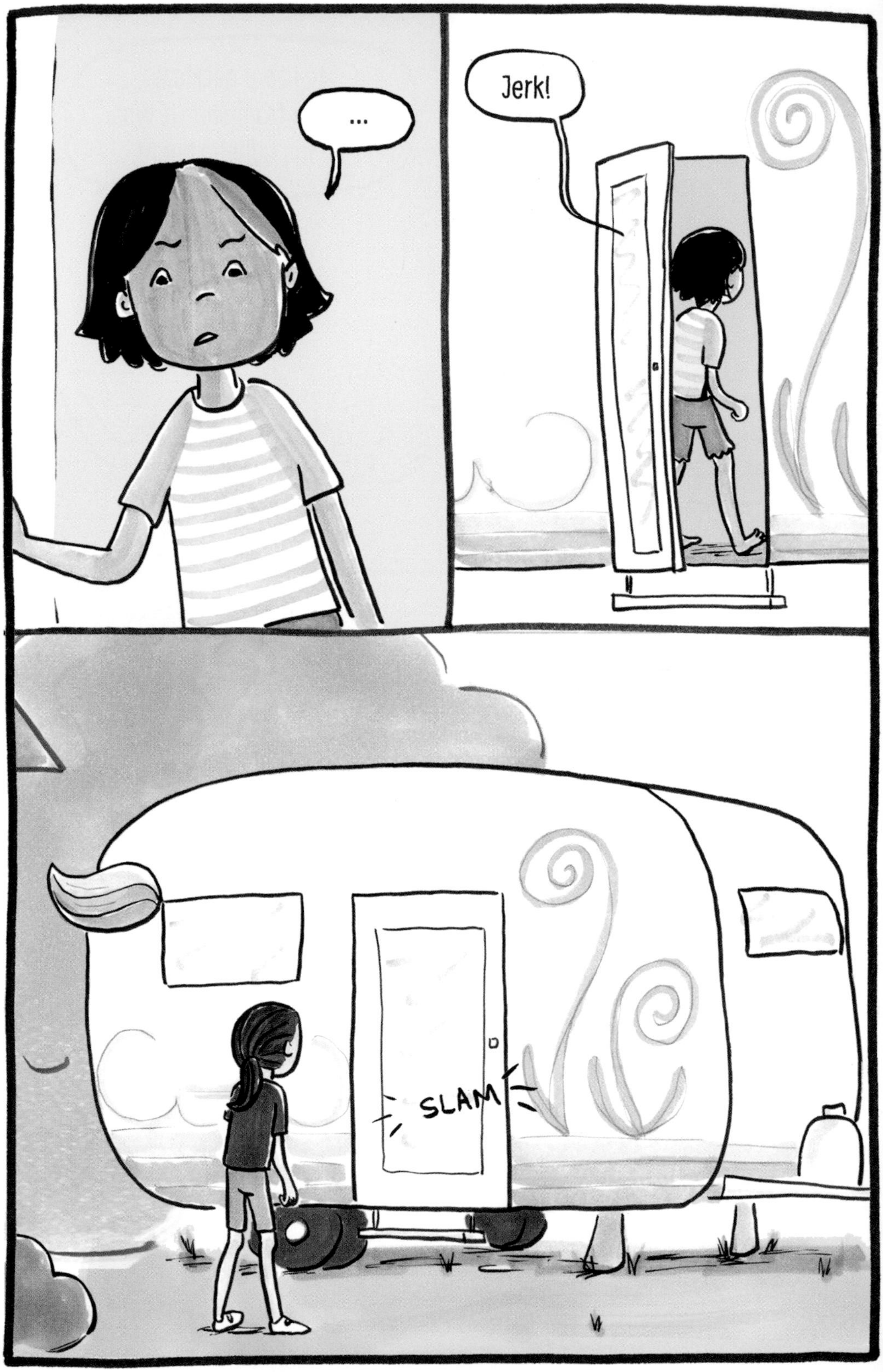
...
Jerk!
SLAM

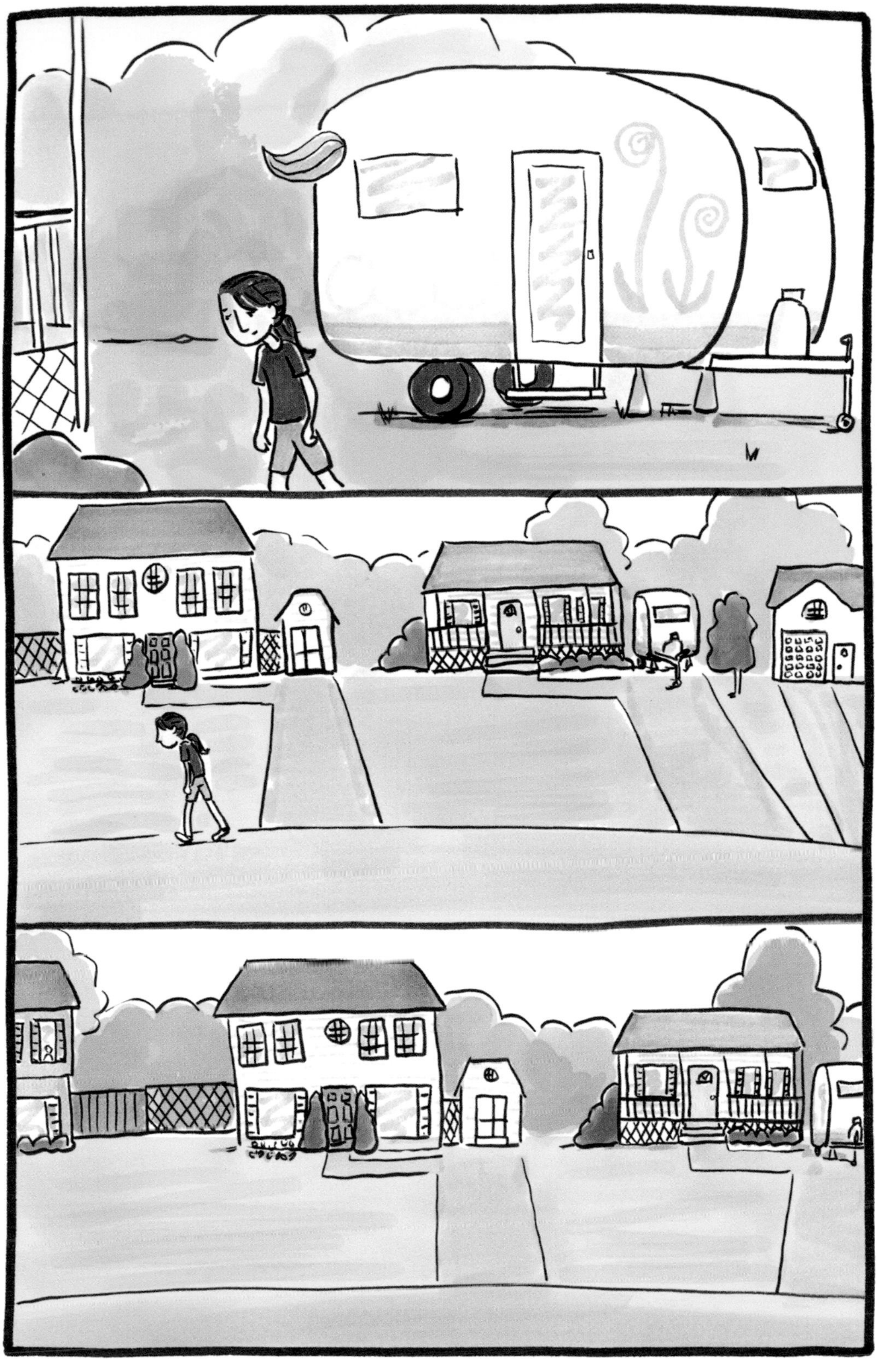

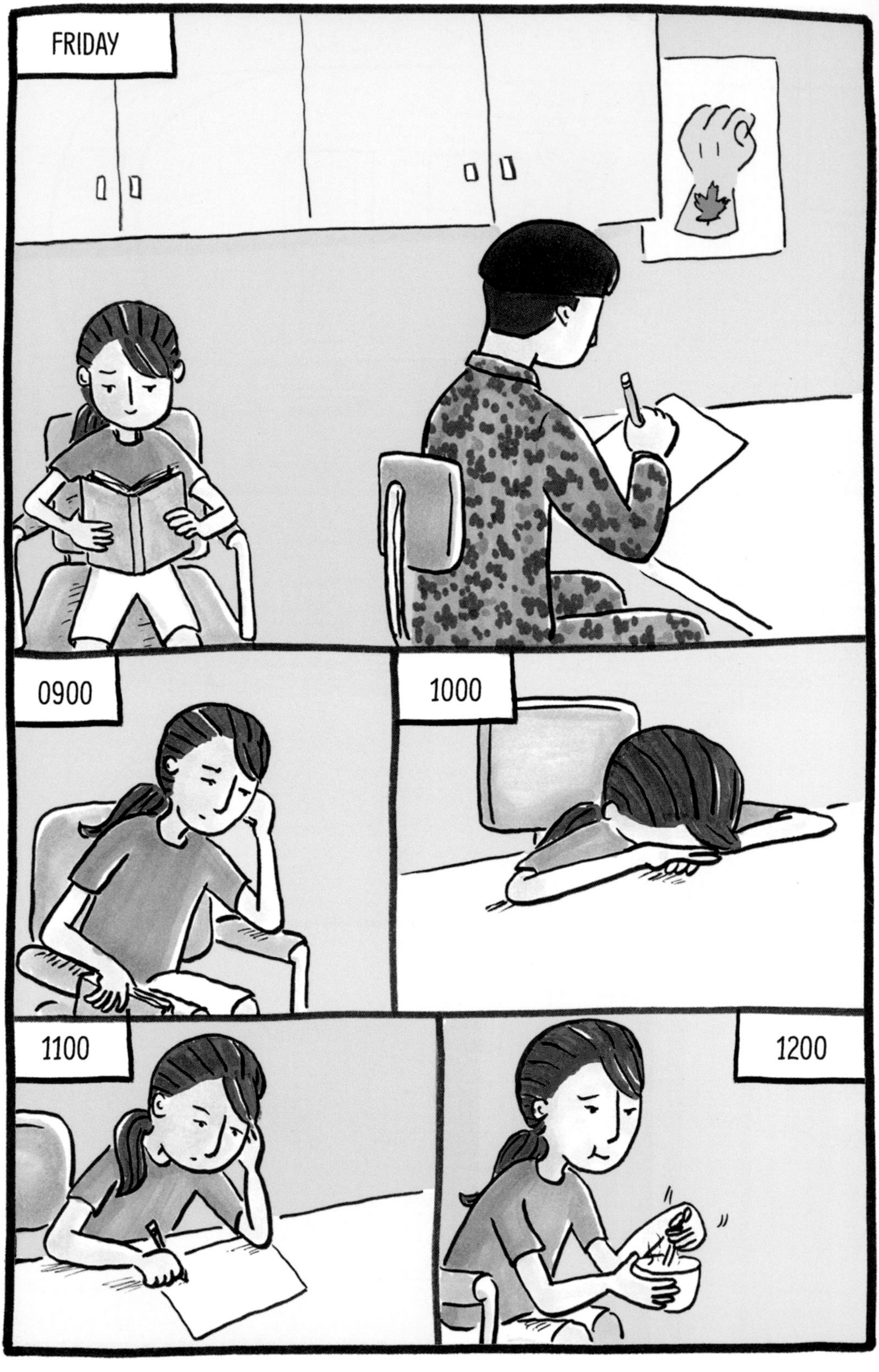
FRIDAY
0900
1000
1100
1200

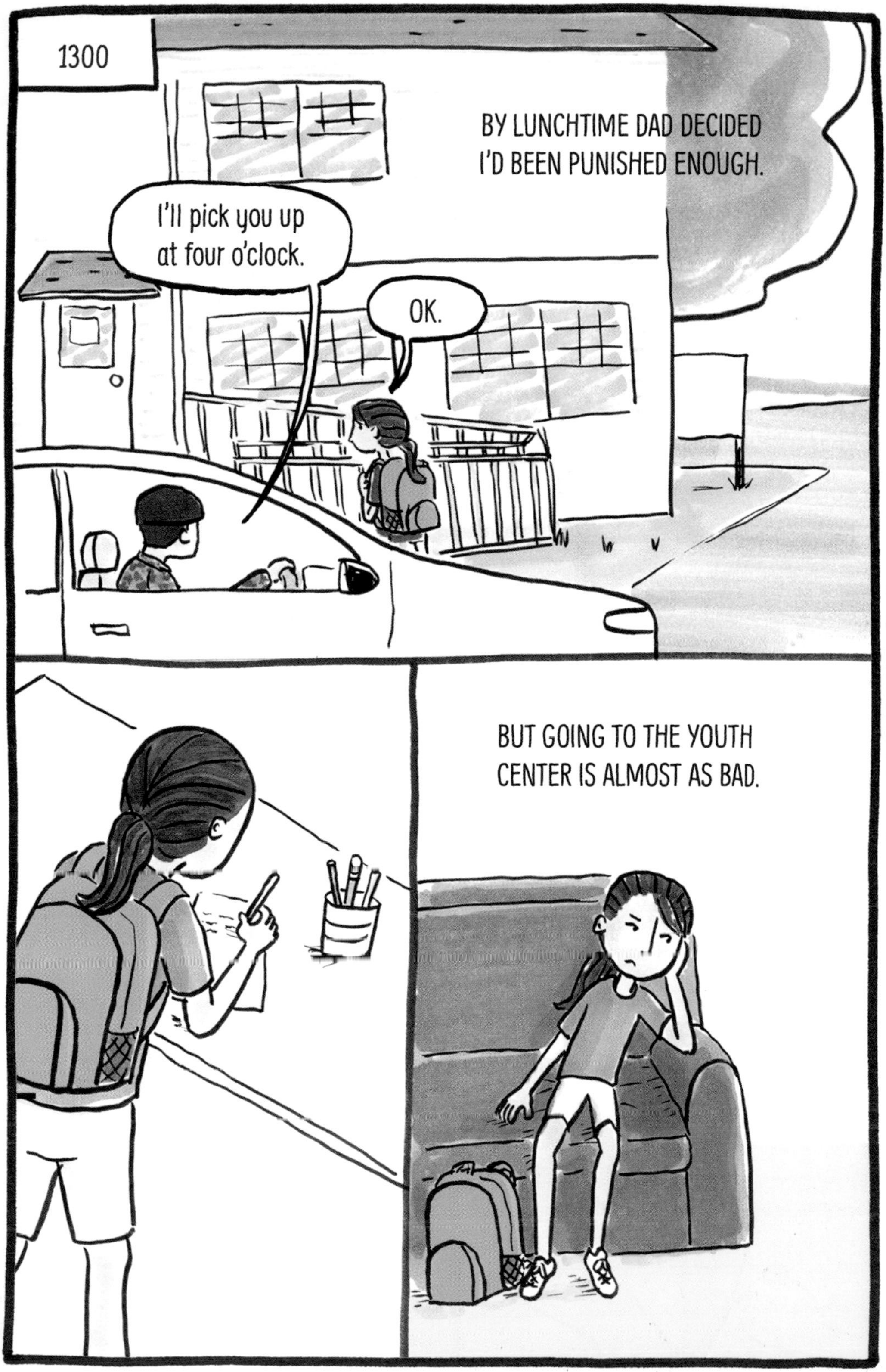
1300
BY LUNCHTIME DAD DECIDED I'D BEEN PUNISHED ENOUGH.
I'll pick you up at four o'clock.
OK.
BUT GOING TO THE YOUTH CENTER IS ALMOST AS BAD.

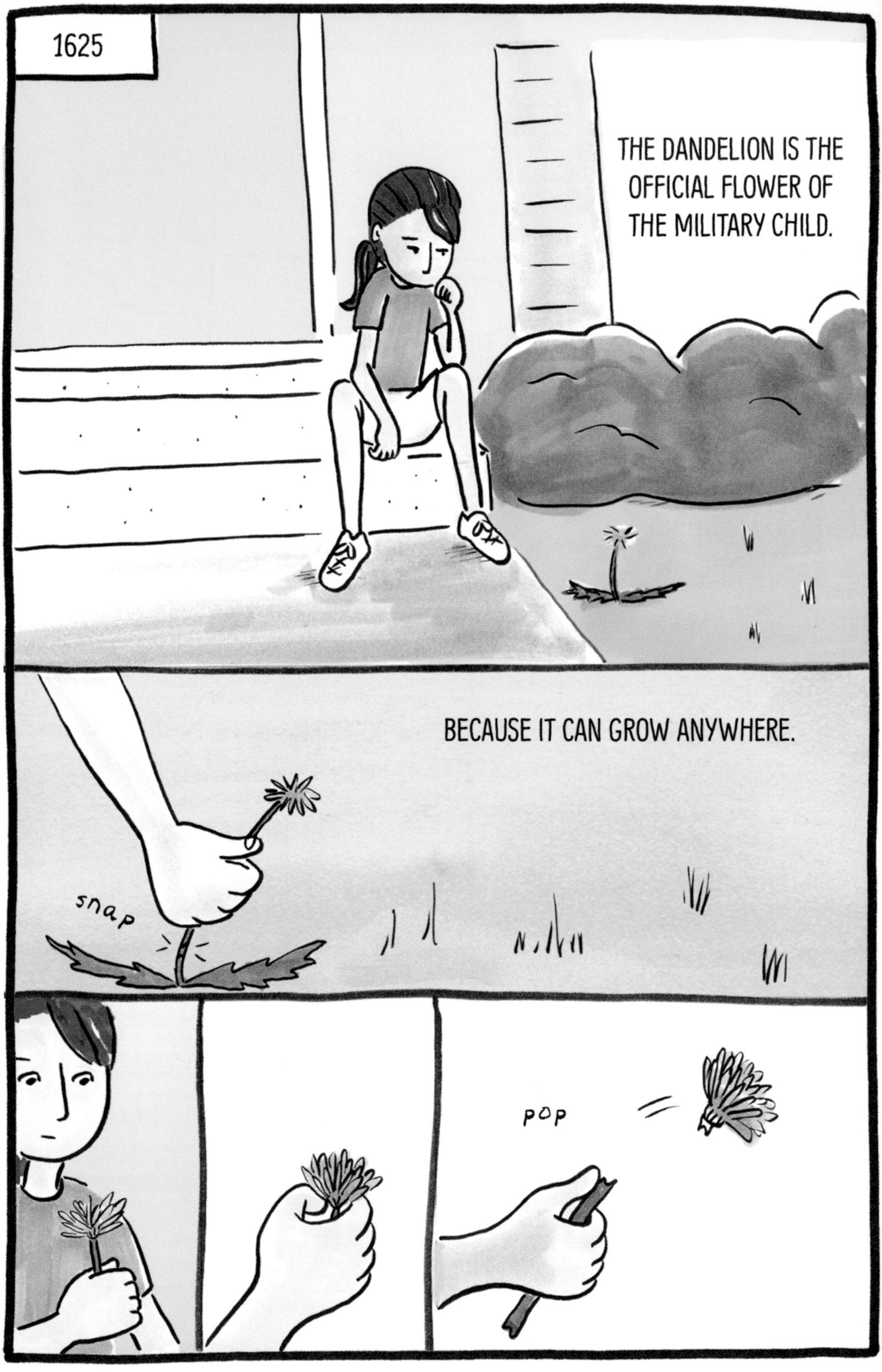
1625
THE DANDELION IS THE OFFICIAL FLOWER OF THE MILITARY CHILD.
BECAUSE IT CAN GROW ANYWHERE.
snap
pop

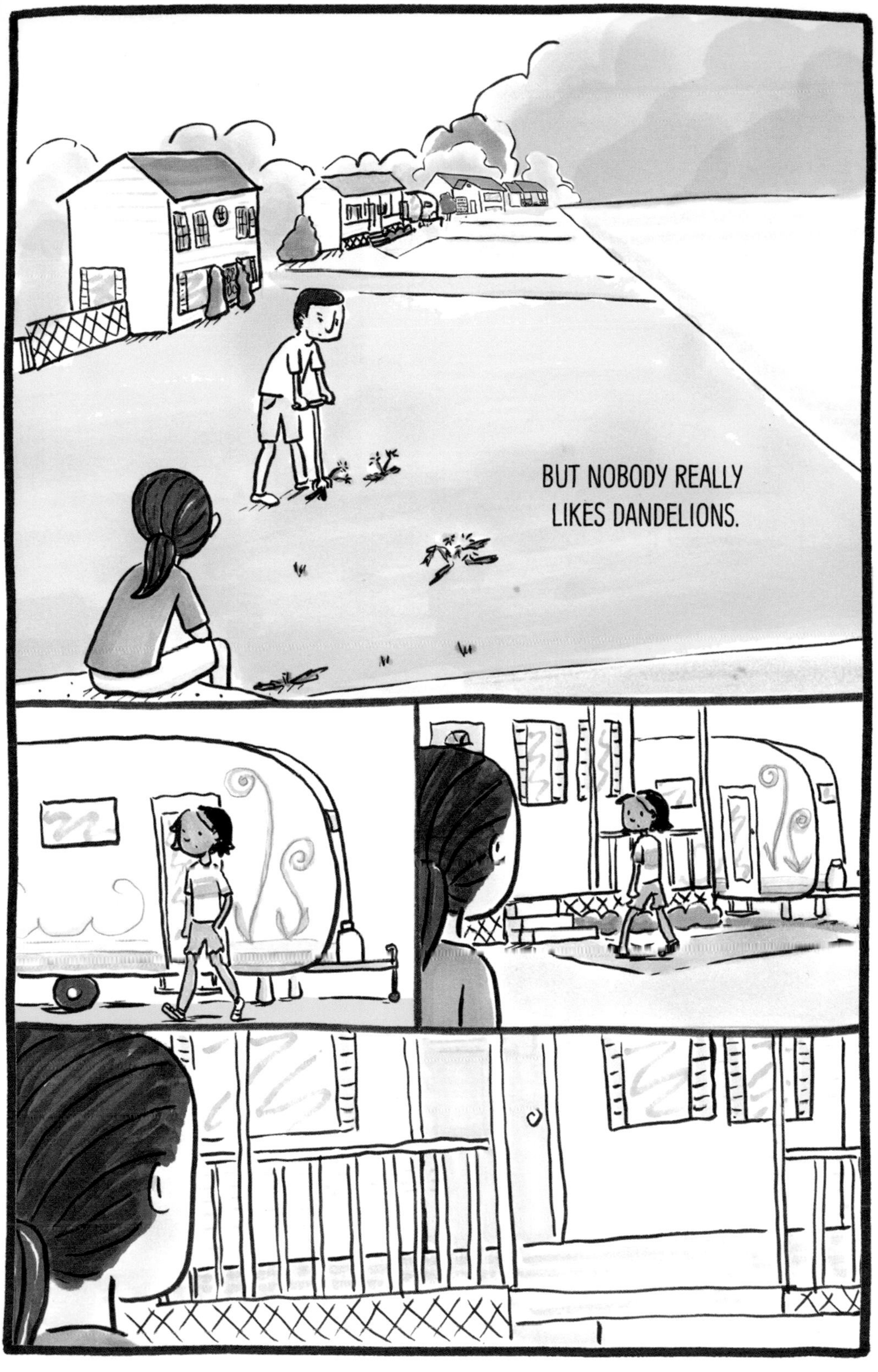
BUT NOBODY REALLY LIKES DANDELIONS.

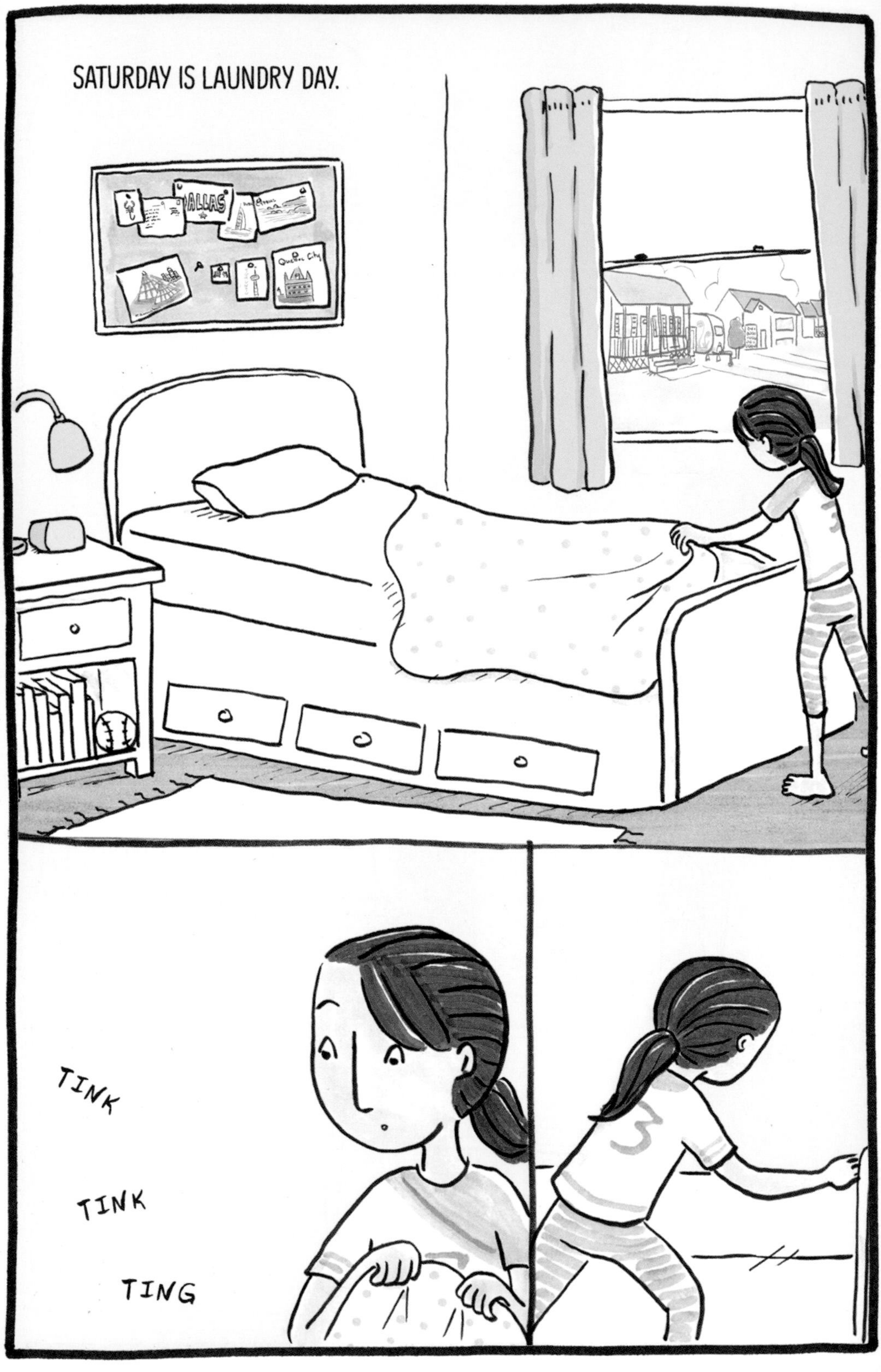
SATURDAY IS LAUNDRY DAY.
DALLAS
Quebec City
TINK
TINK
TING

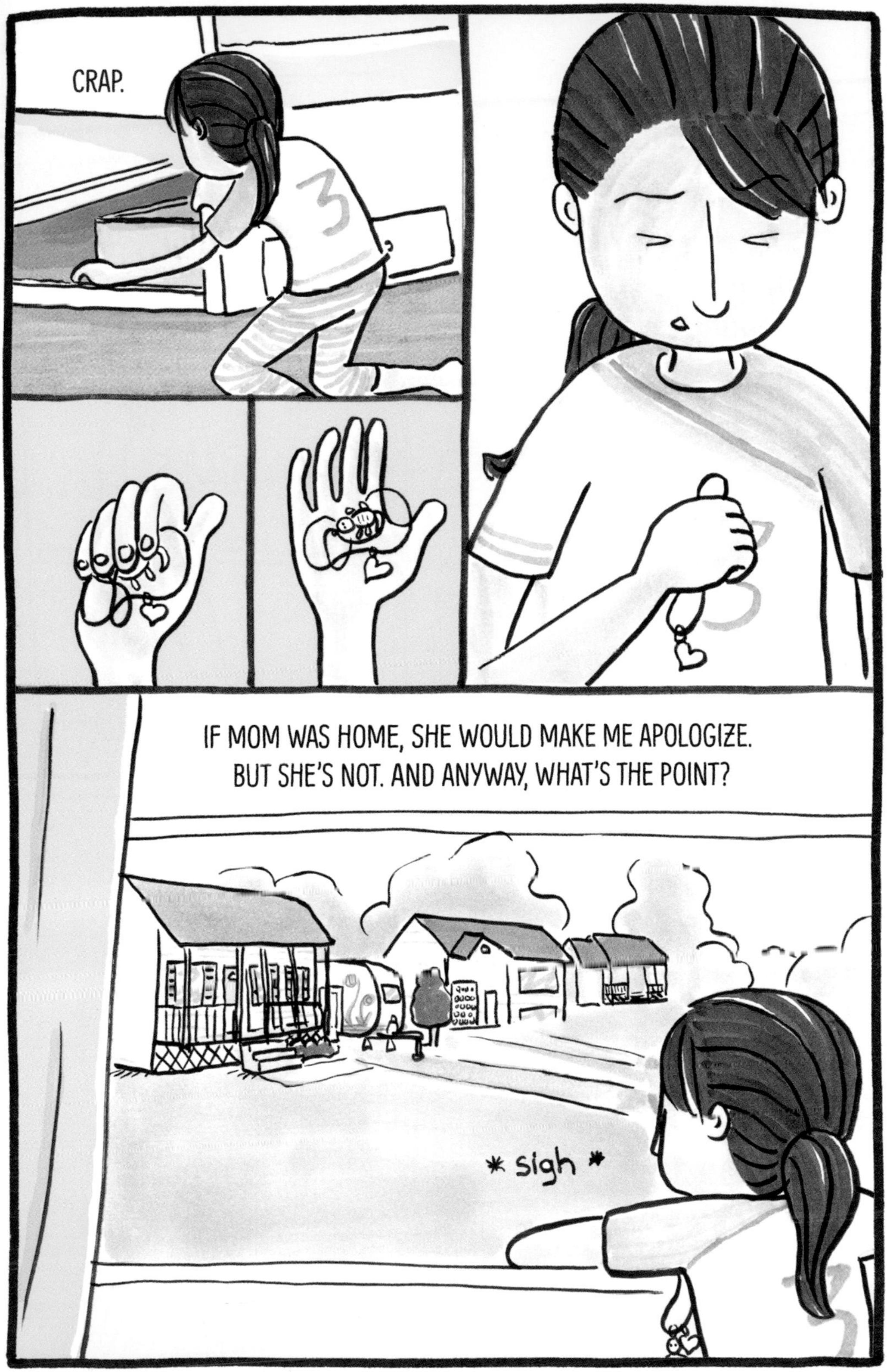
CRAP.
IF MOM WAS HOME, SHE WOULD MAKE ME APOLOGIZE.
BUT SHE'S NOT. AND ANYWAY, WHAT'S THE POINT?
* sigh *

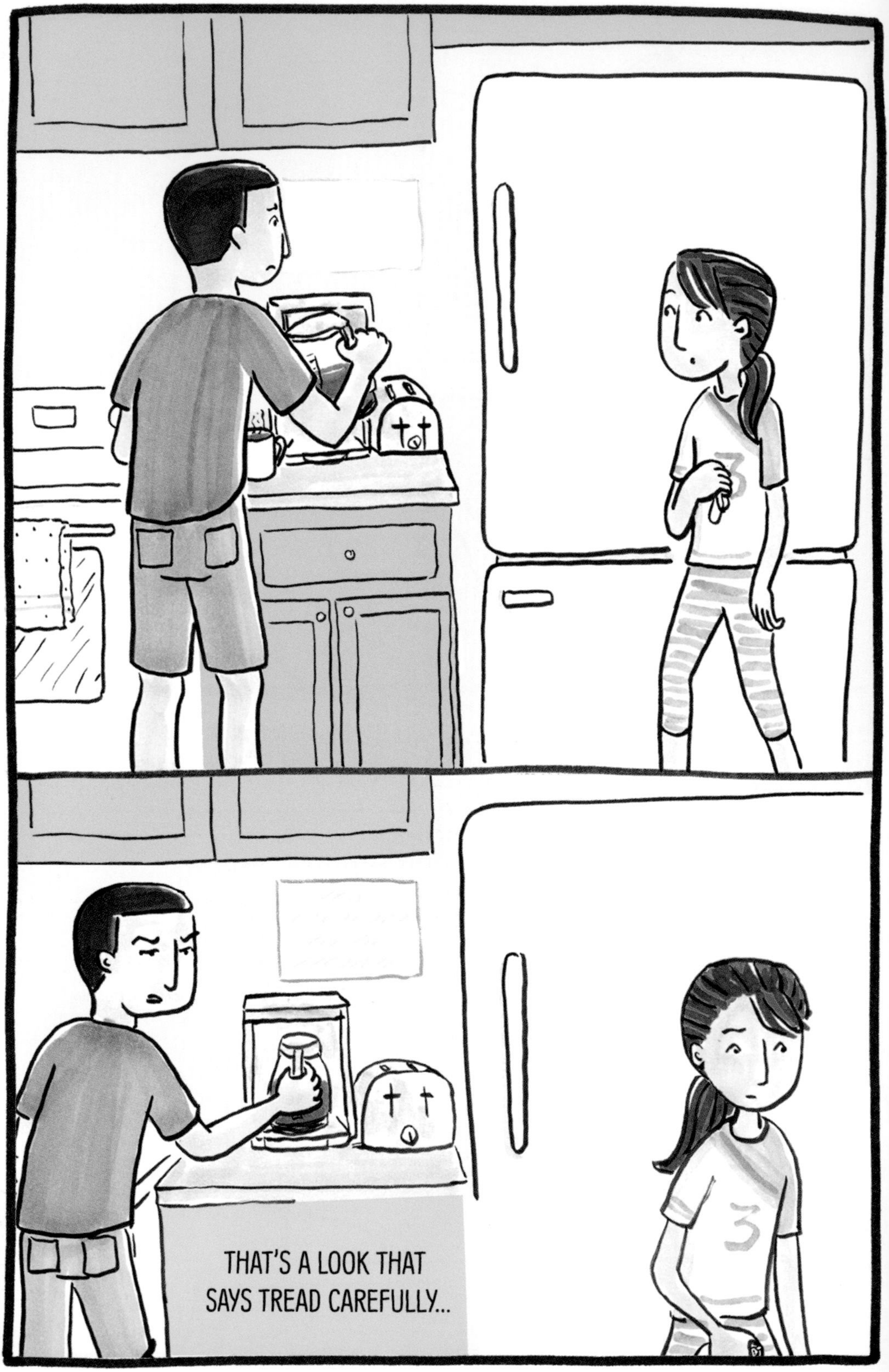
THAT'S A LOOK THAT
SAYS TREAD CAREFULLY...

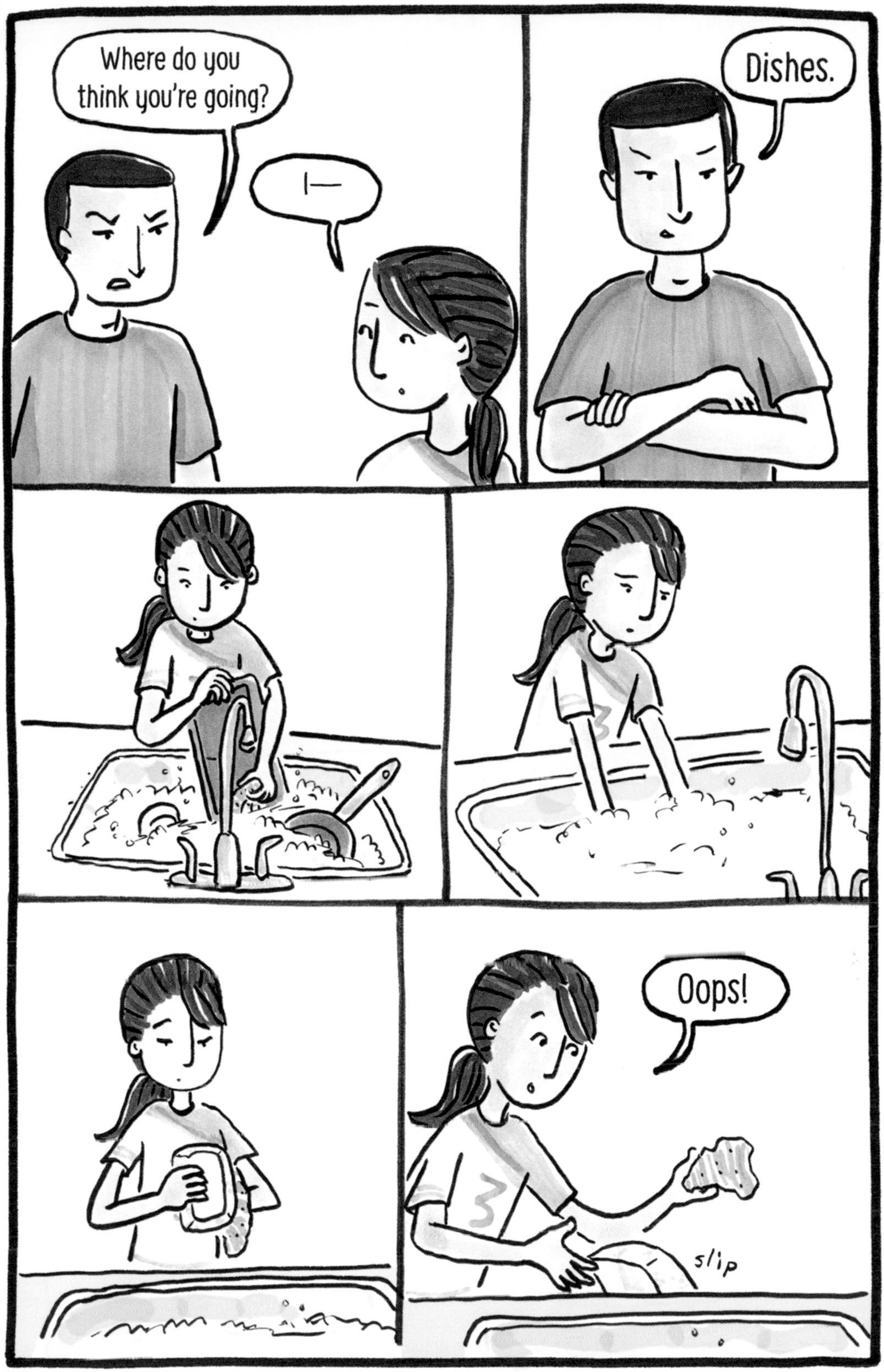
Where do you think you're going?
I—
Dishes.
Oops!
slip

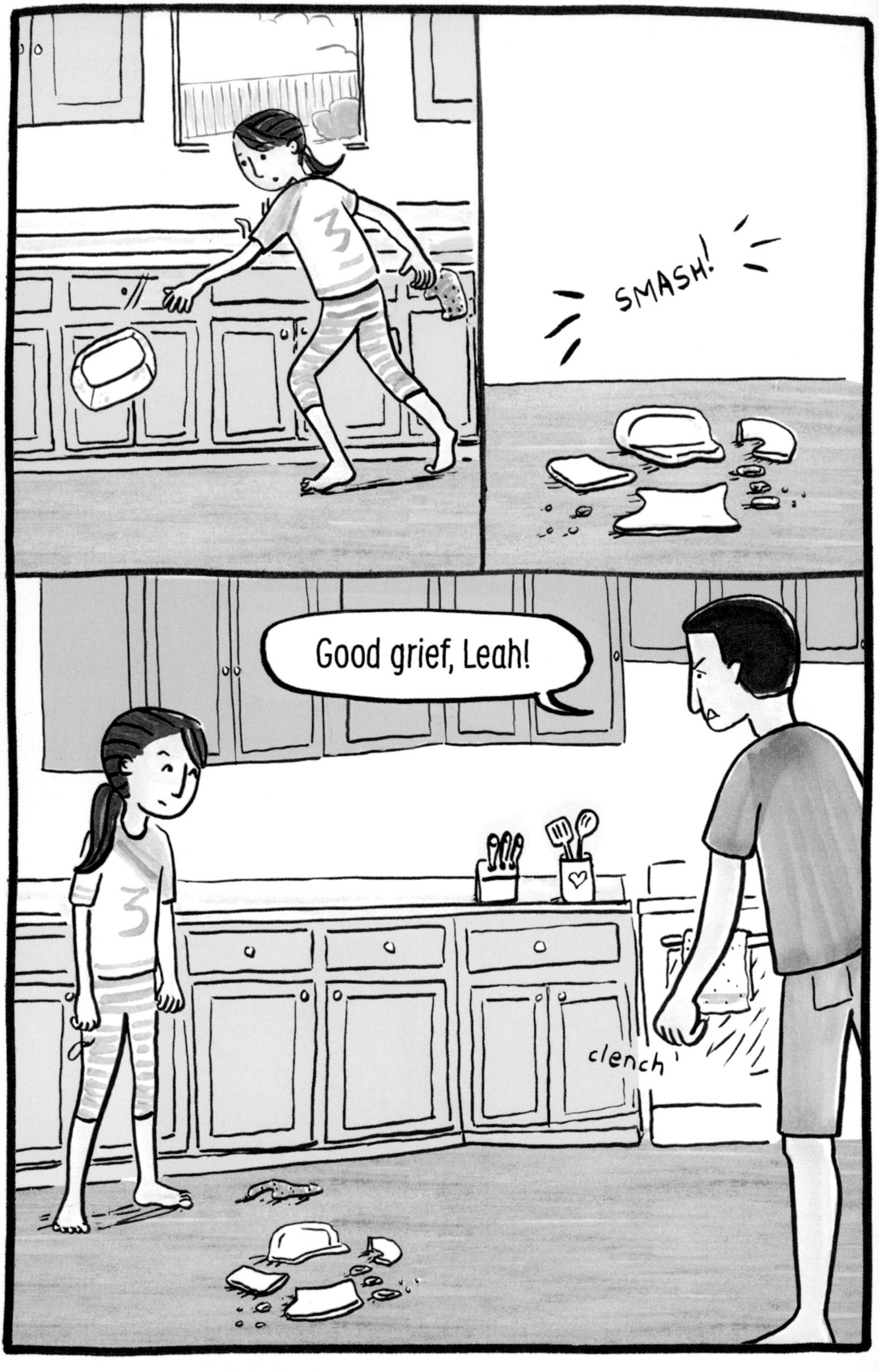
SMASH!
Good grief, Leah!
clench

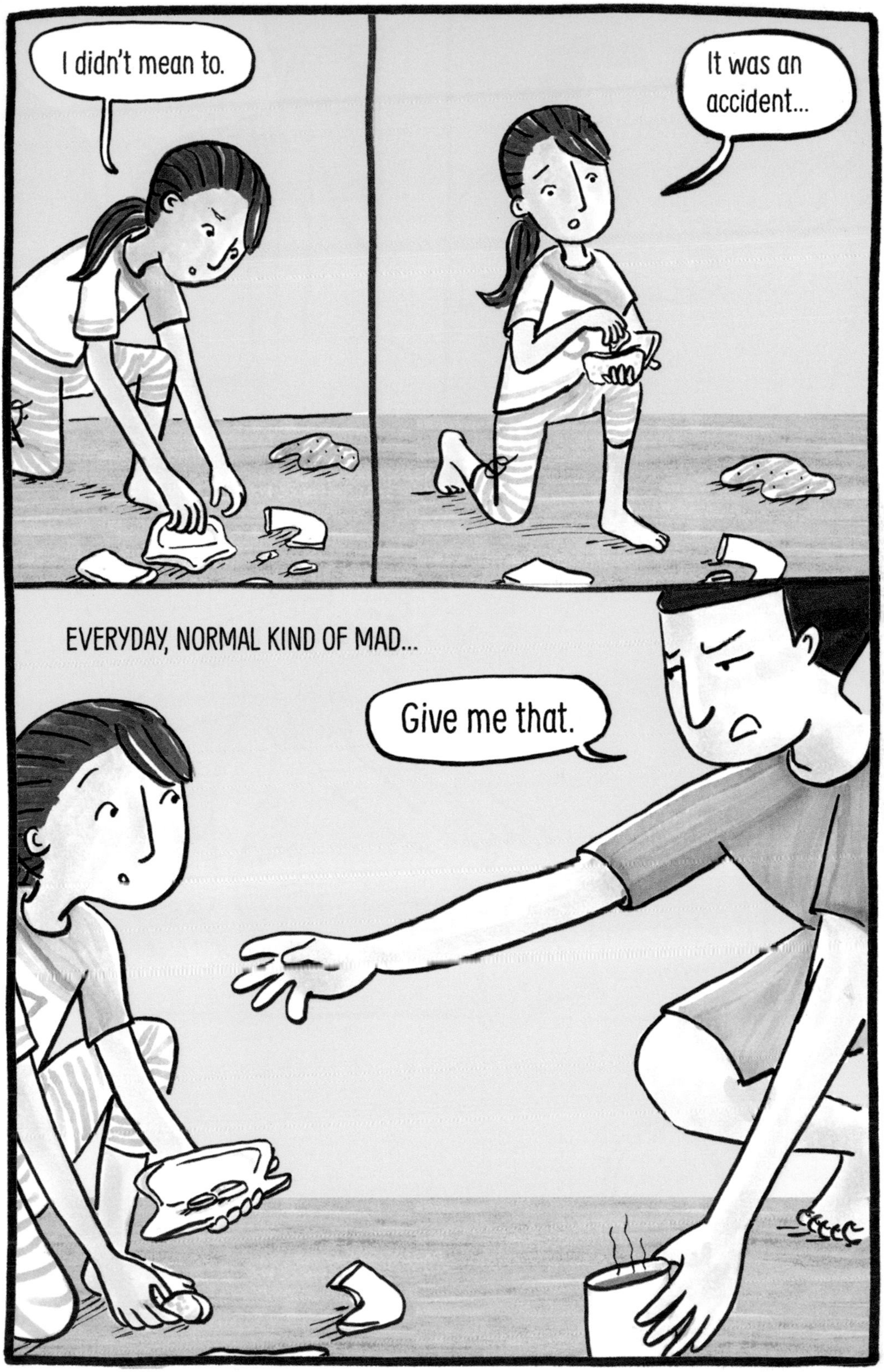
I didn't mean to.
It was an accident...
EVERYDAY, NORMAL KIND OF MAD...
Give me that.

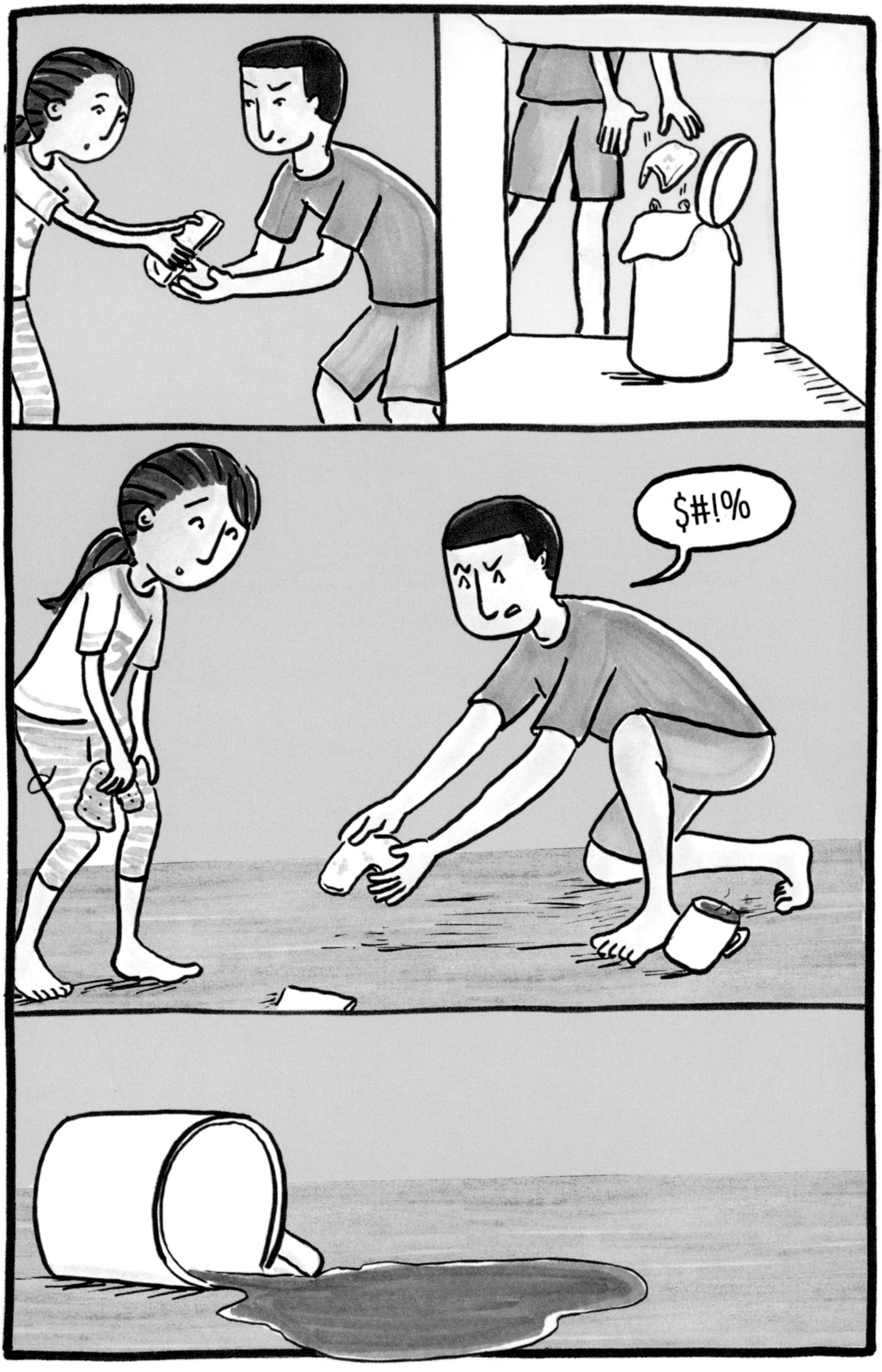
$#!%

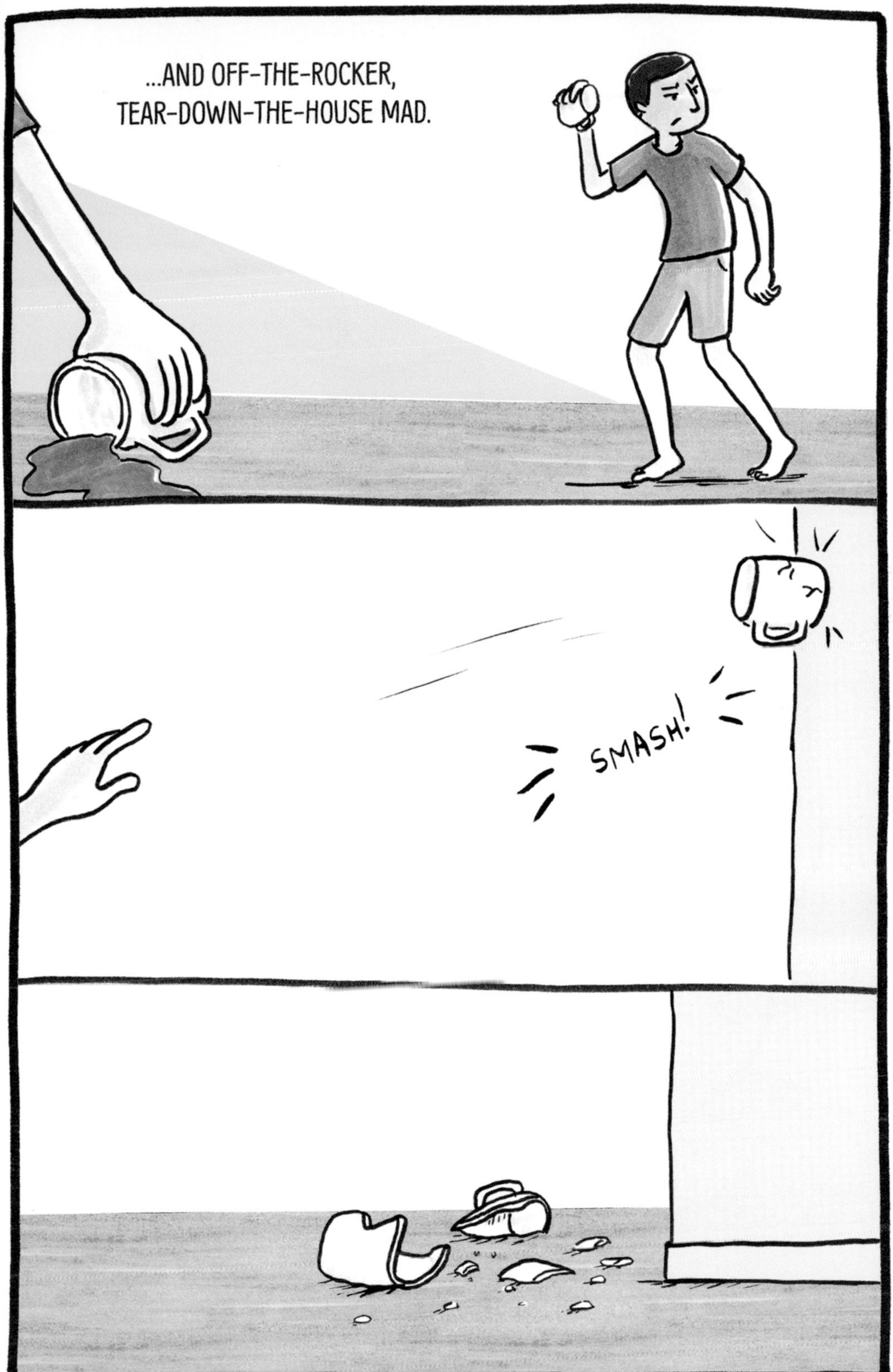
...AND OFF-THE-ROCKER, TEAR-DOWN-THE-HOUSE MAD.
SMASH!

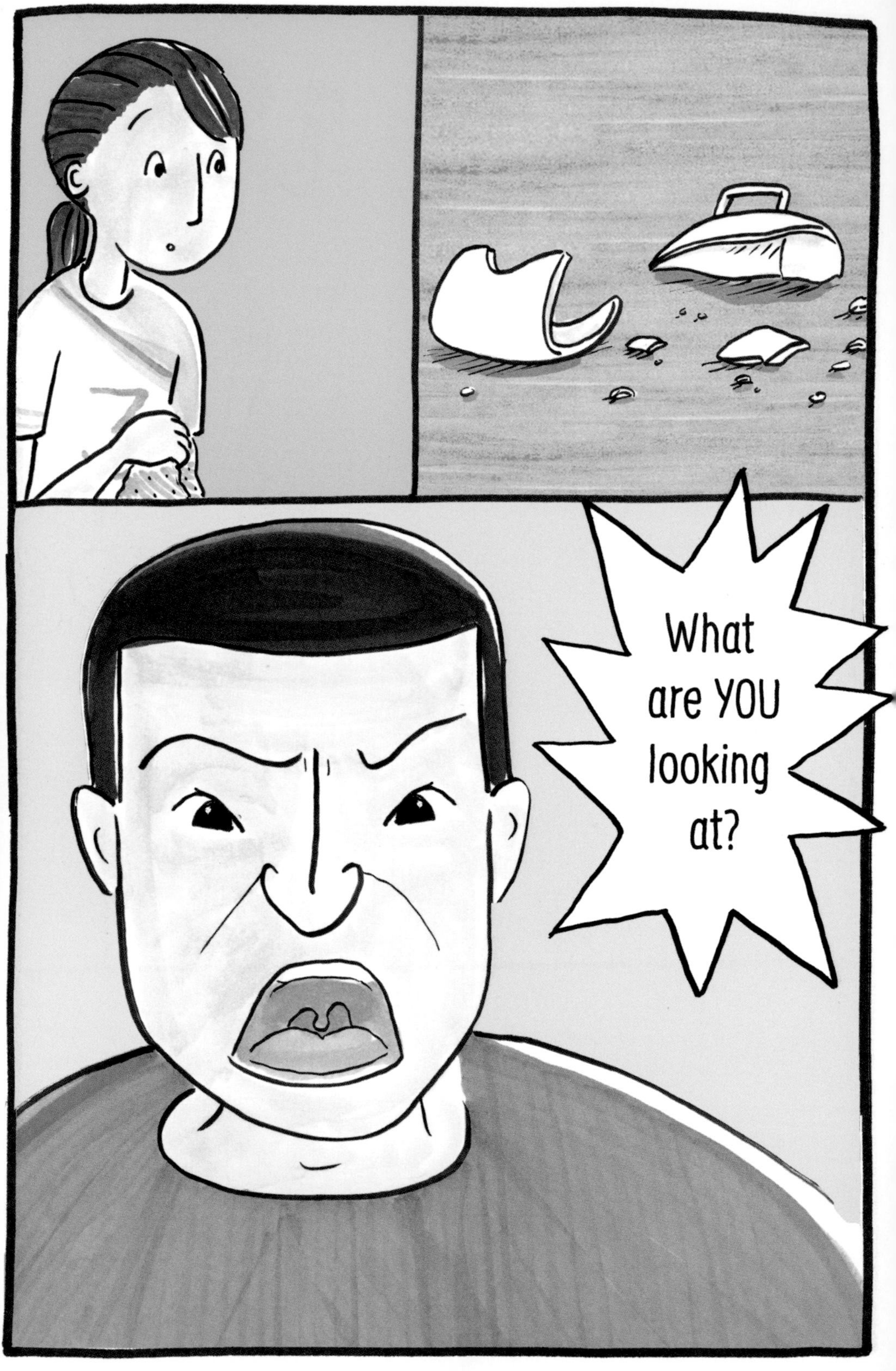
What are YOU looking at?

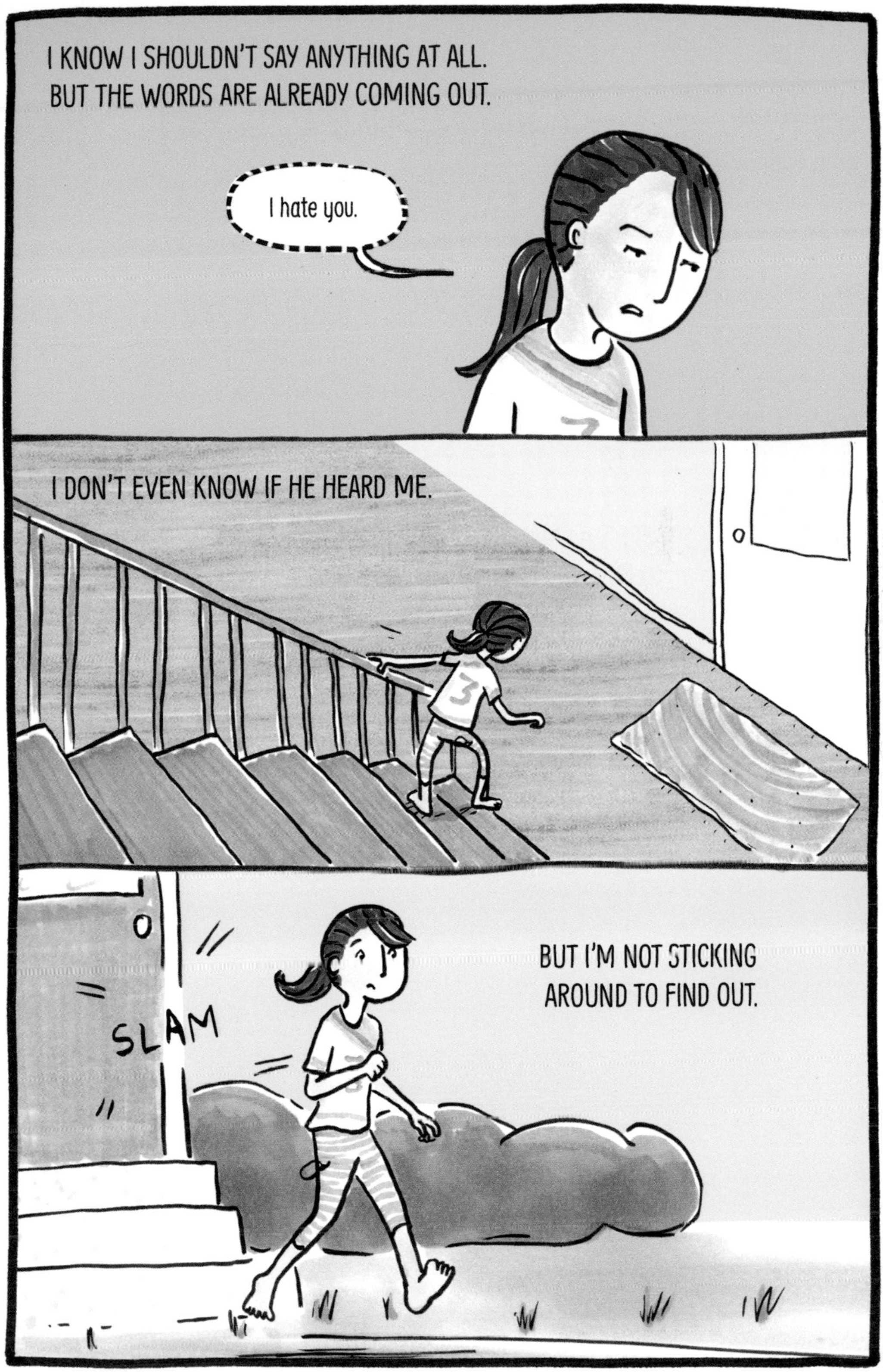
I KNOW I SHOULDN'T SAY ANYTHING AT ALL.
BUT THE WORDS ARE ALREADY COMING OUT.
I hate you.
I DON'T EVEN KNOW IF HE HEARD ME.
SLAM
BUT I'M NOT STICKING
AROUND TO FIND OUT.

THERE'S A SMALL PART OF ME THAT WANTS
TO RUN STRAIGHT TO THAT OLD BRIDGE...

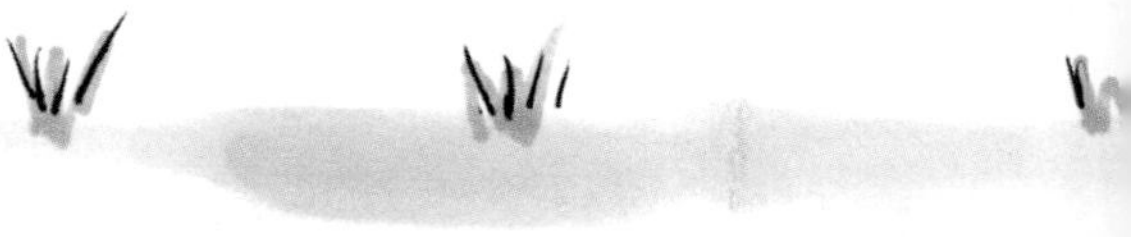

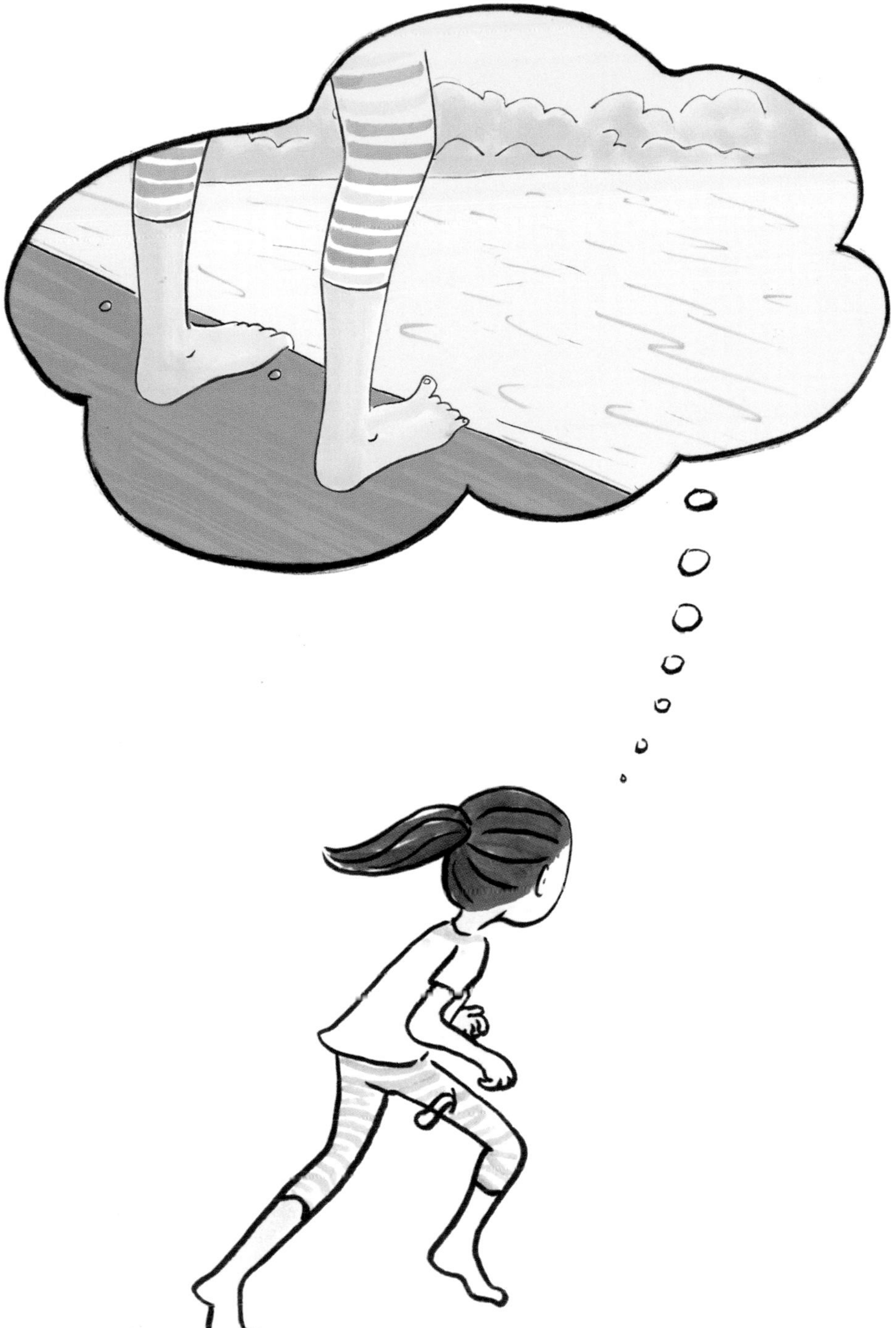

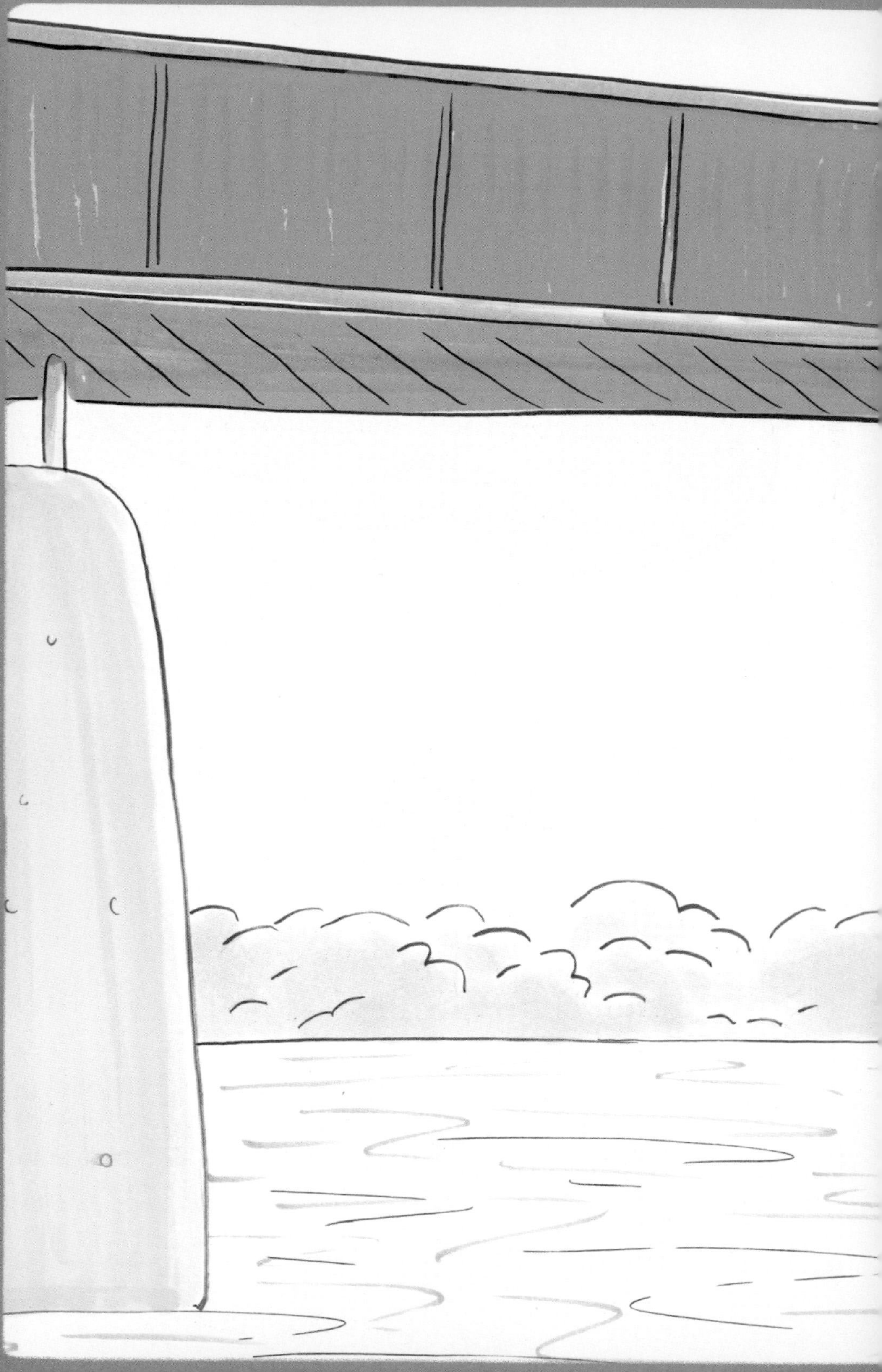

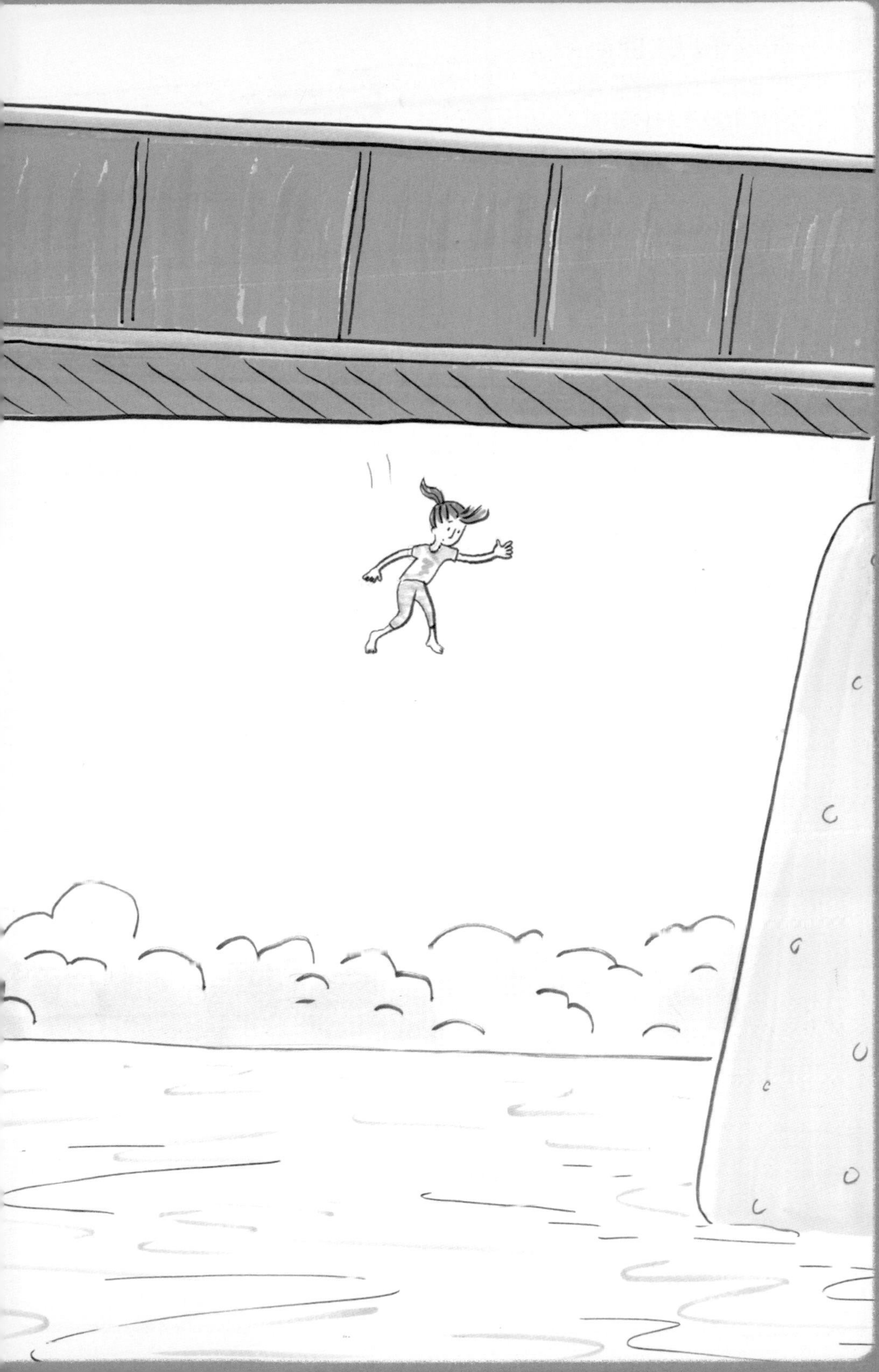

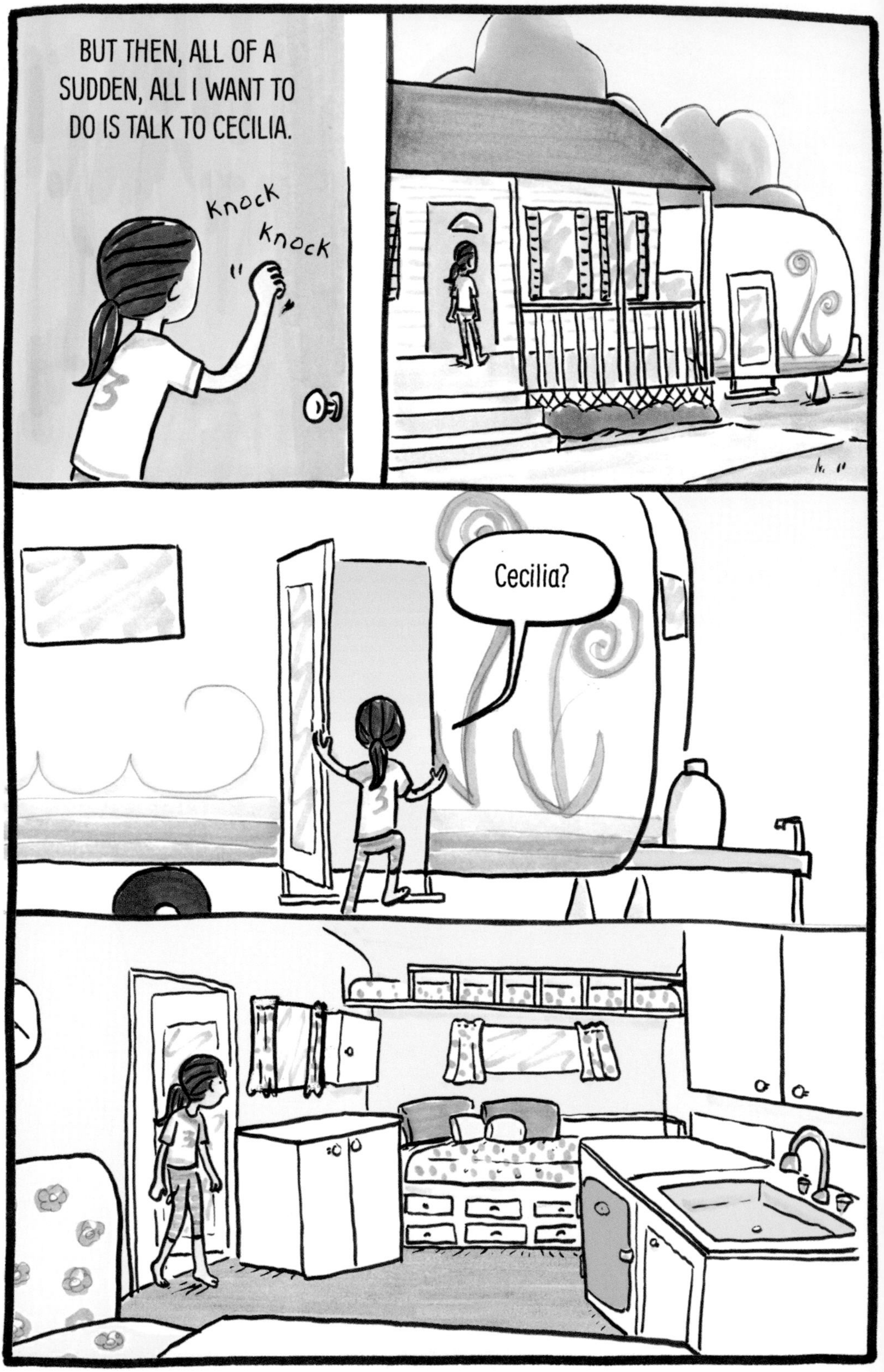
BUT THEN, ALL OF A SUDDEN, ALL I WANT TO DO IS TALK TO CECILIA.
Knock
Knock
Cecilia?

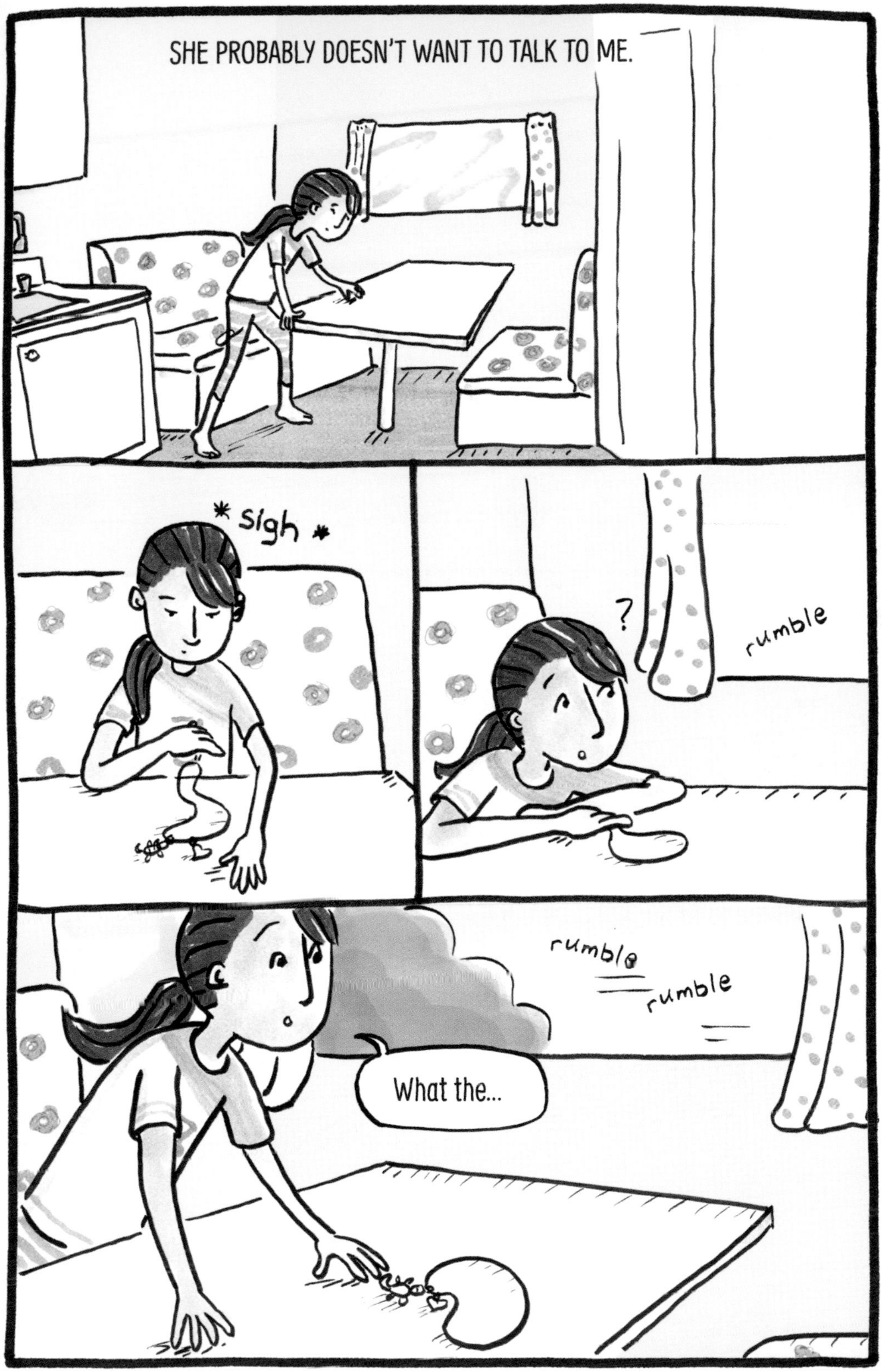
SHE PROBABLY DOESN'T WANT TO TALK TO ME.
sigh
?
rumble
rumble
rumble
What the...

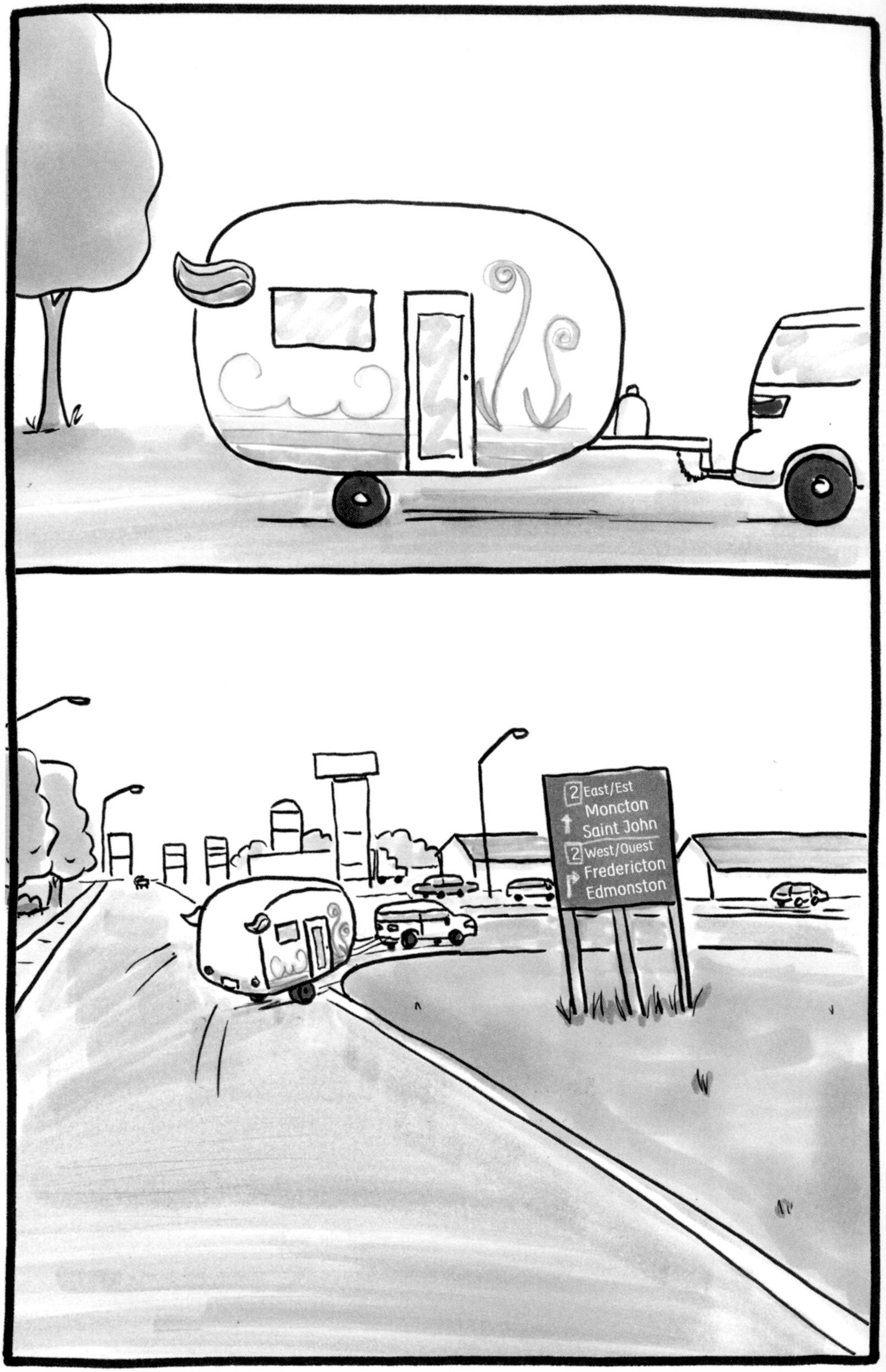
2 East/Est
Moncton
Saint John
2 West/Ouest
Fredericton
Edmonston

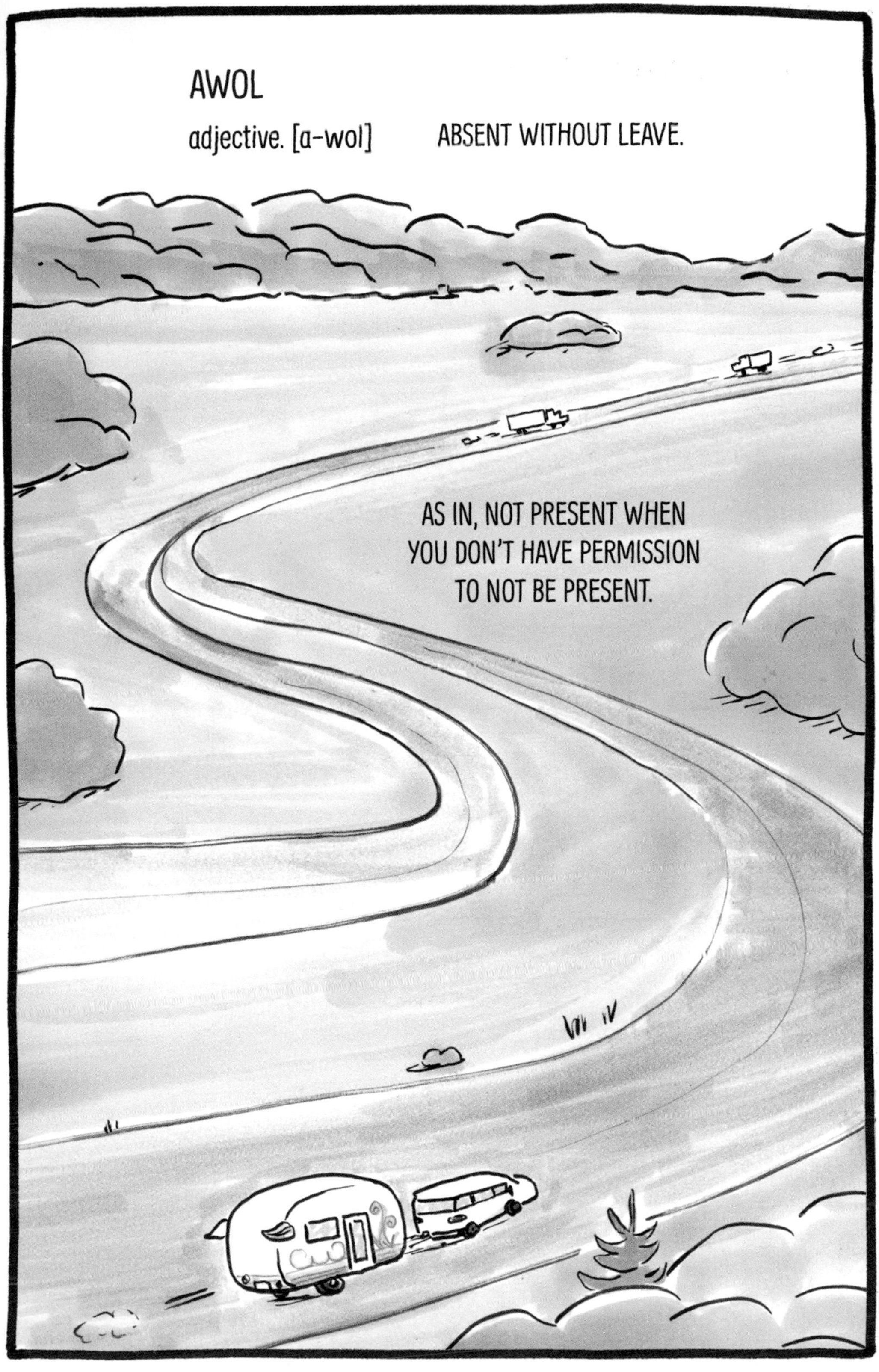
AWOL
adjective. [a-wol]
ABSENT WITHOUT LEAVE.
AS IN, NOT PRESENT WHEN YOU DON'T HAVE PERMISSION TO NOT BE PRESENT.

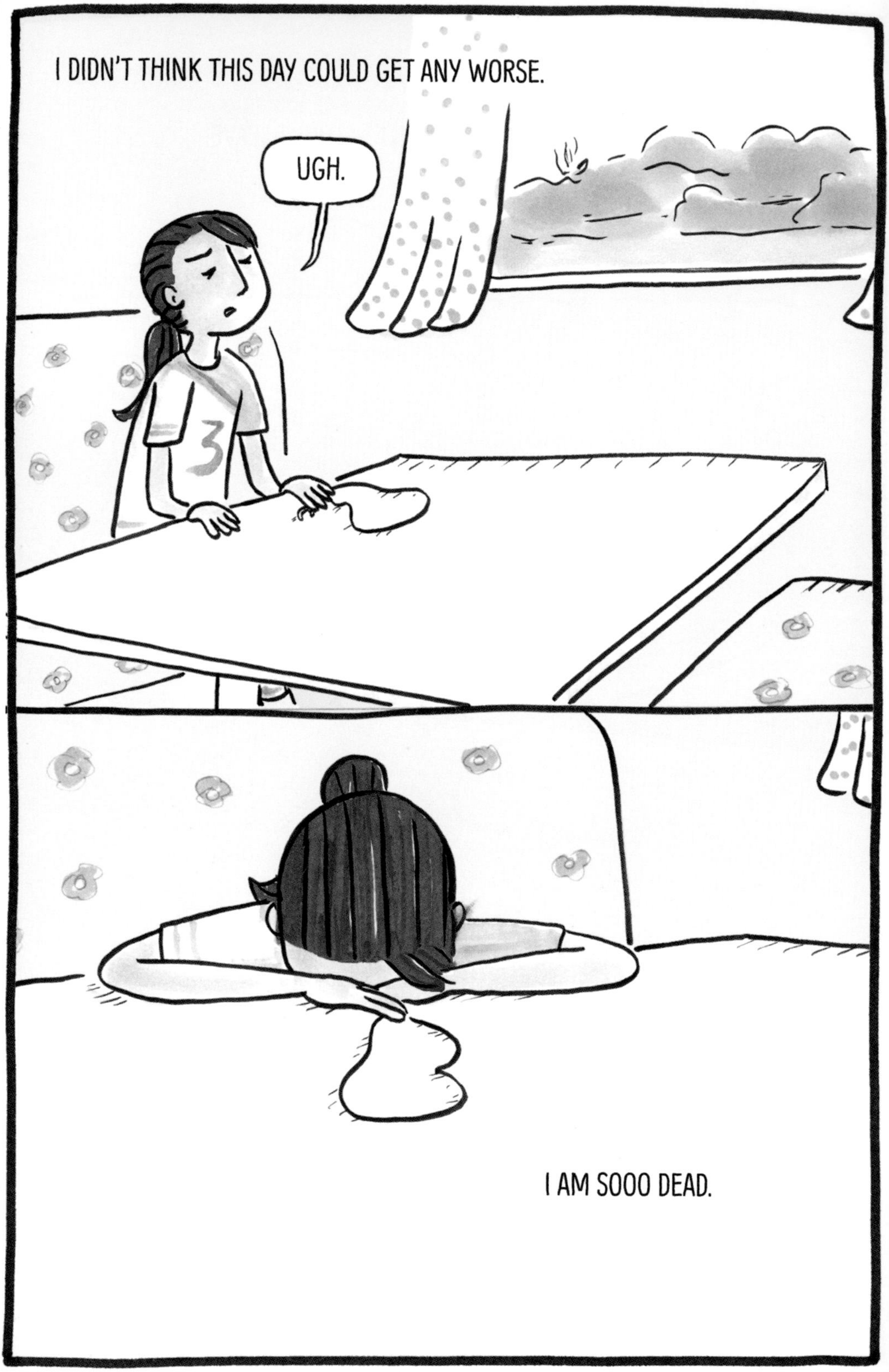
I DIDN'T THINK THIS DAY COULD GET ANY WORSE.
UGH.
I AM SOOO DEAD.

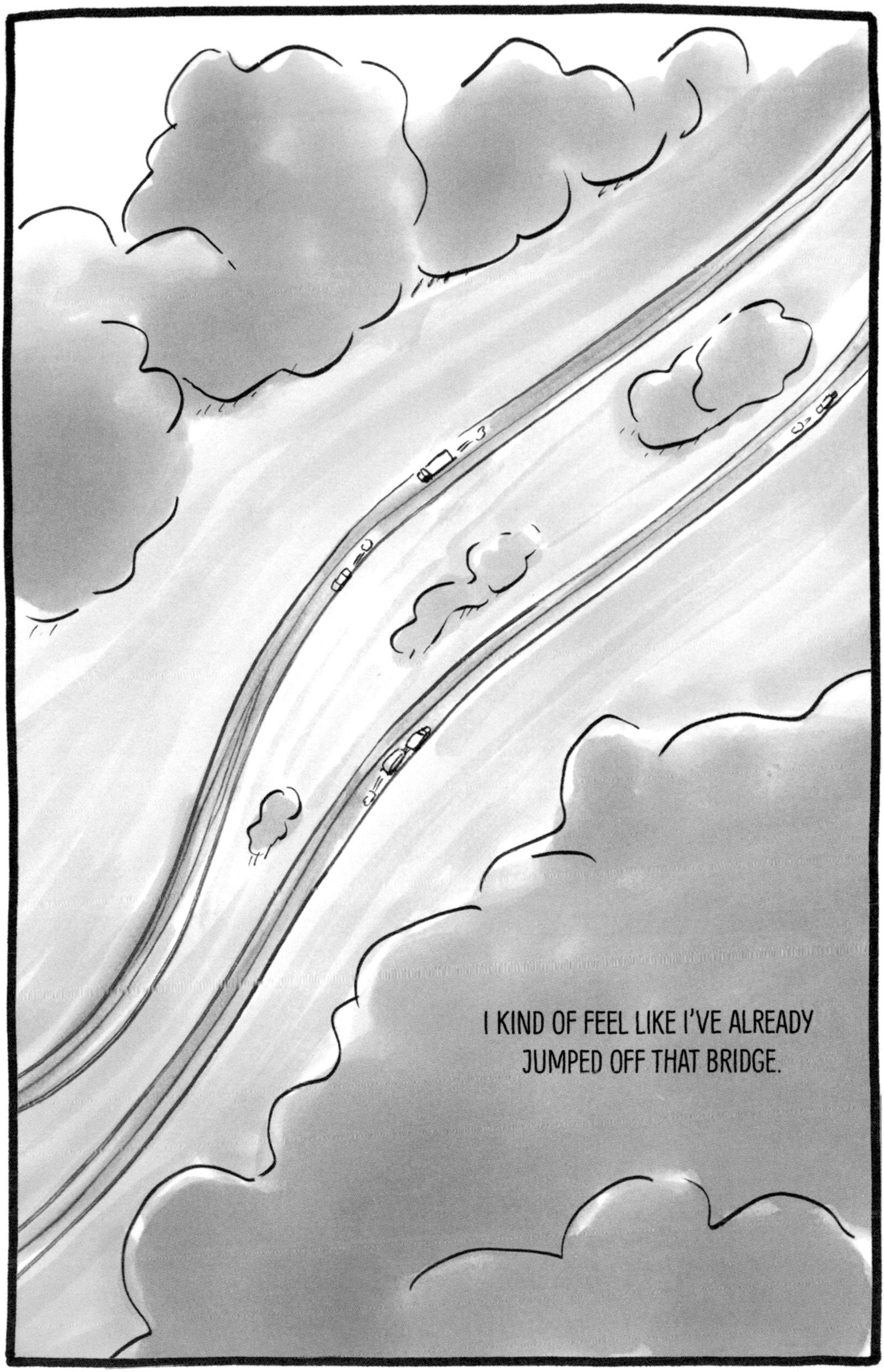
I KIND OF FEEL LIKE I'VE ALREADY JUMPED OFF THAT BRIDGE.

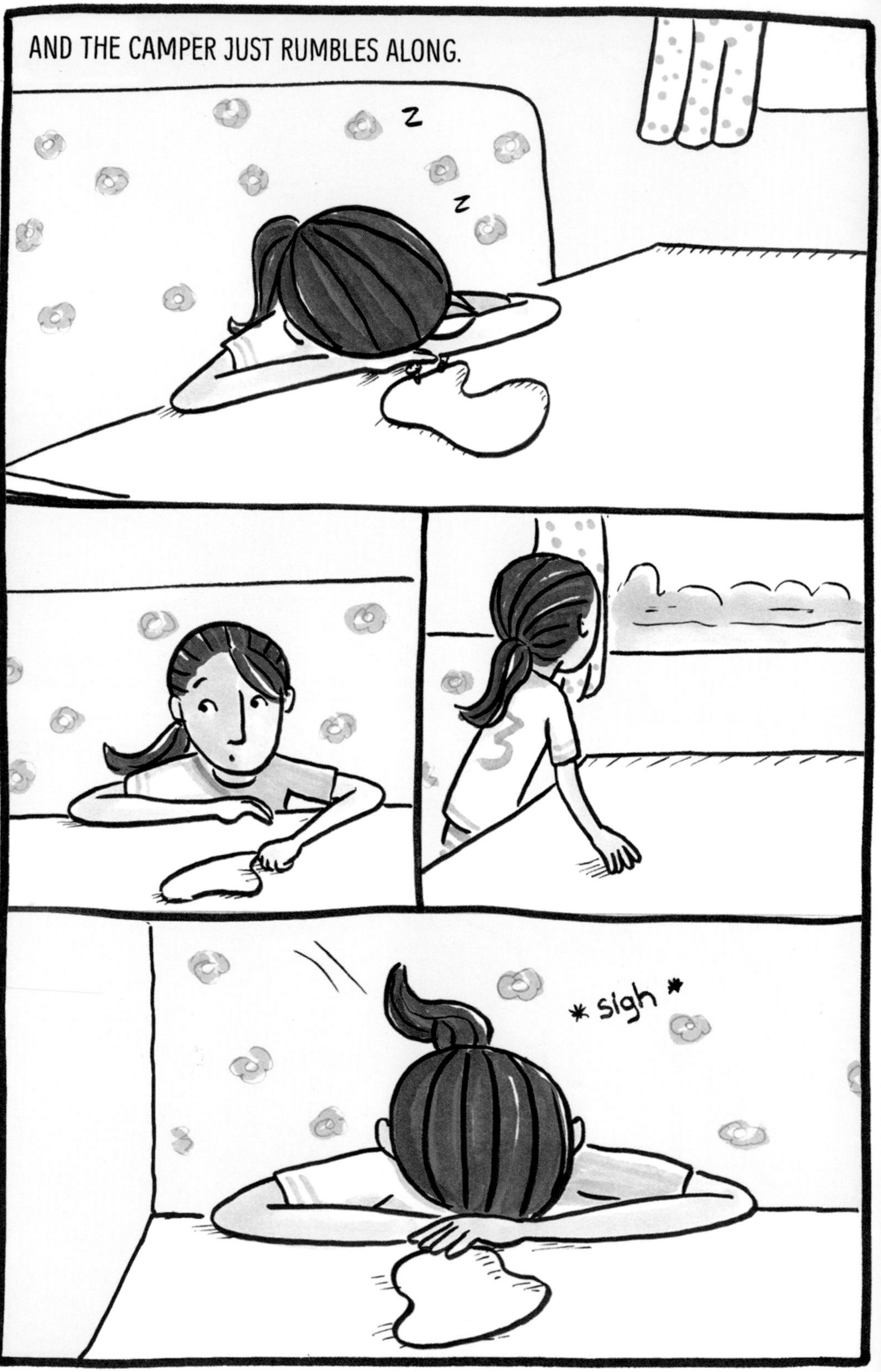
AND THE CAMPER JUST RUMBLES ALONG.
Z
Z
sigh

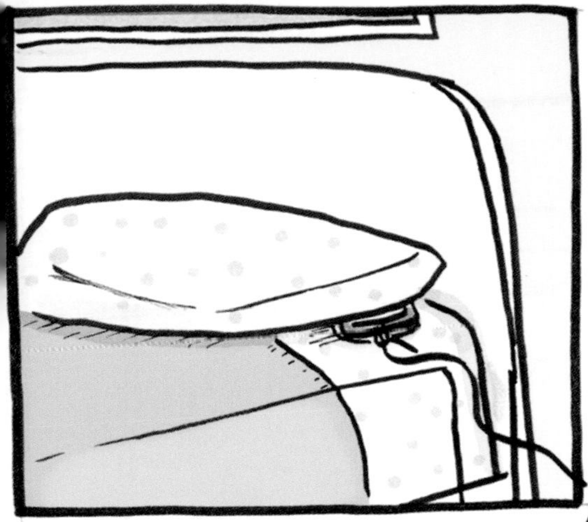

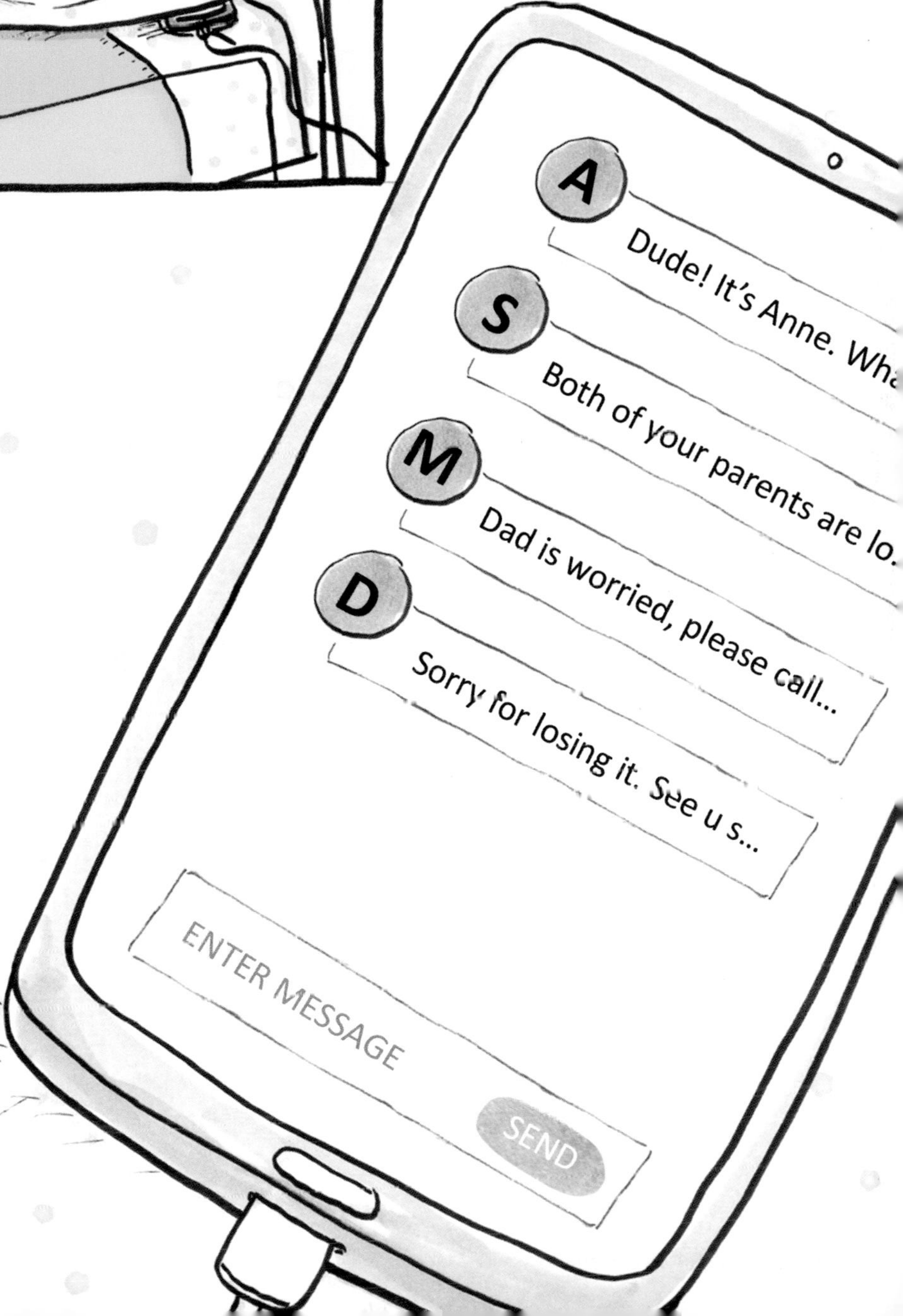

A
Dude! It's Anne. Wha
S
Both of your parents are lo
M
Dad is worried, please call...
D
Sorry for losing it. See u s...
ENTER MESSAGE
SEND

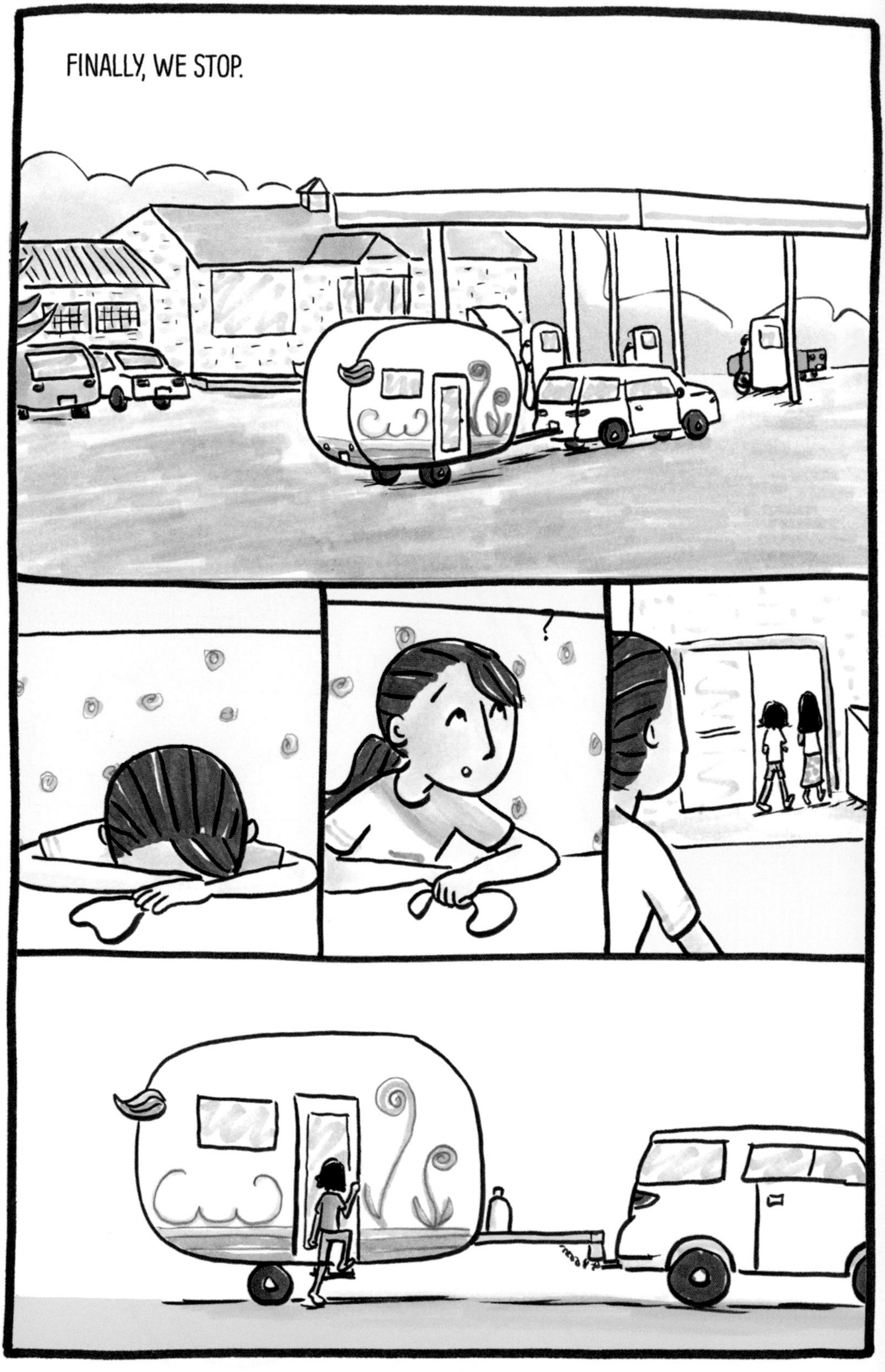
FINALLY, WE STOP.
?

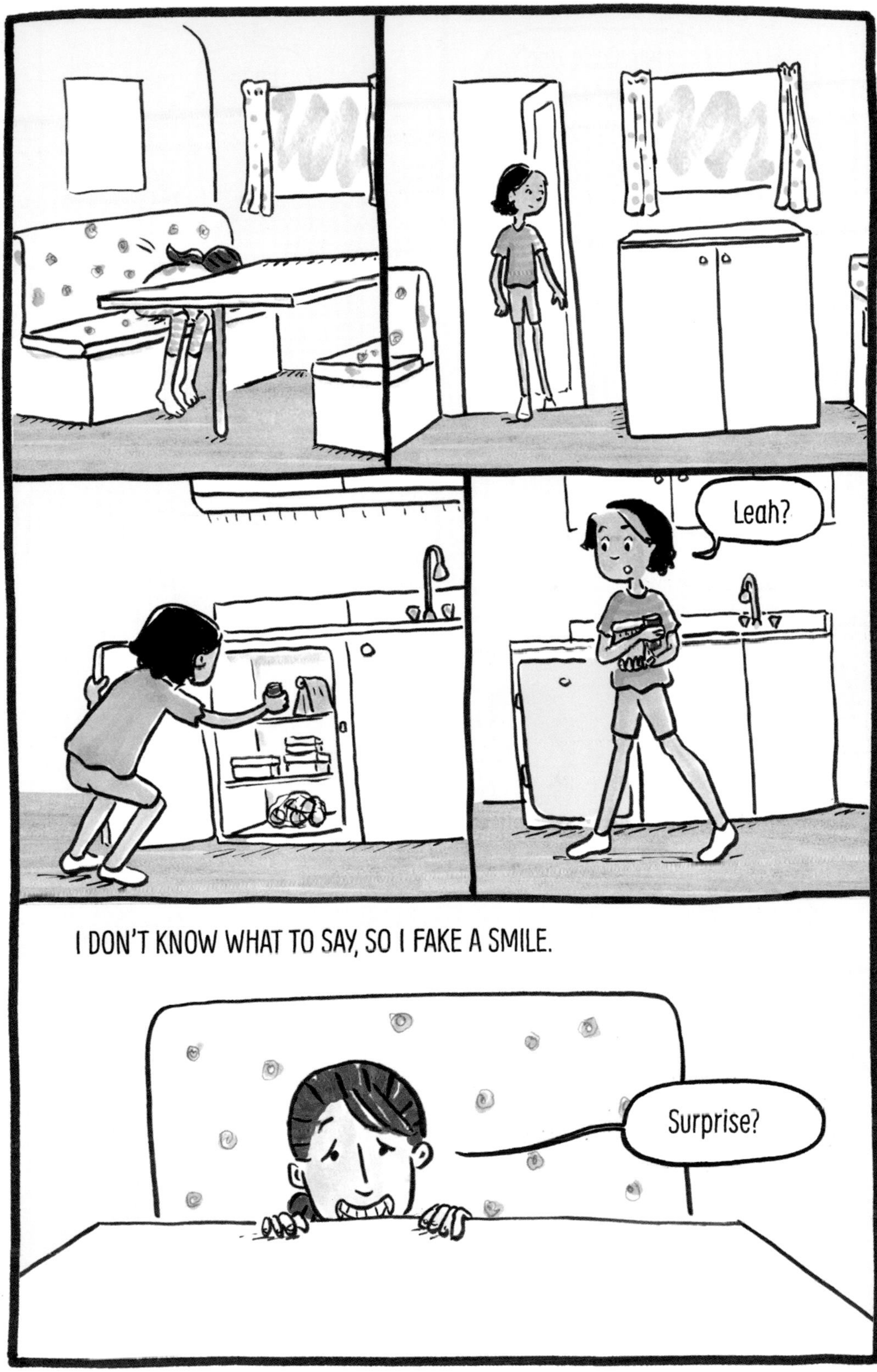
Leah?
I DON'T KNOW WHAT TO SAY, SO I FAKE A SMILE.
Surprise?

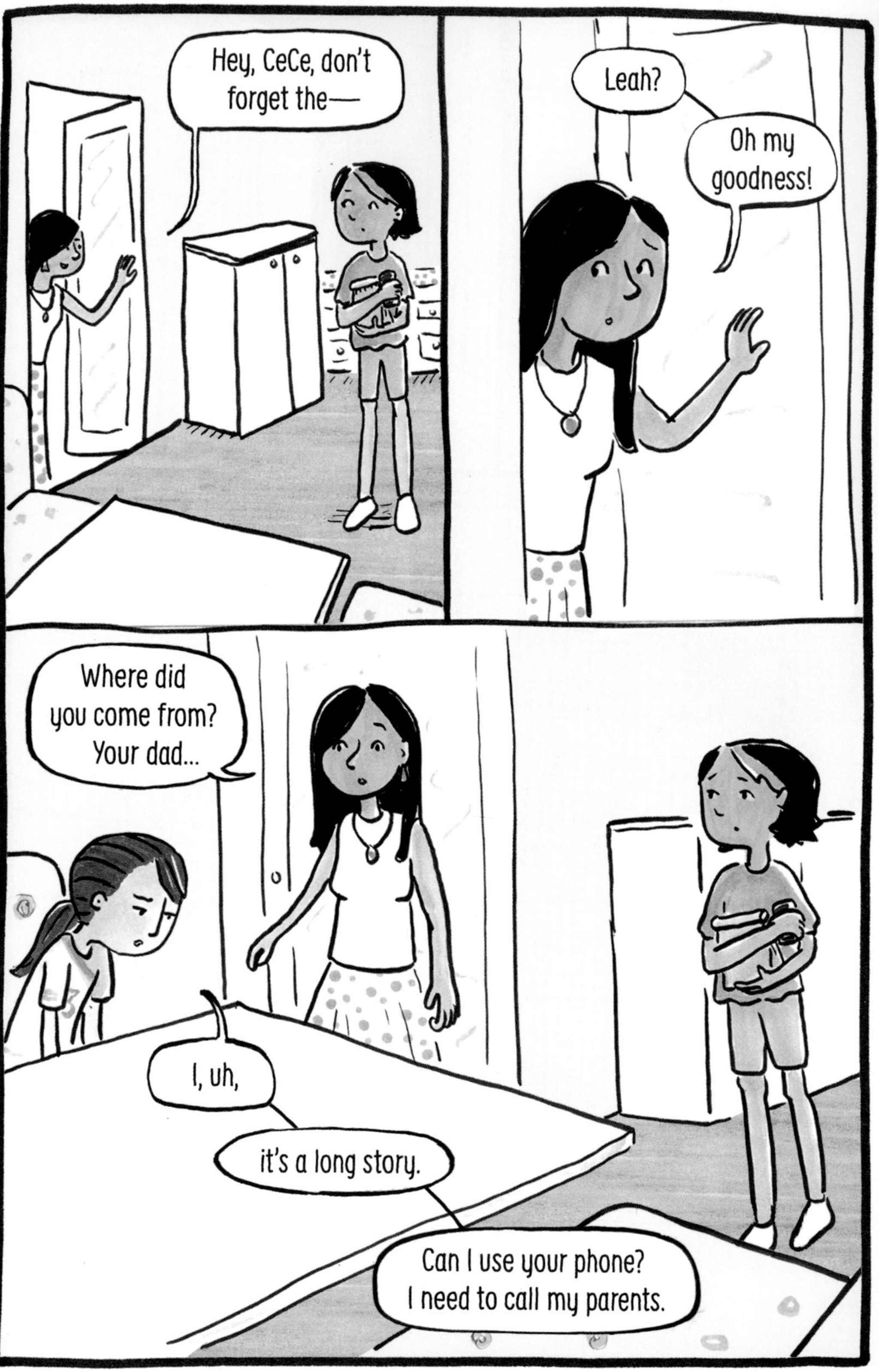
Hey, CeCe, don't forget the—
Leah?
Oh my goodness!
Where did you come from? Your dad...
I, uh,
it's a long story.
Can I use your phone? I need to call my parents.

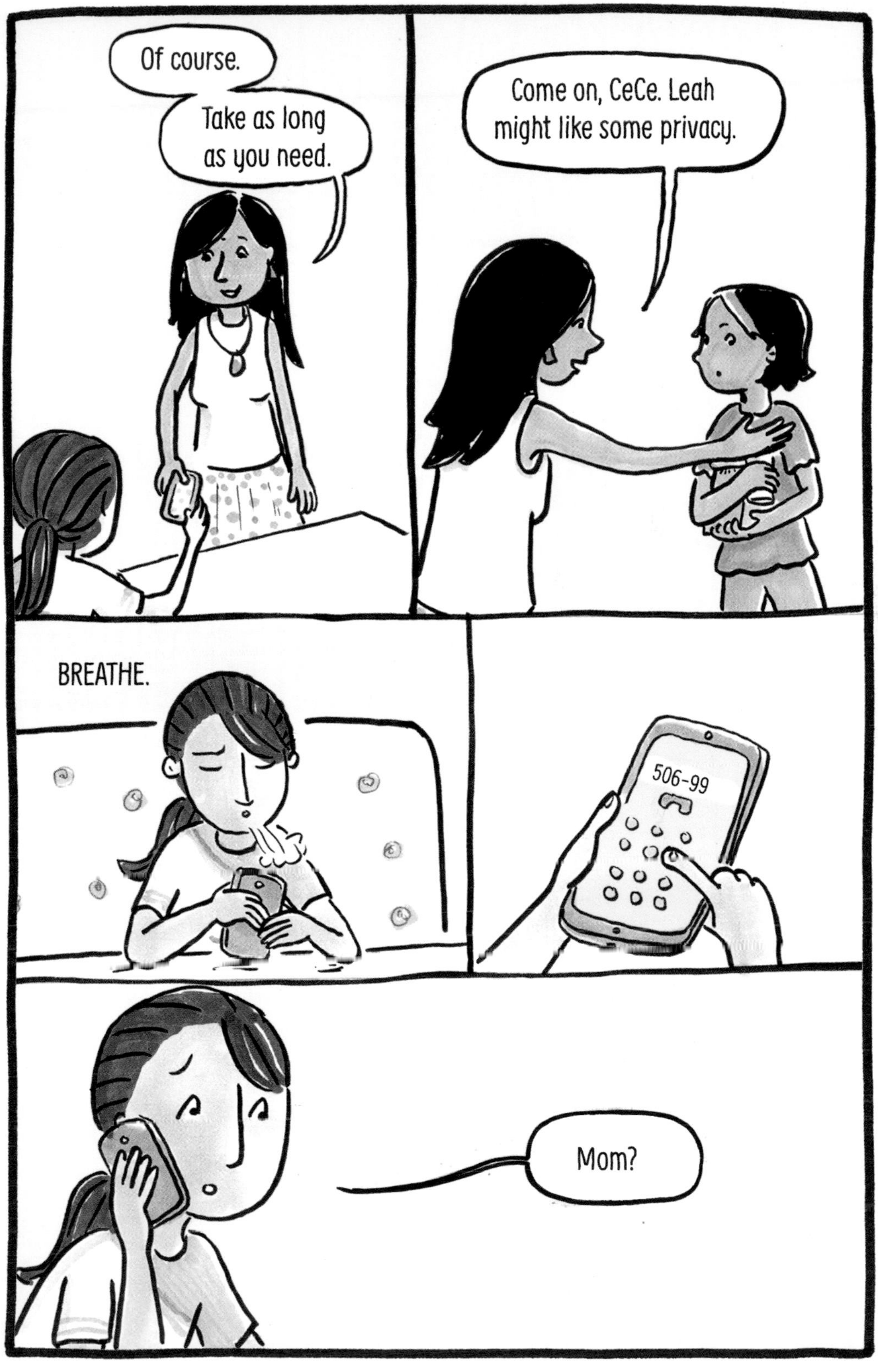
Of course.
Take as long as you need.
Come on, CeCe. Leah might like some privacy.
BREATHE.
506-99
Mom?

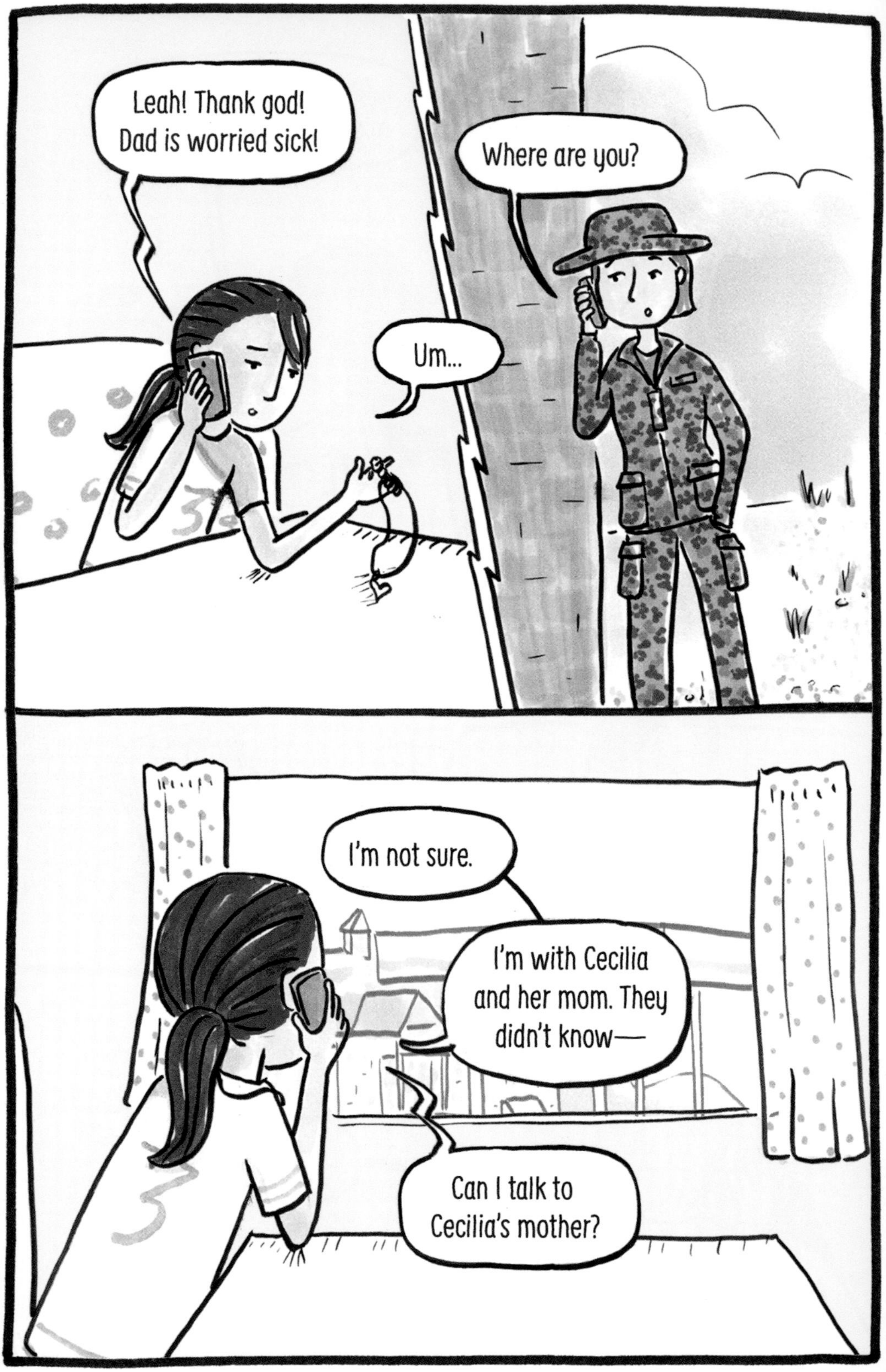
Leah! Thank god! Dad is worried sick!
Where are you?
Um...
I'm not sure.
I'm with Cecilia and her mom. They didn't know—
Can I talk to Cecilia's mother?

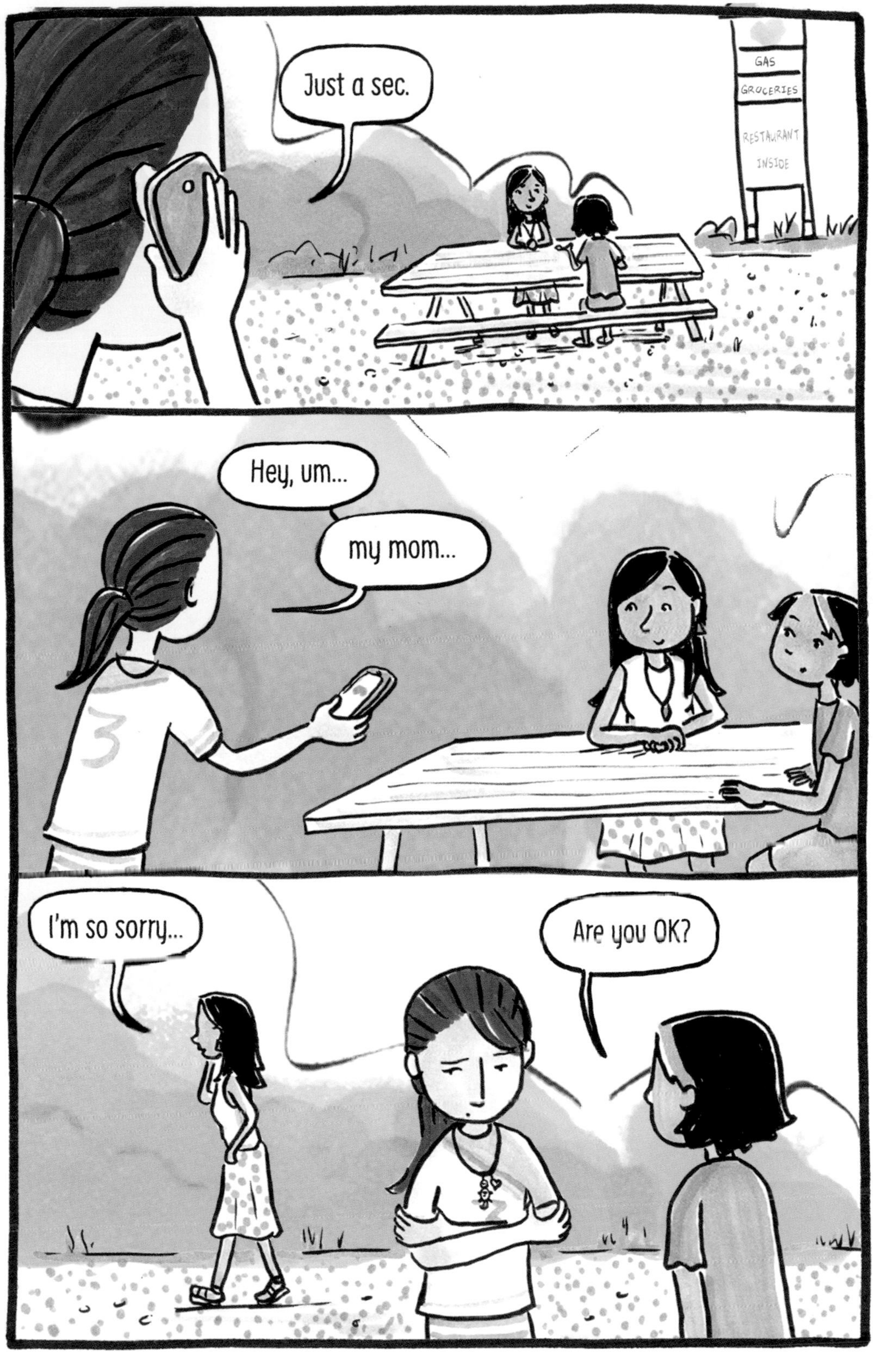
Just a sec.
GAS
GROCERIES
RESTAURANT INSIDE
Hey, um...
my mom...
I'm so sorry...
Are you OK?

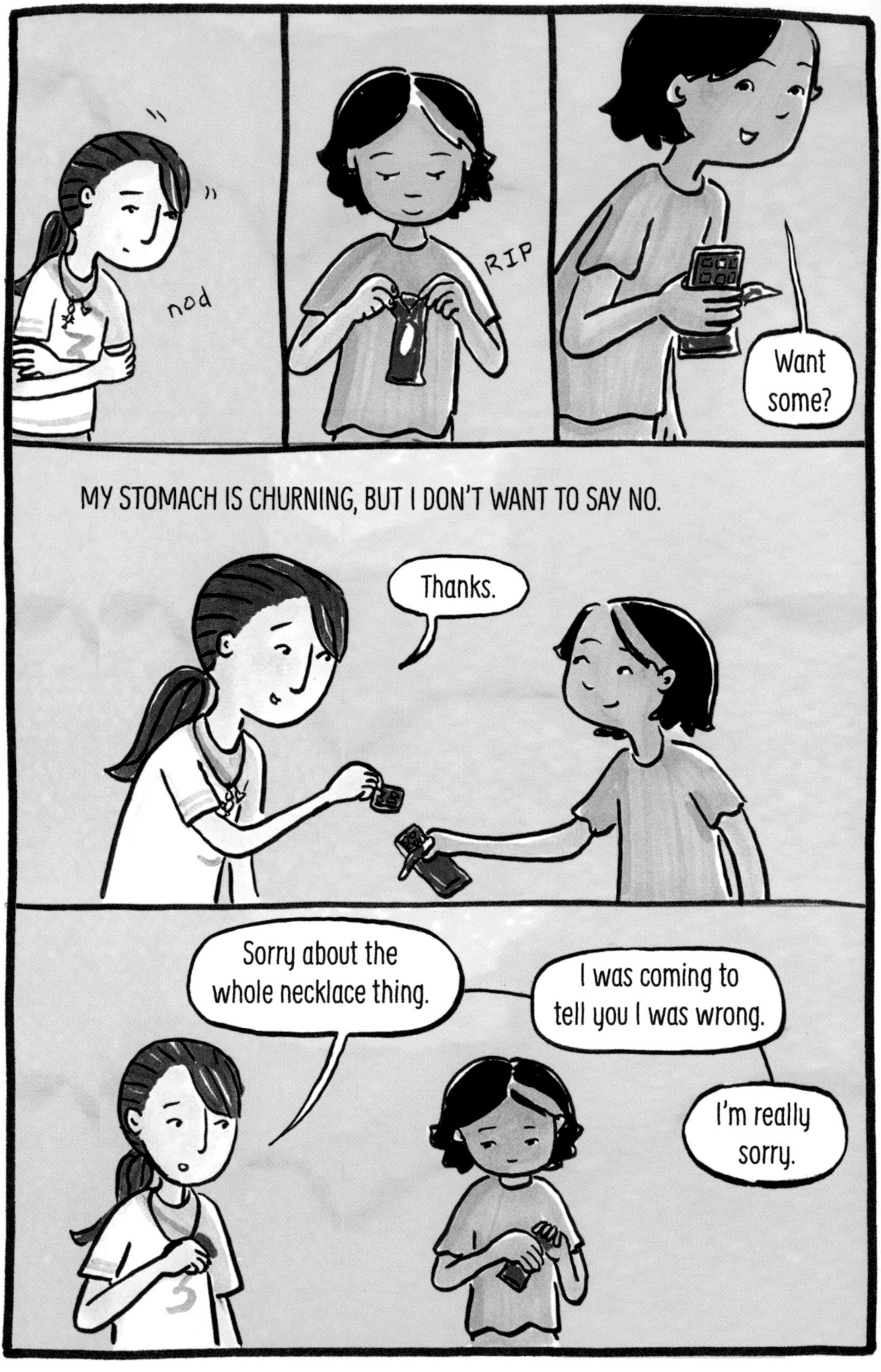
nod
RIP
Want some?
MY STOMACH IS CHURNING, BUT I DON'T WANT TO SAY NO.
Thanks.
Sorry about the whole necklace thing.
I was coming to tell you I was wrong.
I'm really sorry.

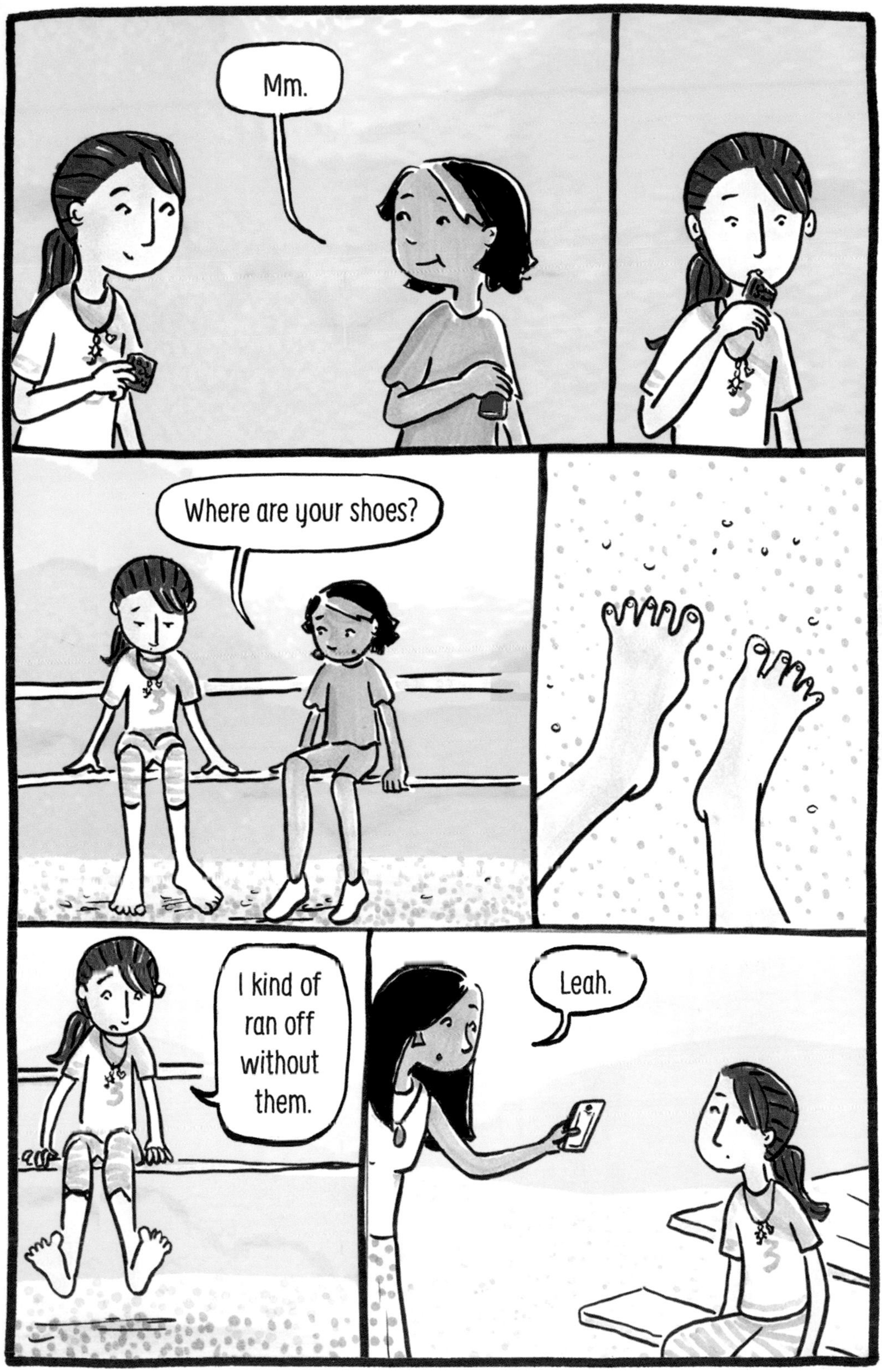
Mm.
Where are your shoes?
I kind of ran off without them.
Leah.

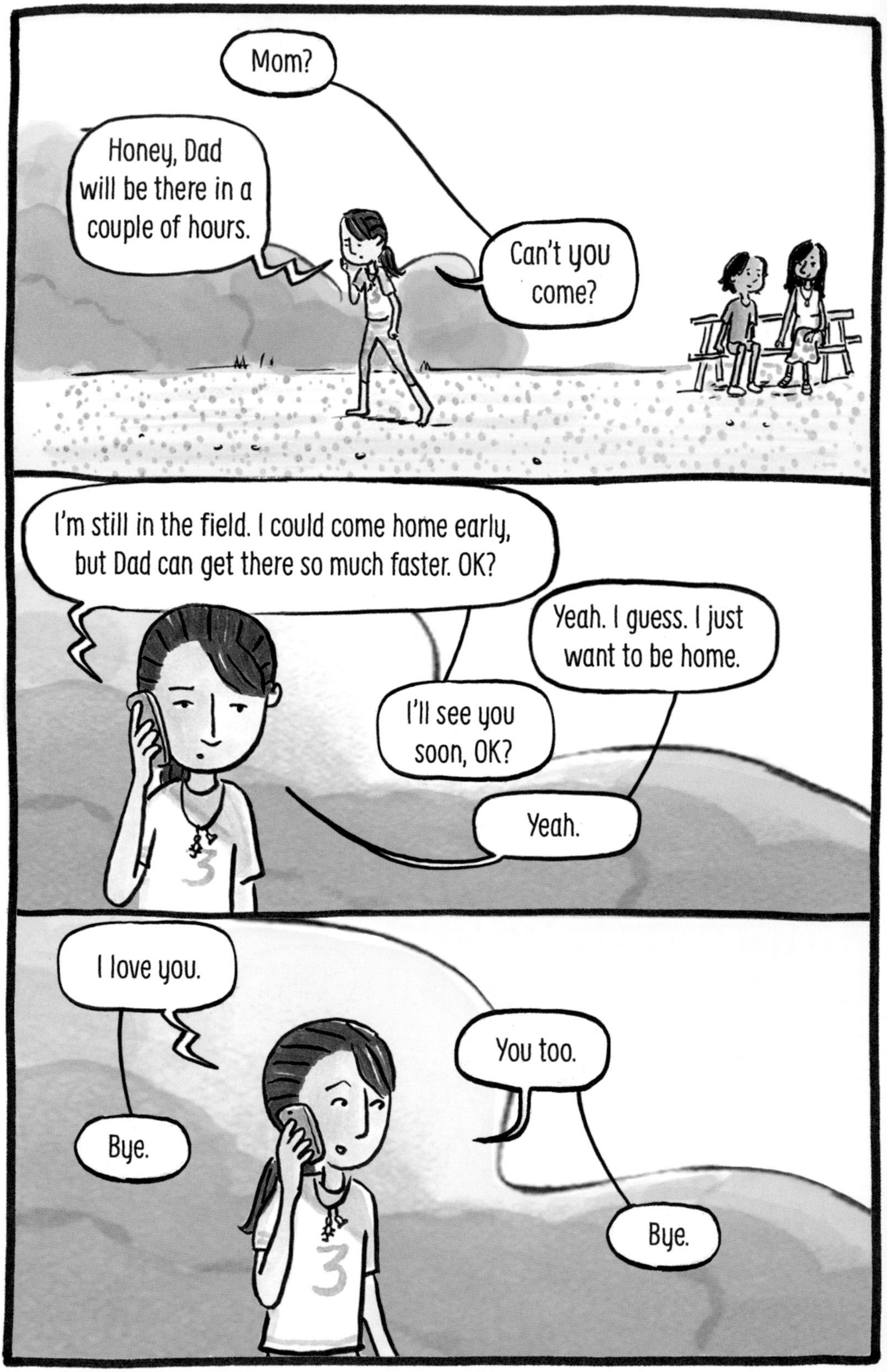
Mom?
Honey, Dad will be there in a couple of hours.
Can't you come?
I'm still in the field. I could come home early, but Dad can get there so much faster. OK?
Yeah. I guess. I just want to be home.
I'll see you soon, OK?
Yeah.
I love you.
You too.
Bye.
Bye.

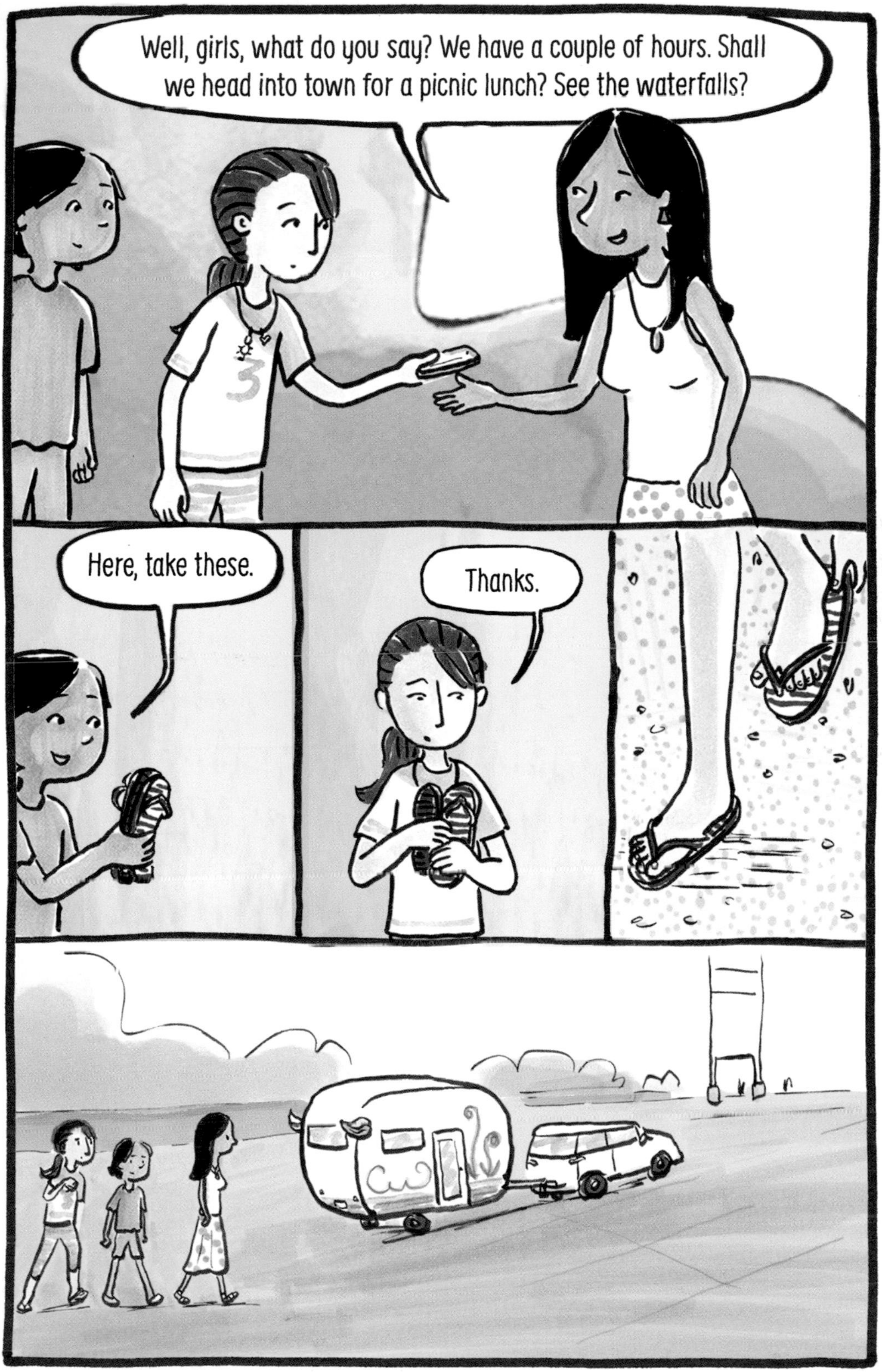
Well, girls, what do you say? We have a couple of hours. Shall we head into town for a picnic lunch? See the waterfalls?
Here, take these.
Thanks.

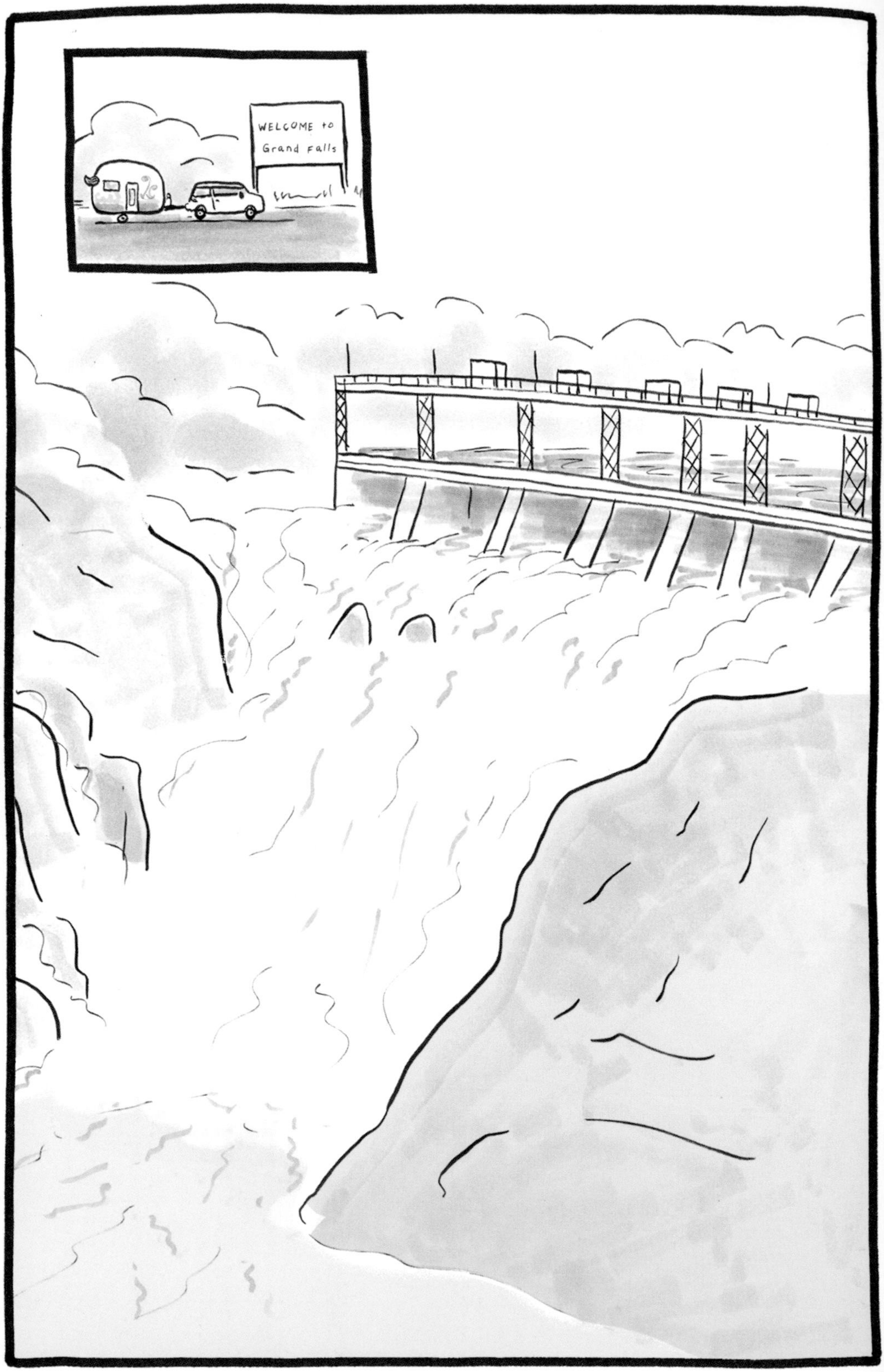
WELCOME to
Grand Falls

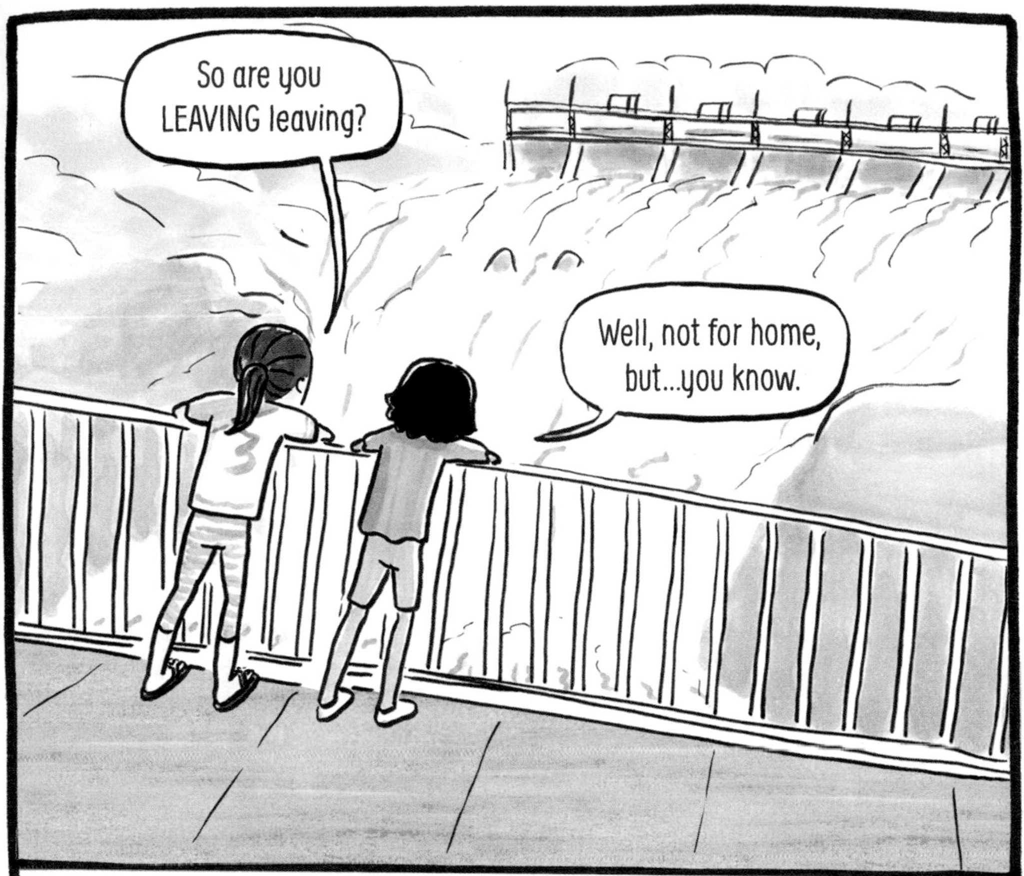
So are you LEAVING leaving?
Well, not for home, but...you know.

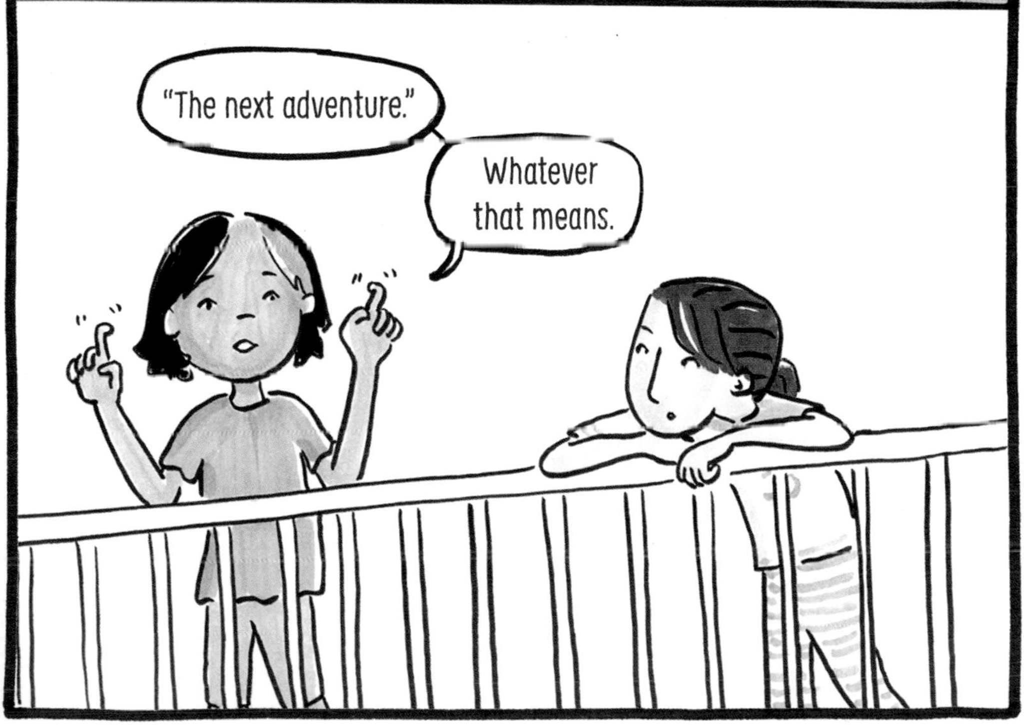
"The next adventure."
Whatever that means.

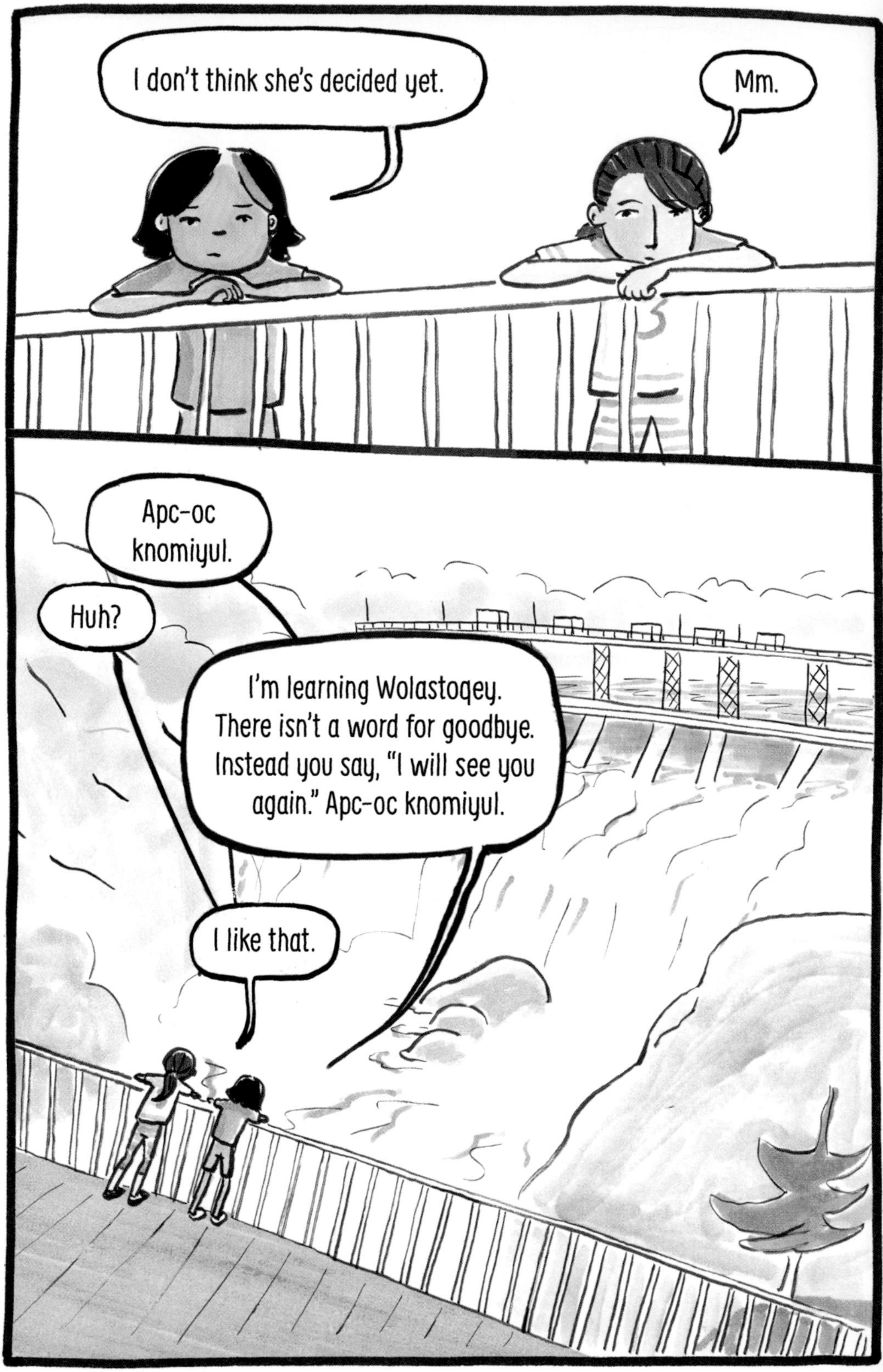
I don't think she's decided yet.
Mm.
Apc-oc knomiyul.
Huh?
I'm learning Wolastoqey. There isn't a word for goodbye. Instead you say, "I will see you again." Apc-oc knomiyul.
I like that.

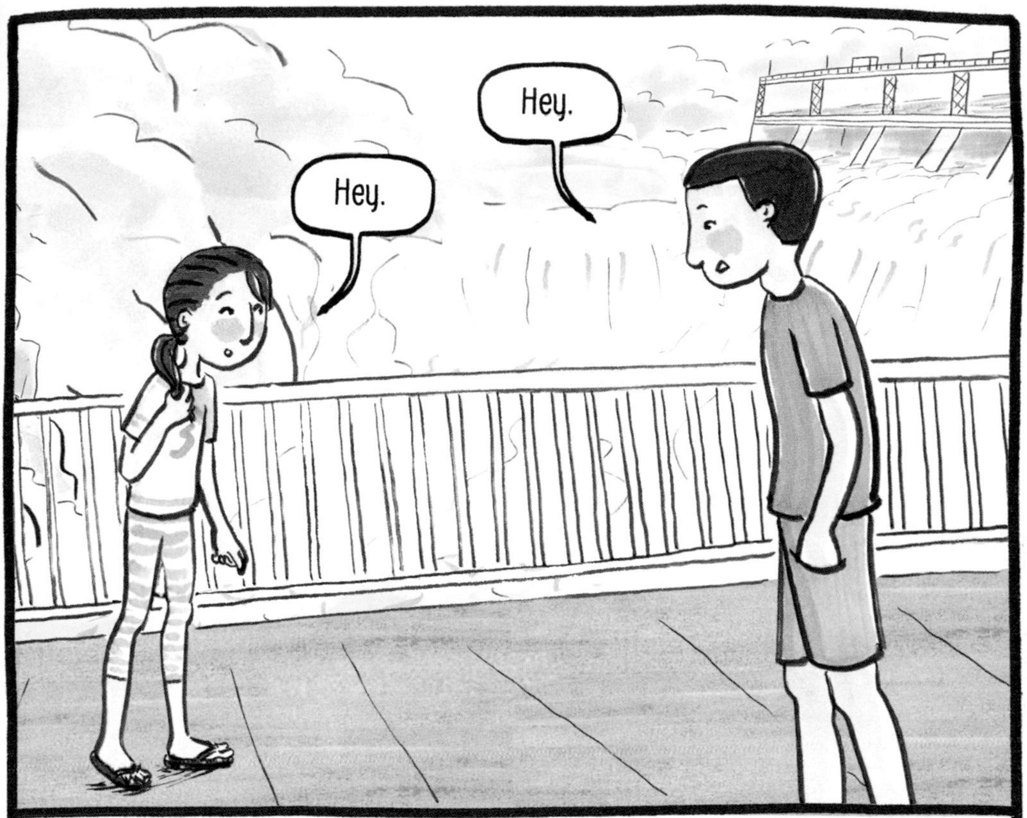
Hey.
Hey.

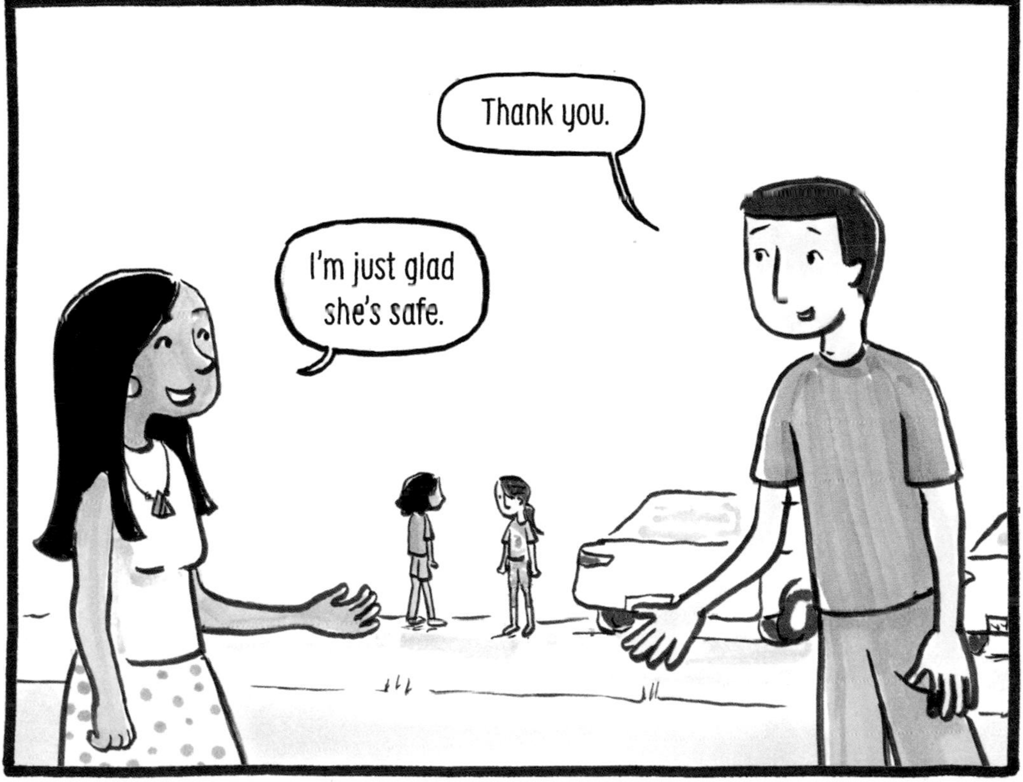
Thank you.
I'm just glad she's safe.

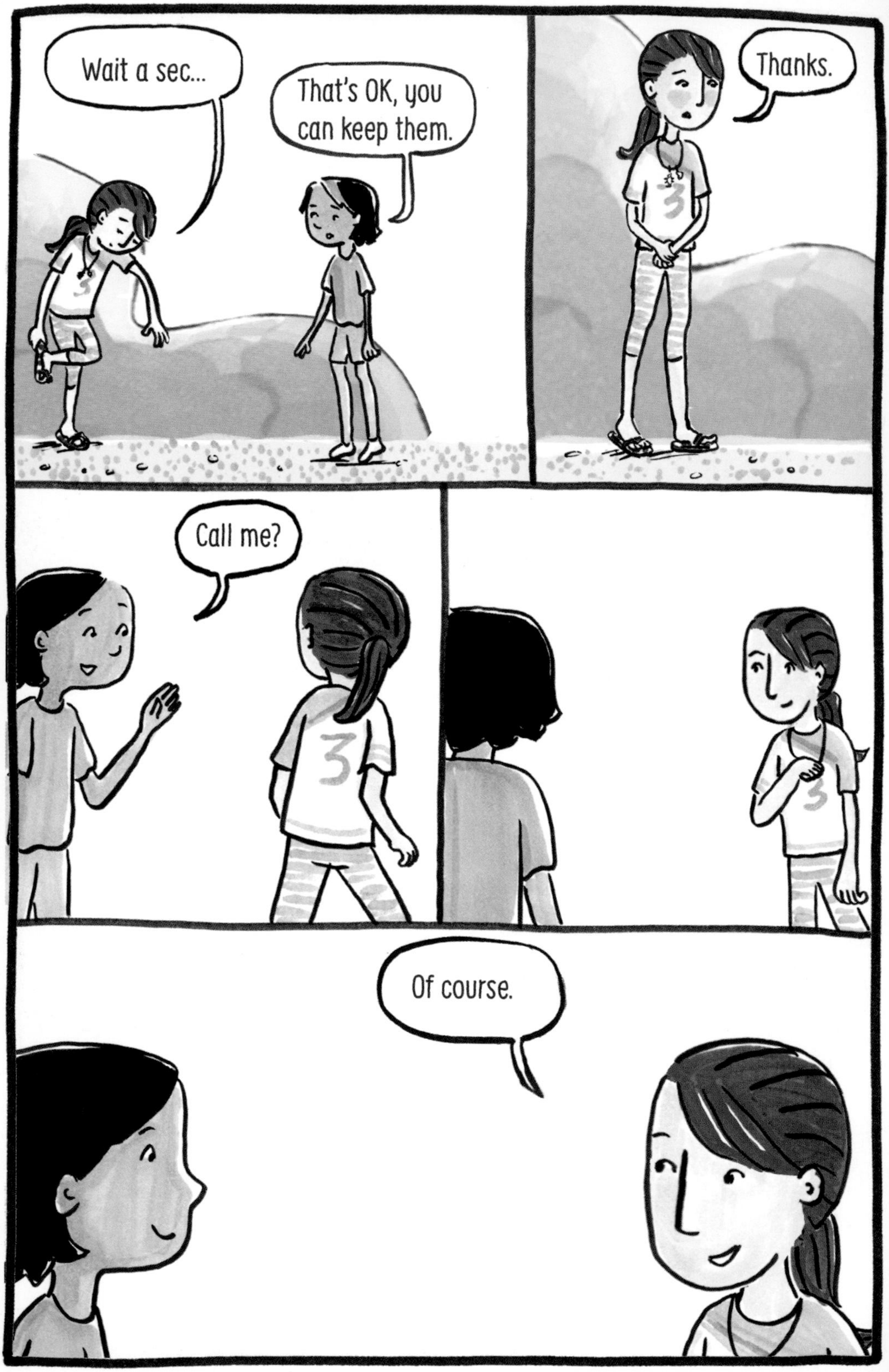

Wait a sec...
That's OK, you can keep them.
Thanks.
Call me?
Of course.

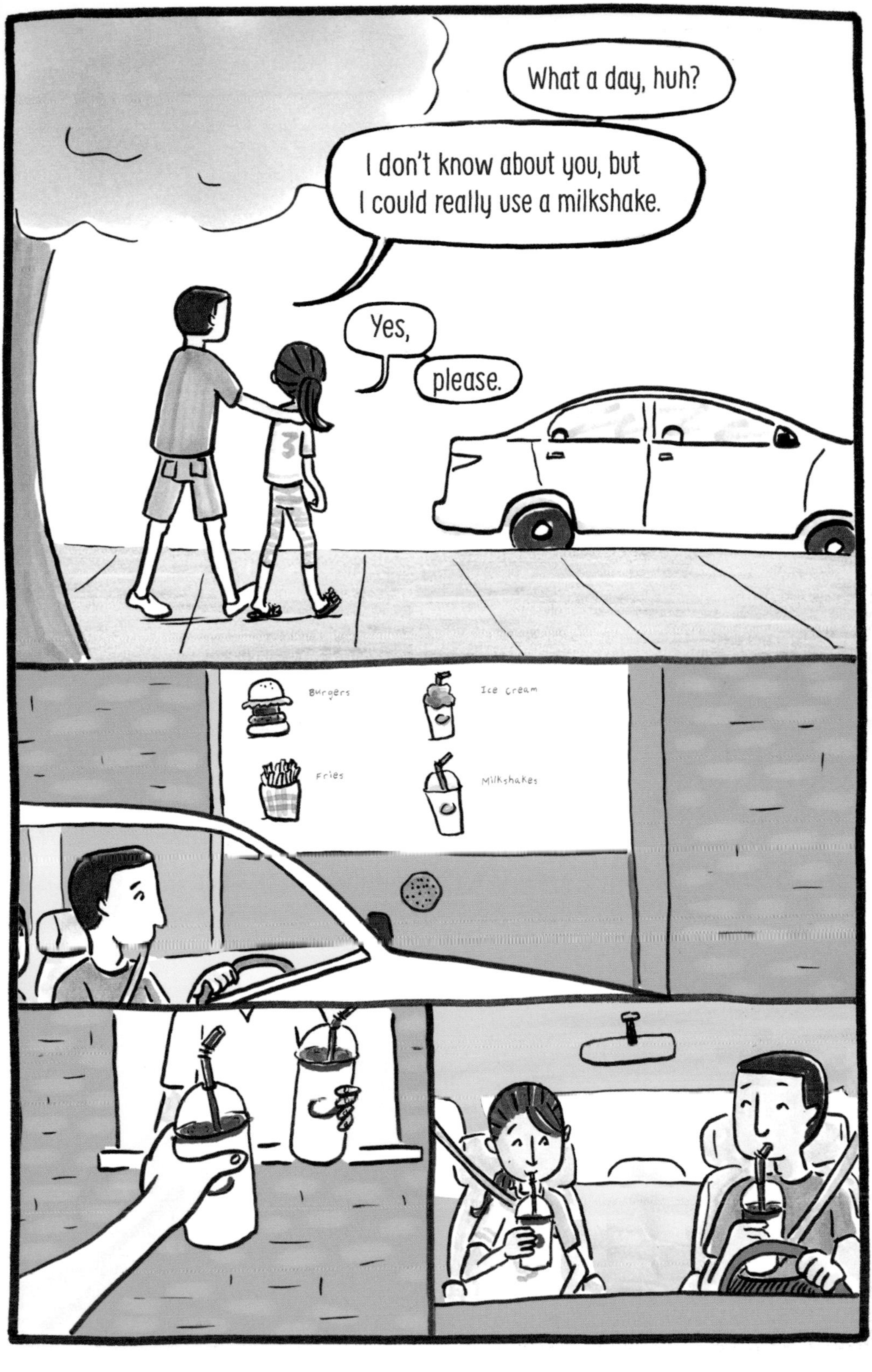
What a day, huh?
I don't know about you, but I could really use a milkshake.
Yes,
please.
Burgers
Ice Cream
Fries
Milkshakes

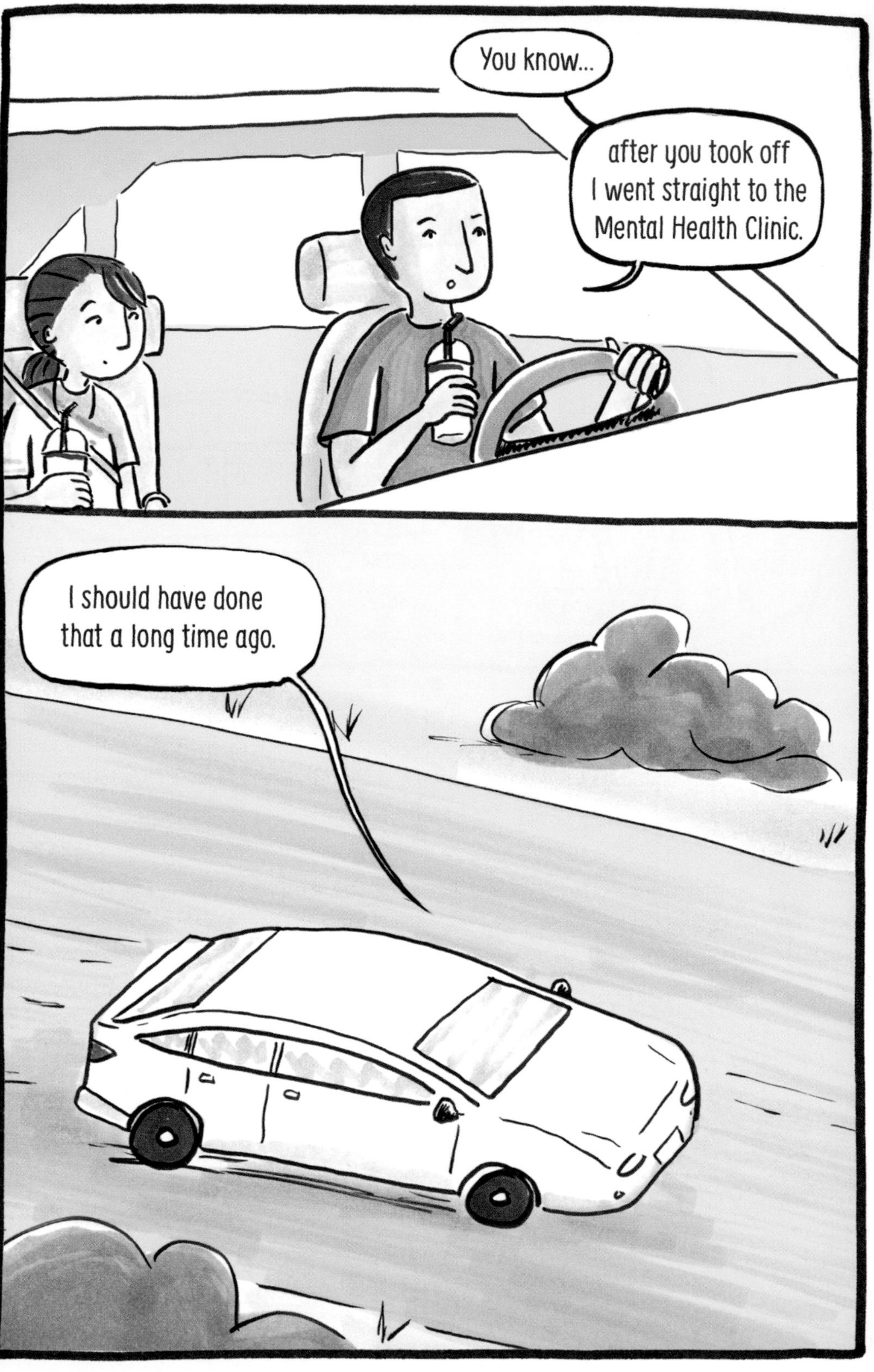
You know...
after you took off I went straight to the Mental Health Clinic.
I should have done that a long time ago.

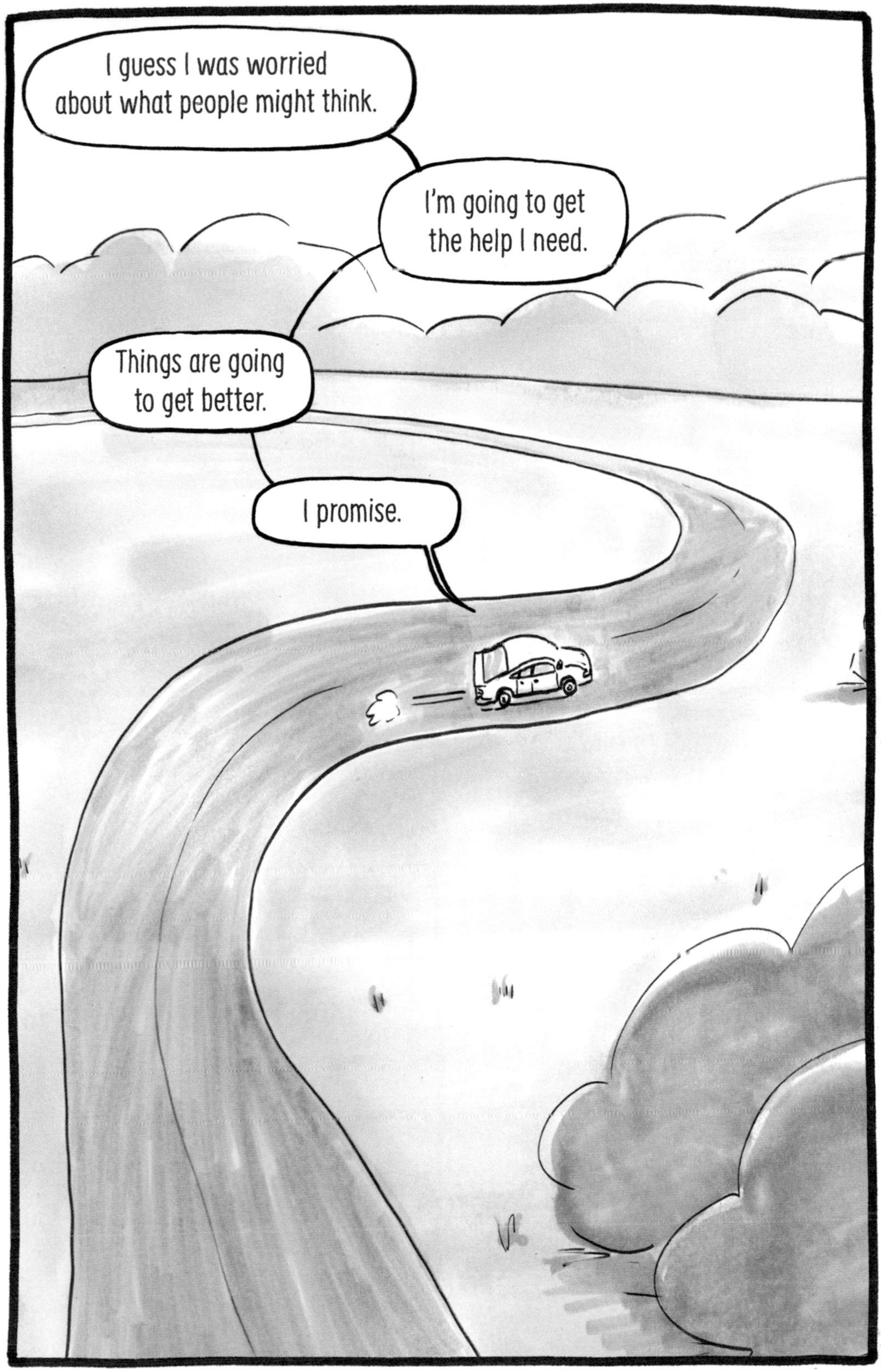
I guess I was worried about what people might think.
I'm going to get the help I need.
Things are going to get better.
I promise.

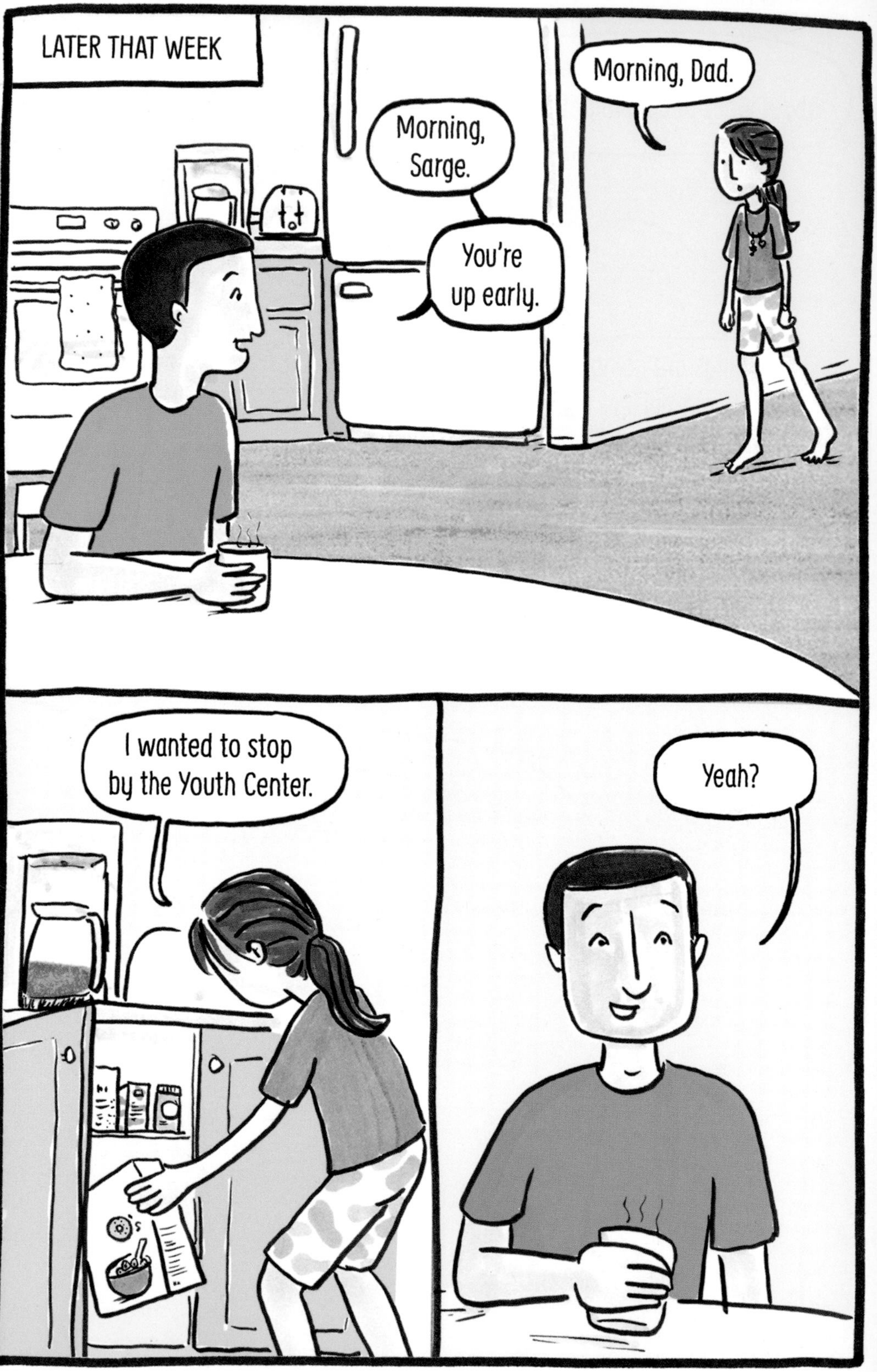
LATER THAT WEEK
Morning, Dad.
Morning, Sarge.
You're up early.
I wanted to stop by the Youth Center.
Yeah?

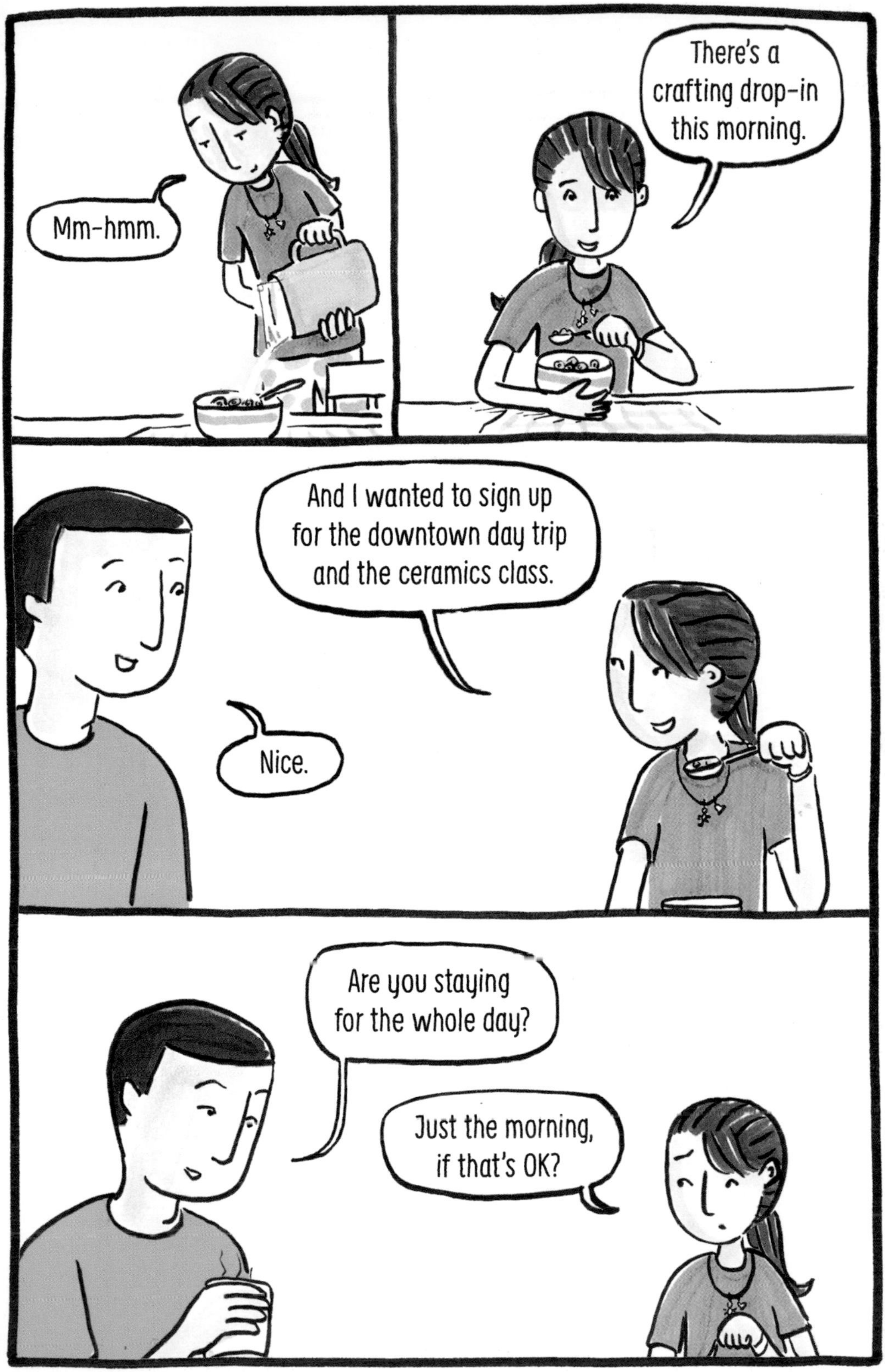
Mm-hmm.
There's a crafting drop-in this morning.
And I wanted to sign up for the downtown day trip and the ceramics class.
Nice.
Are you staying for the whole day?
Just the morning, if that's OK?

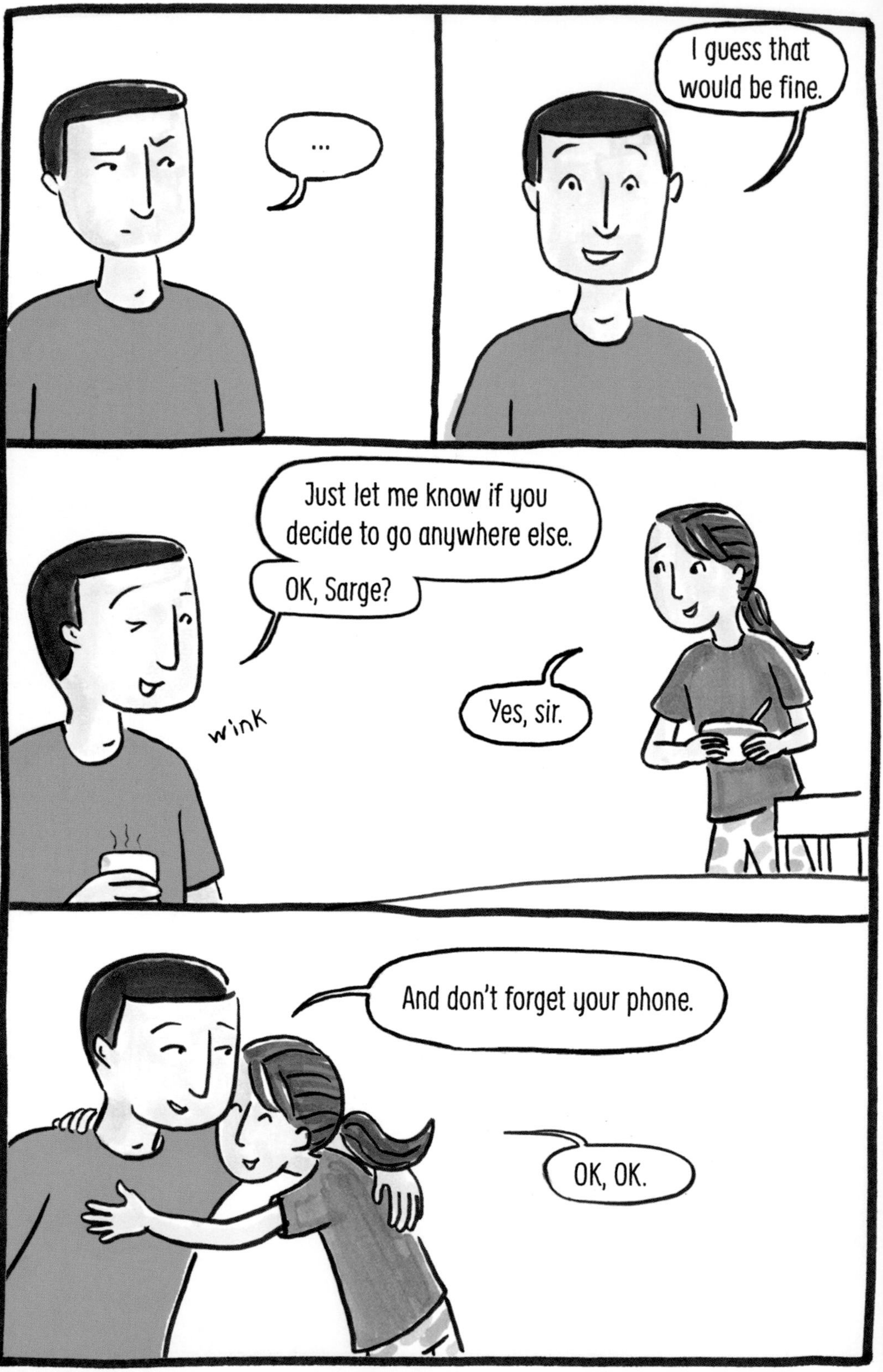
...
I guess that would be fine.
Just let me know if you decide to go anywhere else.
OK, Sarge?
wink
Yes, sir.
And don't forget your phone.
OK, OK.

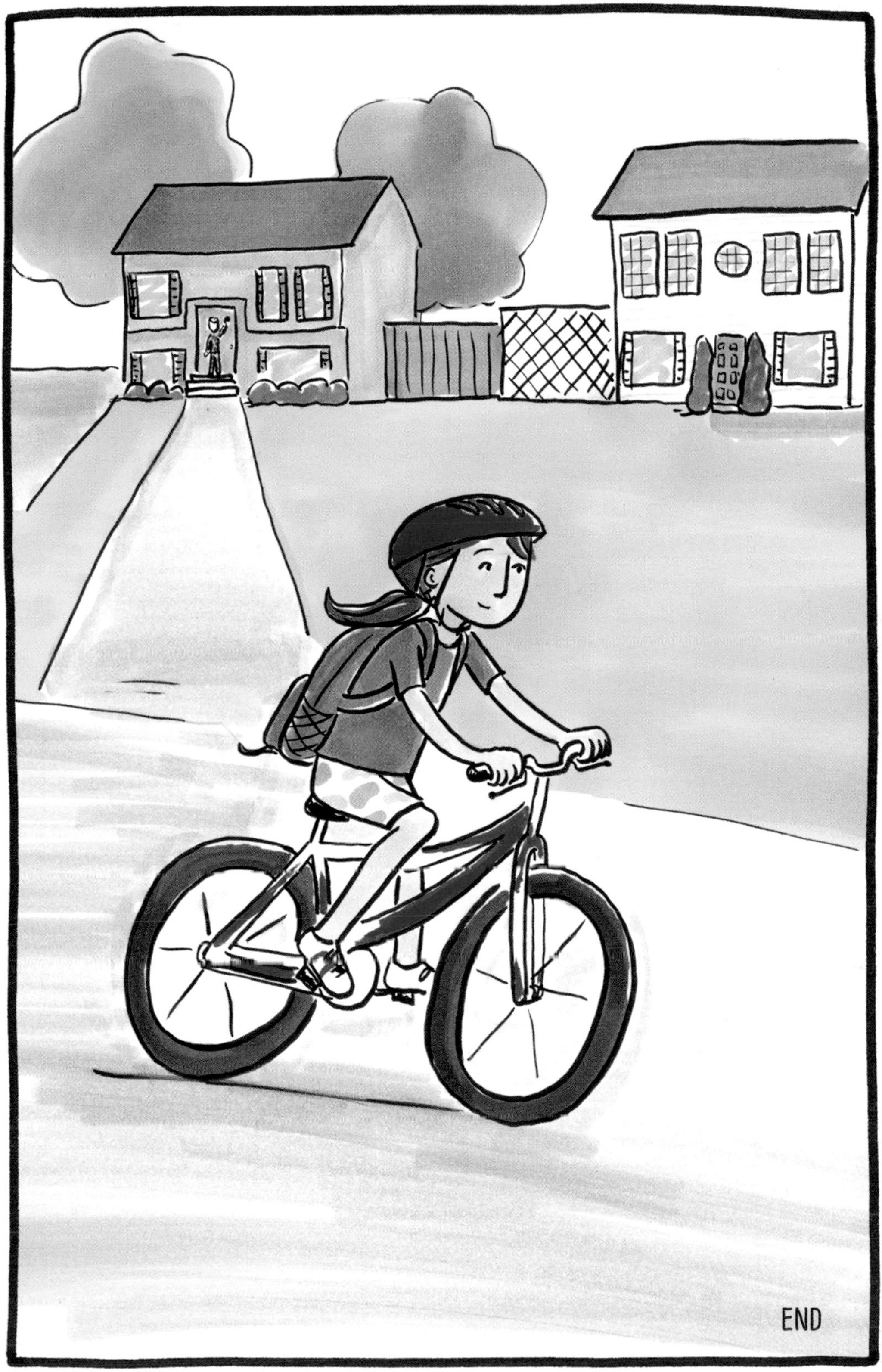
END

AUTHOR'S NOTE

AWOL was inspired by my family's journey with post-traumatic stress disorder (PTSD) and by the many other families with similar experiences. I wanted to write something realistic and familiar so that children who have a family member with PTSD would know they are not alone. In addition to my own experiences and observations, I relied on the book *Growing Up in Armyville: Canada's Military Families during the Afghanistan Mission* by Deborah Harrison and Patrizia Albanese, which presents the real-life experiences of teens who have had a parent return from deployment with PTSD. I borrowed the term *Armyville* for the opening sentence of *AWOL* because I've found that most military communities tend to have a similar feel. Leah's story could easily have been set in any one of them, but I chose Oromocto, New Brunswick, which is close to where I live. Oromocto is home to Canadian Forces Base Gagetown and next door to the Wolastoqey community of Welamukotuk.

POST-TRAUMATIC STRESS DISORDER

PTSD is a mental illness that some people develop after experiencing an upsetting or traumatic event. *Mental illness* is the term used for medical conditions that adversely affect a person's thoughts, emotions and behavior—the brain is not working the way it should. Anyone can develop PTSD, but people in the military and first responders (police, paramedics, firefighters, etc.) are at higher risk of developing PTSD because they are more likely to experience or witness frightening and overwhelming events.

PTSD is an invisible injury, but we *can* see the behaviors it causes. People with PTSD often feel anxious and on high alert. They might avoid or be triggered by things that remind them of the traumatic event, such as loud noises. They might be sad or irritable and have angry outbursts. They might overreact to small incidents like Leah's dad did. Therapy and medication can help people with PTSD learn to manage their symptoms.

PTSD affects the whole family. Children who have a parent with PTSD are more likely to feel anxious or sad. If you have a family member with PTSD, know that it is not your fault. That you are loved. And that help is available.

RESOURCES

If you feel worried or overwhelmed, or are thinking about hurting yourself or others, please talk to an adult you trust, like a parent or teacher. You can also talk to a counselor anytime, day or night, through these resources:

Canada
Kids Help Phone: 1-800-668-6868 or text CONNECT to 686868

United States
Boys Town Hotline (for kids of all ages): 1-800-448-3000
or text VOICE to 20121

Crisis Text Line: Text HOME to 741741

ACKNOWLEDGMENTS

As it often goes, this was not the story I set out to write. But it is the story that kept me up at night, pulled at my heartstrings and demanded to be written. I am grateful for all the people who contributed to its creation.

Thank you to:

All the military children I've met along the way. Especially my own: Henri and Sheila, who have had the opportunity to settle down and make roots but still dream of the excitement of moving away; and Emily, who has probably moved as much as Leah and once declared that she was never making friends again but keeps making them anyway.

My husband, Marc, for always supporting my endeavors with an enthusiastic smile, even when it probably looks like I'm doing nothing at all.

My agent, Elizabeth Bennett, for believing in Leah's story and helping find it a home. And the wonderful crew at Orca Book Publishers for giving it a home and helping polish it into its best possible self.

I never would have had the courage or the skills to start or finish this story without the guidance, support and encouragement of the kidlit community. I'm especially grateful to all those people who took the time to read the entire manuscript and provide valuable feedback.

I'd also like to thank Brandon Mitchell for his insightful input.

And, of course, my thanks to you, the readers!

MARLA LESAGE is a registered nurse who loves to tell stories, both real and imagined, through urban sketching, painting, illustration and words. Her art can be found in private collections in Canada, the United States and Australia. She also wrote and illustrated *We Wear Masks*, which won the Alice Kitts Memorial Award for Excellence in Children's Writing. Marla lives with her family near Fredericton, New Brunswick.

ORCA HAS STORIES
from the heart

"A heartfelt tear-jerker about love, friendship, and courage."
—*Kirkus Reviews*

THE KING OF JAM SANDWICHES

"Tug at the heartstrings and tickle the funny bone."
—*School Library Journal*, starred review

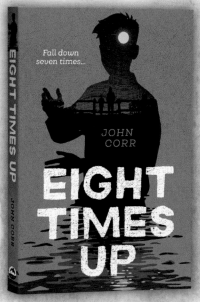

"Addressing mental health with empathy."
—*Kirkus Reviews*

"A sincere story about hope, healing, and a blooming friendship amid grief."
—*Booklist*